Praise for

Ghost of the White Nights

"Completes a fascinating trilogy of ghosts and zombies in a Dutch-flavored alternate history world. . . . The atmosphere and characters are superb. Eschbach's mild-mannered style conceals a dangerous opponent, while Modesitt's mild-mannered style conceals some wild adventure." —*The Denver Post*

"Modesitt's latest addition to the 'Ghost' series exhibits the author's graceful storytelling and unique vision. Fans of alternate history should enjoy this tale of deception and intrigue." —*Library Journal*

"[Modesitt] lets readers savor detailed characterization and world building that includes gourmet meals. [*Ghost of the White Nights* is] smart and absorbing." —*Booklist*

GHOST

OF THE WHITE NIGHTS

L. E. MODESITT, JR.

A TOM DOHERTY ASSOCIATES BOOK
NEW YORK

This is a work of fiction. All the character and events portrayed in this book are either products of the author's imagination or are used fictitiously.

GHOST OF THE WHITE NIGHTS

Edited by David G. Hartwell

A Tor Book
Published by Tom Doherty Associates, LLC
175 Fifth Avenue
New York, NY 10010

www.tor.com

Tor® is a registered trademark of Tom Doherty Associates, LLC.

ISBN: 0-765-34032-1
Library of Congress Catalog Card Number: 2001042282

First edition: October 2001
First mass market edition: October 2002

Printed in the United States of America

0   9   8   7   6   5   4   3   2   1

To Carol Ann, for inspiration and much more

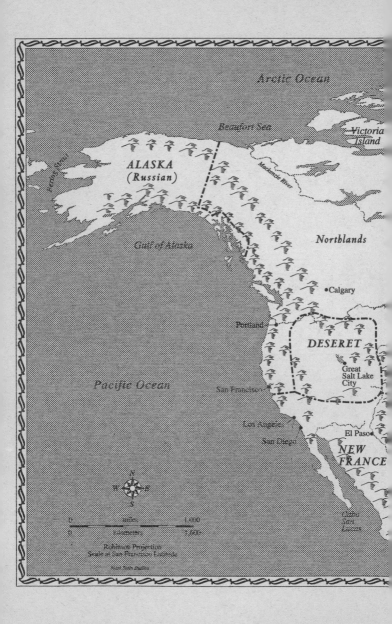

I

I N OUR WORLD there are ghosts and ghosts: those which are real, and those of our own pasts, which are equally real, if less tangible, but often more dangerous.

Why I was thinking about the ghosts of my past—or Llysette's—I wasn't even certain as I sat behind my desk in the early Saturday afternoon of a day in October and looked out through the sparklingly clean panes of the closed French doors at the reds and golds of the turning oaks and maples that lay beyond. If the sun had been shining, it would have been a glorious sight, but the gray skies muted that, although we had not seen rain yet.

My eyes flicked to the Asten *Post-Courier* on the side table. Reading it had been depressing, as it had been for months, with the stories about the continuing buildup of the Austro-Hungarian fleet and the maneuvering over petroleum supplies. The Mediterranean was already Ferdinand's lake, not that the outdated Russian Southern Fleet had dared venture forth from the Black Sea in more than a decade. The Austrians had completed turning the Red Sea into another such lake, and with their Seventh Fleet controlling the Indian Ocean, that meant that they could shut off the flow of petroleum to Great Britain or the

Swedish confederation at any time. Or to Columbia or Quebec, for that matter.

The sounds of a Poulenc piece drifted in from the parlor where Llysette was practicing. I couldn't remember the name. Every so often the song would stop, and she would play a section on the Haaren, as if to check the phrasing or the notes, and then she would resume. I couldn't help smiling as I listened.

Before me on the desk was a brown manila envelope, one with the return address of Eric's law firm in the federal district that held Columbia City. I picked up the disk case that I had set there on the envelope and turned it between my fingers so that the cover shimmered in the light of the desk lamp—*The Incredible Salt Palace Concert: DuBoise and Perkins*. The picture above the incandescent green of the title showed Llysette and the Saint composer Daniel Perkins, both standing at the front of the stage, smiling. I smiled, too, once more and for perhaps the thousandth time, as I set the disk case down on my study desk beside the SII difference engine. I picked up the royalty statement that the disk had accompanied.

It was hard to believe that Llysette's first three concerts in Deseret had been close to a year ago. So much had happened since then. Hartson James had insisted on her doing a segment on one of his videolink Christmas specials—it hadn't been that long, less than fifteen minutes, but TransMedia had paid her two thousand and reimbursed all our expenses in going down to New Amsterdam to record the show, including a suite at the Stuyvesant Grande. James hadn't missed a bet, and Dennis Jackson, the smooth-voiced crooner and host of the special, had even made a big plug for the Salt Palace Concert disk.

Late February had found us back in Deseret. True to his word, First Counselor Cannon of the Deseret Republic had ensured that Llysette had her performance at the St. George Opera House. After that, she'd followed me to Eastern Deseret for my delayed tour of the synfuels plant. I couldn't say that I'd understood all the technicalities, but the engineers from the Columbian Ministry of Interior and the one from Columbian Dutch Petroleum had been most interested.

Then there had been Llysette's appearance in Philadelphia, and the long overdue vacation in Sint-Maarten ... followed by the meeting of the trustees of Vanderbraak State University in May, when they had voted to grant Llysette tenure—and a raise. The raise had been welcome because concert engagements weren't exactly the steadiest of work, as both Llysette and I had discovered.

By midsummer, despite all the publicity, and the favorable reviews, Llysette had exactly five concerts scheduled for the fall and winter. That made almost ten paying concerts in a little more than a year, when she hadn't seen any in almost a decade. A great improvement, but certainly not enough to consider us wealthy.

The song coming from the parlor stopped, and I looked up to see a dark-haired and green-eyed lady in a soft gray sweater step into the study.

"Johan ... worried you look."

"No. Just reflective." I stood and gestured toward the paper. "Ferdinand and his power plays. The world gets more dangerous every day, it seems."

"You ... you are not the minister, *n'est-ce-pas?* Not even a spy any longer." She offered an almost impish smile, one that I was seeing more often the longer we had been married, as if she could finally show some of the playful side that she had probably never been allowed to indulge. Then, I was never certain how much had come from Llysette and how much from Carolynne, the family ghost whose soul was now part of each of ours. I laughed softly. It didn't matter ... now. I slipped out from behind the desk to give Llysette a healthy hug. Of course, I kissed her as well.

She returned the kiss, warmly, but not passionately, before tilting her head to the side. "*Non* ... I must try the Mahler song ... and you would have me ... *impossible homme* ... "

I grinned and released her after another squeeze. She was right. I was impossible, although I loved the way she pronounced the word in French, and I would have been even more impossible had she given me any encouragement. Being married to a beautiful soprano creates great temptations. "Are you hungry?"

"*Mais oui.* Why do you think I came to your door?"

So, while she went back to practicing, I headed into the kitchen.

There was some veal, and some lemon, and we always had wine, although I had to go down to the cellar and pull out a light sherry. Before long I was pounding the veal flat, and then sautéing it, while steaming some late beans. I'd already put on some basmati rice. A simple meal, but that was fine because we had to attend the dean's reception at the theatre before the orchestra concert.

Absently, I wiped a droplet of something off the white enamel of the windowsill. Over the summer, I'd stripped all the trim in the kitchen and repainted all the white so that it would be smooth. I suppose I still had enough Dutch in me that I hated anything that didn't look, feel, and smell spotless. I'd never been a particularly neat cook, and that meant I always had a great deal of cleaning up to do, both near the end of the preparation and especially afterward.

Then, in no time at all, it seemed, everything was ready, and I called toward the parlor. "Mademoiselle la diva . . ."

"Johan . . . *les langues* . . . you are mixing them." Llysette was shaking her head and smiling at the same time as she slipped into the kitchen and sat at the small table that was almost too big for the small half-bay window overlooking the north lawn.

"I know, but I love the sound of that." I slipped the plate of veal and rice and the beans almandine in front of her. I had already poured her tea.

I had fixed myself chocolate, the heavy warm kind composed of near equal portions of chocolate, cream, and sugar. My mother had always said I had to have some English ancestry somewhere because no proper Dutchman could drink chocolate that sweet. I wasn't sure about that, but I wasn't about to argue the point.

"The veal . . . it is wonderful. You could have been a great chef, Johan."

"Only at a very small bistro," I conceded. "I worry too much about things like petroleum shortages, and Ferdinand's fleets."

"Why . . . the news in the paper, does it trouble you so, Johan?"

"I suppose it shouldn't. I can't do anything about it, but I still worry."

"Will not the plans you provided—?"

"They're building the plant, but it will be another year before it's operating, and one plant will only produce a few percent of Columbia's kerosene needs."

"You, *mon cher,* can do only so much." Llysette took another sip of tea from the porcelain cup that had come from the set left to mother by my aunt Willimena. Mother had sent them to Llysette—not me—right after we were married, saying something to the effect that, since Llysette didn't have any family, someone needed to provide her with beloved heirlooms. Llysette hadn't said much, but whenever she had tea, she'd requested one of the cups, so often that I'd just made it a habit to serve her tea in it. "You cannot save the world."

"No, but one hopes." My head agreed with her words, but I couldn't help worrying. I'd hoped that Llysette's and my efforts in reducing tensions between Columbia and Deseret, and even slightly between New France and Columbia, might have strengthened Columbia's position, but Ferdinand's actions suggested otherwise.

"The reception . . . you do not have to go . . ." Llysette ventured.

"I'm supposed to sit here and wonder what new scheme the dean is hatching?"

"Most kind she has been."

"I'm sure she has." I snorted. "You've been good for the university."

The university's visibility, and particularly the reputation of the Music and Theatre Department, had soared with the regional and national news stories about Llysette. Applications for Llysette's studio had doubled, and some were even from as far away as Kansas and Newfoundland. There was even a letter from Daniel Perkins requesting that Llysette take a student from Deseret University for a semester as an exchange student.

After our meal, Llysette practiced another hour, and then took a bath and dressed.

I finished checking her royalty statements, and turned to correcting quizzes from my environmental politics class. I'd asked for a series of short answers, and no one seemed to have gotten the third question: What was the most immediate result of the naval oil reserve scandal?

I thought that would have been simple—the resignation of Interior Minister Fell. I would even have accepted an answer that claimed it had been the defeat of Speaker Roosevelt's administration. Only four papers out of twenty-three had either answer. I shook my head. The republic's only major political scandal of the first third of the century, and the one that had led to the creation of the entire energy oversight function of the Ministry of the Interior, and no one even remembered or thought it important.

After the environmental politics quizzes came the essays from my natural resources introductory course. Since it was a general education requirement, I expected and got some interesting essays, like the young man who wrote that detailed measurements of subsurface hydrology were only possible after the invention of the water table by Daffyd Browder in 1870. I had to admire his inventiveness, but I wasn't grading on gall or inventiveness.

I didn't get through all the essays before it was time to dress for the reception and concert. All too soon Llysette and I were sitting in my red Stanley, because that was its normal color, unless I flipped the switch to use the thermal paint option. After the relatively short drive down the hill and over the bridge into Vanderbraak Centre and around the square, I was still able to find a space in the lower car park.

While the clouds had lowered and thickened some, only a slight breeze ruffled Llysette's hair as we walked toward the music and theatre building that still resembled the physical training facility it had once been. The reception was in the small anteroom off the foyer to the theatre.

We had not stepped more than a few paces inside before Katrinka Er Recchus slithered up, if an overly ample administrator could ever be said to slither. "Llysette! Johan!"

The dean's welcomes had become most effusive in the past year, not surprisingly. Her floral perfume was as pungent as ever, and her auburn hair was pulled back into a bun that seemed to make her eyes bulge out above the white lace collar.

"Dean Er Recchus." I bowed.

Llysette offered a charming professional smile.

"I am so glad to see that you both could make it to the reception. President Waafl had hoped you would be here, dear Llysette."

"Miss this I would not," Llysette said gently.

"I don't see Alois," I added.

"Didn't you hear, Johan? They've called up the New Bruges Guard, and the national commandant wired Alois, and asked him to serve as acting commander for the second echelon reserves. So he's gone back to work on weekends." The dean smiled. "He's pleased that he can still be of service."

I hadn't seen anything about calling up the Guard, and I read the *Post-Courier* fairly thoroughly. "When did this happen?"

"Well . . . it hasn't. Not yet. Alois said that the Guard would announce it in the next few days. I shouldn't be saying much, but I know *you* would be the last person to tell anyone, Johan."

I just nodded.

"If you will excuse me . . ." The dean bobbed her head. "Here come the vanEmsdens."

Llysette and I eased toward the table holding the punch. Blanding Aastre—the orchestra conductor, attired in his performance white and black—stood back from the punch bowl, facing Donnel Waafl, the current president of Vanderbraak State University.

"The arts are important," Waafl was saying. "Every student needs a well-rounded education, and that's just not possible without an understanding of the arts. . . ."

I wanted to laugh. That was his standard line. Whoever he talked to, that was what he said. I glanced at Llysette, but her smile was perfectly in place. I rolled my eyes.

"Johan . . ." she murmured.

"All right," I replied pleasantly.

Blanding bowed to Waafl as we neared. "If you will excuse me, President Waafl . . ."

"Of course, of course . . . I believe you have an orchestra to conduct." Waafl laughed heartily, then turned to us. "Professor duBoise . . . I am so glad to see you. The trustees have been so pleased to hear about your upcoming concerts."

"As am I," Llysette said softly.

"We're all looking forward to another videolink performance. . . ."

"Alas . . . now there are none scheduled."

"She has appearances in Schenectady, New Amsterdam, Asten, and Philadelphia," I interjected.

"Good . . . very good. The arts are so important, and it's vital that students know how strong our performing arts program is here." His head bobbed almost the way the dean's had. Was that something they taught administrators, assuming that administrators could learn anything?

The lights flicked on and off, and the five-minute bells chimed.

"You will keep me informed, will you not?" Waafl's eyes centered back on Llysette, as if I had been dismissed and immediately forgotten.

"*Mais oui,* President Waafl. That I will do."

The lights flicked again, and we bowed again to Waafl, before turning and heading toward the doors to the theatre.

2

M ONDAY MORNING CAME too early, and with it came a cold mist, not quite rain, but heavier than fog. As I guided the Stanley down the drive and onto the narrow road, I could barely see the trees in Benjamin's orchard beyond the stone fence.

"Another cold winter will we have, Johan." Llysette shivered inside her coat.

"You may be right." I paused before asking, "Lunch at Delft's at quarter past?"

"*Mais oui.* That I will need."

"You have ..." I couldn't remember the student she taught at eleven, only that she was the one who had no rhythm and probably wouldn't make it to her junior recital.

"Sweet, she is, but she cannot count, even watching a metronome." Llysette sighed.

"You don't have so many like that anymore."

"*Non* . . . but one, she is too many."

After dropping Llysette off at the music and theatre building, before putting the Stanley in the faculty car park closest to my office, I headed down to the not-quite-garish red and gold sign that marked the Shell service station. Why Columbian Dutch Petroleum had decided on the trade name of Shell, with its simplistically scalloped edges, rather than keeping the sedate and familiar Standard lamp logo after the merger between Royal Dutch and Standard had always baffled me, but I supposed it was a memorial of sorts. For a time, because of my objections to the merger, I'd gone to the AmeriSun station, but the prices were higher, and the service nonexistent.

Almost before I turned off the burners and opened the window, Piet had the filler hose out. "Good morning, Doktor."

"Good morning, Piet. How is business?"

"Not so good. Columbian Dutch raised their prices to me again, and so did Dauvaart. Bruno at AmeriSun said his prices went up more than mine. Shady types at AmeriSun, if you ask me." The stocky station owner carefully squeezed the cleaner onto the windscreen, making sure that the liquid didn't touch the shimmering red surface of the Stanley's bonnet. "They're all shady. Guess you have to be."

"I thought they did that two weeks ago?"

"They did. And they did last week, and again this morning." Piet finished wiping the windscreen with the soft cloth that he always used, another reason why I went there to fuel the Stanley. "That will be thirty-seven fifty, Doktor."

The price of kerosene kept climbing, or so it seemed to me, but I handed Piet two twenties. "The best of luck."

"I'll be needing that, Doktor."

After Piet's came the stop at Samaha's Factorium and Emporium, for my copy of the Asten *Post-Courier*. I left my dime on the counter and walked back out into the mist that was threatening to turn into a colder rain.

Although my environmental economics course didn't meet until eleven, there was little point in stopping by the post centre, since the mail was never ready until after ten, and I was supposed to be in my office for office hours no later than ten. So I put the Stanley in the upper car park and made my way to the remodeled three-story old Dutch

Republican house that held the the Department of Political and Natural Resources Sciences.

Gilda of the frizzy hair looked up as I walked in. "Don't forget the faculty meeting at four thirty, Doktor Eschbach."

"I wouldn't miss it for the world." I grinned as I started up the stairs to the third floor—except I would have avoided it if I could have because there was going to be another fight over Natural Resources 3B.

Once inside my office, I laid out the quiz papers and essays in their folders for each of my classes before opening the paper. I couldn't have missed the headline: "Speaker Hartpence Calls Up Guard."

Federal District (RPI). Defense Minister Holmbek firmly denied that the federalization and mobilization of four state guards was a response to Austro-Hungarian provocation. "The Austro-Hungarian decision to send the First Serbian Cavalry to the joint Austro-Arab base at Basra has nothing to do with the Speaker's decision. By temporarily federalizing several state Guard units, we can provide the intensive training necessary in new equipment and tactics far more quickly than otherwise possible." Holmbek repeated the Speaker's assurance that the government did not intend to federalize any additional Guard units at this time.

In an action that the defense minister declared entirely unrelated, the House unanimously passed an additional defense appropriations measure that would procure fifty more Curtiss turbojet heavy transports, ten more fast frigates, three additional nuclear-electrosubmersibles of the *Hudson* class, and two icebreakers of the *Arctic* class. . . . Holmbek also announced the that the new fifteenth and sixteenth Army divisions would be trained in cold weather and mountain operations to remedy "a shortfall in capability". . . .

I didn't care for the implications either way. A smaller story on page two caught my eye.

Central Northlands (WNS). The fire that laid waste to Columbian Dutch Petro's natural gas processing facility under construction in Enuak has been traced to an improperly wired electrical conduit. . . . Stephanie DerRaalte, speaking for VanderWaal, the construction firm, stated, "This will create some delays, but we've already moved in additional crews to make sure that we can make the contractual deadline. . . ."

The plant is designed to turn northlands natural gas into commercial grade kerosene and turbofuel. . . . Miss DerRaalte also noted that steps have already been taken to remedy the deficiencies that led to the fire and explosion in the second and third conversion plants under construction.

Maybe the story caught my eye because the plant was the first one being built from the plans I'd obtained from Deseret, or because of the rapidly escalating price of kerosene, or because building three plants of a design not implemented in Columbia seemed a bit out of the ordinary. Or, mostly, because I was too skeptical to believe in coincidences. The third story was just odd.

St. Petersburg (WNS). Austrian tracking ships reported a dawn launch from the Ural research center, and identified the booster as the secret Perun rocket, rumored to have been in development for more than a decade. The Austrian Foreign Ministry decried the launch as a violation of the High Frontier Treaty forbidding military use of missiles or the development of military rocketry.

According to the Russian Naval Ministry, the Perun's mission was to test the lower stage booster to determine its feasibility for launching a Russian satellite communications system. . . .

How could the Russians even consider a satellite communications system when half of Russia still had minimal or nonexistent wirelink service?

"Johan!" Regner Grimaldi peered in through my open door.

I laughed. "Yes."

"Yes what?" He actually looked puzzled.

"I will tell our beloved chair that he cannot zero out Natural Resources 3B. Then you and Wilhelm can argue over who will teach it next semester."

Regner arched his eyebrows in an exaggeratedly regal manner, which, for him, as the heir pretender to the princedom of Monaco, wasn't difficult. "Wilhelm has seen the light."

"You'll teach it this year?"

"He will."

"Ah . . . there aren't enough junior majors, and the registrar will zero it out until next year."

"Johan . . . how could you think that?" His tone wasn't quite wounded enough.

"I already checked. You got half the sophomores into it last year when you taught it."

"Only you, Johan . . ." he said mournfully. "Only a former spy—"

"Only you, Regner . . ." I grinned, because Wilhelm had it coming, and because I wasn't sure I could take another pontification from Wilhelm on the greatness of The University—Virginia, that is, that great and wonderful creation of the illustrious Thomas Jefferson. "Only royalty learns tricks like that in the cradle."

"You would think I had been born in Vienna . . . or St. Petersburg."

"You're not tall enough for a Romanov, nor autocratic enough," I quipped back. "And you don't appreciate really good singing. You haven't been at either of Llysette's last recitals."

"As I said . . . only a former spy knows where everyone is all the time. And Tzar Alexander thinks the height of musical perfection is *The 1812 Overture* or perhaps *Boris Godunov*. I did see your lovely wife's production of *Heinrich Verrûckt*, you may recall."

"You're forgiven," I answered, "but only if you're there the next time she sings."

"Would I miss such beauty?"

"Yes—if I didn't twist your arm." I only paused for a moment. "And don't say it." The last thing I needed was to be reminded of my years with the Republic's Sedition Prevention and Security Service. I'd almost managed to bury those—until the events of the previous year. Now most of Vanderbraak Centre had heard something about my years as a Spazi agent, very little of it accurately reported, for which I was probably better off than if an accurate account had been available and circulated.

Regner grinned, then shook his head, before vanishing.

Not a single student showed up during office hours. I used the time to set up the next quiz for the honors course in Environmental Studies 4A. Then it was time to march over to Smythe 203 and Environmental Economics 2A. I didn't see the two groundskeeping zombies I knew best—Gertrude and Hector—but that might have been because they were working behind the science building and because the rain and fog were getting thicker.

While the students were milling in the corridor and filing into the classroom, I went to the ancient blackboard and laboriously chalked a phrase on it: "In a technological society, the practice of completely private property cannot exist."

After the bell rang and most were seated, I pointed to the phrase on the board. "This is the issue for the day. Some of you may ask what private property has to do with environmental economics. I suggest you think about the issue some before asking a variant of that question. I'll give you all a minute or two to consider the implications."

Then I waited for the empty expressions to fade, glad that there were several faces on which puzzlement warred with interest.

"Mister Spykstra . . . what are your thoughts about that concept?" I finally asked.

"Sir?" Damien Spykstra was a tall korfball player, a great defender, I'd heard, but not much in the scoring department. He didn't appear able to score in the classroom, either. He just looked at me blankly.

"Mister Ostfels?"

"Ah . . . your question, sir . . . well . . . it seems to say that if we have technology we can't have private property, but we have technology and private property."

"I'll accept most of that," I said mildly. "What about the term 'completely private property'?"

"But we do, Doktor Eschbach," replied Hans Ostfels. "We're not like New France or Russia."

"Russia, I'll accept. We are very much like New France in the conceptual and legal fashion in which we handle property." I turned and inclined my head. "Miss VanderWaal . . . why?"

"We both place restrictions on the use and transfer of property?"

"That's correct. Why might that be?" I kept looking at Miss VanderWaal.

"You wouldn't want a prison next to a girls' school or . . . a petrol farm beside . . . much of anything."

"Miss Regius . . . what does all this have to do with economics, environmental economics?"

Elinor Regius looked as helpless as the star korfball player.

"Is it a good idea to put a dairy beside a sewage treatment facility?" I asked. "What does that do to the value of the dairy property? Or to the purity of the milk?"

"But we have regulations to keep the milk clean," pointed out Lucia vanEmsden, a cousin of the dairy family, I thought.

"Ah . . ." I pounced. "So . . . if you have a dairy, Miss vanEmsden, you cannot run it however you want?" I could see a few faces beginning to get a glimmer.

"Doktor Eschbach . . ." Then she stopped. "That's what

you meant by completely private property . . . that everything anyone does affects everyone else, and the more technology there is, the more dangers, and the more restrictions. . . ."

At that point, everyone wanted to get into the discussion, and that was fine with me.

"I'm paying for technology I'm not using because . . ."

"An excuse for taking away personal freedoms and rights . . ."

"Governments always do that . . . why we have a Spazi . . ."

There was a momentary silence after that, but I just nodded to another student, and it wasn't long before they were at it again.

In time, I called a halt to the discussion. "The next assignment deals with external diseconomies . . . Excuse me, I just read in the journal that the preferred term is now 'negative externalities.' In any case, you need to know both labels for the problem and why society needs to understand and deal with it." I surveyed the class, the young faces conveying expressions of worry and boredom. "And yes, external diseconomies will be on tests, in essays, and your mastery of the concept will determine a significant fraction of your grade." I just smiled.

After most had left the classroom, I hurried from Smythe down to the post centre, ignoring the fine, almost ice-like needles that bounced off my head and my black trenchcoat.

Maurice must have seen me coming because he peered out from the window. "Got some more posts for the lady, Herr Doktor, and some bills for you." Maurice grinned at me from behind the window. "And a fancy one for the both of you."

"It's about time we got something more than bills. You should do better for us, Maurice." I couldn't quite keep the smile out of my voice.

"We just deliver, Doktor."

I took a quick look at the stack, riffling through the

envelopes. The first one was addressed merely to Mme. Llysette duBoise, Vanderbraak Centre, New Bruges. No address, no box, no street, no postal code . . . but there it was. Somehow, I doubted that one addressed that way to me would ever arrive. The only people who knew my name that well were the type from whom I'd rather not receive anything.

The "fancy" one was from the Presidential Palace, and it was addressed to us both.

The Honorable Johan Eschbach
The Most Honored Mme. Llysette duBoise

An invitation, it looked like, but the sight of the gold-foiled stationery bothered me. I snorted. Every invitation we'd received from the Presidential Palace had led to troubles. Rewards, also, but the price for those rewards had been high.

From the post centre, I climbed the lower hill to the north of the square, up to Delft's, and found myself in the foyer. Llysette wasn't there, and two couples were standing in front of me.

Victor appeared almost immediately and beckoned. "Doktor? Will the lady—?"

"I'm expecting her."

He smiled. "I have the table by the woodstove for you." Then he offered an even broader smile.

I turned to see Llysette stepping into the foyer and shaking out her umbrella before slipping it into the rack by the left side of the doorway.

"Could it snow? *Non*, ice must fall." She patted her hair, but I couldn't see that it had been disarranged at all.

"You look wonderful."

"You would say such, Johan . . ." She shook her head.

We followed Victor to the table nearest the woodstove.

"The stove . . . this table, it is the best, Victor, and you are so kind." Llysette's smile would have melted solid ice.

"It is for my special customers." The proprietor ex-

tended two menus. "The special today is the wienerschnitzel in lemon caper sauce with an Alfredo pasta,"
Victor beamed. "It is very good, mademoiselle."

"That, I will have, with tea." Llysette smiled and handed
back the menu she had barely scanned, but then, we knew
the bill of fare by heart.

"I'd like the special also, Victor, with chocolate."

He bowed, mostly to Llysette, and slipped away.

Only then did I lift the envelope. "We got this."

"And it is what?"

"An invitation, but I didn't wish to open it because it's
addressed to us both."

"I am here." She lifted her eyebrows. "You may open
it." She spoiled the serious tone with a touch of a giggle
in her last words.

I eased open the outer envelope, and then the inner one,
before reading the engraved script.

> *The President and Mrs. Armstrong*
> *request the honor of your presence*
> *at the Thirty-fourth*
> *Annual Dinner for the Arts*
> *Thursday, November 2, 1995,*
> *at seven o'clock.*
> *Répondez, s'il vous plaît*

I tried not to frown as I extended the invitation across
the table.

Llysette took it and read, then looked at me. "I do not
have to sing for my food this time, no?" A twinkle glim-
mered in her deep green eyes.

"No one has mentioned it this time," I replied with a
smile.

Victor reappeared with my chocolate and Llysette's tea.
"Mademoiselle . . . Doktor . . ."

"Thank you," I offered.

"It is always a pleasure." He inclined his head to Llysette. "Especially for one who has preserved *la gloire* that was France."

"Thank you, Victor," Llysette replied quietly.

Victor took two small green salads from the tray held by a waiter and slipped them onto the white linen. "Your dinner will be soon ready." With a bow and a smile, he turned.

"You have to be Victor's favorite."

"One of them, *peut-être*," she acknowledged.

"More than one of them," I joked. "But we do get wonderful tables and service, and I owe it all to you." My eyes dropped to the foil-stamped envelope on the table.

"The invitation, it worries you?"

"Nothing in the federal district happens by accident or without a price," I said dryly.

"The post?" Llysette's voice took on a note of concern. "Have they sent you clippings? You have not heard from Minister Oakes?"

"I don't imagine I'm one of Harlaan's favorites." I laughed, once, reflecting on how I'd inadvertently set matters up so that he'd gone from being the president's advisor to the deputy minister in charge of the Spazi—under an opposition Speaker. "No clippings, either. No briefing material, but I still worry."

"We do not have to attend."

I wasn't about to agree to that. So I smiled. "After all these years . . . I think we're going."

"Could we stay with Judith and Eric?"

"They've said we can stay anytime, even if they're not there. I'll wire Eric tomorrow, but I'm sure it will be all right."

Victor appeared with our meals, and the wienerschnitzel and Alfredo combination was indeed tasty. I didn't bring up the invitation again, but I still worried. Nearly thirty years in and around government, from the Republic Naval Air Corps to the Spazi to being a subminister, had taught me the value of worry.

3

TUESDAY CAME AND went, and so did Wednesday. On Thursday morning I was sitting in my second-floor office at the university, reading the Asten *Post-Courier* before I got back to work on yet another quiz—this one for Natural Resources 1A—the introductory course. I glanced toward the small window, but the way the rain was running down the panes, I really couldn't see anything. So I looked back at the national news section.

> Federal District (WNS). "Austria has absolutely no interest in interfering in the affairs of other nations," declared Ambassador Schikelgruber upon his return to Columbia from Vienna, where he had met with Emperor Ferdinand for consultations. "We wish a world at peace, as do all thoughtful peoples."

I snorted. The Austrian definition of peace was not quite the same as that of other thoughtful peoples. I wondered if anyone thought of asking the zombies in the work camps across what had been France and the Netherlands. Or the Bavarians who'd thrown their lot in with Austria more than a century earlier when the Swedes had repulsed the attack on Denmark, and who now found themselves under a far worse tyrant than the unfortunate Otto van Bismarck ever could have been. Then, Ferdinand's predecessors had been intelligent enough to coopt the Prussians, so much so that it was probably more accurate to call it the Austro-Prussian Empire. Especially since most of the elite military units were either Prussian or trained by the Prussians.

I forced myself to finish the article.

... the emir of the Arab Protectorate has requested Austrian aid to ensure the sanctity of the lands of the Protectorate ... Schikelgruber assured reporters that Austria was only rotating individual units and not increasing total Austrian forces ...

Just like the movements of Austrian forces ten years earlier had only been a redeployment. I shook my head. Strange ... I'd been in France, and so had Llysette, and neither of us had known the other even existed. But that had been in a different world.

The other stories weren't much better.

St. Petersburg (WNS). Early reports about the casualties from the student protests held at St. Petersburg University were highly exaggerated, according to Kyril Lamanov, minister of communications for the tzar. "Only one student was killed, and that was because he fell from a balcony in the excitement." Lamanov invited foreign correspondents to tour the university grounds. He pointed out that if the White Guard had actually fired on students in the way that had been reported, there would certainly be student ghosts visible. . . .

That was true enough. I couldn't imagine there not being ghosts on the grounds of the university if the tzar's White Guard had actually shot down scores of students. Almost always, when a self-aware individual died violently and knowledgeably, there was a ghost formed. Of course, it had taken the Spazi and Ferdinand's scientists to start meddling and trying to create artificial zombies by using technology to remove a live spirit from a live body. Now, although the Hartpence administration had declared a ban on ghosting and de-ghosting research, I had no doubts that it continued on the dark side of the intelligence operations. I still had the files I'd lifted from the covert research operation concealed at Vanderbraak State . . . before Branston-Hay's death had forced its closure. And I certainly hadn't told anyone about certain devices based on that research, not when they'd saved Llysette's life and mine in Deseret.

In any case, I had the depressing feeling that Russia was more than filled with ghosts, and that there were so many that they had a far less mitigating effect than in Columbia. Like many, I wondered if and when Russia would ever change, even as the Romanov tzars approached their four hundredth year of ruling.

The next story was closer to home and worried me a bit more.

Citie de Tenochtitlan (NFWS). Amid rumors that a New French task group sank an Austrian submersible off the coast of Venezuela, Marshall deGaulle refused to comment directly. "Austrian submersibles do not belong in the Caribbean," announced deGaulle. "I cannot imagine that there have been any here in years."

Unnamed Republic intelligence courses claim that the carriers *Buonaparte* and *St. Louis* used antisubmarine aircraft and air-launched Perseus torpedoes to sink a submersible less than one hundred kilometers from the rebuilt Languanillas oil depot. Austrian Minister of Defense Stepan denied that Austria had lost any submersibles. . . .

The next story confirmed my concerns.

Federal District (RPI). Accusing Speaker Hartpence of covering up the critical petroleum shortage facing Columbia and the inadequacy of the Republic's naval defense capabilities, Representative Patrice Alexander (L-MI) today released a controversial analysis by the Touchstone Institute. The analysis claims that three missing Columbian naval vessels were not lost to the causes previously identified by the Ministry of Defcnsc, but to hostile covert action by the elements of the Austrian second and fourth Atlantic fleets. . . .

Speaker Hartpence had no comment. Columbian Minister of Defense Holmbek dismissed the analysis as "flawed sensationalism" and totally unworthy of comment. . . .

Congresslady Alexander was my favorite Liberal, perhaps because she was always saying things about matters that no one wanted revealed, and perhaps because her efforts had saved my unworthy neck once upon a time.

Putting it all together, the way I read the news stories, the Austrians had lost a submersible and didn't want to acknowledge that they were once again targeting the Venezuelan oil supplies to New France and Columbia. Columbia and New France were tacitly colluding to try to keep Ferdinand's forces at bay, and no one wanted any details revealed, probably because the petroleum shortage was so severe that Columbia didn't have adequate supplies for any sustained hostilities.

I put down the paper. The news hadn't improved in three days, but it hadn't gotten as bad as it could have gotten. Yet. But there wasn't too much I could do personally.

The wireset buzzed. I touched the red intercom button and picked up the handset. "Yes?"

"Professor Eschbach, there is a Harlaan Oakes on the wire for you. Line one."

My stomach tightened. "Thank you, Gilda." I touched the only amber lighted button on the wireset. "Hello."

"Johan . . . Harlaan Oakes here."

"What can I do for you, Harlaan?"

"I understand that Llysette and you have been asked to the annual arts dinner. The president asked that I call you. He really hoped . . . strongly suggested . . . that Llysette be there."

"Oh? . . ."

"Johan . . . I really can't say more, except that I think that Llysette deserves to be there."

Deserves to be there—those were provocative words. "I've almost always trusted your judgment on matters like that."

"I trusted yours after you came back from the first concert tour in Deseret."

Harlaan would have to have reminded me about that. "And you're handling the job far better than your predecessor," I replied.

"I don't know that I'm handling the ulcers any better." His tone was rueful.

"We'll be there." I blocked the sigh I felt. "What else did you have in mind?"

"Since you're coming to Columbia City in a few weeks, I was hoping you could drop by."

"I might be able to do that. . . ." When Harlaan had wanted me to drop by, even when he'd been an assistant to the president, and not the deputy minister of justice in charge of the Spazi, it had always meant trouble. I couldn't imagine that changing. "You have something in mind?"

"As a matter of fact, I do, but we can talk about it then."

"Who took your place with the president?"

"Alyster Potts. You knew him years ago, I think." There was the briefest of pauses. "I see that Llysette will be doing a concert in February at the Theodore Roosevelt Centre. Caron and I already have our tickets. She was one of the first to buy the Salt Palace disk."

"I'm glad she likes it."

"So do I, I have to admit, Johan. Llysette's quite something, and it would be a shame for more people not to hear her. Both the president and the Speaker think so."

I managed not to wince. "She has a number of concerts lined up—in between teaching."

"That's good. There will be more, I'm sure." He paused, but only fractionally. "Well . . . the dinner's on a Thursday. If you could stop by around three that afternoon?"

"I'll be there."

I knew I'd been right to worry about the damned invitation. Yet not all of what Harlaan had intimated was bad. He'd really seemed insistent that Llysette attend the dinner. Not me, Llysette. I just wished I knew what he had in mind. With the state of the world, it could be anything, but war seemed to loom ever closer, and, in those sorts of matters, what mattered the life and future of a retired spy— or even a rediscovered diva? And why us?

I stared at the quiz, lying on the desk before me, looking insignificant. Insignificant or not, I still needed to revise it. Also, I needed to talk to Llysette, but that would have to wait until dinner, because our normal luncheon date had been disrupted. I had to attend an informal luncheon in the president's conference room and hear a presentation on the proposed integrated difference engine network that was to be installed over the next several months.

Networks I distrusted, either of people or difference engines, but I still had to go, just as, it appeared, Llysette and I had to go to the federal district.

4

THE RAIN HAD subsided to a drizzle by the time I eased the Stanley to a stop outside the music and theatre building at six o'clock. Llysette didn't even take out her umbrella. She just marched from the entryway through the rain to the steamer. Then, she opened the rear door of the Stanley and flung her briefcase and a large cloth bag containing papers of some sort into the rear. Without a word, she slammed the rear door, yanked open the front door, and threw herself into the passenger seat. She also slammed the front door.

"It was a hard day?"

"*Difficile, ce n'est point . . .*" She didn't even look in my direction.

"Ah . . . did I do something?" I asked as I began to guide the Stanley out of the car park and down toward the square.

"*Non . . .* you it is not. Doktor Geoffries . . . *il est un cochon.*"

"What did he do? Tell you that you were a good little girl, but you didn't understand . . ."

"*Oui!*" She paused, and then two very cold green eyes turned in my direction. I wasn't looking, but I could feel them. "How did you know, Johan?" Her voice turned softly cold.

"I didn't. But that's what administrators do when they're caught out, especially by women, and Dierk's very traditional." I decided not to mention Harlaan's call until later. "What happened?"

"George Dwyer . . . he asked if he could study with me next semester."

"He's an older student, isn't he? One of Beau Jonn's? I take it that George isn't happy with Professor Jonn?" Beaufort Penn Jonn had been a last-minute replacement, hired in haste by Dierk over Llysette's objections. One reason Dierk hired him might have been that Beau had studied with a cousin of Dean Er Recchus.

"Not a one of the good male voices they are pleased," snorted my diva.

A line of steamers appeared before me, and I had to brake hard as we neared the west side of the Wijk River bridge. Then we inched forward through the rain. The irregular screaming of a siren ululated just ahead of the ambulance that rushed past us in the oncoming lane.

"It must have been a bad accident," I said.

Llysette stopped talking, and we both peered forward through the rain. As we drew near the far side of the bridge, I could see the figure of Constable Gerhardt directing steamers past a Reo that had swerved into the stone wall of the bridge. The constable must have been at it for a time, because his rather ample mustaches were definitely drooping from the rain, despite the bill on his watch cap.

I swallowed. I could see the crushed frame of a bicycle half-pinned between the Reo and stones—and a shimmering white figure that seemed to shiver in and out of existence just behind Constable Gerhardt. Beyond the Reo was another bicycle, its frame also bent.

"Two of them?" asked Llysette.

"It looks like the Reo plowed into both of them." The ghostly figure meant that one of the cyclists had been killed on the spot, while the other was being rushed to the hospital.

"On such wet roads . . ." Llysette shook her head as we passed the constable and headed toward Deacon's Lane.

"There's always some idiot." Seeing ghosts wasn't that infrequent, but it always sent a chill down my back, because it meant someone had died violently, knowing they were dying. I didn't want to think about it, not when I didn't have to, and I returned to the subject we had been discussing. "So Dierk told you that this male student couldn't study with you?"

"*Non!* I must teach all women, because the women at the . . ." Llysette paused.

"At the University of New Bruges?"

"The man who taught voice took a student as a mistress. Because trouble is there, I cannot teach a man here?"

"Dierk is very cautious," I temporized.

"His own shadow would frighten him."

"So . . . if you teach more men, Beau would have to teach women to balance the loads, and since he is young and good-looking, Dierk worries about some student throwing herself at him?"

"That is what he said."

"You think he doesn't want you teaching any more men?"

"They would learn more, but learning, it does not matter. His fears are what matter."

The steam, figuratively speaking, was no longer shooting out from Llysette's eyes and ears, but I could sense the smoldering from the passenger side of the Stanley as we turned on to Deacon's Lane and started up the long hill to the house.

"*Un gros cochon . . .*" muttered Llysette.

I decided not to say more.

Neither did Llysette.

I eased the Stanley into the long drive, and then stopped as close to the back door of the house as I could. I'd put the steamer in the car barn later. I carried Llysette's bag and my own briefcase into the warmth of the house. Marie had to have stoked up the woodstove before she had left. There was also a pie—apple, from the smell—still cooling on the rack on the counter, and something simmered in the Crock-Pot.

The house, of course, was spotless, as it was on the days that Marie had been there. Having a housekeeper was one of the few luxuries I had indulged even before we had married.

While Llysette went upstairs to wash up and change, I rummaged around, finding lettuce, a winter tomato from Florida not quite as hard as a rubber ball, hard yellow cheddar, an apple, and a few other items to combine into a salad. Then I added two more short logs to the woodstove in the parlor.

When I got back to the kitchen, Llysette was already there, dressing my impromptu salad. So I hurried down to the cellar and pulled out a bottle of a Washington cabernet that Eric had recommended. After I uncorked it in the kitchen, I motioned for Llysette to sit down. I served the stew right from the Crock-Pot.

"You don't have a recital rehearsal tonight?" I asked.

"*Non.* Tomorrow night, and Friday."

"Good."

"It is not good. I will suffer, and the students, they will complain."

"I meant it was good that you don't have one tonight." I poured Llysette a healthy glass of the cabernet. I took a much smaller amount, then sat down and passed the salad bowl to her.

We both were hungry and ate for a time without talking, unusual for us, but I suspected Llysette hadn't eaten lunch, and I'd had very little of the rubbery chicken served at Donnel Waafl's informal faculty get-together, probably because my feelings had alternated between boredom and anger. I'd said almost nothing, because it wouldn't have done any good. Waafl never met a good idea he'd liked and seemed intent on proving it.

I glanced across the table. Llysette's plate was empty. So I got up.

"Just a little, Johan."

After a bit, I ventured, "You know the arts dinner in the federal district?"

Llysette's *oui* was very wary.

"I got a call today. Someone wanted to make sure *you* would be there. Not me . . . you."

"Because if I am there, so will be you." Llysette held her wine glass without taking a sip.

"That might be, but I don't think so. Rather, they may want me to be there, but the president wants you there, especially."

"He is married, and so am I." There was a hint of a twinkle in her eyes.

"Not for that reason."

"And who was it that called you?"

"Harlaan Oakes," I admitted.

"The minister of the Spazi. And what has he to do with the arts dinner?"

"He's the only cabinet minister placed by the president, and that means if the president wants anything, he'll go to Harlaan when he can. Harlaan also wants to see me."

"What does he wish of you?"

"He didn't say. He wants me to stop by his office before the dinner."

"That is not good."

"No. But I don't know as I can refuse."

"Never can we refuse. Would that we could."

I nodded in agreement with that, and refilled Llysette's wine glass. Then I refilled mine.

5

THE RAIN FINALLY blew itself out late Thursday, and Friday had come in bright and clear, and colder than normal for mid-October, with patches of solid black ice on the roads. My morning run through the hills and lanes was more cautious, and slower. Because of a bonnet-boot smash on the east side of the river bridge, it was almost ten past nine before I dropped Llysette in front of the music building and headed back to Samaha's for the paper. I didn't even look at the headlines, but eased the Stanley back to the upper faculty car park. The campus sidewalks were worse than the roads, and I was muttering by the time I stepped into the natural resources building.

I wasn't three steps inside the foyer before David appeared. "Johan? I got your note."

I frowned. There shouldn't have been any problem in dealing with a two-day absence to attend the presidential dinner. I had already arranged for my classes to be covered. Still, with David, one never knew. He closed the door to his office behind me, then settled behind his desk, fingering the meerschaum pipe he'd given up smoking years before. I took the chair across from him and waited.

"President Waafl wired me yesterday afternoon."

I nodded, having no intention of saying anything until I knew where David was headed.

"He was most concerned that you offered nothing at the get-together on Wednesday. You know that he values faculty input."

"He values being able to say that he offers faculty the opportunity to make suggestions. Can you recall the last time he took any faculty suggestion—unless he'd already proposed it?"

"Johan . . . a university must operate on a carefully developed consensus."

"I agree. I just don't see any consensus being developed. I can see an attempt to impose one, but that's another issue." I could see the blank expression on David's face. "What do you want? Waafl's a slithering idiot who never had an original idea, and couldn't recognize one if it were delivered to him by an express steamer and wrapped in red ribbon. I didn't say anything like that. I didn't tell the group that his idea for multidisciplinary lecture classes of two hundred students plus was idiotic. Nor did I suggest that expanding class sizes for economic reasons was equally idiotic, since one of the biggest attractions we offer to incoming students is small classes."

The blank look was replaced with one of stunned shock.

"Instead, I was quiet, restrained, and polite," I pointed out.

"Your . . . attitude is uncalled for, Johan. The president and dean have been most supportive of both you and your wife, even at times when . . . well . . . matters were less than conventional."

I could feel my blood pressure rising, but there wasn't any point in saying more. There hadn't been any point in saying what I'd said, now that I'd thought about it. David and Waafl were cut from the same mold—ignore reality, follow tradition, mouth platitudes, and try to save money at the expense of both faculty and students. Oh . . . and increase administrative costs, staff, and perks, while economizing on everything else. "You and they have been very supportive," I acknowledged. "And we have reciprocated by mentioning the university most favorably in many places where it would otherwise have been impossible for the university to obtain publicity or favorable notice." I took a slow breath. "You may convey to the president that I was not feeling as well as I might, and, if you would like, I will send a brief note conveying the same."

"That would help, Johan. You know that the legislature is talking about reducing state support for the university system this year."

"I'll send a note today," I conceded.

"I would appreciate that." David stood. "I look forward to hearing about the arts dinner, and I know the dean will also."

"I'll give you a memo on the dinner for the file when we get back."

David nodded, and I slipped out of his office. I even closed the door gently before I headed upstairs to my own far more modest cubbyhole.

I should have graded the natural resources quizzes, but I was too angry. So I turned to my first avenue for cooling down, and that was the paper. I looked at the lead story.

Asten (NBNS). As fuel and heating oil prices have soared across New Bruges, service station owners and operators have begun to hear more than the sounds of coins in their tills. Phrases like price trupps, black-mailers, and profiteers . . .

Steamer and hauler drivers don't accept the explanations of the petroleum companies, such as the explosions at Venezuelan refineries and the reluctance of Japanese consortia to increase exports to Columbia from Southeast Asia . . .

"They got money for a new building in Asten, don't they?" asked one customer. . . .

I couldn't read much more of that, but the story below the fold wasn't much better.

Federal District (RPI). "The Speaker is not considering increasing conscription levels or recalling soldiers
and airmen recently released from active duty. There
is absolutely no truth to that rumor," stated Defense
Minister Holmbek. Holmbek was reacting to a news
report first aired by TransMedia's federal district subsidiary WFD that the Speaker would soon put before
the House a measure to increase conscription levels
and to extend terms of service for reservists now serving.

Holmbek also denied that the federalization and
mobilization of two additional state air guards was
anything other than a need for advanced training.
"The transfer of the Austro-Hungarian First and Third
Elite Cavalry to the border west of the Russian town
of L'Vov had nothing to do with the Speaker's decision. . . ."

Somehow, I recalled reading something else along that
line not too long before. I hadn't believed it then, either.
After reading just those stories, I suddenly wasn't terribly
angry at David and Waafl. Disgusted, but not angry. The
world was tottering closer to conflict and conflagration,
and the two of them were wondering how they could water
down education more and get away with it, when a decent
universal education might be the only long-term hope for
anyone.

I shook my head and opened the folder with the natural
resources quizzes in them.

6

OVER THE NEXT week, I kept looking in the post for envelopes with briefing materials, the way Ministers VanBecton and Jerome had sent them to me when they had run the Spazi. Not an envelope, nothing. On Wednesday, I offered an official RSVP, and then, on Saturday morning, before noon, while Llysette was practicing in the parlor, I forced myself to sit down before the wireset in the study to finally call Eric and Judith. I'd checked with Llysette twice. It was still strange, but she had no problems staying with them, and they always seemed glad to see us.

"Judith? This is Johan."

"It's good to hear from you. With Eric handling all of Llysette's legal work, I almost never hear from you. You're coming down for the president's arts dinner? Both of you?"

"Does the whole world know?"

Judith laughed. "It could be. Marjorie Rusterman wired, wanting to drop in when Llysette was here. She's got a daughter who wants to sing. Nancy Nollen called also. Eric even got a call from Dmitri Volkogonov, asking when Llysette would be singing in the federal district."

"Volkogonovitch? Should I know something about him?"

"Volkogonov," Judith corrected me. "He's the military attaché at the Russian embassy. Eric sees him now and again. I met him at a reception at their embassy once. We got invited because Eric's firm handles commercial legal work for PetroRus. He even knew who Llysette was, and who you were. He said you were a lucky man."

"I am, but that amazes me. Eric's involved in everything."

"Not everything." After a pause, she went on. "Would you two like to stay with us? That's why you're calling, isn't it?"

"Yes, I have to confess. I put it off, because . . . it's just . . . I feel strange."

"We'd love to have you. Llysette's such a dear, and I can't tell you how much I enjoyed hearing her play and sing the last time you came."

"You don't have to twist my arm." I laughed. "If you're sure, we'll be down on the Wednesday afternoon. We'll take you and Eric out to dinner then. It's the least we can do."

"I won't turn that down. We'll be looking forward to it, and I won't tell Nancy. If you remember, you could bring a brochure that tells about the school and the music program."

"Llysette's department put out something this summer." I wrote a note on my "to do" pad.

After I finished talking to Judith, since Llysette wouldn't be practicing that much longer, I went into the kitchen and studied the refrigerator, finally deciding that I could rejuvenate the potato soup and add bread and a salad. We'd need something to eat before driving down to Zuider. We needed odds and ends that no one in Vanderbraak Centre carried. I'd thought I'd stop by my old friend Bruce's establishment, just to see the latest in difference engine technology, and to say hello.

By the time Llysette stopped practicing and peered into the kitchen, everything was ready.

"A hot soup will be good."

"It's not that cold out." Grinning, I gestured outside to the bright—if cold—sunlight.

"You mock me." She offered a pout that wasn't even an attempt at real hurt or anger.

"Only because I like to tease you. You're cute."

"Like the baby ducks, no?"

I winced.

She laughed and slipped into the chair.

I served the soup, then the salads and the hot bread, and sat down across from her.

"Eric and Judith said they'd be happy to have us," I finally said, as I finished the soup. "Is that all right with you?"

Llysette laughed. "Three times now you have asked. You wish I should say no?"

She took some things far better than I would have— such as my friendship with Elspeth's sister and her husband. Very few women would be comfortable staying with her husband's former in-laws, but after what Llysette had been through, she seemed far more focused on what she found important—her singing and teaching, and, thankfully, me.

"The problem with Beau Jonn, you recall?" asked Llysette.

"That Dierk wants him to teach mostly men? You weren't too happy about that."

"*Non.* We may have a larger difficulty, now."

"What's that?"

"He belongs to the reserve forces in Ohio."

"Is that one of the units the Speaker is mobilizing? Does that mean you'll have to teach both his men and your studio? Until the end of the semester, anyway?"

"I would judge yes." Llysette shrugged. "There is little we can do if he must go."

I stood and began to gather the dirty dishes. "Do you still want to go to Zuider?"

"There are no stockings here."

"No water filters, either."

We both laughed and finished the dishes together. While Llysette was gathering her jacket and purse and whatever else, I pulled on my trench coat and stepped out into the bright afternoon and brisk wind that had begun to strip the leaves from the trees and strew them across the lawn. I eased the steamer out of the car barn and turned it around, then went inside to tell Llysette. She was already standing in the foyer at the foot of the steps. She glanced up the stairs, with a look I didn't recognize.

"Are you all right?"

"I am fine." A faint smile crossed her lips. "There are times when . . . there, I look, and expect to see Carolynne."

"I know. Sometimes, I still have images, things that she must have seen, that I never did."

"Moi aussi."

Then, it was strange, and probably always would be, to have the memories of a ghost who had haunted the house for generations before I was born, and even stranger to know that Llysette and I shared those memories of a person neither of us had ever been or known, except as a ghost. But, then, that had only been one of the results of my desperate early attempts with ghost handling, and far from the worst. I still had scars on my shoulder from Llysette's nearly too successful attempts to kill me with a luger, but I wouldn't have given them up for anything.

"Pauvre femme . . ."

We stepped outside, and I locked the deadbolts.

I whistled a five-note unfinished melody, just to be perverse, as I drove the Stanley out onto Deacon's Lane. Llysette elbowed me, but she smiled.

One of Benjamin's sons, Luke, I thought, waved as we headed down the hill toward Route 5. Before long I found myself behind another of the ubiquitous vanEmsden milk haulers, with a long line of traffic headed north. It was definitely going to be a slow trip to Zuider.

"How's the Poulenc coming?" I asked.

"There is one part . . . but it is almost ready, not like the Rachmaninov."

I hadn't realized she was even working on a Russian piece.

"It is . . . *plus difficile que j'ai crois . . .* "

We talked about what songs she planned for the concerts ahead, and I finally got around the hauler, and passed Three Loon Lakes, just after the point where the road turned from the Wijk River and headed due east. The closer we got to Zuider, and Lochmeer, the less traffic there was.

Bruce's establishment was on the west side of Zuider, well away from the lake, identified only by the simple LBI logo. The only steamer in the small car park behind the building was the ragtop Olds that was Bruce's. Sometimes, I wondered about the oddities of things. Both Reos and Oldsmobiles were popular vehicles, but Ransom Olds had created both companies. He'd lost the first through financial chicanery, and yet had persevered to create the second.

Bruce must have seen us coming, because he actually opened the door—for Llysette, although he was gracious enough to keep holding it for me. He still bowed to Llysette after we entered. "It is always a pleasure." He turned to me questioningly. "You don't need insurance, special equipment, miniature devices?" His eyes twinkled.

"Not today," I replied. Bruce had provided all of the above, although his reference to insurance referred to a different type—his willingness to distribute certain information should anything happen to me. Then, we'd known each other for nearly twenty years, back to a time when we'd both served in the Spazi. Bruce had been in the technical side, and had left earlier, and more wisely, but I'd needed the government insurance for Elspeth. "We're shopping for more mundane things . . . water filters, stockings, conservative cravats. But you did say I should stop

by and see what else you had in the way of difference
engines."

He led us to a spotless workbench in one of the rear
rooms, where a difference engine, without its cover, sat
next to a screen. "Here's a version of the newest SII model.
It could handle three of your special requirements at once."

"That is impressive. I'll keep that in mind."

"If you got it now," Bruce added, "you wouldn't be
calling me to ask for the impossible in a week's time."

I laughed; Llysette smiled. Then I stopped laughing.
Bruce never said anything without a reason. "What do you
know?"

"Nothing that you don't." He shrugged. "I read the papers. Matters are getting tight. When that happens, people
look for experts with experience. You have expertise and
experience, and you're unfortunately loyal."

"That is unfortunate?" asked Llysette.

"When a government needs someone it can trust, it is."

"So, wizard technical expert, where are they sending
me?"

Bruce laughed. "How would I know? I can tell you that
it will be someplace where they can't send anyone else."

"You must be having hard times," I replied, "if you're
trying to scare a poor university professor into buying the
latest electrofluidic technology."

"I do have to stay in business," Bruce pointed out.

"I'll contribute," I said. "Fix it up with what you think
I need, and then add more."

For the first time, Bruce did look surprised. "Johan . . .
I didn't mean . . ."

"I know, but I've needed a better machine for a while."
What I wasn't saying was that I'd learned a long time ago
that Bruce was an optimist. Things were usually worse
than he figured.

"Why don't you bring down the special items I made
for you, then," he suggested. "I'll look them over, and see
if perhaps I can't improve them."

Llysette looked from Bruce to me, and then back to Bruce. "You are two just alike."

"I learned it all from Johan," Bruce replied, deadpan.

"After I first learned it from him," I countered.

"Assez!"

We both smiled. After a moment, so did Llysette.

"I'll let you know when the machine is ready," Bruce promised.

"Thank you."

With that, Llysette and I went off to find more harmless items, like water filters and stockings, and I tried to forget what Bruce had said.

7

O N SUNDAY, LLYSETTE and I were even virtuous
   enough to attend the Dutch Reformed service, where I
enjoyed Klaus Esterhoos's sermon about "immeasurable
compassion," the idea that caring for others shouldn't
weighed by time spent, intensity of feelings, or quantifiable
results, because such caring had an effect beyond the present and calculable results and because measuring compassion defeated its very purpose. That kind of sermon was the
type I liked, perhaps because I preferred goodness and
ethics that could stand without deistic support. Unhappily,
Sunday didn't last, and the week began damp and unevent-
ful, before the sun returned on Wednesday.

Bruce did wonders in his procurement efforts, and on
Thursday afternoon I left right after my Environmental
Politics 2B course and drove down to Zuider to pick up
the new SII difference engine—and to drop off the calculator and hair dryer that were more than just what they
seemed to be for Bruce to overhaul and improve. Then I
drove right back to Vanderbraak Centre through more rain,
hard bullet-like drops from the dark clouds that had gathered from nowhere while I had talked to Bruce.

While I wondered about the arts dinner, and worried

about my meeting with Harlaan, I couldn't very well wire Harlaan and demand the explanation he'd already refused to give me. So I taught and fretted, and went on with life. I'd set up the new SII difference engine beside the first in my study and began to edit and transfer files.

The next Monday, I was back in Zuider, in the early evening, while Llysette was giving extra time to one of her upper level students who was preparing for a recital. Normally, Bruce and his brother Curt closed at six, except on Fridays, but Bruce had agreed to meet me. That bothered me a little as well, but Bruce had always been accommodating.

With that faint smile he gave when he had more on his mind than he wanted to reveal immediately, Bruce escorted me back to his own laboratory-workroom. He closed the door.

"I'm not that secretive, Johan, but someone else might decide I'm open if they saw us, and that creates ill feelings if I don't answer their knocking when they see me."

I understood that. It was like refusing to talk to a student, even if you were late for class.

"Here we are." Bruce gestured to the items sitting on the green cloth at one end of his workbench, which was piled high with equipment even I couldn't recognize.

Four of the items I recognized, because I'd brought them to Bruce the previous Thursday. One looked like a pocket calculator, and two of the others looked like ballpoint pens, except they were special projectors Bruce had made for me when we had gone to Deseret. When the pens went into the decorative slots on the sides of the device and the delete key was pressed, the calculator became a zombification device, or a ghost-removal projector. The same was true of the hair dryer, except it took two switches to turn the hair dryer into a ghosting weapon. The pens, calculator, and hair dryer functioned as they should, otherwise.

"What did you do to them?" I asked. "The calculator and the dryer look the same."

"More powerful storage cells, a bit better projection

coils," Bruce replied. "They were in good shape, and it didn't take much to upgrade them."

The device I didn't recognize looked like an antique fountain pen, faintly bulbous, and yet distinguished in its bulk and style. The casing was black, chased with gold swirls. "What's that?"

"The same as the calculator, except it's an emergency, single-jolt zombifier. One battery, one jolt, *maybe* a second weak jolt, but you don't have to fiddle with anything."

I sighed. "What do you know that I don't?"

Bruce smiled. "Not a thing. Or not much. Someone's monitoring the LBI wiresets, and it's through the circuits at New Bruges Telewire, from what we can determine. There have been several gentlemen, and even a lady, of the type we both recognize, who have been observing us. Ergo . . . you mean a lot to someone." He fingered his beard. "What do you know?"

"I don't. The only contact either of us has had was one wireset call from the present head of our previous agency. He practically insisted that Llysette had to go to the arts dinner . . . said she deserved it. Then he asked me to drop in for a chat."

Bruce winced. "Do you have any ideas about what he has in mind?"

"None. No mysterious briefing materials, no wireset calls . . . nothing."

"They have a very big problem, Johan. So big that they don't want anyone to know, or have any idea of what it is. They also can't use any existing agent, for some reason." His smile turned crooked. "They need the best, and you were among the best."

"Thank you. That's a distinction I'd like to put behind me."

"So would they, but they don't have any choice. And they need both of you."

I nodded slowly.

"I'm glad I beefed all this up." Bruce gestured toward the gadgetry. "I'd carry the big pen with you all the time.

Replace the battery once a month, whether you've used it or not. And . . . remember . . . if you have a choice, don't use these where someone is using radio or videolink equipment nearby. The harmonics in some of the frequencies will create a rather large burst of static on most equipment."

"You didn't tell me that before."

"I didn't think about it. You're the one who did the original designs, remember?"

"You would remind me." Actually, the late Professor Branston-Hay had come up with the basics with his dark-side research, and I'd pirated them just before his Spazi-arranged "accident."

"You could have been a very good designer," Bruce said. "You see formulae and figures and your mind comes up with gadgets. I just refine them."

"You've come up with more than a few of your own, as I recall."

"Don't remind me." Bruce glanced toward the door. "You'd better go. If I have any other ideas, I'll let you know."

"And if I do, I'll be back."

"That's what we both should be afraid of," he returned with his off-center smile.

I just nodded. Bruce always got the last word. So I clipped the bulbous pen into my shirt pocket and eased the rest of the equipment into the small box Bruce had set out. The drive back would be long enough, with more than enough time to worry about what he'd pointed out.

8

F OR NEARLY TWO weeks, setting up the new equipment took all my free time, what with transferring my files, overt and hidden, from the older SII model to the new one. Then I ended up having to program more things than I'd ever thought because improvements in difference engines are not always as time-saving as their creators believe.

By that time, I'd thought that I might have been able to dismiss Bruce's concerns. But the events conveyed by newspaper headlines and stories, while not worsening noticeably, were not improving, either. My instincts, and paradoxically, the continuing silence from Harlaan Oakes, convinced me that I had best refresh and improve my understanding of that subject about which I was one of the few living practitioners.

I had once thought, foolishly, that I'd be done with ghosting and de-ghosting technology and projections and creation, and all the other ramifications of the Spazi research undertaken by the late and unfortunate Professor Branston-Hay. But the events in Deseret had disproved that. I might be wrong, but I decided to do a bit more research into the technical ghost-related files and material I had.

Because Llysette had several students doing recitals later in the year, she ended up going in to the university several nights each week. There wasn't much I could do to help Llysette with the recital preparation, except make sure she got fed and rested, but it did leave me more time to learn about the new machine . . . and, after that, set it up for "ghost" operations and to allow me to look into some additional possibilities. I still had a "ghost" profile of Carolynne, and I kept that saved and safe, but I wasn't about to project it. Who knew what might happen? Conceivably, I might even partly zombie myself or Llysette.

I also had the compressed files of the ghost of justice I'd worked on, and I could use that as a possible starting point to see about improving projection capabilities, except I would have to change that radically if I wanted to avoid the self-zombie problem. So I did, first replacing the image with that of a Norse barbarian, because I had a good illustration from something called *The Dark Hammer*. Then, using the actual internal structure of the real Carolynne's scan, I created all the supporting details. The idea was to replicate what I'd done in Deseret without overloading and destroying the equipment, as had happened in the Saint Tabernacle. While there might be a rough equivalency in destroying a difference engine and the field projection equipment for each ghost projection created, it wasn't the sort of equivalency a university professor could afford.

That was how I found myself sitting in my study on a Wednesday night, a week before we were to leave to go to the federal district, looking at a mass of code, an improved—I thought—projection cone, and wondering if I really wanted to do what I was about to do. Finally, I fed power into the cone and entered the execution codes.

The hazy mist formed right in front of the French doors, the whiteness of the initially indistinct form made sharper by the darkness outside. Then, I could begin to see two figures—one the Viking-like warrior, and a softer, smaller form that was vaguely familiar.

I swallowed and flipped the difference engine's power switch—as quickly as I could.

For a moment both figures lingered, then slowly faded. I took a very long and deep breath, glad I was still myself.

Once again, I was in over my head. If what I'd seen happened to be what I thought I'd seen, the structural arrangement of projected data was as important as the data itself, and by using the structure of Carolynne's template, I'd almost re-created the ghost of a ghost.

So I went back to Branston-Hay's files again . . . but the material I had didn't mention anything about what I thought of as the lattice-structure effect. I tried an arrangement based on the ghost of justice structure, but with modifications, and I got a Viking warrior squeezed into a dumbbell. Another rearrangement got me a trapezoid, and I was getting the impression that I was either going to need to be very lucky or find a text on topographical mathematics, but still hadn't figured out a workable structure when I saw the headlamps and heard Llysette's Reo.

She was already easing the Reo into the car barn, but I went out and opened her door. "How did it go?"

"*Comme ci, comme ça* . . . but I am tired."

I closed the car barn doors, and we walked through a light but cold wind to the steps and into the house.

"*Tres fatigué?*" I took her coat and hung it in the closet in the front foyer.

"*Oui* . . . the recital, it will be good, if they progress as they are, but never do they understand until the last how much effort, it is required."

"That's true of students everywhere, I think. I was like that once."

"*Non* . . . I think not."

I wasn't about to argue that. I knew I had been, whatever she said, but trying to convince a loving spouse that I'd been an impatient idiot student was a losing proposition. So I merely asked, "Would you like some chocolate, or some wine?"

"My heart longs for the wine, and my head says the chocolate. The chocolate, I think." A smile—half impish, half tired—followed her words.

I eased my singer into a chair at one end of the table. I hadn't been terribly successful in rejuvenating my ghost-related equipment and skills, and I couldn't help with re-citals, but I could make good Dutch hot chocolate—if a bit sweet.

9

ANOTHER WEEKEND CAME and went, with more late student recital rehearsals for Llysette, more quizzes and tests for me, more silence from Harlaan, and only marginal improvements in my efforts in improving my ghost-creation operations. Before either of us knew it, it was Wednesday again, and I was packing valises into the Stanley well before dawn for the drive to Lebanon to pick up the Quebec Express to New Amsterdam.

The sun was shining through a bright blue fall afternoon sky when we stepped out of the Baltimore and Potomac station on the north side of the Mall in the federal district. I was carrying my valise and the long hanging bag that held Llysette's gown and my black-and-white evening wear for the dinner. There were more cabs than normal, and we found ourselves being helped into another of the ubiquitous dark blue Piet's Cabs.

"Where to, sir?" asked the square-bearded cabbie, who wore a brown vest and a yellow cravat.

"Upper northwest. Spring Valley. Sedgwick just off Forty-seventh and New Bruges."

"That's a minimum of seven now, sir."

"When did that happen?" I asked, showing a ten. The

year before the minimum had only been five, and that had been a dollar increase from the year before.

"Last month, sir. The kerosene price increases, you know."

The cabbie checked the valises in the boot, then closed the doors, and we were soon headed west on Constitution Avenue, passing the Dutch Masters wing of the National Gallery, my own *bête noire,* since the Congress had accepted the design despite my artistic and environmental objections when I'd been subminister. But then, the post had almost been given to me as compensation for Elspeth's and Waltar's deaths in the Nord affair, and few had expected me to take the position seriously. I'd no sooner gotten myself taken seriously than the Hartpence administration had been swept into office in the elections as a result of popular revulsion, and I'd retired to Vanderbraak Centre.

At Llysette's suggestion, we did stop at the Ghirardelli Chocolatiers off Dupont Circle to pick up a box for Judith and Eric. Embassy Row was little changed. The section of sidewalk in front of the embassy of Chung Kuo was still cordoned off, although in the bright sunlight I couldn't see the ghosts of the Vietnamese monks who had immolated themselves there nearly fifteen years earlier.

When we got out of the cab in front of Eric and Judith's, Judith was waiting on the front porch, her silver hair cut shorter than I recalled. She was wearing a black suit, with a red and silver scarf, as if she'd just come from the gallery, which she probably had.

I let Llysette tender the chocolates while I paid the cabbie and struggled with the luggage.

"You shouldn't have," Judith protested, but her gray eyes sparkled. She was pleased. She followed us inside the Tudor-influenced dwelling, into the two-story foyer and under the crystal chandelier.

"I can take these upstairs," I said to them.

"You are certain, *mon cher?*" asked Llysette.

"Let him," suggested Judith, with a laugh. "Every man

needs to do something to prove he's still masculine and vigorous, and Johan's still young enough that he has to prove it."

"For now," I quipped back, before heading up the wide stairs to the second level. After laying out the valises, and unpacking the hanging bag so that our formal wear wouldn't get more wrinkled, I came downstairs. Llysette was sitting at the table in the nook off the kitchen, and Judith was preparing chocolate and tea.

"While I'm getting this ready, there's a story in the *Columbia Post-Dispatch* that you ought to read," Judith said. "It's about the dinner. I saved it for you. It's over on the counter there."

I skimmed over the boilerplate of the introduction, about speculation over the awards for achievement and then the quotes from all the notables about the need for support of the fine arts, before I got to the part that concerned us.

"Among the distinguished attendees will be the Russian violinist Solomon Volkov, who recently fled tzarist Russia, and Llysette duBoise, the former First Diva of Old France. Her recent performances have electrified audiences, and her Salt Palace disk threatens to break all records for a recording of a single live classical performance. She will be accompanied by her husband, Johan Eschbach, former minister in the Vandenburg administration. An expert in environmental technology, Eschbach is vonBehn Professor of Natural Resources at Vanderbraak State University. . . ."

Actually, I was officially the vonBehn Professor of Applied Politics and Ecology, but I could see that whoever had written the story had wanted to emphasize my technical expertise in ecology, not my technical expertise in other areas. Afra Behn would have understood, I thought.

I passed the paper to Llysette.

She read through the article slowly, then looked up. "Johan . . . if so many of these disks I am selling, why are we not rich?" Again, there was the glint of humor in the dead-pan delivery.

"Two reasons," I replied, equally deadpan. "There are very few recordings of classical live performances. That means you can break records and still not make a lot of money. And second, the contracts say that you don't get paid until six months after each accounting period. So . . . if you're rich, we won't start finding out until next April."

Both women smiled as Judith seated herself in the chair with her back to the island.

After waiting for Llysette to lift her cup, I took a sip of the chocolate from the heavier mug. "It's very good." It was, as always, but I would have said so in any case. "And I'll try not to eat all the butter cookies this time."

"You don't look so nervous this time. Things are much easier this year?"

"Not totally," I admitted. "Harlaan Oakes asked me to stop by tomorrow afternoon."

"The new Spazi director?" asked Judith.

I nodded. "He used to be a special assistant to President Armstrong. You might say that Llysette and I got him his job."

"You never mentioned that," Judith said. "Then, there's always been a great deal you haven't mentioned." She smiled at Llysette. "That is true of you as well, I have this suspicion. Both of you keep secrets well, so well that un-less you want something known, it isn't." She shrugged. "And . . . no . . . I don't know anything that might bear on Minister Oakes and you two."

"Harlaan didn't say anything at all, just that he wanted to see me." I paused. "He was very insistent that Llysette be at the arts dinner."

"That would make sure you were there."

"Exactement," murmured Llysette.

"I still think there's a reason they want you there," I told Llysette.

"Moi . . . I think not, except as an adornment."

I had my doubts, but just asked, "How is Suzanne doing?"

"She and Alex love Savannah. We went down there last month. It's far too hot for me."

How long we had been talking, I wasn't certain, but I'd been through three cups of chocolate when the door opened and Eric stepped into the kitchen.

I stood. "We're here, looking for lodging at the best place in the federal district."

"You're welcome, but in the wrong place for that." He laughed. "This time, you came with fewer portents of trouble."

"There's not anything else in the paper?" I asked Eric. "Or any other media?"

"Not that I've seen." My former brother-in-law grinned.

"Where would you like to go to dinner?" I asked. "It's our treat."

"What kind of food would you two like?" countered Judith, her eyes on Llysette. "French?"

"A good French meal . . . that would be most enjoyable."

"How about *Les Myrmidones*?" asked Eric. "It's not that far. It's quiet and very good."

I looked at Llysette. She nodded.

"Let me wire them." Eric walked over to the wireset, then flipped through the directory.

Judith rose and collected my mug and the cups, and the chocolate pot and teapot.

"The name is Elsneher, four of us . . . in fifteen minutes?" Eric hung up the wireset and turned with a smile. "They can take us now. Later would be tight. You don't mind, do you?"

I shook my head.

"I left the steamer outside," Eric added.

I reclaimed Llysette's coat and my own black trench coat, and we preceded Judith out the side door to the rear drive, where Eric stood holding open a rear door to his steamer.

"Is this new?" I asked, raising my eyebrows, as I looked over the sleek steel gray lines of the Stanley, although it wasn't just a Stanley, but the Broadmoor luxury sedan.

"Ah . . . yes." Eric's boyish grin was sheepish.

"The older they get," observed Judith, "the more expensive the toys."

"Et comment," seconded Llysette.

It was my turn to offer a sheepish smile as I thought about my new and all-too-expensive SII machine. I helped Llysette into the large and luxurious rear seat, then shut the door for Judith and climbed in back myself.

"We can talk about it later at the house," Eric said as he eased the Stanley onto Sedgwick and around the corner onto Forty-seventh, "but TransMedia sent another contract. An addendum, really, but it covers sales in South America and in Australia. There's an advance cheque as well. Nothing huge, but significant. Five thousand."

Llysette looked at me and rolled her eyes. To us, five thousand was still a large sum.

"I know it sounds large, but the cover letter estimates that next year's royalties from South America alone will be five to ten times the advance. Hartson James is really behind Llysette."

I hadn't much cared for the way that the media type had looked at Llysette, but he'd always been a gentleman, and he'd certainly been more than fair in his business dealings, according to Eric and my own feelings.

"He should. So should Maestro Lockhart," offered Judith. "He's the new conductor of the Columbian National Symphony."

I'd never heard of Lockhart, but, then, before Llysette, I'd heard of almost none of the renowned performers or conductors, and I was still learning.

Les Myrmidones was more toward Chevy Chase, off Northlands, just outside the border of the federal district. Eric looked a bit reluctant to turn his toy over to the parking valet, but compromised with a large tip. "Take very good care of it."

"Yes, sir!"

The foyer of the restaurant was paneled in dark wood on two sides, and the panels were bordered by heavy dark blue velvet hangings, edged in gold. In the center of each of the wooden panels was an angular Greek warrior bearing a shield, and in the center of the shield was a stylized golden ant, outlined in black.

"Welcome to *Les Myrmidones*." The maitre d'hotel gave a well-practiced smile, and his eyes flicked across each of us in turn, lingering on Llysette fractionally longer, unsurprisingly to me, since she looked stunning in the pale green traveling suit.

"Elsneher . . . I had called earlier."

"Ah . . . yes. If you would follow me . . ."

After the maitre d'hotel settled us in a corner table, a tall dark-haired waiter appeared with menus and the wine list. "Perhaps something to drink?"

"In a moment," Eric suggested.

"Yes, monsieur." The waiter bowed, his eyes taking in Llysette, before he slipped past the empty tables toward the foyer, where he murmured something to the maitre d'hotel, who in turn stiffened, momentarily, then smiled broadly and vanished, only to reappear at our table.

"Mademoiselle duBoise . . . ," he held up a copy of the Salt Palace disk. "You are she, are you not?"

Llysette nodded modestly.

"*Magnifique!* Would it trouble you . . . mademoiselle . . ." He extended the disk and a pen.

"*Inscrivez á vous?*"

"*Á Les Myrmidones, s'il vous plaît.*"

As Llysette signed the disk, I leaned toward Eric and murmured, "Did you two set this up?"

Eric grinned. "Much as I'd like to be able to reassure you that I did, Johan, I didn't. You're just going to have to get used to being married to a celebrity."

That I could get used to, or hoped I could. But I still couldn't help worrying about the next day, and what Harlaan wanted.

10

THE ELEVATORS IN the Sedition Prevention and Security Service building still smelled of disinfectant, and the carpet leading into the deputy minister's office remained dark rust-red, not quite dark faded blood-red. The pinch-faced clerk peered over the wireline console at me, just as she had in two previous encounters, and I almost could have been persuaded it was a year earlier and I was headed in to see Minister Jerome. But I wasn't.

"Minister Oakes expects you, Minister Eschbach. You may go on in."

"Thank you." That I was being called "minister" again worried me, but I stepped through the half-open door.

"Johan!" Harlaan stood from behind the desk and greeted me with a smile. His square goatee was grayer than when we had last met, in a secure limousine on Llysette's and my return from Deseret. "You're looking good."

"So are you." I closed the door and settled into the upholstered wooden armchair across the desk from him. "What do you have in mind? You don't do courtesy visits."

"Good old Johan . . . always the same." He grinned.

"We have a proposition for you. Or rather, for you and your talented and charming wife."

"What sort of proposition?"

"A performance for the tzar of Imperial Russia, as part of a cultural exchange already set up by the Ministry of State. The fee is fifteen thousand Columbian dollars, plus turbojet transport on Republic Air Corps Two to and from St. Petersburg, residence in the Embassy's guest quarters, and whatever trinkets the tzar or his tzarina might add. A state dinner, and a single performance in the refurbished Mariinsky Theatre."

"And?"

"You provide some technical assistance."

I worried about exactly what kind of technical assistance. "Why?"

"You've followed the news about the Austrian stranglehold on the Persian Gulf oil supplies, the polite refusal of the Japanese to increase their petroleum exports to us, and the rising prices for petroleum products here in Columbia?"

I nodded and waited.

Harlaan extended a single sheet. "You know about the fire at the northlands kerosene conversion plant—the one you obtained the plans for? Here's some background."

More background was exactly what I didn't want. "It was in the paper." I skimmed the sheet. While the newspapers had reported it as an industrial fire, Harlaan's report made it very clear that the fire had been nothing less than industrial sabotage, as had been the rupture in pipeline from the Hugoton fields in Kansas, and the explosion at the Languanillas oil depot in Venezuela.

I finally looked up. "That's not good, but what does all this have to do with a cultural exchange in Russia? They've got all sorts of problems with their own petroleum sources, and they certainly don't have a surplus, even if there were anywhere in Russia that we could ship it from."

"Columbian Dutch Petro has been undertaking a quiet exploratory venture in Russian Alaska. There are enormous oil fields there, and we can run an overland pipeline south to connect to those in Saskan and Northlands."

"That would make Columbian Dutch even more impossible," I pointed out.

"They're the only one big enough to fund something like that," Harlaan countered. "Neither AmeriSun nor Penncon could raise the capital for something that big, and they don't have the expertise, either. AmeriSun's more of a chemical cartel, anyway."

I debated, and then asked. "Doesn't AmeriSun have some Russian ties?"

"Not in petroleum." Harlaan shook his head. "They took over the Putilov chemical and munitions cartel when it went bankrupt fifteen years ago, but that's strictly a chemical operation."

"They wouldn't want to use that as a lever?"

"They might, but they don't have either the capital or the expertise." His voice was calm and firm, as if restating a fact.

"The tzar will agree to something because Llysette sings?" I shook my head.

"Of course not." Harlaan laughed.

"I'm missing something." I was missing more than just something. I didn't like that at all.

"The singing is to get you there."

"For what?" Even as I asked, I had a sinking feeling I knew why and wasn't going to like the answer, but I'd known that before I'd walked into the building.

"The tzar's government is short of hard currency. The rouble isn't that firm. The one thing that Russia could export for hard cash over the next few decades is oil, but all Russian oil is controlled by PetroRus—which is thirty percent owned by the Romanov family. They don't have a surplus in Europe or Asia, and they don't have a trans-Siberian pipeline. So . . . Columbian Dutch develops the Alaskan fields. That doesn't cost PetroRus a single rouble, which is necessary because they don't have any, and then PetroRus and the tzar get paid for the oil they can't develop and can't use, and we get oil that Ferdinand can't block. Columbian Dutch can start paying royalties immediately. They have the cash. That's very important, with Ferdinand controlling the Persian Gulf. The Swedes and Finns, Ireland, and Great Britain all face severe dislocations if Ferdinand cuts off their petro imports."

"They have the North Sea fields."

"The North Sea fields just don't produce enough for either Great Britain or Sweden, let alone the Irish Republic or Iceland," Harlaan said.

"Ferdinand could shut down the North Sea fields in days," I pointed out. "Except he'd rather not lose the oil."

Harlaan raised his eyebrows, then laughed. "You would know that."

"I still don't get it," I said. "If this deal is as good as you've said, why do you even need anyone to help?"

"We're short of oil . . . very short."

"Shorter than we're saying? You're already tapping the Dome reserves?"

"Just enough to keep the price increases from spiking too quickly, and to keep the Liberals from demanding some form of rationing." He cocked his head to the side. "Why don't you let me tell this my way?"

I motioned for him to continue.

"The Austrians have always kept their conquests piece-meal . . ."

I winced. I didn't interrupt, but I couldn't see how the fall of France and the Low Countries had been piecemeal.

"There's an exception to every rule, Johan. Ferdinand would prefer not to start an all-out war right now, much as the Austrians are posturing. We can't afford one, not without severe rationing and hardship. The Brits would go down like a rotten wooden yacht hit with a Perseus torpedo, and the Scandinavians can't stand forever against a Europe united under Ferdinand. The Russians would lose even more territory, the last of Poland, and the western sections of the Ukraine at the very least. Ferdinand wouldn't want any more than that right now. He's too smart to take on the Russian winter. Instead, he'd make Tzar Alexander attack him, and the tzar would lose, and we don't have the resources to support Russia right now. And that's the *best* projection. A longer war in Eastern Europe, and there well might be a revolution in Russia. Even if the tzarists hold on, that would hand more of Europe to Ferdinand. One way or another that would make the Alaskan venture very chancy. The hard-line tzarists would oppose the Alaskan agreement, and if the revolutionaries won, we'd be faced with either trying to annex Alaska, and that's almost as bad as fighting in the Russian winter, or losing all hope of energy independence."

What Harlaan was also saying was that if Columbian Dutch got into Alaska, and all those catastrophes happened later, the Speaker would have grounds for that annexation . . . and probably Columbian Dutch would have put in the infrastructure to support just that.

"If we can work out this oil arrangement," Harlaan continued, "we can offer technology to improve PetroRus's European oil production levels within the year, if not sooner, in a way that is acceptable to everyone. Except Ferdinand, of course. You and Llysette are critical to getting this done in a low-key fashion. We'll let it be known to certain people in the Russian upper levels that you have some expertise in environmentally sound oil reclamation techniques. Everyone knows that PetroRus needs more production from the Caspian fields. If the question comes up, they can claim behind the scenes that you're really there to deal with the Dnepyr River problem, but no one has to admit that publicly. A former minister of environmental affairs—"

"Subminister," I said automatically.

"That's better. Then the tzar doesn't have to acknowledge you in that capacity."

I shook my head—again.

"Matters are strained between Russia and Ferdinand, and Ferdinand keeps the pressure on the tzar. This time, Ferdinand's claiming that the effluent from the Dnepyr is affecting the Romanian fisheries, and Austro-Hungary is demanding the Russians do something. The Russian prime minister is trying to pacify the Austrian ambassador, and by bringing you in . . ."

The more I heard the worse it got. "Harlaan . . . I hear all the problems. Just what am I supposed to do?"

"Johan . . . the president—and the Speaker—are giving you a free hand. *Anything* you can do will improve the situation. Ideally, we'd like the agreement on the Alaskan oil sale and pipeline. We were also hoping that you could get the Ministry of State's negotiating team into PetroRus. They've been sitting in St. Petersburg for two months."

"I'm supposed to do that when our own ambassador and minister of state can't manage it? That's hard to swallow."

"They have to be invited, and the tzar isn't about to invite anyone. The only people with enough stature in Columbia to negotiate with the tzar are the president and the Speaker. The president can't, by law, and the Speaker can't afford to go to Russia in the current situation we face with Austria. That doesn't even take into account the other problems with the Alaskan issue. If we send anyone over there overtly on the ministerial level, then the Mir Party will oppose the agreement in the Duma as granting us concessions, and reopening the Alaskan question. Senator Lincoln's efforts to buy Alaska have not been forgotten. If you can get into the Russian Interior Ministry on the Dnepyr question, then you can slip the right people a suggested approach that puts them in the apparent high ground, and they'll offer it to us on a take-it-or-leave-it basis."

"They'll listen to a broken-down former junior acting deputy minister? I have my doubts."

Harlaan shook his head. "We've put a lot of thought into this. We can send all of the equipment as the ionization and filtration systems for the Dnepyr cleanup, but there will be oil improvement technology there as well."

"And that will get me into the Interior Ministry?"

"We think you have a chance. The Tzar's cousin is the

chief executive of PetroRus. PetroRus created the Dnepyr mess."

"And he will be so grateful?" I asked. "If the Romanovs are half so arrogant as you think . . ."

"He's also desperate. The tzar doesn't really want to know about the mess. Pyotr Romanov—he's the head of PetroRus—doesn't want to face the tzar on it, either. Both the Septembrists and the Liberalists are looking for an excuse to bring up a motion to further curtail the tzar's powers. They can't do it without a cause . . . overt misfeasance, and cousin Pyotr can't keep the Dnepyr mess out of the Duma for much longer."

"That's all well and good. I don't know Russian— merely German and inadequate French, and we're in a situation where everyone all over and around Europe is ready to pounce or react without thinking, and where, if it happens, Ferdinand will probably own all of Europe and the Mediterranean. Unless we all decide to turn dozens of cities into black glass, in which case, everyone loses." I snorted. "None of this even takes in what those idiots in Columbian Dutch might do."

"I know you're not fond of them, but they lost the Southeast Asian fields to the Chinese and Japanese, as well as what interests they had in the Persian Gulf, and they took a huge hit when the Languanillas refinery was destroyed."

"That's not enough. What else is going on?" I frowned. "Holmbek wants the Soviet rocket technology . . . is that it? From the Goddard offshoots?"

"That's not something we need discuss."

"All right. We won't." He wouldn't anyway. "Can we just say that there are other aspects to this operation I don't know and don't need to know?"

"Why would I say something like that?"

"To reassure me that the entire civilized world is at stake—or something like that."

"It could be worse than that." Harlaan actually sighed. "Alexander wants to turn back things a century, to when the tzar was the total autocrat, as opposed to merely being the wealthiest man in Europe, commander in chief of his own army, and the only head of state besides Ferdinand with an absolute veto over his legislature."

"The Duma never did like that."

"It was actually an improvement in 1912 . . . a radical one, but we can discuss history some other time. The tzar's facing unrest among what educated middle class there is. The peasants are muttering about the need for greater land reform. Most of the budget increases have gone for military equipment and research, but that's also resulted in a larger and larger army because there's not enough of a civilian technology base to absorb those technically trained people. PetroRus has bought the rights to import SII technology, and it's likely the military will bleed off trained people for that. We need to buy time for initiatives like that to bear fruit."

"Will they?" I was skeptical, to say the least.

"We don't know, but the alternatives are worse. The PetroRus approach offers some hope, and without support there . . ." Harlaan shrugged. "You're an intelligent man, Johan."

Even with the enticement of fame, money, and prestige for Llysette, the idea of going to St. Petersburg had a definite lack of interest. "Why would I want to do this?"

"Because no one else can. And because you're still a loyal Columbian."

He would have to make an appeal like that.

"And because, if you manage to pull it off, International Import Services will pay you a handsome success fee, commensurate with the degree of success. A *very* handsome fee."

"Money and patriotism." I sighed. "So when do I see Minister Vandiver?"

"You don't. You don't see anyone else but me. Tomorrow morning, Llysette and you will have a very open and public meeting with Vandiver and his cultural affairs deputy, and there will be lots of media types around, and it will all center on her and her invitation to St. Petersburg. Any equipment you might need will go to the embassy in St. Petersburg through us. I'll hand you one stack of briefing materials here, and another will show up on the turbojet with later updates. This afternoon, you'll leave here by my private elevator. My own limousine will take you back to the Elsnehers'. We're old friends, remember? There arc only three others at the highest levels who know about this, and no one else will. Minister Vandiver isn't one of them. He's only been told that this is something the Speaker and president want."

I definitely had my doubts about the degree of secrecy, but I also didn't want to see my own country energy-starved and at Ferdinand's mercy. Nor would a concert in St. Petersburg exactly hurt Llysette's career.

So I took Harlaan's offer, his packet of briefing materials, and his private limousine . . . and worried all the way down to the underground garage and all the way out Constitution and up New Bruges Avenue. The driver didn't say anything, and I wasn't in the mood to open a conversation. So the ride was very quiet.

Judith had obviously been watching, because she opened the door before I reached it. She didn't say anything until I was inside. "That was an armorcd limousine, wasn't it?"

"I don't think Harlaan has any other kind," I pointed out. "Thc head of the Spazi isn't usually the most popular member of the administration."

"Are you two into something again?"

"I'm not sure we were ever out."

"Oh . . . Johan. I'm so sorry. Neither you nor Llysette deserve this."

"She doesn't," I admitted with a rueful smile, "but it's not all like that. It looks like she may get an invitation to perform in St. Petersburg, both for international exposure and a healthy fee. It's not certain yet."

"I won't say anything, except to Eric."

"I need to tell Llysette." So I put on a smile and headed

up to the guest suite, where Llysette was removing herself from the rather hot and steamy tub.

"You . . . you are *impossible*!"

"Only sometimes." I enjoyed the view for a moment.

She flushed . . . momentarily. "Minister Oakes . . . what did he wish?"

"You're going to be invited to do a cultural exchange concert at the Mariinsky Theatre in St. Petersburg. For lots of money and international exposure."

"He wants something from you."

"He does. I'm supposed to help the Russians clean up the mess they've made of the Dnepyr, without letting anyone know that's what I'm doing."

"Why does he wish this?" Llysette's voice hardened, with a great deal of skepticism evident. "Not from the goodness of his heart, I do not think."

"To let the Russians mollify Ferdinand enough so that he won't invade Russia, or part of it, over the environmental mess, and in turn that will allow them to use related technology to boost oil production in the Caspian and in the older Russian oil fields. That will free up other oil that can go to Scandinavia and the Brits, which will hopefully mean more oil here." I was definitely shading what Harlaan had said, but I needed a consistent cover story.

"Johan . . . it is not that simple, *n-est-ce-pas?*"

"No. It's much more complicated. Getting it done is going to be . . ." I shrugged. "Like everything."

"And we do this? . . ."

"And you get more press and stardom, and fees. They're paying fifteen thousand dollars, our lodging in the embassy's guest quarters, and all our transportation on Republic Air Corps Two to and from St. Petersburg."

"War is very near, is it not, Johan?" Her voice was calm but sad.

"It could be. They're hoping I can head off some of the things that might trigger it."

"It will be dangerous."

"Not so dangerous for you, I think, as Deseret was."

She laughed. "An optimist, you are." She shook her head.

While she continued to get herself ready, I took a quick shower. I'd always felt like I needed one after leaving the Spazi building. Then I donned my black-and-white formal wear. By that time, Llysette was dressed, and stunning, in a dress that was half green, half black, but the colors were set on a diagonal, with a green-trimmed black jacket. The green set off her eyes, making them look deeper and more alive than ever, and that was saying a great deal.

As Llysette swept down the steps, she was every inch the diva.

Eric, who was standing in the front foyer, even stepped back a pace, before grinning and giving a sweeping bow. "Your carriage is waiting."

"You are most kind—" Llysette started.

"You don't—" I began.

"I insist," Eric said, still smiling broadly.

"We won't stand on ceremony," I replied with a laugh. "That is, if you're sure, and not just making a gallant effort."

"Eric is known for such," Judith admitted from the archway that led to the kitchen, "but this is not one of those times. He makes such offers far more stiffly. With a touch of insulted righteousness."

"Alas . . . has a man no dignity?" questioned the solicitor. "No secrets?"

Judith and Llysette rolled their eyes almost simultaneously.

So the four of us walked out to the Stanley, and I helped Llysette into the luxurious rear seat of the Broadmoor luxury sedan before getting in myself.

"When are you going back?" Judith asked as Eric guided the steamer out of the rear drive and toward New Bruges Avenue.

"Tomorrow sometime. We have passages on the mid-morning express, but I may have to change them."

"Perils of fame," suggested Eric from the driver's seat.

"I can take you, whatever time it may be," Judith suggested.

"It will be perfectly safe," Eric added. "There's an undercover Spazi car trailing us. I imagine that it's one of those watching the house." He laughed. "We're always safe whenever you two come to town."

"I suspect you're even safer when we don't."

"No. There have been more than a few smash-ins in the neighborhood in the past year, much worse than any time I can remember," Judith said.

"Why might that be?" asked Llysette.

"Fewer jobs," Eric said. "The petroleum thing. It's not as bad here, but several of our clients in places like Chicago and Denver, and even Vicksburg, have talked about how lower-end jobs are drying up. People can't get work, and the dole isn't enough . . . crime goes up."

There was a slight line of steamers on Pennsylvania, but not a huge number, and within minutes Eric stopped at the curb opposite the east gate of the Presidential Palace.

"Have a good time, and show them what a real diva is like!" Eric said in parting.

Judith just smiled.

We stepped away from Eric's Stanley and began to walk toward the well-lighted east gate, where more than a few media types were gathered, standing behind a cordon. As we neared the gate, there was a flash from a camera.

"There she is! The diva—duBoise!"

Several other photographers turned, and there were more flashes. Llysette paused for a moment, then, giving in to my gentle urging, kept walking toward the gate and the pair of security guards with the attendance list.

Amid one or two more flashes, I caught the faintest wink of blue-green. That was enough, and I yanked Llysette flat against the granite pillar beside the entry station, shielding her as well as I could.

Crack! Crack! Two shots slammed against the stone, less than a foot from my shoulder, and there was a needle-like stab on my cheek. To our right, behind the informal cordon line, the press types and the photographers scattered or flattened themselves. Two more shots followed and then one more—and then the roar of an internal engine cycle rose and vanished. The follow-on shots didn't seem to have come anywhere close to us.

I studied Llyscttc, then, in the momentary silence, jerked her toward the gate, which I thought would offer more protection, and practically jammed the invitation, my ID, and her passport at the two guards. One had already pulled some sort of alarm, and a pair of internal combustion engine pursuit vehicles roared up from somewhere.

The other gate guard hurried us inside, where less than ten yards inside the grounds we were met.

"Minister Eschbach! Mademoiselle duBoise . . . this way." There were four guards in the white and gold of presidential security. Between them, we were escorted to a much nearer side entrance.

Once inside the palace walls, I fumbled with my handkerchief and dabbed my cheek. A faint red splot showed on the handkerchief. Probably a stone fragment.

"Are you all right, sir?"

"Just a tiny stone splinter, I think."

Llysette peered at my cheek with worried eyes, then nodded. "It is but a small scratch."

As we were hurried along the back hall, I avoided frowning, but I had to wonder about the shots. There were far better places to shoot at us than from somewhere near the Presidential Palace. Or had the shots even been meant for either of us? Or had they been a warning? But who would risk getting caught to deliver a warning? And the motorcycle indicated that someone had figured out exactly the best way to get away from our Spazi surveillance.

Just before we reached the formal area of the palace, the first functionary to greet us was Alyster Potts, the blond and balding special assistant who had taken Harlaan's place. He wore a worried expression that appeared habitual from the lines in his face. "Mademoiselle . . . Minister Eschbach . . . are you all right? I just heard about the shots.

I've had the presidential guards doubled. I can't believe it—just outside the Presidential Palace—and with the Speaker already here." He shook his head. "There's never been anything like that." He paused. "Are you certain you are both all right?"

"We are fine," Llysette offered. "Johan, he received a slight scratch. I am untouched."

"Rock chip," I explained. "It's already stopped bleeding."

"Are you sure?" asked Potts.

"I'm fine."

"I am so sorry. Something like this . . ." He shook his head. "I can't believe it."

I could, unfortunately.

"Minister Vandiver has been waiting for you, Mademoiselle duBoise. Would you see him before you enter the reception area? Would that be acceptable?"

"Of course." Llysette presented a charming smile.

As Alyster turned, I leaned toward Llysette and murmured, "Minister of state. Probably to ask you to perform."

"That I had determined, Johan."

I flushed, but I got a warmer smile, and her lips brushed my cheek.

A tall white-haired and distinguished-looking man in evening wear appeared and stepped toward us, followed by Alyster, and flanked by two men in the dark suits and white shirts of the Spazi. He smiled broadly. "Miss duBoise . . . I must introduce myself. Mitchell Vandiver, minister of state." After a pause, he added, "I am so glad that you escaped that . . . incident . . . outside." He frowned. "I'm sure that the Security Service will take care of matters." Another smile followed. "But you are here, and as charming and beautiful as everyone has said."

I didn't nod, but could have. A semipublic invitation, set up so that it would be almost impossible to refuse and also so that it was widely covered by the media.

"This is perhaps not the best time, but matters being as they are, I would like to request that you consider joining

... in fact, being the showpiece, the star of our cultural exchange concert in St. Petersburg on Thursday, December seventh." He beamed.

"That ... I would be delighted ... except ..." She glanced at me.

"Oh, I should have made that most clear. We would also want Minister Eschbach as well. I understand his presence has been requested in conjunction with some sort of environmental seminar. And we are not requesting your services on a gratis basis. All Columbia knows how much you have sacrificed for your art. I will not go into details at the moment, but you will receive all the benefits you deserve." He finished with another beaming smile, the kind I'd seen enough and probably delivered too often myself, where the official is pleased with having delivered the message and relieved to have completed the task. It's not obvious, or that obvious, unless you've been there.

"You are most kind, and Johan and I will be most honored to represent Columbia in St. Petersburg." She inclined her head. "You will work out the details, no, with Johan and my solicitor?"

"We had thought perhaps tomorrow morning, at ten-thirty." Another professional smile followed. "But the president and Speaker had hoped for your answer before the dinner."

"I understand. We will do this if all is as you have said." Llysette matched his professional smile with one equally professional but warmer. "You are most kind."

"You are most charming, and we are very grateful." Vandiver bowed. "I look forward to seeing you tomorrow in my office." Yet another smile followed.

As the minister bowed and turned, Alyster Potts reappeared. "If you would follow me ..."

We did. The formal state dining room was already three-quarters full, and from the moment Llysette stepped through the squared archway, eyes followed her from all across the room, those of men in black and white and those of women in all colors and shades of formal dresses.

We were seated near the end of the head table, in the only two vacant places. I was actually at the end, across from a woman I didn't know. Llysette was seated between me and Halston Vandaagen, the minister of justice, and as such, Harlaan's superior, and across from a man whose face was vaguely familiar.

"A pleasure to meet you, Miss duBoise," offered Vandaagen, overly loudly, as if he were making a public introduction. "I so enjoyed your performance last year here, and I bought one of the first disks."

"You are too kind," Llysette demurred.

As Mrs. Armstrong lifted her fork and people began to nibble on their salads, I could catch several murmurs.

"*That's* Llysette duBoise?"

"Beautiful . . . in a cold way . . ."

"Best keep your interest in your eyes, dear . . . say her husband was a spy and an assassin . . ."

"Heard someone was shooting at people on Pennsylvania Avenue . . . him, you think?"

I managed not to wince as I took in the gray-haired but young-faced woman across the table, impeccably coiffured, in a silver-gray dress with a matching jacket. "I probably should know you, but I don't. I'm Johan Eschbach."

She smiled, an actual smile. "There's no reason you should. Not personally. I'm Patrice Alexander."

I laughed. "I'm very pleased to make your acquaintance, Congresslady. I appreciate all that you have done over the years. Professionally," I added.

"You're not what I would have thought, Minister Eschbach," she returned. "But then, not much in the federal district is." She turned to the younger man at her side, the one whose Latin-like face had seemed familiar. "This is my son, Estefan Alexander. Estefan, this is Minister Johan Eschbach, and his wife, Llysette duBoise."

"Pleased to meet you both," replied the younger man. "Mother has been a fan of both of you . . . for different reasons, of course."

"I'm sure Llysette is flattered," I said quickly. "I'm just happy to be her husband at this stage of my life."

"Just her husband?" Patrice Alexander lifted one eyebrow. The gesture was most effective.

I laughed. "What can I say?"

"Best you don't," replied the Congresslady.

The salad was a walnut hearts of palm that I could have done better, and the main course was a filet mignon that I couldn't have bought anywhere, with a bearnaise that was too lemony, accompanied by slightly overcooked beans almandine and potatoes gratinée.

The conversation was slightly arch and slightly false, as expected, and I didn't hear much more about the shots, although everyone in the dining room doubtless knew.

"Adjusted for inflation, kerosene prices aren't that much higher. . . ."

"Schikelgruber is such a charming liar you almost want to forgive him. . . ."

"Main Line musicals aren't what they used to be. I can remember . . ."

"You knew Speaker Colmer intimately, didn't you? Of course, that was well before my time. . . ."

After the pêche melba, a bell rang faintly, and President Armstrong stood and moved to a podium at the end of the table. From there he gestured toward the Speaker, who had been seated across from him. Speaker Hartpence stepped up beside the president.

"The Speaker and I have our differences," Armstrong said, pausing for a moment, before adding dryly, "although you can't attribute the shots outside a while ago to those." He waited a moment for the brief chuckles and light laughter to pass. "We do have our differences, and there isn't any secret about those. We also share a number of beliefs and feelings. These don't make for vivid headlines or videolink stories, and so most people don't realize that. This is one of those times, and, for once, I'm going to let the Speaker have the first and last words on the next subject, which is one about which we both agree."

There were more than a few puzzled expressions around the head table and around the others, from what I could see.

Speaker Hartpence smiled broadly as he stepped up to the podium. "Thank you, Mister President. I hadn't expected such an explosive opening to the dinner, but it may just serve to emphasize the importance of what we're here tonight to commemorate." He nodded to Armstrong before continuing. "The arts are fundamental to who we are as a people. They are also fundamental to the survival of a civilized world. When the arts and those who create them are disgraced, or used as mere political tools and propaganda, we all lose. When we fail to recognize and exalt those who struggle to perfect the best in their art, those who often risk their lives rather than compromise their art, we become far less than we should be and can be. Too often we do not recognize the contributions of those in the arts. Tonight, I am most pleased to make a special presentation of the Columbian Medal for Achievement in the Arts. The recipient has had a unique career, which has spanned early fame, years of suffering for her art, years more of teaching success, unrecognized except by her students and colleagues, and then, once again, great, well-deserved, and long-overdue acclaim."

I swallowed, glancing sideways at Llysette. She was swallowing, too, as eyes turned to her.

Speaker Hartpence gestured toward Llysette. "Mademoiselle Llysette duBoise . . . all Columbia . . . indeed, all those who follow music anywhere, thank you for the spirit; the excellence, and the dedication that your life has exemplified . . ."

The president stood once more, and he also motioned for Llysette to step forward.

I eased out her chair, but did not stand, so that all eyes would be on her as she walked along the side of the table toward the podium.

"We are both pleased to be able to make this award," offered President Armstrong, "and to say that it is small enough repayment for all that you have given to us."

Llysette swallowed, but she did step up to the podium and the microphone. "Speechless . . . I am . . ." She smiled. "Almost. A great honor this is, and I thank you all. Most of all I thank Johan. All would have been lost without him." She inclined her head, then stepped back.

The applause filled the room.

For a moment, I could not see.

As Llysette turned to head back to her seat, Patrice Alexander leaned across the table. "She's right, even if but a few of us know."

When the applause died away, the Speaker stepped back to the podium. "I also have another announcement concerning Mademoiselle duBoise. She has most graciously agreed to perform on behalf of Columbia in St. Petersburg next month at the cultural exchange concert before the tzar . . . and I might add that she agreed to do so long before she ever knew about the award tonight. In fact, we took great pains to ensure she did not know about tonight's award." Hartpence smiled boyishly. "Now, I'd like to relinquish my moment in the light to the president for the rest of the awards and the program."

I frankly didn't recall much of the rest of the evening, except that the singer was from the Philadelphia Main Line, and she sang a medley from the season's early hit, something called "Always Tulips." She couldn't compare to Llysette, and, in a way, I felt sorry for her.

And, as could only be expected in a land settled by both Dutch and English, very little more was said about the shots outside the Presidential Palace.

Then we were being escorted to another limousine, one with a plainclothes guard in the front beside the driver, and were driven through a clear night, unseasonably chill for so early in the fall in the federal district.

"Johan? Why did you laugh when you and the woman across from you began to talk? You did not know her, but that is not how you acted."

I laughed again. "Patrice Alexander is the Liberal Congresslady from Michigan. I've never met her before to-night, but she's the one . . ."

Llysette laughed as well, both in humor and, I thought, in relief, but I had no idea why. My diva remained the most beautiful woman in the world, and the only one with whom I ever could have shared my life.

I almost forgot that we were in an armored limousine.

11

When the Spazi limousine dropped us off, Eric was at the door immediately, and Judith was waiting for us, standing by the table in the kitchen nook. A pot of chocolate, with vapor seeping from the spout, was set on a brass-edged trivet in the middle of the table.

"You're both all right, I see," offered Eric, "and with an armed escort. We were worried after the late news stories. I almost couldn't believe it when I heard about the shots."

"You are all right?" asked Judith. "The news reports didn't say much."

"Johan got a scratch on his cheek. . . ." Llysette volunteered.

"It's just a scratch. Probably from a stone chip. Some of the bullets hit one of the pillars by the east gate," I explained.

"I saw all the sirens just after I pulled away," Eric said. "When I got back, I checked the videolink. It was a while, but there was a report on the news. All the reports said was that shots were fired, and that no one was injured, except one photographer in the shoulder. I take it that one of you two happened to be the target?"

"Probably," I admitted, "but I have no idea whether it was a warning or a serious attempt. Whoever it was was using a blue-green light sight."

"Semiprofessional, then, or a warning. About what were you being warned?"

"Can we find out what happened?" interjected Judith. "From the beginning? Johan and Llysette have had a long day, and I'm sure they'd like to sit down." She motioned to the other two chairs around the table, and we sat down. "Chocolate or tea?"

"Chocolate . . ."

"Moi aussi," Llysette looked at me. I was supposed to give the report on events.

"We arrived," I began. "Someone fired shots in our direction and escaped on a motorcycle. We got an immediate presidential security escort into the palace. The minister of state personally cornered Llysette before we got to the actual dinner and asked if she would headline the cultural exchange concert in St. Petersburg next month. Then we went to the dinner."

"And the Congresslady Alexander took great interest in Johan," Llysette said blandly.

"Only professionally. She was there with her son Estefan Alexander."

"He's supposed to be quite something," rejoined Judith. "He's a rising videolink star on one of the daytime romance epics." She poured Llysette's chocolate, and then mine.

I took a slow sip, enjoying the taste, even if it didn't happen to be quite as sweet as I would have preferred. "We had dinner. Then the first award was the one for Llysette. The Speaker gave her the special medal for achievement in the arts. She accepted it, and then they gave a few more awards—"

"And, according to the news, she said she owed it all to you," Judith said.

"That I do, and Johan, he knows such." Llysette smiled, then stifled a yawn. She hadn't touched her chocolate.

"We're meeting with the minister of state tomorrow at ten-thirty, and I think there might even be more media there. They claim that they'll pay Llysette a great deal for the performance."

"Always the politics," Llysette said.

"Always," Judith concurred, "but isn't it better to get paid through politics than never to be recognized or paid? It's sad, but great artistry isn't ever enough. You have to have great artistry to get that far, but the artistry alone . . ."

"It got me to Columbia, and no farther," Llysette said. "Johan, he did the rest."

"No," I protested. "I helped, but the artistry is yours, and you got the invitation to Deseret on your own, because you worked with Perkins's student."

"You are kind, Johan."

Judith laughed. "I think she's telling you that you're offering false modesty, Johan."

"They've got that picture painted," added Eric.

I think I flushed, and I took refuge in another sip of chocolate before continuing. "Anyway . . . after the awards and songs, they bundled us into the limousine and carted us back here. Tomorrow morning, we go to the Ministry of State, and then catch a train back home."

"Will you get some sort of protection there?" asked Judith.

"Even before what happened tonight, Harlaan Oakes had said that there would be a team watching us. Now . . . there might be more."

Llysette smiled sadly.

"That's another price for fame and artistry," Judith said. "I'm very glad we live a more quiet life."

"We used to," I said.

Eric laughed. "When?"

Both Llysette and Judith smiled. After a moment, so did I.

After another yawn by Llysette, Judith stood. "Your lady needs some sleep, and so do we."

"It has been a long day," I admitted.

"Tres long . . ."

So we staggered to our feet and made our way up to the guest suite, where I helped Llysette out of her formal gown. "You looked wonderful tonight."

"That you say because you love me."

"I do, but you still looked wonderful."

That got me a smile and a gentle kiss.

As we lay there in the darkness after I'd turned out the lights and pulled up the covers, and the extra comforter, because Llysette was cold, she turned to me.

"Johan . . . I know what you must say. But the artistry, it is not all mine. And I would be dead, *mort,* in the soul if you had not done what you did." Her lips brushed my cheek, and I could feel the wetness on her face. "Never can I say such . . . *sauf* . . . *seulement* . . . to you."

"To do what you do takes great courage," I said softly. "I could not get up before hundreds or thousands of people and sing. I couldn't open my soul that way."

"A soul to open, I would not have . . ."

We fell asleep holding each other.

12

I WAS UP early on Friday, first so that I could call the B&O to change our return tickets to Vanderbraak Centre, and second to find out what had been reported in the *Columbia Post-Dispatch* about the dinner and the events of the night before. I let Llysette sleep while I had chocolate and something to eat with Eric and Judith, since the B&O recording told me that the wireline reservations office did not accept wirecalls until eight o'clock.

After Eric left, I went back over the news stories. There were two in the *Post-Dispatch,* both on the front page. The lead story focused on the sensational.

> Federal District (RPI). Shots rang out on Pennsylvania Avenue, right in front of the Presidential Palace just before the president's annual arts dinner. Although a number of noted artists and political figures were entering the east gate at that moment, none were struck by the handful of bullets fired. District police and federal officers were unable to determine who fired the shots and have no suspects. "Most likely, it was a disenchanted artist or a supporter," suggested

Alberto Lucio, head of the Federal Investigatory Service. . . .

Lucio worked for Harlaan, and I could see Harlaan's fine hand, but I doubted that the shots had come from any artist. The rest of the article detailed how no one knew anything, and how everyone was confident the shooter would be found. I had my doubts about that, and then some.

I liked the second story, the one below the fold, a great deal more.

Federal District (RPI). Last night President William L. Armstrong and Speaker Gerald Hartpence jointly awarded the Columbian Medal for Achievement in the Arts to Llysette duBoise, the diva whose Salt Palace recording has actually topped the classical charts and even appeared low on the popular charts. The award took some observers by surprise. "An outstanding singer, to be sure," declared one noted art critic, who declined to be quoted by name, "but she's only been a Columbian citizen for the past few years."

Others were overjoyed. "It couldn't go to a more worthy singer," declared TransMedia mogul Hartson James. Then, James should be pleased. His company has produced the Colombian version of duBoise's best-selling Salt Palace disk. . . .

"An example of talent and determination for young singers the world over," added Columbian Minister of State Mitchell Vandiver. . . .

I almost laughed out loud at that one as I skipped through the other items in the column to the last paragraph.

DuBoise and her husband Johan Eschbach were among those entering the Presidential Palace when an unknown gunman fired two shots and vanished. Eschbach is a former subminister who was the focal point of the Nord scandal when he was wounded and his first wife and son were killed. Later investigations revealed that Colonel Nord ordered the shootings in an effort to silence the former Spazi agent. . . .

I winced at that. Wouldn't they ever let that die?

When the grandfather clock in the hall struck eight, Judith peered into the kitchen at me.

"Is it all right if I use the wireset?" I asked.

She nodded, and I did. After I wired the B&O ticket office and got our passages changed to the one o'clock New Amsterdam Express, my next wirecall was to Harlaan. I even got through.

"Harlaan . . . what do you know about last night?"

"Nothing, Johan. I mean that. From what we can tell, none of those who might have once been your . . . competitors . . . had anything to do with it. Al Lucio is steaming like an ancient flash boiler without safeties. It just wasn't from any source we've been able to track."

"Now what?"

"You may see a few more gray steamers."

That didn't exactly reassure me.

"Isn't Llysette meeting with Vandiver and his deputy for cultural affairs this morning?"

"At ten-thirty. She's very pleased with the concert side of matters."

"It will be wonderful for her career. The president is also very pleased, I understand. I know the Speaker is. He wired me again this morning, and he's most appreciative."

I didn't tell Harlaan that we hadn't had that much of a choice, being who we were and where we were in life. He knew that already, and he was probably happy to repay me for setting matters up so that he was the Spazi director. "I'm glad. I know Llysette is happy to represent Columbia, and you know I'll do anything I can to help."

"I know that, Johan." There was a pause. "Have a good meeting, and if I don't talk to you later, a good trip to St. Petersburg."

After hanging up the wireset, I headed up the stairs to wake Llysette, but she was not only awake but emerging from the steam of a hot bath.

"Johan . . ." She raised her eyebrows.

"I know. My timing has always been . . ." I leered.

"You are a naughty man." But there was a twinkle in her eyes.

"What can I say?"

"Say that you will have tea and something to eat for me." After the words, she did kiss me, and I wasn't terribly forward—somewhat, but not terribly—before I went back down to start something for Llysette, except that I didn't have to, because Judith had returned to the kitchen.

"Just sit down and talk to me," she said, easing cheese into an omelet. "I didn't tell you last night, but Nancy Nollen and Marjorie Rusterman both wired while you were out yesterday. You didn't happen to bring—"

"There are two packages about the university. I left them on the side table in the bedroom." I started to get up.

Judith motioned me to stay at the table. "That's more than they deserve. I'll get them later, and let them pick them up after you and Llysette are safely away."

"I'm not sure we'll ever be safely away from anything."

"That doesn't sound like you, Johan. Do I hear a hint of self-pity?" Judith laughed good-naturedly.

"Probably. I have to wonder. . . ." I let the words die away, perhaps better unspoken in any case, as Llysette appeared, this time in a darker green traveling suit.

"Good morning," Judith offered cheerfully. "I have an omelet ready for you, along with toast and some peaches. They're tinned, but it's hard to get produce this time of year."

"*Merci . . .*" Llysette was almost shy in her response as she seated herself. "Is there not something I could do?"

"Not a thing." Judith slipped the platter in front of Llysette. "The article about you was very flattering."

I poured Llysette's tea.

"It was a great surprise." Llysette lifted the teacup, then

glanced at me. "You are most certain that you did not know?"

"All I knew was what I told you, that the Speaker and president wanted you at the dinner. Harlaan never even hinted at why, and I certainly didn't guess they'd honor you so."

"When one is honored so, Johan, the price is always high." Llysette smiled and shrugged. "Yet it is better to be honored than not, and so we shall do as we can." She looked down at the platter and cut a section of the omelet with her fork.

After Llysette ate, and we finished packing, I carted our valises, and Llysette carried the hanging bag down from the guest suite. Judith was waiting with her smaller Stanley—more the size of mine, except newer. When we pulled out of the drive and turned onto New Bruges Avenue, behind us, an older and grayer steamer appeared—definitely government procured.

"I see we have an escort," Judith said dryly.

"We may have them for a while," I answered. "Minister Vandiver wants very much for Llysette to perform in St. Petersburg next month." So did Harlaan, but I didn't mention that.

The Ministry of State was a long gray building at the northwest end of the new Mall, overlooking both the Potomac and the recently completed Washington Memorial. From the outside, the structure didn't appear all that different from the Dutch Masters wing of the National Gallery, whose design I'd disapproved. For my pains, Speaker Ashbrook had overridden my decision, just before the complete and confidential report on the Nord affair had surfaced before the elections and defeated his administration, and now the federal district had two long and gray ugly stone buildings on the north side of the Mall.

"I worry about the luggage," Judith said. "Couldn't I just wait somewhere and keep it."

"No. We'll manage. You've done enough."

So I marched up the steps with the two valises, and Llysette carried the hanging bag.

Someone had been alerted, because a thin red-haired young man stepped out of the main entry into the gray morning with a most professional smile "Mademoiselle duBoise, Minister Eschbach." He bowed, leaving the smile in place. "I'm Corliss Corson, special assistant to Minister Vandiver."

"I apologize for the luggage," I offered, "but there was no way to make the meeting and our return train without bringing it."

"Minister Vandiver had thought that might be the case." Corson raised a hand, and two zombies in gray singlesuits appeared. "Please take the valises and bag and follow us."

"Yes, sir," the two replied in unison.

I was happy enough to surrender both, and Llysette tendered the hanging bag with a warm and broad smile. The zombie smiled back. Llysette had that effect. I could even remember Gertrude, one of the university zombies, crying after hearing my soprano sing. Was it because Llysette now put so much life into her songs? Into all she did?

The foyer inside the double doors was two stories high, extending almost the entire length of the building. The solid stone facing of the second-level open balcony at the back of the foyer was decorated with the flags of every sovereign nation on earth—or so it seemed. For all its length, the foyer itself was almost deserted, and Corson led us to an elevator guarded by two Republic Marines in dress blues. "The minister's private lift."

The lift went up to the fourth level, and to another foyer, also guarded by a pair of armed Republic Marines. The luggage and the zombies trailed—I hoped. We followed Corson through the double doors and down a corridor carpeted in deep blue to yet a third guarded door, which he opened with a punch combination of some sort. We found ourselves in an anteroom.

There a single clerk smiled professionally at the three

of us. "Minister Vandiver is waiting." She opened yet another door.

Mitchell Vandiver did not stand behind his desk but stepped forward toward Llysette. "Miss duBoise . . . or Mademoiselle or Doktor . . ." His shrug was rueful, natural, doubtless well practiced, and, combined with the white hair and open smile, disarming. "Even after last night, I scarcely know how to address you, but I am happy that you were able to see me this morning."

"I am pleased to be here." Llysette returned the minister's greeting with a smile more reserved, if charming.

"Please be seated." Vandiver gestured to the man beside him. "This is Deputy Minister Drummond Kent."

Llysette and I were ushered into the two seats closest to the desk, while Corson and Kent took the seats flanking us, and Vandiver settled back behind the empty polished wood surface of his wide minister's desk.

"You have made quite an impression on the world, and we are pleased that you have agreed to help us." Vandiver smiled, but I could sense the slight unease behind the practiced expression. "We find ourselves in a difficult situation, because the tzar sent the Ballets Russes here last spring, and expects us to provide our best in return. You are our best." Another pause followed. "As I mentioned last night, the exchange concert in St. Petersburg is most important. You are one of the most noted singers in the world today, and your presence would make a great difference."

Llysette nodded.

"Pardon me for being direct, but we understand that you received fifteen thousand dollars for performing in Deseret. We could do no less, especially after the worldwide reception of your disk." Vandiver smiled again. "We have a packet for you. There is a contract there . . . merely a formality . . . you understand, but the solicitors insist, and a retainer cheque as well. There are also schedules, background information on what you may encounter in St. Petersburg, and detailed information on the rest of the performers on the program. You would be the last performer, of course. We had hoped that you could do fifteen to twenty-five minutes of songs."

"That I can do . . . if all is as you have said." Llysette inclined her head to me. "Johan must agree to the details."

"I'm sure there will be no problem," Vandiver replied smoothly. "We would like to request two additional . . . considerations from you. If you could, your program by a week from now, and we would like at least one Russian song, or two if you could manage it."

"One I can do, and more, *peut-être*. We will see."

"Do you have any questions?"

"There is one," Llysette ventured. "A good accompanist is necessary."

"If you have no objections, we had thought that Terese Stewart . . ." Vandiver glanced to Drummond Kent.

The deputy minister nodded. "You have worked with her before. If she is not satisfactory, we could see who else might be available."

"Fräulein Stewart, she will do well, but we must practice before the performance. You have said that the performance, it must be the best."

Drummond Kent cleared his throat, looked at Vandiver, then spoke. "Fräulein Stewart will have her expenses paid to come to Vanderbraak State for the week prior to your departure to work on your program. We'll also pay her fees, as well."

"We want this to be an outstanding concert," Vandiver added.

"The tzar should hear our very best," added Minister Kent.

"Who else will be performing?" I interjected quickly.

"The noted pianist Robert Thies and a chamber group— the Black Mesa Quartet."

I'd never heard of either, but Llysette nodded.

"The information packet for you," Vandiver continued smoothly, "has the details on the concert and the itinerary. You can look it over at your leisure. We had planned to have Republic Air Corps Two put down at Asten on Saturday night, December second, to pick you and your husband up. I understand that also allows us a greater flight range as well." Vandiver turned to the deputy minister. "You have the information packets, Drummond?"

"Yes, sir." The wispy-haired deputy minister smiled and lifted two folders.

I took them and leafed through them. They were thick and heavy, the kind that had always bothered me. The retainer cheque was for five thousand dollars, and the contract was a simple one-page affair, seemingly without catches, but Eric would have to look at it before I had Llysette sign it. There were also briefing documents, including street maps of St. Petersburg, a map to the federal aerodrome at Asten, and a diagram and some printed material on the Imperial Mariinsky Theatre. "We'll send the contract back as soon as Llysette has had the time to look it over and sign it."

"Splendid!" Mitchell Vandiver even looked pleased. He waited almost thirty seconds before looking at the clock on the wall, the signal that the meeting was over. "You have return passages to Vanderbraak Centre . . . or Lebanon, I gather."

"We do," I answered. "On the one o'clock New Amsterdam Express."

"I'll have my steamer take you to the B&O station." Vandiver stood and bowed, and the bow was directed clearly to Llysette. He paused, looking almost embarrassed. "Would you mind if . . . there are several reporters in the outer office. I told them you were on a tight schedule . . ."

Llysette looked at me.

"A few minutes," I said, "and whatever photos they'd like."

The next minutes were a blur, as I followed Llysette into the anteroom, where she was showered with a flare of camera flashes. Once my eyes cleared, I realized that there were only four or five photographers and maybe a few more reporters.

"Mademoiselle duBoise will answer your questions for a few minutes," Drummond Kent said. "She has to make a connection to return home."

Even before Kent's last words ended, the first questioner fired his words at Llysette. "Miss duBoise . . . why did you agree to go to St. Petersburg?"

Llysette smiled, an expression warmer than professional but still slightly guarded. "Columbia has been good to me, and I would repay that."

"Some say it's because people here like musicals better. How do you feel about that?"

Llysette offered the hint of a frown. "There are beautiful songs in many places. Some musicals, they also are beautiful. I sing where those who enjoy what I sing would like me to sing."

"That sounds like not everyone likes what you sing. Is that so?"

"Everyone . . . all people have different likes. I am told that the tzar likes the music I sing. So I will sing there." She smiled more broadly. "Many in Columbia like what I sing. They have bought my disk, and I will be singing in many places in Columbia in the next year."

There was a laugh from one side of the anteroom.

"Did you get the medal for political reasons?"

Llysette laughed, humorously and ironically. "I knew no one in politics until I sang for the president last year. I saw him at the dinner this year. My Johan, he has not been in politics for ten years, and the other party he was representing. Is that politics?"

Another laugh followed.

"One more question," announced Drummond Kent.

"You were badly treated by Emperor Ferdinand. The tzar is an autocrat just like Ferdinand, but you'll perform for him. Why?"

"I will sing before the tzar. I sing for the people of Columbia." She paused, and her voice chilled with the next words. "The tzar, he is not Ferdinand."

I wondered if the two were that different, despite the muted hatred in Llysette's voice.

"That's all," Drummond Kent announced.

"What about the shots last night?" called a voice.

"That's all," repeated Kent.

"I know nothing about that," Llysette replied with a smile.

Corson led us out into a back corridor.

Deputy Minister Kent followed, then bowed to Llysette. "I look forward to seeing you on the turbo to St. Petersburg."

Our valises and the hanging bag, and the two zombies, were waiting farther down the corridor. That the two zombies were there was especially important, because zombies were trustworthy to a fault, and literal minded.

"Did you have any trouble with the bags?" I asked. "How did you bring them up?"

"No, sir. We had to take the freight elevator."

"Thank you."

Of course, they had to carry them back down again, trailing us.

Llysette was being treated like ancient royalty, and while she deserved it, I was quite certain I didn't like the implications. Someone knew I was protective of her, and they wanted her—and me—to be pleased, very pleased, and no one did that in government out of kindness or generosity.

Desperation, yes . . . calculation . . . but not kindness.

13

A T EIGHT O'CLOCK Friday night the Quebec Special finally eased to a halt in Lebanon. A chill and damp wind gusted around us as we stepped onto the platform. I beckoned to a porter and watched as the zombie put both valises and the hanging bag on his cart, then fell in behind us.

"Déja, c'est l'hiver." Llysette pulled her coat tightly around her.

I left my topcoat folded over my arm. The chill felt momentarily welcome after the heat of the train. "Not yet."

"It will be colder in Russia, *n'est-ce-pas?*" After a moment, she added, "What one must do to sing . . . it never ceases."

A six-wheeled steel gray Stanley was parked in a space directly behind mine, and a squarish man in a gray topcoat nodded to me as I turned to the porter. "Everything's fine, Minister."

"Thank you."

Llysette smiled politely and nodded her head in thanks.

I opened the Stanley's boot and watched while the porter loaded the valises. I gave him three dollars.

"Thank you, sir."

Llysette didn't say anything more until we were inside the Stanley with the doors closed and headed eastward on the Ragged Mountain Highway.

"Johan . . . there is much more than a concert in St. Petersburg, is there not?"

"I told you that," I said reasonably.

"Johan . . . do not humor me. A child I am not."

Concealing a wince at the chill in her voice, I answered. "I've told you most everything I've been told. Columbia needs petroleum and kerosene desperately. It will be another year before the plants we got the plans for come on line. The Japanese won't export more to us, and neither will the Austrians. We're getting additional supplies from Deseret, but not enough. We need Russian oil very badly, and there are more than a few people who don't want us to get it."

"But . . . how would they know . . . my concert?"

"Spies . . . of one sort or another. Certainly, enough people know that we worked out the arrangements with Deseret. Now . . . you get an arts medal, and a concert in St. Petersburg . . . and there is already a negotiating team from Columbia in Russia—"

"That, you did not mention."

"I'm sorry. Part of what I'm supposed to do is make it easier for them to get to see the right people." I had to slow the Stanley as we came up behind a Columbian Dutch Petro hauler.

"Oh? And you will meet them at my concert?" At least, there was a hint of amusement in the question. "They will like Rachmaninov? Or will they sit and murmur of petroleum?"

"You've told me that the *Vocalise* is beautiful and difficult, and that you've always wanted to do it in a performance. You already know it. They'll love it. Remember, they're not just petroleum types. Several members of the Romanov family are connected with the Russian petroleum industry. The tzar's cousin is the head of PetroRus."

"Worse than the Bourbons, they are . . ." Llysette shook her head.

"The Russian aristocracy has always been a small society." I finally was able to pass the lumbering kerosene hauler on a straight-away. "They do support the performing arts, though."

"Performers are their play dolls, no? Is not the prima ballerina of the Ballets Russes paid to be the mistress of the tzar?"

"That was his father, or his great-great uncle." It might have been farther back than that. Having a prima ballerina as a mistress had been one of the more notable accomplishments of the ill-fated Nicholas, who had probably done his country a favor by dying of intestinal typhus. Then, rumors were that one of the grand dukes had ensured that the ailment had been fatal before the ardently disliked Alexandria could provide an heir. As it was, his far more gifted younger brother Mikhail had barely survived the restructuring of Russia in the early years of the century. Unhappily, the current tzar was bent on emulating the autocratic ways of the early Romanovs, although Alexander had continued the rocket development initiative begun by his grandfather. And he did support the arts—more than did my native Columbia.

"The same he will be."

"It could be." I laughed. "How would we know?"

"I will know. Carolynne knew."

"I'm sure you will." I hadn't searched the memories of the family ghost whose spirit had melded with mine, not in depth. It was hard to take some of them, especially those intensely female recollections, probably because they showed my own inadequacies all too clearly. Then, as I got older, there was more and more that revealed inadequacies, such as my inability to protect Llysette in Deseret. "Just don't encourage the rascal." I smiled as I said the last words.

"Even the tzar . . . he would not . . . not when I am sent by your Speaker."

"I would, if I were tzar," I joked, even as I wondered. The Romanovs had not exactly been a dynasty known for moderation. Then I had to concentrate on driving as we'd caught up with an intermittent line of haulers, probably headed to Asten, and the road got more winding.

The clock was striking nine-thirty by the time we reached Vanderbraak Centre and I was carrying in the second valise to take it upstairs to the master bedroom. While Llysette began to unpack, I stoked up the woodstove in the parlor. Next, while the stove was heating up, I moved the steamer into the car barn, topped off the water tanks, then returned to the house.

Driving always left me keyed up, and I certainly wasn't ready for bed. So I began to fix chocolate and get out some biscuits. While the milk for the chocolate was heating up, I carried the two briefing packets into the study and set them on the desk. I looked around the study. Everything seemed to be in its place, but it didn't feel that way. So I turned on all the lights. That didn't help.

I flicked on the new difference engine and waited. My telltales didn't show anything either.

"Llysette?"

After a minute or two she slipped into the study, still wearing her suit jacket. "It is cold."

"I've stoked up the woodstove. It should be warming the parlor before long." I paused. "Something feels different, but I can't figure out what."

She sniffed. "It looks the same, but the same it does not smell."

Smell hadn't occurred to me, but she was right. I checked the lock on the French door and looked out to the patio but could detect nothing different and out the place, although it would have been difficult with the limited range of the lights and the swirls of fallen leaves across the lawn.

The questions were simple enough. Who had been in the house, and why? It had been a professional, or a team of professionals, because nothing was out of place, and that made it seem unlikely that it was the same person or group who had shot at us outside the Presidential Palace.

"Harlaan's boys," I murmured.

"You think so?"

I nodded. They'd done it once before, and I had no doubts that they now had every file on my difference engine. This time, I couldn't figure out why. The Spazi knew everything I did about ghosting and de-ghosting and zombification. Surely, they didn't think that I had come up with some new breakthrough.

"I like this not at all, Johan."

"Do you want to cancel the performance?"

"*Non!* Who would ask again? And when?"

She had a very good point there—very good. I flicked off the difference engine. "Let's have some chocolate."

"That would be good."

It would be, especially since there was little else we could do at the moment.

I4

SATURDAY WE SPENT recovering, although I did handle some chores, as well as correct some quizzes and make a trip down to Vanderbraak Centre to the post centre and to Samaha's for the back issues of daily newspapers Louie kept for me. Unlike with Llysette's earlier performance in the federal district, the Asten *Post-Courier* had no references to her in any of the issues put out while we had been gone, not even the one on the shots at the Presidential Palace.

On Sunday, I made a quick trip to pick up the paper, but neither Llysette nor I happened to be in the mood to attend church. Instead, we sat in the parlor, warmed by both sun and the woodstove, and sipped chocolate and read the Sunday paper. It was impossible for me to ignore the headlines and front-page stories in the *Post-Courier*.

Peiping (WNS). Warlord Minister Wei Deng Tsao claimed that a Russian Perun rocket had crossed the northern borders of Chung Kuo before exploding . . . Little is known about the Perun. With a range of less than eight hundred miles, it is not a military threat except to Austro-Hungary, Chung Kuo, and the

Swedish confederation. Despite last month's apparent nuclear test in Siberia, experts believe that Russian scientists have been unable to develop an atomic device suitable for a warhead.

Austro-Hungarian Foreign Minister Erich von-Braun reiterated the Viennese position that deployment of missiles with nuclear warheads would violate the High Frontier Treaty and the older Treaty of Warsaw, which concluded the Summer War. . . .

Russian Minister of Communications Lamanov denied that there had even been a launch of any rocket. He also stated that the purpose of the Perun program was "purely scientific" and denied that the Perun would ever carry warheads.

Skeptic that I was, I suspected that either the Russians had a bigger rocket under development based on what they'd learned from the Perun program or the Perun couldn't carry a big enough payload to make its development and deployment militarily useful.

A smaller article did catch my eye.

Athens (WNS). King Constantine and his consort Arianna saw their twin daughters off to school today. Both will attend the University of Virginia . . . Earlier Crown Prince Nicharos began graduate studies at Washington and Hamilton University. . . .

I set down the paper. I must have sighed.

Llysette put down the Culture section. "I should be the one sighing, Johan. Barely one word is there about my award. . . ."

I took the paper from her hand and pointed. "I see a picture. I also see a beautiful woman in it, and a story about how she'll enchant all of Europe—"

"Johan . . ."

I almost missed the twinkle in her eye. "Go ahead and sigh. Do you really want more than this? Do you want every moment of your life in newsprint?" I deepened my voice. "Noted soprano Llysette duBoise is spending a quiet morning with her husband, the former secret agent and assassin. DuBoise is known for her incredible voice and for her lack of judgment in marrying former minister Eschbach. . . ."

She did laugh.

"Seriously," I pointed out. "That's your choice. Have every moment reported by someone, or risk dropping out of sight."

"C'est so triste. . . ."

"It is, but that's Columbia. You'd have more of a private life in Britain or Russia, or even New France, but I don't know that you'd want to live there."

"I should think not." Llysette paused. "Some did go to St. Petersburg, but it is colder there than here." She shivered, although the woodstove had the parlor very comfortable. "The Russians, they are so filled with gloom."

With the history of Russia, anyone raised there had to be gloomy. There must have been thousands of ghosts haunting Moscow and St. Petersburg over the centuries. Maybe it wasn't so bad in the summers, during the white nights when it never got dark. Most ghosts would be hard to see then. I took a sip of chocolate before I turned on the sofa and asked, "Have you thought much about your program in St. Petersburg?"

"Oui . . . I had thought of doing *seulement* the Russian songs."

"You'd said you'd do the Rachmaninov *Vocalise*. What else?"

"The song of Mignon, 'None but the Lonely Heart.' That is Tchaikovsky. . . ." She sang a phrase, clearly in Russian, because I didn't understand a word, then shook her head. "So long it has been."

"You know Russian?"

"Only the songs. A singer would be a diva of France, she always hoped to go to St. Petersburg." Llysette shrugged. "Never like this."

"Then you won't have to learn so much so quickly."

"I must talk to Terese Stewart."

"Her number is in the packets we received from Vandiver. You could wire her later today. She lives out in West Kansas."

"Not today, Johan. Today, it is for us."

I wasn't about to argue with that. Instead, I inched closer to Llysette and kissed her neck.

"*Aprés* . . ." she replied with a throaty and gentle laugh, leaning away from me. She held up a section of newspaper. It wasn't the *Post-Courier,* but the twelve pages of the *Tower*—the student paper.

I raised my eyebrows.

"They are writing about the play. . . ."

"Gregor's production of *Hamlet*? It doesn't open for two weeks."

"He talks about ghosts . . . and the need to understand." Llysette shook her head.

So did I.

Gregor was from the west. He had seen one or two ghosts in his life—and thought he knew ghosts. We understood ghosts—all too well. And neither of us wanted any closer or greater understanding. I massaged Llysette's neck, gently, while I waited for her to finish the article.

15

MONDAY MORNING CAME, and with it, the obligatory visit to the most honorable Herr Doktor David Donniger. So, after dropping off Llysette, I hurried in and picked up the paper at Samaha's, folding it shut and not even looking at it because I was running late. I drove back up to the faculty car park where I left the Stanley—again—in the last row and then walked through a clear bright morning, marred only by a cold and gusty wind out of the northwest.

Gertrude and Hector were working on the lilac hedge beside the walk from the car park to the converted Dutch Republic dwelling that held my office. Both zombies had their rakes out and were attempting to remove all the leaves from beneath the hedge. The cold wind was light enough that leaves were not flying. Neither zombie looked up as I passed, but that was normal.

When I stepped into the front foyer of the building, I could see that the door to David's office was open. Sooner was better than later. So I stopped just inside his door. "David . . ."

"Yes, Johan?" Herr Doktor Donniger looked up from

the oh-so-neat stack of papers before him with a look that suggested he really didn't want to talk.

"Llysette will be singing in St. Petersburg on December seventh. St. Petersburg, as in Russia."

"I'm glad for her." A bemused smile crossed David's face. "Dierk may not be so glad, from what I've heard."

"The Ministry of State has set it up as a cultural exchange program," I added.

"I suppose you want to go along. That would make matters a bit difficult here, you know?"

"I've been requested to accompany her. One of the major Russian companies has an environmental problem. The State people thought I might be of assistance."

"Outside consulting is frowned upon during the school year, Johan. The trustees have pointed out that we are a teaching institute, not a research university." David smiled blandly.

"I understand," I replied, just as blandly. "Still . . . the minister of state met with us both personally on Friday. He expects us both on Republic Air Corps Two on the Sunday before Llysette's performance. He and the Speaker think that it's important enough to fly us there on government turbo at government expense. If you would like me to convey your concerns . . ."

"Ah . . . Johan . . . I'm sure that won't be necessary. Even though we are not a research institution, both the dean and the trustees will be more than pleased to know that we have two faculty members so distinguished that the federal government has requested them specifically."

"I'll do my best to make sure that the university is mentioned, David."

"That . . . ah . . . would be helpful."

David was reaching for the wireset even before I left his office, doubtless to report to the dean. Dear Katrinka would prefer the publicity and the indirect spotlight for the university far more than perfect attendance by her faculty.

Once upstairs in my small office, before unfolding the paper, I picked up the handset and wired Bruce, wondering if it were too early, and whether he happened to be in.

"LBI."

"Bruce . . . Johan."

There was a low chuckle. "I *said* something was up. I presume you were the target of that anonymous shooting attempt?"

"Llysette, I think."

"I don't like that."

"Neither do I. She's been picked to sing in St. Petersburg, a cultural exchange concert next month. I'm supposed to go along and help with some environmental matters."

"I see."

I could tell he did. "Believe it or not, I still don't know much more than when we talked, except that they seem to think that if I solve some environment negotiation problems they have, the tzar's people might figure out a way to help us with some energy concerns."

"Have you looked at the morning paper?"

"No. I called you first."

"You ought to. What I said before still holds."

I reached for the paper and opened it. I winced at the headline: RUSSIANS GO NUCLEAR. "I just read the headline. You're right, but I still don't know the angle."

"I have every confidence in you, Johan. You'll figure it out."

"Thanks."

"No problem. Let me know if you need anything else."

"I will, but I honestly can't think of anything else. The new difference engine really is a marvel. You told me that it was better to get it before I needed it, and you were right about that."

"We do our best. . . ."

When I hung up the handset, I smoothed out the paper and began to read, knowing that I didn't have that much time before getting down to working up lesson plans and quizzes for whomever would cover my classes while we were gone. I still swallowed the second time I read the headlines, even before I got into the story itself.

Vienna (WNS). Austrian Foreign Minister vonBraun revealed a series of high-altitude photographs of a purported nuclear detonation at the Lobachevsky Proving Grounds in Siberia. "We will not stand by while the tzar threatens all of Europe. Nuclear weapons have no business in a civilized world." For decades, Austro-Hungary has announced that it will not use such weapons on a first strike basis. . . .

Independent scientific observers questioned the success of the test, noting that the seismic recordings showed a low yielding device, or one poorly designed for weapons usage, combined with an excessive amount of electromagnetic radiation. Initially, the electromagnetic pulse that created more than a minute of intense static in eastern portions of Austro-Hungary was what called scientific attention to the blast. VonBraun's statement did not comment on the effectiveness of the device. Other observers suggested that the Russians were attempting to develop a nuclear warhead that could be mated to the Perun rocket. . . .

In reaction to such a question, Russian Communications Minister Lamanov strongly denied that Russia was developing nuclear warheads for the Perun, saying it was "absolutely ridiculous . . . totally out of the question. Russia has no desire to turn Europe or anywhere else into black glass or a radioactive wasteland. We Russians have always loved the land. We would not do that."

I shook my head. With that strong a denial, the Russians were attempting something—and probably failing, given the observations in the newspaper. The smaller RPI story noted that with the Russian detonation, there were effectively five nuclear powers, although the Japanese had never detonated a device. But then, where could they have detonated one?

The rest of the news was comparatively placid—another set of stories about the price of kerosene, and a semi-feature devoted to the growing influence of the Greek trupps. The story did note in passing that such criminal elements were a small segment of Asten's burgeoning Greek population and that the immigration from Greece had continued to climb, often illegally, as Greece became more and more of an Austrian puppet state.

The story below the fold on the second page dealt with the Asten Aerodrome, and the wasteful nature of the long runways required by turbos, and the huge amount of re-fined kerosene-based fuel gulped by the handful of civilian turbos and the military turbo transports. That provoked a few thoughts, which, an hour or so later, in my eleven o'clock environmental economics class, led to a diversion . . . of sorts.

I asked a related question, near the end of the class, since almost all the faces appeared bored or blank "Mister Unduval, would you care to explain why, in some senses, the title of this class is an oxymoron?"

"A what, sir?"

"An oxymoron, a contradiction in terms . . . such as a straightforward politician, an interesting professor, a hard-working student."

I got laughs on two of the three examples, but then, most students *think* they work hard. I know I had. I didn't find out I was wrong until much later.

"Miss Zand?"

"The most environmentally sound way of doing some-thing should be the most economical?" The petite blonde swallowed after she answered.

"That's very carefully and very well phrased." I couldn't help smiling, despite the other blank faces. It was good to get a solid answer without having to go through student after student. "The word 'should' is especially important. Why? Mister Denheider?"

The gangly korfball player gulped. After what seemed minutes but was less than thirty seconds, Alden Denheider finally stuttered. "Ah . . . Professor . . . because . . . well . . . I mean . . . the cleanup costs for oil spills and chemical leaks . . . they're not included in the prices of things."

For Mister Denheider, that was eloquence; it was also proof that he'd read at least some of the assignment, because originality wasn't exactly his greatest strength. "Exactly," I said with another smile. "If . . . *if* . . . all the costs of producing and distributing goods, including all the environmental costs, were included in the price of the good, then it would be to each producer's advantage to produce products in the most environmentally sound manner." I paused. "So why doesn't this happen?" I gestured to Miss Vught.

"Sometimes price isn't as important as other things?" asked the redhead in return.

"Can you give me an example?" I looked around the class.

"What about military aircraft, sir?" asked the clean-cut Verner Oss. "A dirigible is more economical and efficient, but it won't stand much chance against a high-speed turbo fighter." Oss was an older student, one who'd registered late, and I actually had him in two classes, practically back-to-back—both the environmental politics and environmental economics.

"So economics has to defer to survival?" I shot back.

"Well, sir, if a society doesn't survive, its economics won't, either."

Once upon a time, when I'd been a Republic Naval Air Corps pilot, I'd have probably given the same answer, but a few years had taught me that simple and accurate answers usually left out a great deal. "If the political and economic structure results in wholesale destruction of the environment," I pointed out, "then the society won't survive much longer."

Mister Oss looked vaguely troubled at my response, but no one wanted to comment on that one, probably because it was two minutes before the bell was due to ring.

I fingered my chin, grinning. "All right . . . what about this? The ultimate environmental economy is surviving."

Several students nodded. Most were looking at the wall clock yet again.

"That's the topic of a thousand-word essay due a week from today."

The sighs and groans were muffled, but most dutifully wrote down the assignment.

The wind had picked up and was colder when I stepped out of Smythe. Gertrude and Hector had pushed off their wheelbarrows, and the roots of the lilac hedge were clean and waiting to trap more leaves as I headed down to the post centre. There, I found only circulars and three bills, plus a thick envelope for Llysette from the New Bruges Association of Teachers of Singing.

Llysette had the table by the stove when I got to Delft's.

Victor was explaining the special. "The crabmeat is . . . just so . . . mademoiselle, and with *les champignons* . . . "

"Whatever it is, Victor, it sounds wonderful." I slid into the chair across from Llysette.

"Ah, Herr Doktor, it is."

I glanced at the menu, noting it was new, and that the prices were higher, but, in the end, we both ordered the special, which Victor had probably created especially for Llysette. She had tea, and so did I, and we sipped it, waiting for the French onion soups that we ordered in place of salad.

"Did you tell Dierk about St. Petersburg?" I asked.

"*Mais oui.* He was pleased, and he was not pleased."

"Is that because with you gone, and with Beau Jonn being called back onto active service, he has no one to teach your students while you're gone?"

Llysette offered a Gallic shrug. "More professors we have needed. He has not asked."

"The department keeps growing. You can't keep adding music majors without adding faculty," I pointed out. "Not when each one requires an hour of private studio lessons a week."

"*Non* . . . but the dean he did not wish to upset."

"Now, he'll have to, and she'll be much more upset than if he'd explained the problem last summer, when he learned that enrollment had gone up by twenty more majors."

"It was thirty, Johan."

"Mademoiselle . . . monsieur . . ." Victor appeared with the baked French onion soup. "The cheese, the Gruyere, is not aged as it should be, but I cannot get the proper cheeses."

"Are you having trouble with supplies, Victor?"

"Only with the special items, Doktor . . . beef I can get, but not good veal. *Les champignons* . . . those I get from my wife's brother . . . and without my spice garden . . . all would be lost." He shrugged. "We do what we can."

"You do it very well, and we appreciate it."

Victor beamed, if only for a moment. "The special . . . you will like it." Then he vanished.

I tried the soup. Despite Victor's protestations, it was excellent, the onions neither limp nor too crunchy, and the Gruyere melted just right over the crouton cover that was also perfectly crisp. We ate silently for a time. It had been a long morning, in its own way.

"Dierk didn't say that you shouldn't go, did he?"

"That, I did not allow." Llysette arched her eyebrows. "*Il n'est pas fou.* He would not wish to cross the dean . . . or you, Johan."

"David wasn't exactly pleased when I told him."

"Your David, he is a fool. Do you not always have the full classes?"

"Usually." I laughed. "I'm not sure why. I probably mark the hardest, and ask the most of the students."

"Even the Dutch dunderheads, they can understand who can teach," Llysette pointed out. Her mouth turned up in an impish smile. "And the young girls, they think there is mystery in a professor who was a spy."

"There's not much glamorous about it. You know that."

"They do not." She tilted her head slightly. "You show . . . the danger, Johan. The girls can feel it. A safe danger, you are."

"Because I'm married to you?"

"*Exactement.* Do not forget that." She spoiled the effect by smiling. "Herr Doktor Donniger cannot see. The most dense of your girl students see, but he cannot."

"David can't see much beyond David and faculty politics." I looked up to see Victor approaching with a tray.

"Power there is. Politics are not power."

I nodded. She'd put it succinctly. Too often, especially in democratic societies, people mistook the mechanisms of power for power itself. "Did you get in touch with Terese Stewart?"

"I did. She is most excited." Llysette smiled. "More than am I. She has done the *Vocalise,* but not 'The Lilacs.' The others, *elles ne sont pas si difficile.*"

As Victor set his special *champignon* dish down before us, I decided to set aside musico-political ruminations and concentrate more on gourmet gustatory explorations, inhaling the fragrance that steamed up from the plate. "It smells wonderful."

Llysette took a bite, then smiled and looked up at the anxious Victor. *"Merveilleux."*

Victor bobbed his head. He was happy.

And, sitting across from Llysette, with great food before me, so was I.

16

T HE REST OF the week passed uneventfully, and so did the beginning of the following week. In fact, we got to Thursday in blissful quietude. Neither rain nor snow fell on Vanderbraak Centre, and while it froze at night, the frost was gone before we left the house in the morning.

Llysette reported that Dierk Geoffries had located a former choral director at the University of Assen who had retired the spring before and who was willing to fill in for Beau Jonn. No one sent me any mysterious packages or letters or briefing materials. As Harlaan had promised, I did see a few gray steamers, but at a distance—except for the one hidden under the maple across the back lawn and the field beyond, an older gray Spazi steamer that was there almost all the time.

I'd also done some more ghost-projection-related research and by Wednesday night had come up with a system. By scanning an image, then converting the codes to a log base, which reflected the image parameters, and then changing certain aspects, by feel, nothing more, I got so I could create projected images that looked like what I'd scanned. Complex, but it did work. A good mathematician could have done it in an hour or so, but . . . it worked, for whatever reason, and I've always been one for making things work first and worrying about how I got there later. That, I reflected, was also how I'd gotten into a lot of trouble, and on more than one occasion.

Since that Thursday was the third one of the month, when the Music and Theatre Department had its monthly faculty meeting, I didn't get lunch with Llysette. I made do with a sandwich from the student centre and graded essays and quizzes until it was time for Environmental Politics 2B. Because the temperature was just above freezing, the classroom in Smythe was boiling. I couldn't believe Mondriaan thought the room was cold, but as we passed in the entryway, he had his winter coat buttoned up to his chin. It was a good thing his family had fled west, rather than to Russia—and that they'd escaped before the fall of the Low Countries. Ferdinand didn't care that much for painters and their families, but then, Ferdinand didn't seem to care much for any kind of art except for instrumental suites that glorified the Hapsburg empire or statues of its heros and emperors.

Class went as planned, if more smoothly, because the korfball team had left at noon to travel to Asten for some sort of preseason tournament. After class I graded a few more papers, and then went to pick up Llysette. Dinner would be rushed because Gregor Martin's production of *Hamlet* opened that night, and Llysette had promised to attend. I would have gone with her, regardless, but I was interested in seeing the production, because Gregor had set it in the mid-1800s. That should have made sense, since the Swedes had faced a similar crisis with the sudden death of Charles XIV in 1835, except young Oscar I hadn't had to contend with an uncle, only the Prussian-backed coup and attack against Denmark that had required Sweden to effectively annex Denmark after the assassination of the Danish royal family and the murder of far too many Danes. Still . . . I wanted to see how Gregor managed to integrate it with history.

Llysette, surprisingly, was waiting as I drove the Stanley

up to the music and theatre building. She was also smiling.

"Good day?" I asked as she slipped into the front seat and leaned across to brush my cheek with her lips.

"*Mais oui.* Marlena vanHoff, she won the New Bruges competition for the Association of Teachers of Singing. Also, Terese Stewart will be coming on Monday, or earlier, and already the music she has."

"Is she staying with us?"

"*Non.* This I did not know, but her sister lives in Zuider, and with her she would rather stay. I told her that we would drive her to Asten when we go to St. Petersburg. You would not mind that, Johan?"

"Heavens, no." I did like the idea that she wouldn't be staying with us, since Fraulein Stewart was a most astute woman, and might well notice our protective Spazi detail, something I really didn't want to explain. "That only makes sense."

The wind was stronger up on the hill, and almost blew Llysette's scarf right off her when she stepped out of the Stanley in our driveway. I left the steamer by the door.

Llysette shivered even after we were inside, and made for the parlor and the woodstove, still radiating some heat. I followed her and added two more logs, before heading to the kitchen, filled with the aroma of baking and spiced beef.

I'd asked Marie to make us a beef pie for dinner—I paid extra for that, but on nights like this one, when we were rushed, it was well worth it. So I had the salad ready, with a glass of wine—Sebastopol cabernet—and the whole dinner on the table even before Llysette was quite sure she wanted to leave the comfort of the parlor.

"First diva of Columbia," I called, "dinner is served."

"Johan . . . that is not of humor." Those were her words as she entered the kitchen.

I grinned because she couldn't keep the smile out of her eyes.

"*Impossible* you are."

"To impossible academics." I raised my wineglass, and we both laughed.

Llysette took a sip of the cabernet, then several bites of the meat pie before she spoke. "I was hungry, I think. A long day it has been. Good, but long."

"You wish we didn't have to go to the play tonight?"

"I promised that we would go. We did not see his last."

"No, we didn't." Gregor's last production had been something by the rising West Kansas playwright J. Francis Hogan, but I couldn't remember the title. That had been when Llysette and I were in Deseret the second time, and she'd performed at the St. George Opera House.

So, after eating and a quick cleanup of the dishes, a few moments of stacking papers in the study and unloading my briefcase while Llysette freshened up, we were back in the Stanley, heading down Deacon's Lane and over the River Wijk bridge back into Vanderbraak Centre. We got one of the last spaces in the lower car park and struggled to the music and theatre building against the gusty wind, not particularly cold, but strong.

While I was getting the tickets, Llysette stepped aside to say something to Dierk Geoffries, who was standing to the left of the box office wicket, doubtless waiting for his spouse.

As I turned, tickets in hand, I saw Gertrude—one of the university zombies—marching toward the main door to the theatre.

"Gertrude?" I asked gently.

She stopped and turned. "Yes, sir?"

"If I might ask, why do you come to operas and plays?"

"Professor Martin said I should, sir. He said I would feel better." Gertrude waited, as zombies always did, for the next question or order.

"Do you?"

"I don't know."

"I hope you do tonight."

Gertrude just waited.

"Go and enjoy the play."

She turned from me and headed for the door.

"How terrible," Llysette said, slipping up beside me.

"I don't know. I've seen her cry at your opera and when you gave a recital. I've never seen a zombie cry. Maybe Gregor is right."

"Peut-être . . ."

"You think he just wants a bigger gate?"

"Even Gregor . . . I do not think—" Llysette stopped and touched my arm, turning as a small and dapper man with wispy silver hair stepped toward us. "Georges, this is my husband Johan. Johan, this is Georges Almorire. He is the new choral director."

"Pleased to meet you, Doktor." Almorire gave a quick bow from the waist and straightened with a warm smile. "You don't look as imposing as your reputation, and that probably means you're more so."

I wasn't quite sure how to handle that. "In a college, students always creatively expand things, particularly reputations. I'm just a professor of applied politics and ecology, trying like every other professor to impart some glimmer of enlightenment." I laughed gently.

"Don't we all? Don't we all?" Almorire replied. "Your lady is most accomplished, and I understand that she will be singing at the Mariinsky Theatre in St. Petersburg in a few weeks."

"She will. I'm looking forward to it."

"You should. You should." He bowed and then eased away toward Blanding Aastre.

Blanding merely inclined his head to us as the two handed their tickets to the student usher and entered the theatre. We followed. Our tickets put us halfway back in the two seats closest to the aisle on the left.

Gregor had definitely made changes. Fortinbras was no longer a Norse fortune-seeker, but an Austrian archduke eager to expand the empire's borders, while Polonius wasn't so much an old pompous fool as a scheming courtier looking to position himself to survive the coming disaster. Ophelia's madness came as much from her insight into her father's duplicity as from Hamlet's indifference and apparent cruelty, and Claudius had poisoned Hamlet's father because the old king refused to understand the danger from the south—Austro-Hungary. In a way, it made sense historically, but Gregor's substituted lines, few as they were, weren't up to the original.

Afterward, we went to find Gregor, which wasn't hard, because he was standing on one side of the lobby, surrounded by a mix of students and university faculty. Once the crowd thinned out, we stepped forward.

"Most powerful," Llysette offered.

"Congratulations, Gregor." After looking over my shoulder, I asked, "Why did you tell Gertrude to come to the plays?"

"Who?"

"The zombic woman groundskeeper."

This time Gregor was the one to lower his voice. "Because I thought it would help her. I told her to come to the music concerts and the plays, especially the musical events."

I didn't know quite what to say to that.

"If good music won't help a zombie reclaim her soul, then it certainly can't hurt her."

"Gregor!" someone called.

"A good performance," I reiterated as I stepped away.

Llysette gave me a quizzical look, one I didn't respond to, except by squeezing her hand. I needed to think for a minute—or longer.

I left the theatre that was really more of a recital hall than a true theatre still pondering Gregor's words. The drama professor had never been one of my favorite people, arrogant as he sometimes was, but I'd seen Gertrude cry at Llysette's recitals and productions, and zombies weren't supposed to cry. Emotion was beyond them. Certainly, Gertrude mostly acted like a zombie . . . but was she becoming more human? Was Gregor onto something?

When we were in the Stanley on the way across the

river and back up Deacon's Lane, Llysette finally broke the silence.

"You are thinking, Johan."

"About zombies, about what Gregor said."

"Johan . . . a zombie, she does not have to remain such."

I winced, if silently. In a way, Llysette had been part zombie, part of her soul stripped away by Ferdinand's torture chambers and ghosting experiments—until I'd given her back part of another soul, not that I'd intended quite that. "We know that. I'd just never thought that music and drama might have the same effect . . . over time."

"That . . . it would make sense," Llysette pointed out.

"It would. And no one would ever think of it, because who would expose zombies to the passion of music and drama?"

"*C'est vrai. . . .*"

I reached out across the seat and squeezed her hand. She squeezed mine in return, and for the moment we were almost as one.

The wind on the hilltop was stronger than when we'd left. While I moved the Stanley into the car barn and then topped off the water tanks, Llysette opened the house.

When I finally finished and entered the house, she was standing in the archway between the parlor and my study, her head tilted, her brow furrowed. "Someone, like before, *je crois . . .*"

While everything in the study seemed to be in its place, as had Llysette, I felt like something was different. I touched the casing of the difference engine, but it was cool and had not been used recently, not in the last half hour in any case.

Llysette frowned. "Someone, they have been here."

After checking all the outside locks, I returned to the study. "The locks were still set."

Llysette raised her eyebrows.

"I know. That doesn't prove anything." Next, I turned on the lights and looked out onto the terrace from the study. The terrace was empty.

Then I went out with a hand-flash. Llysette, shivering without her coat, followed. There was a single set of footprints in the frost on the grass. The footsteps vanished at the edge of the lawn, where the intruder had stepped over the low stone fence into the field beyond.

Back inside, after relocking the doors, I turned on the difference engine, but so far as I could tell, nothing had been altered, and none of the hidden files had been opened. That meant only that the intruder hadn't found them, or was far better at difference engine programming than were Bruce and I. So I turned the machine back off, checked all the locks once more, for all the good that would do, and then turned off the lights in the lower level before climbing the steps to the master bedroom—and Llysette.

Who had it been? What had he wanted? I doubted that this intruder had been a Spazi type. Given the Spazi surveillance, I had to wonder how he'd gotten in, and especially how he'd gotten away. That the intruder had managed it didn't exactly boost my faith in Harlaan's operations.

Still . . . there wasn't much else I could do, not then. But . . . I worried, and it took a long time to drift off to sleep, even with Llysette's help.

17

T HE NEXT MORNING was sunny, warmer, and calm, and the footprints in the frost had vanished before I went out to fire up the Stanley. The gray six-wheeled Spazi steamer was under the trees on the far side of the field, but I had to wonder exactly how much good Harlaan's surveillance detail was doing.

When I went to the door to call Llysette, she was standing by the foyer closet, wearing a gray woolen skirt with a green blouse, and a gray jacket, in which she looked wonderful, and which she promptly swathed in her winter coat before stepping outside to get into the Stanley.

"It's not that cold," I said cheerfully, as I eased the Stanley down the drive and out onto Deacon's Lane. "And, besides, it's Friday."

"The north pole, you would say it is not cold, Johan."

"Remember—in two weeks or so we'll be in St. Petersburg."

"Do not remind me what I do for art."

"All right. I won't," I said cheerfully.

"Johan . . ."

I laughed, and so did she.

I really didn't need the kerosene, but after I dropped off

Llysette, I headed down to Piet's Columbian Dutch Shell
to top off the Stanley's tanks. What with rising prices and
unsettled times, I didn't want to be caught short, although
I did have two ten-gallon tins stored in the car barn.

Piet was alone, and as he started washing the windscreen, I asked, "How are things with your suppliers?"

"Prices keep going up. Not much at any one time, Doktor, but they never go down." Piet wiped the Stanley's
glass dry. "Widow Huerlein, she saw the prices and backed
right out of the station. Went down to Bruno's. Didn't do
much for her. He's running a dime more a gallon than I
am. He's worried. Some sales rep came by the other day.
Asked him a bunch of questions, about what grades of
kerosene folks bought and even about whether you college
professors preferred Shell or AmeriSun. Bruno played
dumber than he already is. Then, the fellow told him
AmeriSun was closing stations in New Bruges, those that
didn't sell enough."

"He sells enough, doesn't he?"

Piet shrugged. "Who can tell what's enough for the bolt
counters in headquarters?" Piet looked at the pump.
"Thirty-one even, Doktor."

I paid him, and he hurried over to the other pump to
catch Fred Jaekels, the korfball coach. Next I picked up
the paper from Samaha's and drove back to the upper faculty car park.

The bright sunshine had me in a happy mood, and when
I saw the zombie workforce, I called out cheerfully, "Good
morning, Gertrude."

"Every morning is a good morning, sir." The zombie
lady smiled happily, then returned to raking, turning over
the bark mulch in the flower bed lining the walk.

Deciding against asking her about the play, I smiled and
replied, "It is indeed." Which, in a way, it was, at least for
me. I mostly enjoyed teaching, and I had a loving and
talented wife, and I'd seen enough of what wasn't so good
in life to appreciate—usually—what I did have.

Just as I was about to enter the natural resources building to head up to my office, two students appeared. One was Verner Oss, and the other was Pietra Zand.

"Professor?" ventured Pietra. "About the essay . . . do you mind if we define the terms you used? Or did you have a definition you wanted us to use?"

For a moment, I had to shift perspectives. "Which terms?"

" 'Survival' . . . sir."

I smiled at the petite blonde, who was one of my better students. "Actually, you can use any definition so long as you make sure you define which one you're using."

Verner Oss blinked, as if I'd surprised him.

"Mister Oss . . . one of the things you learn if you've spent a while in the military is that both survival and victory come in two varieties, long and short term, and you need to consider whether short-term victories, particularly, lead to long-term survival. All too often, they don't."

"Were you in the service, sir?"

"I spent two tours in the Naval Air Corps . . . part of it during the Panama Standoff."

"You were a pilot?"

"FF-7s."

"Ah . . . any decorations?" Oss asked, almost apologetically.

That was a rather presumptuous question, and a bit odd, but the way in which it was asked was clearly one of honest curiosity. For a moment, I wondered whether to answer it, but decided honesty was the best policy. "A few. Nothing terribly glorious. An RAC, with a star, a purple heart, and the usual unit commendations." I paused. "Did you have a question, Mister Oss?"

"I think you answered it, sir. I wondered about defining 'long term.' "

"Define it as you wish, but affirm or attack the proposition and support your argument."

"Isn't the proposition almost a tautology, sir?"

I shook my head. "Not really. You've got a grasp on it already, because whether it is or isn't depends on the definitions . . . and I've probably already given you too much."

"Ah . . . thank you, Professor Eschbach." Pietra almost bowed.

"Thank you," echoed Verner.

"You're both welcome, and good luck with the essays."

I got a nod from Verner, a respectful nod, not a perfunctory one. As the two walked away, I waited by the door for a moment. I couldn't help but overhear their words as they walked away.

"Why did you ask about awards?" That was Pietra.

"Decorations, not awards. Because . . . just because. There's something about him . . . but . . . an Air Cross in an FF-7 . . . they only gave out three in the whole war . . ."

I couldn't hear any more after that, and opened the door and headed across the foyer toward the stairs. Actually, they'd given out four Air Crosses, and it hadn't really been a war, for all the pilots we lost in the Mosquito Gulf, but we'd kept the canal, to the dismay of both New France and Austro-Hungary. I'd been happy to complete my second tour and quietly resign to enter the Sedition and Security Prevention Service. No matter what anyone said, the mortality in the Spazi was far lower than in military flying, and the government health care that Elspeth had needed had transferred with me. Also, the military time had counted toward my federal pension.

I smiled at Gilda, who was listening on the wireset, and headed up to my office, where I took off my topcoat and unpacked my briefcase before opening the *Post-Courier*. There was little new, just more about the unsettled Persian Gulf and speculations on fuel prices.

In the meantime, while the world was teetering on the brink of a conflict over petroleum supplies, the Romanovs were pursuing their quixotic dreams of intercontinental rocketry.

Vienna (WNS). Austrian Foreign Minister Erich vonBraun protested as "dangerous" and "provocative" the latest test flight of the Russian Perun missile. "Launching a military prototype rocket from a base less than two hundred kilometers from another nation's borders is clearly a violation of the High Frontier Treaty," vonBraun claimed. "Russia must cease such behavior or face the consequences of violating international law."

In St. Petersburg, the imperial minister of communications, Ivan Lamanov, denied the charge. "This was a test flight for purely scientific purposes. This missile was never designed to carry warheads."

According to Russian sources, the Perun's missile body self-destructed, while the instrument capsule parachuted to earth near L'Vov, just inside the Russian border, and was reclaimed immediately by troops detailed to the Imperial Astronautics Facility. Unconfirmed reports indicated that the missile may have reached a height of one hundred kilometers. . . .

To me, it didn't make sense—even the launch direction, which had risked losing the test data. Even if the Russians could make nuclear warheads, and there was considerable doubt that they could make devices both small and sturdy enough to be carried by the reputedly finicky Perun, the missile's range was so limited that half of Austro-Hungarian territory was beyond it. Ferdinand had hundreds of heavy high-altitude bombers and several hundred large nuclear devices. While it would have been difficult for him to use them against the Americas, effectively all of industrial Russia was well within range, and the Russian turbo fighters were no match for the Prussian-built Messerschmidts. But then, from the days of Peter the Great, the Romanovs had always been unpredictable, and Tzar Alexander seemed to be cast from the same mold.

I couldn't do much about any of it, and so I began entering grades in my gradebook. The intercom buzzed. I picked up the handset. "Yes?"

"Chief Waetjen is on line one, Doktor Eschbach."

Gilda's voice was cool, and that probably meant that David was standing right beside her desk.

"Thank you." Watch Chief Waetjen? I punched the blinking light. "Johan Eschbach."

"Why is it, Eschbach, that whenever your wife is about to go off and do a concert somewhere, strange things happen here?"

"I'm sorry, Chief. I'm afraid I don't understand. What strange things?"

"Your neighbor reported lights, and strange noises last night. Did you hear anything?"

"No, but we didn't get home until almost eleven. Llysette and I were at the opening night of *Hamlet,* and it's a long production."

"You didn't notice or hear anything strange when you returned home?"

"No." Before he could ask more, I countered. "Could you tell me what this is all about?"

There was a long silence.

"I wish you'd never come home to Vanderbraak Centre, Eschbach. You know that."

"You've made that rather clear, Chief Waetjen. But it's the only family home I have left, and I've always been cooperative." That was politely stretching things, but it was worth saying. "It might be helpful for me to know exactly what the problem is."

"You insist you don't know?"

"Chief . . . I have no idea, and you already know that or you'd have asked me to come down to the Watch station." He had requested that of me several times before, when bombs had exploded and dead bodies had appeared on my property.

"Eschbach . . ." There was a dramatic sigh. "A body appeared in the river this morning. No signs of overt foul play. That is, no bullet wounds, no broken bones, no crushed skulls, but Doktor Waasre also didn't find any water in the lungs."

"Do you know who it was?"

"No identification. Rather, there was a set of papers, and a large folder of bills in his wallet, but the identification was all false. Those all reminded me of you."

I held back my own sigh. "I can't help you, Chief. I don't know anything about this. I can't even guess." That was almost true. I had some guesses, of a general nature, but nothing that could have possibly helped the chief.

"You always say that, but, you know, I can't say that I exactly believe you. Especially when your friends from the federal district are providing, shall we say, a protective detail."

"That's for Llysette. She'll be singing for the tzar of Imperial Russia in a few weeks. The Ministry of State is counting on her."

There was a silence, at least for a moment. "Give her my best, Eschbach. Don't know as you deserve her, but I can't fault a man for doing all he can to protect his wife."

I started to thank him.

"Just keep out of it this time, Eschbach. Let the Spazi do their own dirty work."

"I have no intention of doing anything to upset you, Chief."

"Good. Right here is what I have to worry about. Hope everything goes well for her. Have to run." With a click, he was off the line.

I set down the wireset slowly. Hans Waetjen was no fool, and he was basically telling me that if I kept out of things he certainly wasn't about to drag me in. He was also saying he really didn't care what I did elsewhere—or what I did in self-defense or to protect Llysette.

I had to wonder, and worry, about who the intruder had been, and whether the body in the river had been his. The other question was to whom he belonged. Ferdinand? The New French? Why had he been in our house? Ferdinand's head ghost scientist Heisler doubtless knew far more about psychic research than anything that was in my difference engine files. So did Harlaan's research division.

Yet someone wanted to know what I knew, and, apparently, Harlaan's boys had been more effective than I'd given them credit for in making sure whoever it was didn't pass on much. That, or matters were even more complicated than I'd been led to believe, and while that was usually the case, I had a depressing feeling that there was far more going on than any of the players knew.

Depressing or not, there wasn't much I could do, except finish grading essays and quizzes until it was time to leave for environmental economics.

There, the usual muffled groans greeted me as I handed back quizzes.

The theoretical subject of the day was the economics of electrical power generation. It was a *long* class, and I was very happy to have survived it when Llysette met me at Delft's, where Victor had given me *her* table, by the woodstove, after discreetly asking if she would be joining me. She was a bit late, and I'd already sipped my way through one cup of chocolate and was starting a second when she sat down.

I couldn't help but smile. "You look wonderful." But then, she always did.

"Johan. Always, you say that."

"That's because you do," I pointed out.

She shook her head, but she was still pleased.

I waited until we'd ordered before turning to Llysette and saying in a low voice, "Watch Chief Waetjen called me this morning, just before my office hours."

"Do I wish to hear this?"

"A dead body turned up in the river this morning, with no signs of injuries."

Llysette's hand went to her mouth.

"Later," I said. "We'll talk about it later, but I did want you to know. He seemed to think that any strange happening in Vanderbraak Centre was my doing."

"You did nothing."

"No, I didn't, but the chief is very skeptical of me. He let me know quite clearly that he thinks highly of you, and he understands why I want to protect you. He also knows it wasn't our doing, and he suspects whose doing it was."

"Almost, I would like a glass of wine . . . but then, I have Veronique for my first lesson after we eat."

"The fundamentalist Dutch Reformed child?"

"Oui," Llysette's tone was dry. "All the town would know a glass of wine I had . . . and the dean."

"I'll open a good bottle of Sebastopol tonight. We don't have to go anywhere. We saw the play last night, and you don't have any recital rehearsals tonight, do you?"

"Johan . . . there is a dance tonight. One does not rehearse when one is twenty, and there is a dance. Not in New Bruges, one does not."

Victor arrived with the salads, and I had several bites before I asked, "Speaking of rehearsals, when do you start with Terese Stewart?"

"Tomorrow afternoon."

"I thought she wasn't coming until next week."

"This way would be best, we decided."

I laughed. "What did you promise her?"

"A larger fee."

"You *are* worried," I said.

"Johan, for the first time, I can pay to have the accompanist when I need such. Never will I sing in St. Petersburg but this time. It must be right."

I couldn't argue with that, not at all. "At the house, I hope?"

"In the beginning. I have told Dierk we will need the theatre."

"Are you going to do any other pieces? Or have an encore piece?"

"I had thought . . . *'Adieu Forêt'* . . . "

I was out of my depth with that one. "Another piece I don't know."

"Tchaikovsky, it is, but the French version I will sing. It is the sad aria from *Orleanskaya Deva* . . . *The Maid of Orleans* . . . *trés triste.*"

"Sad, for an encore?"

"Trust me, Johan. The Russians, they will love the aria."

If she said it was so, it was, even if my practical Dutch upbringing wondered about it.

"Mademoiselle, Herr Doktor . . . the *spécialité* . . . " offered Victor.

"Merci," offered Llysette.

"Thank you."

With a smile, Victor was gone, and I decided to enjoy the food and my diva. I had been slow to understand, but I had come to realize that such moments in life were fleeting, and to be savored.

18

WE DID GET to sleep in a little on Saturday morning,
since Terese Stewart wasn't supposed to show up
until two o'clock, and we dawdled for a bit over a pot of
chocolate and some currant scones that I whipped up. They
went well with the last of the orange marmalade that
Mother had sent us at the end of summer.

I took a shower before Llysette did and then hurried
down to Vanderbraak Centre, where I picked up the paper,
the mail from the post centre, and a few odds and ends of
groceries from McArdles'. I'd hoped for some late beans
from Florida or Cuba, but there weren't any, just a lot of
parsley. So I changed plans and picked up a flank steak
and the plain mushrooms, and two pounds of butter, and
what there was for a salad, and then waited in line for my
purchases to be rung up.

"Professor Eschbach!"

I didn't recognize the voice, but I turned anyway. A
slender but very pregnant dark-haired young woman stood
in the line behind me.

"Yes?" I said as pleasantly as I could.

"You probably don't remember me, but I'm Kara La-
compagna. I studied with your wife two years ago, but

then I got married." She looked down. "I saw in the *Chronicle* that she was going to give a concert in Russia, and I was *so* envious."

"I hadn't seen the story," I admitted. Usually, I leafed through the Vanderbraak *Weekly Chronicle* to check on the short section of university happenings, just to see if there were any articles about Llysette or her opera productions, but I hadn't been exactly regular in looking lately.

"It just came out this morning. Anyway, tell her I was thinking of her, and I hope she has a wonderful time."

"Thank you."

On the way out of McArdles', I did pick up a copy of the *Chronicle* but didn't stop to read it, just putting it with the Asten *Post-Courier* on the front passenger seat of the Stanley. When I got back to the house, since Llysette was still upstairs dressing, I unloaded the groceries and put them on the kitchen counter, then went out and tucked the Stanley back into the car barn. There was no reason to leave it out, not when gray clouds were drifting in from the northwest. I'd spent too much on the thermal paint feature to let the weather beat it up unnecessarily.

Back in the kitchen, before I put everything away and started on lunch, I opened the *Chronicle* and skimmed through until I found the College Notes section.

Dean Katrinka Er Recchus announced that two faculty members have been honored by the president and the Columbian Ministry of State. Professor of Voice Llysette duBoise was recently awarded the Columbian Medal for Achievement in the Arts. She is the first faculty member of Vanderbraak State to be so honored. In addition, she has been chosen to represent Columbia in a transcultural arts exchange concert before the tzar of Imperial Russia . . . Professor Johan Eschbach has been picked by the Ministry of State to participate in environmental exchanges between Russian and Columbian experts . . . "This shows the success of our efforts to raise the caliber of the faculty at Vanderbraak State," Dean Er Recchus said . . .

Trust Katrinka to find a way to misstate matters and to take some credit where none was due. After shaking my head and closing the *Chronicle,* I glanced through the *Post-Courier.* The emphasis was back on the economic problems of the Aerodrome, and the local Asten politicians were suggesting that the federal government should be paying more for its usage of the south side of the Aerodrome as a Republic Naval Air Corps base, especially for the wear and tear caused by the more frequent antisubmersible patrols.

That bothered me for a moment, and then it bothered me more. Dirigibles were used for the actual patrols and stayed on station for days. Missions against submersibles were carried out by turbos because they could carry more armament, and return for more quickly, if necessary. That meant more actual missions against Ferdinand's submersibles—or at least more cases of contacts.

After I unloaded all the groceries from their sacks, I threw together a relatively quick chicken pasta, with a salad that was mostly iceberg lettuce, with croutons, dried apples, and raisins for variety, but before I could get the pasta off the stove and onto the table, Llysette was in the parlor, beginning to warm up.

"Mademoiselle la diva . . . your sustenance is ready . . ."

"Un moment, Johan."

It was more than a moment, but not that long before my green-eyed beauty appeared and slid into her seat at the table. After we finished, Llysette warmed up.

A not-quite-dilapidated Reo hiss-whistled up the driveway at ten before two, the hissing signifying less than exemplary performance by the steamer's boiler system. I stepped outside and motioned for Terese Stewart just to stop by the door.

She got out and looked around, then flashed a smile at me. "You'll have to pardon me for the sound effects, but this is the old steamer, and I didn't want to take my sister's good one."

"As long as it gets you where you need to go," I temporized. "Do come in."

The accompanist pulled out a battered leather case, not quite bulging, presumably with music, and followed me into the foyer, where she glanced around, then up the stairs.

I instinctively looked up, as if to check to see if Carolynne were there, but, of course, she wasn't, and hadn't been since she'd become a part of us. But years of looking for the family ghost still had left the habit pattern.

"An impressively modest dwelling, Professor."

"Johan," I insisted. "We're likely to be seeing a great deal of each other. Do come in. Llysette should be down in a moment."

"A moment, and I will be there," Llysette called down. "Johan . . ."

"I'll show her to the parlor." I turned to Terese. "Would you like anything to drink before you start?"

"Just water, if you please."

I returned with the water after Llysette came down the stairs and had greeted Terese.

"Good it was of you to come early," Llysette was saying.

"I wouldn't have missed it." The pianist hadn't changed any in the year since I'd seen her last. She was still small, dark-haired, and determined looking. The one difference was the warm smile. "I can't thank you both enough. I've always wanted to play in Russia."

"Not both of us—Llysette," I said. "They chose her, and she chooses her accompanists."

"My friend Dmitri is a bit jealous. He graduated from the St. Petersburg Conservatory, but he never did get to play in the Mariinsky Theatre."

"He's in Columbia?" I asked.

"Actually, he lives in Dublin. Unlike St. Petersburg, it has a sense of history that mirrors struggles, but not every stone is paved with tears, and not every ghost is bleached out in the white nights."

Llysette inclined her head toward the parlor, and I followed the two. Terese sat down at the concert piano bench, and her fingers ran across the keys, doing, I supposed, the pianist's equivalent of a vocalise. She looked up. "This is a good instrument . . . one of the better Haarens."

Llysette smiled as she moved to the side of the piano, equivalent to where she would be when performing. "Johan gave it to me just before we were married, as a wedding present."

"Quite a present."

"If you'll give me the keys to the Reo, I'll top off the water tanks," I offered. "I have a filtration system in the car barn."

"I can see he's one of those impossibly ordered people." Terese smiled cheerfully.

"Llysette has called me impossible upon occasion," I admitted. "Upon more than one occasion."

"Johan." My lady diva flushed ever so slightly.

"There's a story there," said Terese. "I can see that."

"More than one, but she is right, and I don't need to get in the way of your rehearsal." I held out my hand for the keys to the Reo.

She bent down and fished out a single key from the brown bag she'd placed beside the piano bench, and I took it and got out of the way. I did check over her borrowed vehicle and tightened a couple of hose clamps. My adjustments wouldn't help whatever was going wrong in the boiler assembly, but they would keep the water from vanishing quite so quickly.

Then I slipped back to my study and tried to concentrate on grading papers, except the sound of Tchaikovsky kept bringing back thoughts about what I was supposed to do in Russia. So I took out the box I'd brought back from Bruce's and looked over the matching pens and the pocket calculator, and the hair dryer. I checked them again, and then jotted down the extra batteries I'd be needing, wondering if I should contact Bruce for more hardware. I shook my head. He'd already given me the elegant-looking but bulbous pen zombification projector, and there wasn't much else I could use.

I did manage to finish grading the essays for the honors section of environmental studies. Most were decent, but then, I'd weeded out the worst students long before they reached that level.

The piano and Llysette had stopped for a time, and it was close to four when I eased just inside the parlor. Both women looked at me.

"You're staying for dinner, I presume." That was directed at Terese Stewart. "It's no imposition," I said. "Not at all. Llysette seldom ever gets to have a social occasion with another musician—unless it deals with faculty politics. And she's not cooking."

Terese offered a grin to Llysette. "Is he a good cook?"

"Non . . ." Then Llysette smiled. "He is not good. A chef he could have been."

"I don't know about—"

"You've both twisted my arm." Terese laughed. "Not that it needed much twisting. Cherise and Michael are playing some private function tonight that they couldn't get out of."

"Is your sister a pianist?" I asked.

"She's a violist. Her real job is with the Asten Symphony, but she and Michael have a quartet that pays for the extras."

With a nod, I said, "It will be another hour or so, but I already have the main dish in the oven." While they discussed the program, I repaired to the kitchen and completed making dinner with the light lace potatoes that had always been a family recipe and that I'd learned from my mother when I was probably fifteen.

Before I knew it, it was approaching six, longer than I'd expected, but that was often what happened when I experimented in the kitchen. I uncorked the cabernet, lighted the candles, and summoned my musical charges. "Ladies . . ."

Within minutes, while I was carrying out the crescent rolls I'd just eased into the roll basket, they came into the dining room, sharing one of those glances that it isn't always wise for any sensible male to interpret. I carved the stuffed flank steak quickly, so that it wouldn't get cold, and then added the laced potatoes. "This is simple, but the market was out of what I was looking for," I said as I slipped a plate in front of Terese, and then Llysette.

"You should not apologize, Johan."

"Habit," I murmured. Any man who is a decent cook—and not a chef—had best apologize. After a mouthful of the steak, I took a sip of the cabernet and nodded. It did complement the marinated and parsley-mushroom-stuffed flank steak—just a hint of sharpness, with a smooth fullness beneath.

"Does he always cook like this?" asked Terese, looking at Llysette.

"*Toujours* . . . and always he thinks he should do better. But that is my Johan." I got a fond and warm smile after those words.

"You don't have a brother, do you?" asked the pianist with a mischievous smile.

"No. I was an only child. After my mother spent the first year dealing with me, she decided one was enough."

"Someone said you were an Air Corps pilot, a Spazi assassin, and a minister in the Vandenberg administration."

"Two out of three," I said. "I did work for the Spazi, but just as a covert agent. My more interesting assignments were learning difference engine codes and working as a programmer for an equity assurance company suspected of passing financial information to the Austro-Hungarians. Very dull." That assignment had been dull, relatively free of personal danger, and I would have preferred that all of them had been like that. It hadn't worked that way, of course.

"A real hero and spy." Terese shook her head.

"Not a hero," I protested. "Would you like a little more wine?"

"Yes, please."

With a look at Llysette, Terese asked, "Just how did you land this gig in St. Petersburg?"

"I could not say." Llysette shrugged and gave me a smile.

"Politics! I knew it."

"I wish that were true," I replied, and I meant that, if not in the way that I wanted Terese to take it. "It is political, but not because we know the Speaker or the president personally, but because the Ministry of State needed an internationally famous singer for their cultural exchange with the tzar. He'd sent the Ballet Russes here, and apparently the Russians suggested that Llysette ought to be on the program after her Salt Palace disk started making even the popular charts. They wanted her . . ."

"But Johan said I could not do it unless we were paid," Llysette added firmly. "I cannot sing that many more years. Not singing as one should."

"I'm most appreciative that you two pointed that out." Terese laughed. "Too many people think that we should only get supper for singing and playing."

"Last year, that I did at the presidential arts dinner," Llysette replied.

"They didn't pay you for that?" questioned the petite pianist.

"Non."

"I can see why you were reluctant to give another free performance."

"I sang for many years when only students listened. They listened because they were required to listen."

I remembered part of those years, and the voice that had been so beautiful, and yet lacking . . . something. And the events that had restored it and left their marks on both of us. I still had scars from the bullet Llysette had put through my shoulder, but the inner scars sometimes hurt more, as when a memory of an arc-lit stage I had never seen passed through my thoughts, or a ghostly view of myself as a child reappeared.

"You enjoy the academic accompanying?" I asked Terese.

"Some of it, but working with faculty and the visiting artists are the best part, but unless you're permanent staff, you don't get benefits, or a steady income."

I could see that the life of a freelance pianist could be very uncertain indeed. But then, all life was uncertain. So, I sipped my wine, and mostly listened, as they got back to discussing the beauty and the history of the Rachmaninov *Vocalise,* and the fact that it was perhaps the most beautiful piece of vocal music written without actual words.

19

W E DID GO to church on Sunday, but Klaus's sermon wasn't quite so good, with the emphasis on forgiving the unforgivable. I still wasn't that charitable. Later, in mid-afternoon, Llysette and Terese practiced, mostly the *Vocalise,* and early in the evening, the three of us went to Cipoletto's for dinner.

Monday and Tuesday, Llysette taught and practiced in the afternoon in her studio with Terese. Wednesday, it rained, a cold downpour that would have turned into black ice, except that the sun came out around three for long enough to warm up the sidewalks and roads to evaporate the incipient ice. That was good, because I was already late and didn't get to the post centre until after four, and the way I hurried I'd probably have slipped or skidded into something.

Maurice was almost waiting by the postal wicket. "Couple of big packages for you, Doktor," he offered, with the grin he usually gave me when he could hand over a stack of circulars. "And some letters and bills, too."

"You're so cheerful, you wretch." He was right about the bills, which included one from NBEI for the utilities, one from New Bruges Telewire, and one that looked to be the annual property tariff from the town itself. I eased the envelopes into my inside jacket pocket.

Both boxes were oblong, ten inches by a foot, and a good foot and a half high or long, except the official stickers of the Ministry of Environment were on the short side, as if they were to be opened that way. They were heavy, but the last heavy package I'd gotten from the federal district had literally exploded.

Not without some misgivings, I carried them up the hill from the post centre to the car park and put them in the boot of the Stanley. All that meant that I was late picking up both Llysette and Terese. They were awaiting me at the music and theatre building.

"I thought you were the punctual type," offered the accompanist.

"There were two large packages in the post, and I had to cart them back to the Stanley."

Llysette didn't say anything. She didn't have to; the look she gave me told me to be careful. I didn't get around to dealing with the two boxes until after I finished cleaning up after dinner, when the ladies retired to the parlor to discuss obscurities in phrasing in the *Vocalise*.

So I was finally free to take my packages out of the boot of the Stanley and set them beside the stone foundation of the car barn, close to the corner. Then I taped my new razor knife to a makeshift crossarm attached to my newish rake and rummaged until I found the old mirror, cracked from the last time I'd attempted opening a package from a protected position. This time was different. It took much longer, because nothing exploded. The first box did in fact contain paper, a set of six manuals, all bound.

With a nod, I went to work on the second one. It didn't explode, either. I felt a little sheepish with all my precautions, but better sheepish than dead. Then I had to take apart my contraption and put the tools back in the tool case and close up the car barn. It was well past eight by the time I carried the open boxes into the study.

As I passed through the parlor Llysette looked up, eyebrows arched in a question.

"Books . . . technical manuals, I think."

A faint smile of relief appeared, and then she was back to rehearsing.

In the study, listening to Llysette practicing phrases in the parlor, I took out the envelope that had been tucked on the top of the larger box. Under the Ministry of Environment's seal, it was addressed to The Honorable Johan Eschbach, Minister of Columbia, Retired.

Dear Minister Eschbach:

Enclosed you will find a set of five volumes that outline the Ministry's best technical analyses of the Dnepyr River watershed and effluent problems, along with a recommended technical approach for each of the four most likely contingencies. The sixth volume is the historical background and executive summary.

You should also have received under separate cover a duplicate version of this study in Russian . . . For your convenience, also attached to this letter is a listing of those who participated in the analyses and recommendations, with their areas of expertise, and their addresses and wireset numbers . . . These names are only for your use, but the studies may be distributed as you see fit.

I have been asked to inform you that, in a day or so, you will be receiving another set of documents from the Ministry of Interior dealing with low-cost technical improvements in petroleum drilling and recovery technology.

Our thanks in advance for your efforts to better our world's environment and safety.

The signature was that of Frederic Eisness, Minister of Environment. I had to smile, if ironically, at the last words.

The contact sheet was on white paper, with no identifying letterhead. After setting the letter and contact sheet on my desk, I looked over the manuals. One set, the larger set, was in English. The second set was clearly in Cyrillic.

Belatedly, I noted another matter. Both sets had no identifying names, not even those of authors—nor any ministry contacts or imprints. The appendices listed a complete bibliography of scholarly articles, studies, and references, and their authors, but not the authors of the studies. In short, I'd been handed a set of remedial blueprints all on off-white paper. I had less than two weeks to learn everything in the material—or most of it—so that I could discuss it as if I were the expert the Russians thought that they were being sent. That didn't include whatever the Ministry of Interior was sending.

"Johan. You spent much time outside." Llysette stood in the archway.

I smiled and gestured to the pile of remedial manuals. "Environmental remedial plans. For the Dnepyr River project."

"Outside, you were studying them outside in this cold?"

"No, I was opening them outside. Most carefully."

"Will it always be so?"

I couldn't answer that question. I hoped not, but in the uncertain world in which we were living there was no surety of anything. "Is Terese still here?"

"We have done what we can today. My voice, it is tired."

I stood quickly. "A glass of wine?"

"In a moment. Terese would like to go."

I followed Llysette and Terese out to the front foyer, where I helped the accompanist into her coat. I flicked on the outside lights, and Llysette and I stood on the front stoop, where Llysette shivered as a few lazy flakes of snow drifted past us, while the pianist backed the old Reo down the drive and out onto Deacon's Lane.

"A very good accompanist, she is."

"She's good, but you're better." I ushered my diva back

into the house, locking the deadbolt as I did.

We walked back to the parlor. I added another two logs to the woodstove for the night, before going back to the study, where I turned off the SII difference engine, whose keyboard I'd never even touched because of all the fiddling with the boxes and manuals.

Llysette lifted the top manual and began to leaf through it. Then, her brows crinkled, and she looked at me. "It is as you said."

"They're rather special manuals. They're the best judgment of some of the best scientists in Columbia as to how the Russians can clean up the Dnepyr River."

"Why can the Russians not discover these answers themselves?"

"It's a matter of money. Russia is only a partly capitalistic nation. It has no agricultural surplus to speak of, and the tzars have spent billions of roubles over the last century trying to modernize and industrialize. Studying the environment and how to keep it clean costs money to begin with. Over time, you can save money, but the tzars have never had enough money to keep a large enough military to hold off Ferdinand and the Swedes, industrialize, and study the environment in depth." I didn't mention the millions or billions they'd also poured into the rathole of rocket development.

"Always the money, *n'est-ce-pas?*"

"Usually," I admitted.

Llysette looked at the manuals. "You must learn all this?"

"Most of it."

She shook her head. "Do not stay up too late."

"I don't intend to." I smiled, not quite licentiously.

We laughed together, and it was a moment of warmth we both enjoyed.

20

I STUDIED THE materials on environmental reclamation, practiced some on ghost creation technology, taught my classes, held office hours, and read the newspapers and wondered how long it would be before someone made a mistake and a shooting war erupted. It didn't, and before long, the next week had gone by without much new occurring, except for cold rain and more long practice sessions by Llysette—until Wednesday, when it snowed, a foot of wet snow that turned into a wet slushy mess by mid-afternoon under a warm south wind and a bright sun.

So after my honors environmental studies class, I slogged down to the post centre, every step of my boots spraying slush. From behind his wicket, Maurice greeted me with a broad smile. "Another box, Doktor. Not as heavy as the last one, but it feels like books."

"Thank you." I took the box from him. The label held the seal and address of the Ministry of the Interior.

"Don't forget your circulars," Maurice said, extending a handful of envelopes.

"How could I?" With a laugh, I stuffed them into my inside jacket pocket and trudged back up the hill to the Stanley.

Llysette was alone when I picked her up from the music and theatre building, and she looked tired.

"A long day?" I asked.

"We practiced much of the afternoon. I must preview two students tonight."

"Tonight?"

"On Sunday we leave. For the rest of the week, Johanna must be in Asten." Llysette shrugged. "Dierk has not heard their literature."

"He waited until now?" I shouldn't have asked that question, I realized, almost as the words were out of my mouth.

"Nothing I do is so important as does he. He could not sing his path from a . . . closet with a grand orchestra. Complain he always does, but he does nothing. More faculty we need, but does he ask for such? New pianos we need . . . but he says nothing. For weeks he knows I go . . . and today . . . today, he says he must hear Elfreda and Caron. *Cochon! Non!* Too kind is that."

There was more steam coming from Llysette than probably was in the flash boiler of the Stanley. "An incompetent imbecile?"

"Imbeciles, they have some brains! *Le grand professeur* . . . he has none."

I didn't ask more for a time. As we crossed the Wijk River bridge, I continued to listen, listen and watch the road, because there were sections where the slush had packed into grease-ice. I could see one steamer in a ditch ahead on the east side of the river, although it looked to have been there for a time, because there was still snow melting across the windscreens.

"What did he say?" I finally asked.

"He was sorry, but he had been too busy. He sits and little does, but he was too busy."

I nodded, then eased the Stanley around a hauler half parked, half stuck on the right side of the road just before the turn-off up Deacon's Lane.

"I am sorry. Already, you did not look pleased. I did not mean to speak harshly to you."

"That's all right. I can see why you were upset. Dierk hasn't been exactly the best chair the department could have had."

"Nights I have worked to make sure the students, they get their lessons . . . and he is too busy. Letters he writes about the need to write papers and to go to meetings. *I* need to go to meetings to sing and to teach singers?"

"I hardly think so." The steam issuing from Llysette was beginning to subside as the Stanley sloshed through the driveway I needed to shovel before it got cold and froze into solid ice.

Abruptly, as I stopped the Stanley near the door, Llysette turned and looked at me. "Something was upsetting you, was it not?"

"It will keep until I get the drive clear. I don't want to slide out of here in the morning."

"You are sure?" She raised her eyebrows.

"I'm certain."

"I am sorry," she said again as she got out of the Stanley.

Llysette carried in her case, and I left mine in the Stanley and got to work. It took nearly an hour, and I was soaked in sweat by the time I finished. Then I had to put the Stanley in the car barn and carry in my own papers, and the package from the Interior Ministry.

Llysette had set the kitchen table, fired up the parlor stove, and had gotten herself a glass of wine that she sipped as she sat in the parlor reading through a stack of university memoranda and papers. She looked up. "Are you all right, Johan?"

"I'm fine." I blotted more sweat off my forehead. "I should have changed, but I wanted to get it off the drive so that some of it could dry before it gets cold enough to turn it to black ice."

I shifted the box to my other arm.

"That? *Qu'est-que-c'est?*"

"Oh. I got another package. This one is supposed to contain information about improved petroleum drilling and reclamation technologies."

"Johan . . . I am not a scientist. I am a singer. Even *I* know one does not give away such."

"They aren't giving it away. I'm supposed to be the one offering it as a trade."

"And if the tzar takes the information and does not trade?"

"Then we go home, and I don't get my consulting fee, but you still get your concert fee."

"That simple? I do not think so."

Neither did I, but I went into the study and opened the box. There was a letter, short and to the point.

Dear Minister Eschbach:
  Enclosed is a compilation of the latest publicly available technology dealing with both oil recovery and reclamation techniques . . . Of particular interest might be the cold weather techniques . . .

We wish you the best and trust you will find the information of use.

The signature was that of a subminister of whom I'd never heard.

In short, the Interior Ministry had had its arm twisted—hard—and they were cooperating reluctantly. Even I could tell that some of the newer proprietary techniques weren't there, but what was there was probably years ahead of what PetroRus was using.

I frowned. Quite a contrast to the Ministry of Environment. Was that because the Interior Ministry was older, and more of a captive of the petroleum industry and its lobbyists? Or for some other reason? I just didn't know, and I didn't really have any contacts in that quarter.

But . . . I still had to get dinner and start thinking about what I was going to pack to take to St. Petersburg. Llysette had dresses, suits, and two performing gowns laid out in the upstairs guest room. I hadn't even thought about it, except to make sure my formal wear had been cleaned.

With a sigh, I headed to the kitchen. Dinner would be far easier than packing, especially since I had no idea what "special" equipment I should or could take besides Bruce's gadgets. Given my past experience, whatever I took wouldn't be quite what I needed, and I'd wish I'd chosen differently. But that was life, also.

In any case, I'd have time, since Llysette would be doing her previews.

21

I DID FINISH packing most items, except for toiletries, by Friday, a good day before we were to leave. In the end, I took Bruce's gadgets, although the hair dryer went in Llysette's valise, a flexible plastic knife that fit inside my belt, a small coil of synthetic line, the Spazi vest made of plastique, and the vest liner that was relatively proof against sharp objects, such as knives and against most handguns—if not fired at point-blank range, or at one's head—or an arm or exposed shoulder. I still had the scars from Llysette's luger, although I'd never seen the weapon since that wonderful and terrible night during which she had shot me, and during which my meddling with ghosting technology had merged the soul of Carolynne, the family ghost, with both my soul and Llysette's. I still didn't want to think too long about the implications of all of that, and whatever Llysette had done with the luger—that was her business.

I also had to use one case for all the documents and bring my briefcase as well, which held official looking papers, as well as a number of concealed ghosting and de-ghosting codes. I didn't expect to use the latter, but they wouldn't do me much good in St. Petersburg if I left them home in Vanderbraak Centre.

While we didn't have to worry about tickets as such, we did have to make sure we had our passports, and I was grateful, again, that not only had I been allowed to keep my diplomatic passport, but that the government had granted one to Llysette when she had gone to Deseret. In most places, the diplomatic passports eased matters.

Saturday afternoon was gray, with thick clouds boiling in from the north, promising snow, but not before we were in Asten, I hoped. It was a good two and a half hour drive to the Asten Aerodrome, and I hated to be late or pushed. Also, we had to stop in Zuider to pick up Terese, and who knew whether that would be a ten-minute stop or an hour? So we left at three. Rather, I had the Stanley packed at three. It was quarter past before we backed out onto Deacon's Lane. I did note that the Spazi vehicle wasn't there.

Traffic on the road to Zuider was light, as it usually was on weekends, except in early October when the tourists from Asten came up to look at the colors of the turning leaves.

After a time, when we had passed the Three Loon Lakes, Llysette looked back again, then at me. "Johan . . . are there not two steamers following us?"

"Three . . . if you count the one in front."

"There is one before us?"

"Front tail. You can do it if you have a good idea where someone is going, and I'm sure Harlaan's boys know where we're headed."

"This . . . this I had not expected."

Neither had I, not an escort of three, exactly, although it made sense. "They want you to get to St. Petersburg safely."

"Moi?"

I could feel the raised eyebrows and sense the Gallic cynicism. "You." If Llysette didn't get there to sing, there was nothing I'd be able to do. Nothing at all, and Harlaan's boys knew that better than anyone. That was one reason why a dead body had shown up in the Wijk River. I wasn't sure that was the only reason.

"You are sweet, *mon cher,* but much rests on you. I am but to sing so that you will be in St. Petersburg."

"I'm glad I love you for your terrible honesty," I returned with a laugh.

Her laugh was another kind of music.

Route 5 heading into Zuider was quiet, and just after we passed the sign announcing the town border, I turned off on Island Road, following the directions Terese had written out earlier for us. One of the Spazi tails followed. The other pulled off and waited on the shoulder, and that meant they knew the area, because Island Road was a dead end—a long and curved one, but a dead end all the same.

Terese's sister lived on South Isle Lane, which was about a mile farther, but the house was easy enough to find even in the growing twilight because it was the only white frame house on the lane, sandwiched between two ancient brick structures.

As we pulled into the graveled drive, Terese started down the wooden steps from the open but covered front porch—a southern architectural style not exactly suited to New Bruges except for two months out of the year.

"Quarter past four, just like the man said," the pianist offered as I stepped out of the Stanley.

Unlike Llysette, Terese had but one valise, and a battered brown leather briefcase.

"Music?" I gestured to the case.

"Music, and some books I haven't had a chance to read."

I managed to squeeze the valise into the Stanley's boot, but it was a good thing that it was built with capacious space for luggage, or I never would have managed. Then, we were off, back out Island Road, and onto Route 5 for about a mile before turning onto Route 10, which headed southeast to Asten.

"What are military turbos like?" The pianist laughed. "I should be asking about any kind of turbos. I've never been able to afford to fly even a commercial turbo."

"They're much smaller than trains or dirigibles," I replied. "You're sacrificing space for speed. It took us a little less than five hours on a turbo from Deseret to the federal district. That's more than two days by dirigible or train."

"The seats, they were comfortable," Llysette added, "but all one could do was stand up, and walk down a space, and then walk back to one's seat. Also, one sees nothing."

There was silence for a moment as Terese turned in the rear seat and looked behind us. She said nothing for a moment, then leaned forward. "Llysette, have you found out more about the piano in the Mariinsky?"

"No," I answered for my diva. "I'd guess it would be good, since the Mariinsky Theatre is the home of the Imperial Russian Opera, but the Ministry of State didn't know."

Terese turned in the seat again, looking into the dimness of twilight, deepened earlier by the heavy clouds. She cleared her throat. "Johan . . . would you mind telling me something?"

"If I can."

"Is it my imagination, or was there a steel-gray steamer watching my sister's house? And is there one tailing us?"

"Your imagination it was not," Llysette said. "Johan tells me this concert is most important."

"There are two following us, and one somewhere in front of us," I added.

"Do I want to know why?" questioned the accompanist.

"Llysette said it best," I allowed myself a resigned sigh. "Relations with Russia have been touchy, not because of problems between Columbia and the tzar, but because Russia can't afford a war with Ferdinand. The tzar sent the Ballets Russes to Philadelphia and the federal district last year. The tzar expects Columbia's best classical talent. If anything were to happen to Llysette, it would prove that Columbia couldn't even protect an artist, and would weaken Columbia's negotiating position with Russia."

"That assumes we need something from Russia," pointed out the accompanist.

"At the very least, we need Russia not to become allied with Ferdinand," I replied.

"There's more there."

"Very probably," I admitted. "But they don't tell retired ministers. They just use them and their talented spouses."

"You two are going along with . . . this?"

"What are the real options for professors and artists?" I asked before Llysette could reply. "Llysette gets paid, and she gets exposure. She didn't get any exposure until the friends of the first speaker of Deseret wanted her to perform in Salt Lake. She got a handful of offers in Columbia after that, but nothing new has been offered in four months."

The laugh from the rear seat was harsh and knowing. "You think it's different when you play for a big-name artist, but it isn't, is it?"

"Non." Llysette said. "And I am not a singer that well known in Columbia. No one in Columbia wanted me to perform until someone else asked. That changes not."

"I suppose it doesn't," Terese agreed.

We were still in the midlands of New Bruges, and, once away from Zuider, into the hilly and half-wooded country that separated the lake area from the flatter farming areas north and west of Asten. Although there was no oncoming traffic, even before the Stanley crested a low hill, the glow of tail-lights ahead warned me, and I eased back on the power, ready for whatever had caused the slowdown.

In a moment, even in the dim light just before full night, I could see the tableau on the highway before me. The Spazi front tail steamer had skidded to a stop, just past a long driveway that wound out of a dark wooded area. The rearmost axle was clearly broken, and most of the tires were flat. There were dark blotches all over the concrete of the road, triangular tire spikes—the modern equivalent of caltrops.

"There is an accident, Johan!" Llysette snapped.

From the side road lumbered a huge petro hauler, except that it had turned onto the shoulder of the road—the shoulder on our side—as it accelerated toward us.

One man jumped away from the wrecked Spazi vehicle as the hauler brushed it aside like a pile of rubbish. But the Spazi agent made it clear of the wreckage and began to fire at the hauler. I couldn't see the weapon, only the briefest of muzzle flares and what seemed to be sparks flashing from the side of the big hauler that loomed ever nearer to us.

Slowing down would have been suicidal. We just would have suffered the fate of the Spazi steamer. So I kept the Stanley headed straight down the road toward the hauler and poured on full power, wishing at that moment for the near-instant response of an old-fashioned internal combustion engine. I had less than a hundred yards before we reached the spikes strewn across the road for what I needed, and hoped that what I was about to try would work.

With what seemed less than a handful of yards between us and the hauler, although it had to be more, I jammed on the brakes, starting a fishtail, before angling to the left through the one space on the road clear of the spikes—the space swept by the Spazi steamer's broken-axled skid. From what I could see, while the left-hand lane had some of the spikes, the far shoulder had none.

The hauler turned to my left, trying to cut us off, but I'd timed it right, and his response lagged. He jerked the wheel, and the big rig started to rock.

As we accelerated out of the skid and cleared the end of the hauler's tank trailer, I half saw the Shell emblem of Columbian Dutch Petroleum angled as if the long tanker section were about to fall on us. We squeaked by and onto the far shoulder. I concentrated on navigating the uneven gravelly pavement of the shoulder, trying to dodge the handful of spikes I hadn't seen before.

I must have been successful, because none of our tires exploded. Then we were past the spikes, and behind us flared a brilliant orangish light, followed by a dull concussion.

"My Lord!" murmured Terese. "It exploded."

I was still focused on driving. Just over the crest of the next low hill were temporary sawhorse road barriers, which explained the stretch of empty highway. So I stayed on the shoulder past the barriers and the handful of waiting steamers, slowing only slightly. Once we passed the waiting traffic—on the wrong-side shoulder—I crossed behind them and returned to the side of the road where I should have been driving all along.

About then, I shivered for the first time. After a second shudder, I reached forward, under the dash, and flicked the thermal paint switch, setting it one notch. Within minutes, the red glossy finish had darkened into a standard steel gray that graced thousands of Stanleys. While it didn't change the shape or model of the steamer, it might throw off any other pursuers.

"I can't believe that," Terese finally said. "That hauler—he was trying to ram into us."

"I'm not sure what he was doing," I replied. "I'm just glad we avoided the mess."

"A racing driver, you also should have been, *mon cher*," Llysette murmured. "*Magnifique* you were."

I didn't know about that. I just knew that the combination of past training, instinct, and luck had helped. Maybe the unseen scales of justice had tilted in Llysette's favor this time, so that she could have the chance to sing in St. Petersburg.

The rest of the trip to Asten was rather silent, although one of the escort steamers did catch up with us after about forty minutes. The Stanley's paint change didn't seem to have thrown them.

Because the aerodrome wasn't in Asten proper, but almost due south of the city, I took Route 29, which skirted Asten to the west before turning east on the south side of the river. It was just after six o'clock when we passed the first sign for the aerodrome. Without saying a word, I flicked the hidden switch to let the thermal paint revert to its base red. I doubted that Terese had even noticed in the darkness, and Llysette wouldn't have said a word.

"That sign said it was the main entrance," suggested Terese, almost apologetically.

"It is, but the military terminal is where we're headed, and that's on the south side. I'm told it's much less crowded."

Neither of them laughed.

I'd expected guards at the gate to the Asten Air Corps Aerodrome—but not Republic marines dressed in battle fatigues and carrying Garand fours—the kind that could go to full automatic with the flip of a lever. Nor had I expected another Spazi steamer to be pulled over and to be waiting.

I rolled down the window as the guard stepped forward. "Sir?"

"Johan Eschbach, Llysette duBoise, and Terese Stewart to catch Republic Air Corps Two." I extended my government ID—the one they'd let me keep as a retired minister—rather than my diplomatic passport.

The guard took the ID, scanned it, compared my face to the one on the card, then handed it back. "Ah . . . sir . . . the ladies?"

The guard was fairly quick, but he still used a flash to illuminate Llysette's face and Terese's as well. Then he returned the passports. "Your escort has a word for you, sir. After that, please follow them, sir."

"Thank you."

The squarish man who stepped up to the Stanley was the same one who had greeted us in the car park in Lebanon when we'd last returned from the federal district. "Minister Eschbach . . . congratulations on some very good driving, sir. We also admired your paint job."

"Thank you."

"We've reported the accident, and it was an accident."

I nodded. "I understand."

His eyes flicked to Llysette.

"I think we all understand."

"Good." He nodded. "We'll lead you to the dignitaries' terminal." He turned.

I rolled down the window.

"That wasn't an accident," Terese said.

"It was an accident," I said. "That's the way it will be reported, and nothing will change that now." As I began to follow the Spazi car, I couldn't help but notice in the Stanley's rearview mirror that the link-fence gate closed behind us. I didn't recall the gates being kept closed on my previous visits to the military side of the aerodrome.

"This is more than a concert," Terese said.

I thought she shook her head, but I couldn't see.

"The concert, it is most important," Llyscttc said firmly, not quite in her ice-and-steel voice, but close.

Terese didn't say another word.

As instructed, I followed the Spazi steamer to the compact military terminal—a low brick structure less than two hundred feet from end to end, and with a low cupola tower on the north side. The Spazi steamer turned into the small car park across from the covered entry of the terminal, and then stopped forward of a series of spaces with a sign before them: RESERVED: FLIGHT GUESTS.

According to the briefing materials, I could leave the Stanley in the reserved car park, and I gathered that one of the spaces was for us. So I pulled into the middle one and shut the Stanley down, remembering to make sure that the thermal paint switch was back to neutral. Then I stepped out into the damp breeze. The split-beam beacon from the military tower cast an intermittent eerie glow as I stepped back toward the boot to get out the luggage.

Before I'd taken a step, two guards in greens appeared, both wearing side arms, but not carrying the Garands.

"Minister Eschbach? Miss duBoise? Miss Stewart?"

"Yes?"

"The turbo was delayed a few minutes in the federal district." The shorter marine gestured, and two others in fatigues appeared. "These men will carry your luggage."

He paused. "Ah . . . sir . . . it will have to be scanned. You understand?"

"I understand." I laughed. By the time I had the boot open, both Llysette and Terese had gotten out of the steamer and stood beside me as I handed the valises and the cases to the waiting marines. Then I locked the Stanley.

"We are on the government business . . . and our valises they must scan?" murmured Llysette as we followed the marines.

"It would be most embarrassing if the Russians scanned our luggage and found something," I pointed out.

"The Russians, still they fear all the world," she replied.

"With their history, it's understandable. Regrettable, but understandable."

They also scanned our hand cases, and some of Llysette's makeup and one metallic purse just came out as blurs. They took one look at the metallic sequins and laughed, not even opening the purse. The hair dryer did show up on the X-ray scanner, but, since they plugged it in and it functioned, and since I had taken the precaution of including a current converter, no one said a word, except suggesting that it be left on top where it could be easily reached. No one said anything at all about the extra batteries in my valise. All in all, between carting luggage and scanning it and waiting for results, it was after seven before we were escorted to a small lounge with wide windows that looked out on the empty tarmac. Despite what the lead marine had said, we waited less than fifteen minutes before the whine of turbos penetrated the terminal, followed by the white-yellow flash of anticollision lights as an aircraft eased up before the terminal. The four-engined modified Curtiss 440 didn't bear the standard silvery aluminum finish of a military aircraft, but was painted white, with gold piping, and bore the Columbian seal on the fuselage below the cockpit.

Even before the port engines were shut down, the ground crew had a rolling staircase wheeled up to the side of fuselage just in front of the wing, and what looked to be a Naval Air Corps officer was scurrying down and toward the doorway to our right. When the auxiliary power was connected, the starboard engines went silent, and a fuel hauler rolled up to the far side of the turbo, presumably to top off the tanks.

I rose. "I think they're ready for us."

Another officer appeared at the back of the lounge. "Ladies . . . sir . . . they'd like you to board." He gestured toward the aircraft and the windows, where the marines in fatigues were rolling a luggage wagon toward the rear of the turbo.

The door onto the tarmac opened, and the Naval Air Corps officer from the aircraft stepped into the lounge and toward us. He wore the gold wings of a command pilot, a silver rosette of his rank on his collar, and two and a half black stripes on the sleeve cuffs of his green uniform blouse. "I'm Lieutenant Commander Madley, sir, ladies." The Naval Air Corps pilot saluted me and bowed to Llysette and Terese. "I'm your military attaché."

"You're not with the Ministry of State or the embassy in St. Petersburg?" I asked.

"No, sir. Colonel Sudwerth is the head of the embassy's military contingent. Because he's been rather involved— I'm sure you understand, sir—Defense Minister Holmbek sent me."

"You're on Minister Holmbek's staff, then?"

Madley flushed slightly. "Barely, sir. I just came off the *Yorktown.*"

I nodded. "I never was on the *Yorktown,* just the *Lexington,* the *Calhoun,* and the *Roosevelt.*"

"Good carriers, sir."

"So is the *Yorktown.*" I was afraid we'd need all those carriers, and more, before too long unless matters somehow changed.

"We need to be going." Madley offered his arm to Terese.

I picked up my briefcase and took Llysette's arm in turn, and we walked through the doorway and out onto the tarmac and back out into the raw and damp air. I could smell the jet fuel, probably from the refueling hauler.

Before we were up the portable stairs, the ground crew had our luggage in the hold and had it battened down. A steward in white and gold closed the cabin doorway behind us. We followed the commander from the gray-decked space, almost a foyer, through a doorway to the right.

There, Madley gestured to one side of the turbo's cabin, far narrower than even one side of the promenade deck of the *Breckenridge,* the dirigible that had carried Llysette and me to Deseret. Turbos—even those as luxurious as Republic Air Corps 2—were clearly not designed for luxury, but for speed. Unlike the Air Corps transport that had carried us back from Deseret, this turbo—or the section where we had been escorted—did not have leather seats in rows, but three groupings of four seats around small tables. Each seat was in fact overlarge, luxurious, and upholstered in pale gray leather. All were securely anchored to the deck, and all looked as though they reclined and swiveled. The seats around one table were empty.

"Greetings!" called Deputy Minister Kent from the table seat behind the empty one. "Minister Vandiver sends his greetings and his regrets that he was unable to join us." Kent sat with three aides, two younger men, and the third a gray-haired heavyset man I'd seen somewhere but didn't recall.

"We're happy to be here," I replied.

"Not so happy as we are to see you," Kent replied with a wide smile. "How was your trip?"

"Ah . . . we just missed getting involved in a smash-up with a petroleum hauler. Other than that, it was the normal drive from Vanderbraak Centre."

"I'm very glad you weren't involved."

"So are we." I laughed. "I'd hate to have had to explain that."

"Nor I," added Llysette with a musical laugh that was a great performance in itself.

Commander Madley cleared his throat to get our attention. "The front table area is yours. There's a bin for your cases just forward there." He gestured toward the open bin.

In the end, Terese took the seat closest to the porthole window, Llysette the one directly aft of the table, and I took the one closest to the center of the turbo, leaving the commander with the forward-most seat.

Before he sat, the commander leaned toward me and said quietly. "I have a briefing case for you, which I'll hand over for you to look at as soon as we're airborne."

"Thank you." I was glad that Harlaan or whoever hadn't forgotten that little detail.

We had barely gotten ourselves seated when an air crewman in a shimmering green flight suit stepped into the cabin. "Ladies, gentlemen, if you would turn your seats forward and lock them in place for takeoff, and then secure your restraint belts . . ."

Since our seats were already locked in the proper position, all I had to do was lock the restraint belt—and then show Llysette how to lock hers. By the time we were trussed in, the aircrewman had vanished.

"Dinner will be served as soon as we level off at our cruising altitude," offered Lieutenant Commander Madley. "You'll also notice that these seats are rather large. They swivel and extend into sleeper seats. It is a rather long flight."

From what I'd already figured, it had to be between eight and nine hours, assuming a direct great circle flight path and no delays.

The whine of the turbos increased, and the aircraft lumbered away from the terminal and down between the red lights that indicated the taxiway toward the duty runway. As the aircraft cleared the structures, I could see the commercial side of the aerodrome to the north, where spotlights illuminated a dirigible docking at the mooring mast. Absently, I wondered if it was the *Breckenridge*.

Somewhere ahead of us, I could hear the takeoff roar of at least a pair of military turbo fighters. Then, without any announcements, the big Curtiss swung onto the runway, headed eastward, and the turbos revved into a high-pitched whine. We were pressed back into our seats as the aircraft accelerated at a rate unfathomable to anyone who had only flown in dirigibles. I glanced at Llysette, who had a smile on her face. On the other hand, Terese Stewart's face was totally blank. Commander Madley's head was tilted sightly to the side, as if he were listening to the engines—just as I was.

Once airborne, we were almost immediately enveloped in thick gray clouds. Mist formed droplets that streaked across the cabin portholes. The pilots held the Curtiss in a fairly steady climb for more than ten minutes, although we were above the clouds within a few minutes.

Shortly after the Curtiss leveled off, Llysette tapped my arm, and I turned. She gestured toward the darkness outside. "Johan?"

"Yes?"

"Those are what?" Llysette was pointing into the star-spangled darkness above the clouds toward two sets of unblinking lights, each white and green.

"Probably FF-10s. Fast fighter escorts."

"An armed escort we need?"

"Probably because we have the deputy minister of state on board."

She raised her eyebrows.

I shrugged, because I really didn't have a good answer to her unspoken question. If matters were so important, why didn't Minister Vandiver happen to be on board? But then, I've never been a complete optimist, and I certainly wasn't after the incident with the hauler. Who had been behind it I had no idea, except that it wasn't anyone in Columbian Dutch Petroleum, or the Russian Okhrana. Nor had it been the Spazi, unlike the days of my encounters with vanBecton and Jerome. My best guess was that the Watch Report on the "accident" would find that the hauler had been stolen by a freelance trupp to sell in some black-market fashion, and that, regrettably, the thief had died in the explosion. But it would all be reported as a simple theft and accident, and the planning and the road barriers just would be conveniently ignored.

All I could figure was that it was critical that our deaths not be identified as murder. That was extremely important to someone, vital enough that they'd taken a higher risk and lower probability method to try to kill us. The attempt at the Presidential Palace followed a similar logic, because the shots fired at a crowd of politicians and celebrities wouldn't have been interpreted as a targeted assassination. So someone wanted one or both of us dead, but didn't want the world to know that we were targets. That was interesting, but scarcely reassuring.

22

As Lieutenant Commander Madley had promised, once the Curtiss reached its cruising altitude, dinner was served, on real china with the Speaker's seal and congressional silver. After that, the seats did recline into something resembling a train sleeper. The ubiquitous stewards also supplied pillows and navy-blue cotton coverlets.

Llysette closed her eyes, but I opened the case that Madley had given me. After the first two pages I wished I hadn't. The first folder just held pictures and background material on people I'd never heard of—except for the tzar, Prime Minister Brusilov, and Pyotr Romanov, the head of PetroRus. The tzar looked impressive enough in his formal uniform as commander in chief, clearly a tall and muscular man with a sharpish nose, if with a receding hairline. Brusilov looked more like a general than a prime minister, with iron-gray hair and a square jaw. Pyotr Romanov was tall like his cousin, but there was an angularity in his face that was almost reptilian. The dossier didn't make me think much more kindly of him. Harlaan's analysts had him pegged as a micromanagerial type, and he'd managed to struggle through because he was bright, but he didn't want to spend enough on modernizing the Caspian fields because it would reduce the cash flow to the military. Apparently, some twenty percent of what I would have called gross revenues was earmarked for the military.

I assumed the backgrounders were on officials and others I might meet, or was even scheduled to meet. The second folder had a tentative schedule of appointments that looked awfully slim, but a note at the bottom said that more were likely to have been confirmed. I hoped so.

Another folder updated the political situation with regard to the Dnepyr River. The bottom line was that Ferdinand was continuing to complain about the effluent from Russian factories and facilities and demanding that the river be cleaned up. Either way, he won. If the Russians did spend the money on environmental remediation, it meant they could spend less on military goods. If they didn't, the situation gave Ferdinand a lever to agitate against the tzar, and as Harlaan's briefing background on the tzar indicated, Tzar Alexander IV was not the most temperate or patient of autocrats.

When it got hard to keep my eyes open, I finally tucked away the folders.

We slept, after a fashion, to be awakened at an hour we were told was noon in St. Petersburg, which meant, as I figured it, that we'd gotten perhaps five hours fitful sleep. It still felt like the middle of the night, which it would have been in Vanderbraak Centre. But it was definitely light outside porthole windows of the Curtiss, and there was a steward, bright-eyed and hovering over us beside our table.

"Would you like café, tea, or chocolate?" the steward asked Llysette.

"The tea, if you please."

"Chocolate." I managed not to growl.

"Café," chirped Terese.

I was generally a morning person, but I did wonder how anyone could sound so cheerful after so long a trip and so little sleep—and without a hot shower.

"We're headed east," I pointed out to Madley, when the

steward slipped away after taking the beverage order, "but there's just ice and ocean below. Turbos aren't that slow."

"It takes longer than it used to. It's gotten too risky to overfly the Baltic. Both the Austrians and the Swedes have gotten touchy about their airspace."

"So we're coming in from the north."

"Yes, sir."

After we ate the generous breakfast, with slightly tough grapefruit sections, bacon, two kinds of sausage, individual omelets, and buttery croissants, in turns we did use the facilities aft of the cabin to attempt to return our persons to some semblance of humanity, but my own bleary-eyed visage in the mirror reminded me that while turbos had the advantage of speed, dirigible travel was definitely easier on the system.

I had barely settled back into my seat when the big Curtiss 404 banked into a starboard turn and then settled on a more southerly course. An aircrewman appeared in the forward doorway. "Ladies, gentlemen, we'll be beginning our descent into St. Petersburg in about fifteen minutes."

"Have you ever been to St. Petersburg?" I asked Madley.

"Only briefly. I did an exchange visit after my first tour. I was here just three months."

The patterns clicked. The *Yorktown* had done patrols in both the North Atlantic and off Alaska. So I asked casually, "You speak Russian, then?"

Madley nodded.

"And you're headed for intelligence after this escort job?"

Madley looked at me without speaking for a moment, then laughed. "Sir . . . I believe you should be escorting me."

"I don't speak Russian," I pointed out.

"Just German and French," he countered.

Llysette's eyebrows rose, but she didn't say anything for the moment.

"What can we expect once we land?" I asked.

"They'll scan every bit of luggage. If we were just tourists or visitors, they'd also look at every book. The Okhrana proscribed a number of novels. The one they really look for is almost one hundred and fifty years old." Madley laughed. "Something called *What Is to Be Done* by Chernyshevsky. It wasn't even published. The Okhrana tortured the author to death, but they say there are bootleg copies even today." He paused. "Also, they don't like Russian history books that glorify the Decembrists or the failed Bolsheviks."

"And one, one must have a permit to own a difference engine," Llysette added.

"Is that right?" asked Terese.

"Not any longer," I said. "You can have one without a permit *if* you're not on the dissidents list. If you are on the list, and they find you with one . . . it's off to the Siberian frontier."

"And who is on the dissidents list?"

"Anyone who might criticize the tzar or the government," suggested Llysette, the edge of her voice carrying over the droning whine of the turbines.

Another voice rose over the conversation—that of Drummond Kent. "We are here for a cultural exchange. I would strongly suggest that none of us discuss Russian internal politics while we are guests of the tzar. Strongly suggest," he added for emphasis.

He didn't add any blither about the success of the cultural exchange, I noted, studying Commander Madley's face, which bore a certain expression of relief. I didn't feel relieved at all, only apprehensive, as the whine of the turbines dropped off and the Curtiss nosed down slightly.

The aircrewman reappeared. "We're beginning the descent a little early. Please turn your seats forward and fasten your restraints."

Of our group, only Commander Madley had to swivel his seat into the forward position.

Again, we were enveloped in gray clouds, even thicker

than those coming out of Asten, or so it seemed to me. When we broke out, probably around two thousand feet, it was over a landscape of whiteness and water—presumably Lake Ladoga, which hadn't frozen over, at least not yet.

I could only catch glimpses of what I thought was St. Petersburg through the port windows across the cabin from me, but the little I saw seemed to confirm what I'd read—that St. Petersburg was two cities—a center city of canals and rivers built of granite and an outer industrial city of low monolithic buildings. Both parts of St. Petersburg were partly shrouded in a combination of smoke, haze, and light snow.

Then, the turbo banked back to the west, presumably to line up on its final approach to Tzar Mikhail Aerodrome. The approach was smooth, and the pilot brought the Curtiss down without even a faint jar, not that I would have expected otherwise from an officer detailed to Air Corps 2.

The thrust-reversers shuddered into play, and we slowed quickly before the Curtiss turned off the runway. The open ground out beyond the runway and the taxiways held snow, not a great deal, perhaps two feet or so. The taxiway lights were lit, perhaps because of the light and fine snow that continued to drift out of the clouds.

The Curtiss rolled to a stop. After unfastening the restraint belt, I had to crane my neck to look out at the aerodrome building that resembled a train station, with heavy gray stone blocks and a gray flat roof. I didn't bother to stand. I had the feeling we'd be standing for some time to come, diplomatic mission or not.

For several minutes nothing happened, even though I'd seen a portable staircase rolled forward toward the aircraft. Then a wave of cold air swept into the cabin. Several minutes more passed, and then one of the pilots stepped back into our cabin and walked over to Drummond Kent. He spoke quietly, and I couldn't quite catch the words. As quickly as he had come, he left.

The deputy minister stepped toward our group. "We arrived slightly ahead of schedule, and they are not quite ready."

Kent was being polite. What he meant was that, although we were supposed to be considered diplomats, the Russians had a slightly different view of matters. A diplomat entering Columbia didn't have to undergo customs. He might be later requested to leave, but he wasn't inspected. In Russia, everyone coming in had their luggage scanned. If you weren't a diplomat and you had something in your luggage that was forbidden, you either had it confiscated, and you got fined on the spot, unless they carted you off to prison immediately. If you were a diplomat, you also lost whatever it was, and you ended up on the next departing turbo or dirigible.

"I understand, Mademoiselle duBoise," Kent continued, "that several photographers are waiting for you, once we clear the necessary formalities . . . It should not be long."

"Thank you," Llysette said.

"It is a good sign," Kent replied with a smile before returning to his own seat.

It was very good. If photographers had been told, that meant that the tzar and those close to him wanted the concert to go on, but it also meant that someone didn't, but the only ones I could see that would be opposed would be the Austrians—and they wouldn't have attacked us in the way that we had been. In turn, that meant someone else both knew what was involved and didn't want it to take place. Even more troubling was my own experience telling me that if two parties already knew, so did most of the intelligence community, since two or more people can never keep that sort of secret.

"Not one photographer in Columbia for years," Llysette said quietly, "but in Russia . . ."

"They like culture here, and they've liked French culture since Catherine the Great."

"They're ready for you, ladies, gentlemen," announced the aircrewman.

We walked down the steps—icy—and across the tarmac

toward an open rectangle of light in the pale gray stone of
the terminal building. Even though there was little wind,
the air felt damp and biting.

Just inside the doorway to the terminal stood two
guards, wearing dark brown and crimson uniforms, with
the double-headed eagles of the Imperial Empire on their
visor caps. Beyond them, in a gray walled room without
windows, perhaps twenty feet by thirty, were two inspectors in black uniforms with silver insignia on the lapels of
their dress blouses. The insignia were also the double-
headed Romanov eagles, but of a smaller size.

Our luggage had already been carried off the Curtiss and
set on the counter to the right of the inspectors. There was
a single X-ray scanner, into which one of the Republic
aircrewmen placed each piece, one after the other, including those that had to belong to the deputy minister and his
assistants. The first inspector would study the screen, then
the second, and both would nod before repeating the process with the next piece of luggage.

One inspector took my heavy case with all the papers
in it and looked around, as if to ask to whom it belonged.

I stepped forward.

"What is inside?"

"Papers. Scholarly papers on environmental techniques." That was totally true.

"You are?"

"Johan Eschbach."

He looked at a list. "Minister Johan Eschbach?"

"Yes."

"Ah. All is explained."

I wasn't sure what was explained, but I saw no point in
saying so, and stepped back and waited until the two finished scanning all the luggage.

The taller inspector cleared his throat. "Your passports?"

In turn, the two inspectors looked over every passport,
and they both looked at each one in turn before stamping
them and the attached visas. Then, the two inspectors

turned, without a word, and departed, leaving the door through which they left open.

We let Deputy Minister Kent, or rather, his older assistant, lead the way past another set of guards, stationed in the wide corridor just beyond the customs facility for important functionaries. I didn't really want to consider what happened to regular travelers.

Immediately beyond the Russian guards were four Republic marines in winter overcoats, forty-fives belted in place outside the greatcoats. Standing with the marines was a short square-faced man in a black greatcoat as well as a taller full colonel. Behind them was a crowd—a small crowd. Several of the men held cameras, cameras of all sizes, ages, and shapes.

The shorter man stepped forward to greet us. "Deputy Minister Kent, Minister Eschbach, Miss duBoise . . . we're glad to see you arrived safely. I'm Ambassador Hagcl, Charles Hagel." He turned to the Air Corps officer beside him. "This is Colonel Sudwerth, military attaché to the embassy."

"We're happy to be here, Ambassador." That was as far as Drummond Kent got before voices erupted from the crowd as they caught sight of Llysette.

"A picture!"

"La diva!"

There were other words, Russian sounding. I had no idea what they meant, except in the general sense that they wanted pictures of Llysette, and I stepped back and slightly aside for the photographers.

The flashes were blinding, even momentarily, but Llysette smiled through them all.

After several minutes, there was a growling command from somewhere, and, like magic, the photographers backed away, some smiling, one or two bowing, and within moments the space that led to the outer doors was clear.

As we crossed the polished stone floor of the wide space that was too small for a foyer and too large for a corridor,

I could feel currents of steam-heated air swirled with damp chill air, presumably from outside. Then we were outside, on a granite sidewalk that flanked a drive, where four black vehicles waited. The first was a limousine, followed by three large black sedans of a type unfamiliar to me, and I'd seen many vehicles over the years.

Although it was mid-afternoon, now getting close to three o'clock, the light was more like twilight, but then, I realized at St. Petersburg's latitude it probably was twilight, or at least very late afternoon. The wind was light but bore a chill dampness. Llysette shivered as she stepped toward the embassy limousine, flying the miniature flag of Columbia, with its stars on the blue field, bordered in red and white. Terese followed her into the limousine, and then I climbed in. The limousine was an internal combustion car, not a steamer, but I supposed steamers were less practical in Russia with the winter cold. The Russians also had more petroleum, and a smaller middle class to burn it.

Ambassador Hagel and Minister Kent joined us, sitting on the plush seats facing to the rear, while the three of us sat in those facing forward. Then the driver shut the passenger door. I glanced toward the gray stone of the terminal.

"Colonel Sudwerth and Commander Madley are in the military vehicle. The colonel wanted to brief the commander," the ambassador said. "Very touchy times here, but you know how that can be, I'm sure, Minister Eschbach, especially with your background."

"I'm sure they're quite touchy," I said easily. "Is there any subject we should avoid discussing, besides internal Russian politics?"

"I wouldn't ask about military capabilities, not that such is your field, directly, but the Okhrana can be touchy about that. With your status, they'd just deport you on a slow steamer routed through Stockholm, some Brit port, and Halifax. That happened to our third secretary last year. Ambitious young fellow, he was. I understand he's now teaching at some small college in the west Northlands."

I nodded. "I understand that I might be meeting with a few experts in environmental matters."

"Some Russian environmental and energy types have expressed an interest. Piet Darwaard—he's the first secretary—has been handling the arrangements. You're likely to be rather busy, he says."

The limousine accelerated, with the slight jerkiness endemic to the gears of an internal combustion engine, and we pulled away from the terminal out onto a concrete road dusted with snow. The snow didn't seem that heavy, the way it swirled across the concrete, not compared to a northeaster in New Bruges, but even inside the limousine, the air had a dampness despite the cold.

"When will we be able to practice in the Mariinsky Theatre?" asked Llysette.

"You have several rehearsals arranged, mademoiselle." The ambassador inclined his head. "The second secretary has the exact times. Although he handles cultural matters, I insisted on the need for rehearsals in the theatre for you. Both Frau Hagel and I were most impressed with the disk of your Salt Palace performance, and Ambassador Klein wired me to insist I hear you. Walter is not easily impressed, I must tell you, and when he said you were magnificent, it had to be an understatement."

"Thank you." Llysette smiled, not quite shyly.

Once we left the aerodrome, we began to pass long stone structures, narrow buildings with steep roofs, almost box-like.

"Those are for worker housing. Most were built in the 1930s. The newer ones are south of here, and they're shoddier," the ambassador said. "You can see the train line. It runs right into one of the stations, Tzarskoe-Selo, I think. I'm pretty sure it's not the Baltic or the Warsaw station. Makes it easy for workers in the cities to get out to the industrial plants. The Sikorski aircraft works is only five miles from here." Hagel laughed. "You couldn't bribe your way in there with ten pounds of gold."

"And if you did, I suspect you wouldn't leave," I replied. "But I'm not interested in such. My background is environment, and also where it relates to energy."

"You have a rather broad background, Minister Eschbach," the ambassador said dryly, "but I'm glad to hear that you're here on environmental matters."

"And to support my wife," I added with a laugh and a smile. "I wouldn't be here at all if she weren't singing."

"For her singing, we are all grateful," Hagel acknowledged.

I kept looking outside, just to try to get a feel of St. Petersburg. No matter what so-called experts say, you can get a feel for a country from a closed vehicle—if you know what to look for. What I saw was a great deal of stone, but not much of it comparatively new. There were also very few vehicles out. While some of that might have been attributable to it being Sunday, not all was.

We passed an omnibus stop, where more than a dozen men and women in brown and gray cloaks or coats huddled under a narrow roof, turning slowly. Not one looked up as we passed.

"They've still got sections of the road that are stone paved, part of the old Lvov Prospekt, they tell me," the ambassador added conversationally.

I had no idea what the Lvov Prospekt was, except it had to be an avenue named after the Russian prince whose reforms and work with Count Witte had effectively saved Tzar Mikhail and the Romanovs in the early part of the century, when Mikhail had taken over after the death of Nicholas II. The avenue or highway was relatively broad, and generally uncrowded, from what I could see from the window.

Even through the snow that fell—not quite lazily, but also not in sheets—I could see that St. Petersburg was definitely a city of stone, gray stone facades contrasted with stone panels painted in bright pastels—blues and yellows, particularly—that stood out against both the gray of the building blocks and the somehow slightly off-white of the snow.

I lost track of the canals we drove beside or over, or both, by the time the limousine turned in through an iron gate that opened as we neared, and then came to a stop in a small courtyard. The ambassador almost bounded out, then waited for the rest of us to emerge into a twilight misted with the fine falling snow. The air smelled somehow chill, with a scent of distant burning coal, and yet slightly dank, possibly from the river that had not yet frozen.

"This was once a grand hotel, but when France fell . . . well . . . it came on the market, and we managed to have it remodeled, but they did keep the wonderful 'ancien regime' feel. The Nevsky Prospekt is only a block south." With a gesture to his right, and a laugh, Ambassador Hagel added, "The British embassy is to the north, and beside it, the Austro-Hungarian embassy. The Austrians haven't had an ambassador in residence for almost ten years, and not much of a staff there. This is the private entry to the embassy. The public entry is on the other side. It's closed today, but not much happens in St. Petersburg on Sunday in any case."

With that announcement, he turned toward the covered entryway, where there stood two Republic marines. This pair carried Garands, in addition to their side arms. I glanced back, but another three marines in fatigues were unloading the luggage from the back of the limousine. As I watched, another black internal combustion auto entered the courtyard. Through the passenger window glass I could see Colonel Sudwerth talking emphatically to Commander Madley.

"Johan . . ." Llysette tugged at my arm, and I realized that we had been left by the others.

We didn't miss much, because the ambassador was standing and waiting for the two military officers and Deputy Minister Kent's aides to join everyone in the foyer, a two-story expanse with an inside dome finished in gold leaf and bordered in green faux marble. The floor was real

green marble, inset with what appeared to be bronze curl-
icues.

There were two archways from the foyer, one leading
straight ahead to a metalwork grating. Behind the grating
I could see the public entry area of the embassy. The second archway was to our right and led down a paneled
hallway perhaps fifteen feet wide. Every ten feet or so was
a painting, each set in a lighted recess.

"Ah . . ." The ambassador cleared his throat as the rest
of the travelers who had been on the Curtiss arrived, along
with Colonel Sudwerth. "We will be having a welcome
dinner for all of you at seven-thirty. We will be gathering
in the lounge for drinks between six-thirty and seven. Not
formal, of course."

Not formal meant that a suit was mandatory for me, but
that Llysette could wear either her traveling suit or a dress,
as she wished.

"The guest quarters are down the corridor to my left—
your right. The Ministry of State personnel will be housed
on the third floor. There are placards on your doors identifying your rooms. Oh . . . and your luggage will be
brought up in the next few minutes." Ambassador Hagel
turned toward Llysette. "The guest quarters for you three
are on the fourth floor." Hagel then motioned to the young
man who stood at one side of the foyer. "Minister Eschbach and Miss duBoise have the main quarters, Miss Stewart the smaller suite."

At the end of the corridor was another foyer, with two
other corridors branching off, and two elevators on the
other side.

"The lounge is down the first corridor," Drummond
Kent said to us before he boarded one of the elevators.

The three of us found ourselves on the same elevator
with the ambassador and the unnamed young man.

"Your quarters are up here somewhere?" I asked Hagel
pleasantly.

"The fifth floor. As far as we can get from the day-to-
day hubbub." He smiled. "I'm looking forward to talking

to you all once you've had a chance to settle in."

We got off on the fourth floor, stepping out into another broad corridor. The young aide waited for the elevator door to close before speaking. "I'm Christian DeWitte, and I'm your day-to-day liaison while you're in St. Petersburg." He began to walk along the corridor, which extended only in one direction from the elevator—north as it turned out. "There are three smaller suites on this level, in addition to the main suite, but it's unlikely that there will be anyone else on this floor while you are here. The others in the concert—the pianist and the quartet—they'll be down on the third floor." He grinned, an expression that made him look less than twenty. "Having converted a former hotel offers us certain advantages."

"What's here?" I asked absently, pointing to a stretch of blank wall that looked as though it had held doors at one point.

"Ah . . . just empty space, sir. You see, this was a grande hotel, and . . . well . . . a young man who was reputed to have been a lover of one of Tzar Mikhail's daughters was staying here. The story is that her brother shot him, beginning with his knees. . . ."

In spite of myself, I winced.

"The space is unused. There's a door off the service stairs, and every so often we check, but the ghost is still there."

A good story, and possibly even true, but I wondered.

DeWitte continued on, until he paused at the second door and extended a key to Terese. "Your quarters, Miss Stewart."

"A suite, I can take that," Terese said as she opened the door.

Even from the hallway, I could see that she had a large main room, with an upright piano.

"There is a small grand in the salon space of the quarters for Miss duBoise and Minister Eschbach," DeWitte explained. "It's only a Haaren, but I'm told it is a good instrument, and it was tuned on Friday. So was the one in here."

Leaving Terese to explore her "smaller" suite, we followed DeWitte to the double doors at the end of the corridor.

"This is where any cabinet ministers stay when they come to St. Petersburg." The boyish grin followed. "Not that we've seen any in the year I've been here." He opened the door and then extended keys to each of us. "I imagine you'll need separate keys with your schedules."

Obviously, the main suite had been designed at one point for visiting royalty, or the equivalent. We stepped into an entry foyer with octagonal rose marble floor tiles, and paneled in a rich cherry. There was a coat closet on the right side, and a powder room, papered in a pale blue damask-like fabric, on the left. The archway led into what could only be called a salon or a drawing room a good thirty-five feet long. In front of the full-length windows, curtained in dark-green velvet hangings, stood the Haaren. It looked as though it had just come from the factory, without a scratch upon it.

The couches and empire-style furniture had been arranged as if for a chamber concert. Llysette looked at me and raised her eyebrows, but we followed DeWitte through the end door.

"This is the master suite."

The bedchamber of the master suite was more than thirty feet long and dominated by a massive, triple width, four-postered bed that appeared very Russian. The comforters were rose, trimmed in a muted crimson piping. A small desk stood before the windows, and flanking it was a chaise longue. There were two bath chambers, one with an enormous ceramic tub, the other with a huge shower for two. Of course, there was a walk-in closet.

DeWitte showed us the small kitchen, with a breakfast area overlooking the private embassy courtyard, and the other "smaller" bedroom.

"I hope this will make your stay more enjoyable." Standing in the entry foyer, he bowed.

"It will certainly make it more comfortable," I replied, adding before he could turn and leave. "I presume you're most fluent in Russian?"

"Of course, sir."

"I'm not. My expertise lies much more in environmental fields. Could I call upon you if I need something short translated—or is there someone else I should contact?"

"I'm the one you should contact," he affirmed. "If it's long or you need it quickly, I may call upon some others to help."

"Thank you. I just wanted to know. Will we see you at dinner?"

"Yes, sir."

After we closed the door behind young DeWitte, I turned to Llysette. The guest quarters were certainly the most palatial accommodations in which we had ever stayed. "They are definitely treating you like a diva."

"They want much."

"We'll see."

There was a knock on the door.

"Yes?" I called.

"Your luggage, Minister Eschbach, Miss duBoise."

I looked through the peephole, then opened the door gingerly, but as should have been the case, two Republic marines in fatigues stood there.

"Where would you like these, sir, madame?"

"Actually, just put them right in here. We'll take care of it from there. We appreciate your doing all the hard work."

"Just our job, sir."

"Thank you."

After closing the door, and sliding the bolt into place, we carted the luggage to the cavernous bedchamber, where we began to unpack. I was tired but still keyed up, and I could tell Llysette felt the same way.

Needless to say, my luggage had been opened. There

was nothing missing, and nothing obviously out of place. I didn't say a word to Llysette.

"Johan . . . my valise—"

"I know." I put my finger to my lips.

She shook her head sadly, and we both knew what she meant.

"We can take a nap for an hour or so, if you'd like," I said.

"I would like. There is a clock?"

"I brought one."

"*Bon.*" But she shook her head again.

I didn't, but I felt that way. The next weeks were going to be very long indeed, beginning with the welcoming dinner.

23

LLYSETTE DID BATHE and change, into a high-necked green velvet dress with a lace collar. Despite her tiredness, she looked stunning as we stepped out into the corridor to make our way to the elevator. After my own long hot shower, I'd put on a dark gray suit and a maroon cravat that Harlaan would have admired. Terese must have been listening, because she joined us at the elevator. She'd also changed, into a long black dress trimmed in white, with a patterned green and black matching jacket.

"I haven't been this dressed up when I'm not performing in years." She looked from Llysette to me. "This must be normal for you two."

I could only shrug. What was normal? I wasn't sure I knew.

No one else was on the elevator we caught, and once on the main floor, we followed the sounds of conversation down the corridor and around the corner into another space, what had probably once been a secondary greeting foyer for the hotel that had preceded the embassy. The ceilings were arched and white, with an off-green trim, very simple, compared to the almost rococo paneling and carving in the wood paneling, and I wondered if the arched ceilings had once held murals or the equivalent.

We stepped through the open double French doors into the lounge, a space that had once been some sort of function room in the hotel the embassy had once been, I gathered, with the rich cherry-wood walls, the carved crown molding, and the built-in glass-paneled sideboards that now held leather-bound books, but once probably had held an array of either crystal or perhaps sample bottles of wine or cognac. I shook my head as I reconsidered. The room had to have been a tea room—the woodwork and the shape of the room were too subtle, and those had not been changed since the embassy had taken over. There were small tables arrayed around the room, each with two or three pale blue leather covered armchairs surrounding it. I could almost imagine how it might have been in the thirties or forties, with women of the Russian aristocracy taking tea or chocolate and conversing politely, while their escorts or husbands had cigars and brandy or wine and whatever in an adjoining bar.

"Our guest of honor," called out Drummond Kent, moving away from his aides toward us, or toward Llysette. He bowed. "You look ravishing. And you as well, Miss Stewart."

"Too kind you are." Llysette offered a warm smile and a half-curtsy.

Terese smiled but did not speak.

"You will not even have to sing to dazzle the audience," Kent added, "although all of us look forward to the concert."

Llysette laughed, musically. "My singing is what they wish, not my appearance."

"They will have both, I am sure."

I was, too.

"I did have a question." Kent looked slightly puzzled. "The program lists a *Vocalise* by Rachmaninov, but I've never seen or heard it performed here."

"Most times, it is performed by orchestra with strings," Llysette replied, "but that it is not how he wrote it."

"Tell me more about it, if you would." Kent broke off as Ambassador Hagel appeared with a dark-haired woman. "Ambassador, Miss duBoise was about to tell us about her program."

"I'd like to hear about it." Hagel offered the warm political smile that is a requirement for any successful diplomat or politician. "But I wanted Annette to meet our distinguished guests. This is Miss duBoise, and her husband Minister Eschbach . . . and Terese Stewart, who is the noted accompanist who will be playing for Miss duBoise."

Everyone murmured polite words of greeting before Llysette began her answer to Drummond Kent's question.

"The first song, it is one by Rimsky-Korsakov called 'The Nightingale' . . ."

"Are all your songs Russian," asked Annette Hagel. "I mean the ones you'll be singing?"

"One I may do, it is by a Russian, but in French . . ."

In the momentary pause, I bent toward Llysette and asked in a whisper, "Wine?"

"A white . . ." she murmured.

"I'll be right back." I wouldn't be, but I hoped my detour wouldn't take too long, not so long as it would for Llysette to explain her program. I'd already spied Christian DeWitte standing beside the small bar and slipped toward him before I got tied up with any other functionaries.

"Minister Eschbach, sir." He straightened as I approached.

"A few details, Christian, if you would? Housekeeping . . . so to speak. Breakfast, for example?"

"Breakfast is served for senior staff in the same room as tonight's dinner. That's from seven to nine. You're senior staff. After that, there is a canteen in the basement."

"But I take it that's only for the truly desperate?"

"It's not quite that bad, sir."

But almost, I gathered. "Newspapers, news services?"

"I can have you get what the ambassador and senior secretaries get. That's a summary of major stories from everywhere, plus those that bear on Russia, and a copy of the wire edition of the *Times* of London. It will be outside your door by six-thirty, if that's all right."

"I'd also like to change some dollars to roubles."

"If it's not a large amount, we can do that through the embassy accounting office."

"Just a few hundred. We may not even need it, but we'd both feel better." I smiled apologetically. "Being in a strange city without local currency . . . roubles aren't exactly easy to get in either Asten or Vanderbraak Centre."

"We can do that, sir."

"That's very helpful. Do you know when I'm supposed to meet with the first secretary?"

"Piet Darwaard? It's on his schedule for nine-thirty. You also have an informal meeting at PetroRus at eleven o'clock and another at the Ministry of Interior at two. Piet has the details, though. I don't know more than that."

So I had another appointment beyond those Harlaan had laid out. That was slightly encouraging. "Thank you."

"Anything I can do, sir."

For all that, he looked slightly uncomfortable, and I didn't press. "That's all. Sometimes people overlook the little details. Thank you again." With another smile and a nod, I slipped to the bar, where the bartender was a senior enlisted marine, I would have bet, probably from the embassy's security detail and moonlighting for extra income.

"What sort of white wines do you have?" I asked.

"A Washington state chardonnay, Hague Valley, and a Samvian pinot grigio."

"Two of the Samvian, if you would."

"Good choice, sir."

With the two wineglasses in hand, I edged my way past the aides of Drummond Kent, whom I'd never met, and back toward Llysette and Drummond Kent. Ambassador Hagel, his wife, and Terese had moved aside and were talking separately.

"Piano for years," Annette Hagel was saying, "but I didn't have that burning desire. . . ."

"I can talk to large groups of people," Minister Kent

was telling Llysette, "but the thought of singing, of having people judge . . ." He shook his head.

I slipped up beside Llysette's shoulder and extended the wineglass. "Your wine, dearest."

"Merci, mon cher."

I glanced around the lounge again, taking in the detail of the carved crown moldings and of the sideboard.

"You look bemused, Eschbach," offered Drummond Kent.

"Looking into the past, in a way," I replied.

"It's easy to do here. This whole country's in the past."

"Is that why Minister Vandiver didn't come? Or because he's too much of a southerner to deal with the combination of Russian bluntness and deviousness?"

"That was the Speaker's decision." Kent laughed lightly, suggesting I was probably right. "You'd best ask him."

"By the time I could, we'll both know, I suspect."

Llysette laughed politely.

"That may be." Kent coughed slightly. "I see that Colonel Sudwerth is moving this way." He turned. "Colonel, you look most distinguished."

Sudwerth was wearing undress blues, the military equivalent of a dark suit, with the only insignia the gold wings of a command pilot. Above the navy blue double-knotted cravat and white shirt he was smiling, as if he'd just heard a good joke and was still enjoying it. "The advantage of uniforms, Minister Kent, Minister Eschbach. Never have to ask what to wear. That's a great benefit in St. Petersburg, where there's a proper and an improper attire for everything."

Kent inclined his head. "If you two will excuse me, I believe the ambassador has someone for me to meet."

The someone was Terese Stewart, whom he'd already met several times, but I merely smiled and took the barest sip of the pinot grigio, a 1988, I thought.

"I understand you also were once a Naval Air Corps aviator, Minister Eschbach." Sudwerth's tone was jovial, just like vanBecton's had been, although the former Spazi director and the colonel looked nothing alike.

"A number of years ago," I admitted, stepping aside a little as Lieutenant Commander Madley eased up to join the three of us.

Madley offered a slight nod, enough to suggest respect, but not to require a response that would have interrupted the colonel.

"You aren't old enough for Singapore," suggested Sudwerth.

"Panama Standoff." I took but a sip of the wine.

"There was an Eschbach," offered Madley, "awarded an RAC. Was he any relation?"

Llysette glanced at me. I'd told her that I'd been decorated, but not the grisly details.

"Guilty as charged," I said dryly. "It was a long time ago."

Madley's eyes widened, if fractionally, while Sudwerth's narrowed, also but fractionally.

"Then you got into politics?" Sudwerth pursued.

"All government is politics, Colonel," I said cheerfully. "Even the Air Corps, isn't it?"

"I suppose you're right about that." He laughed, not quite heartily. "What sort of government politics did you specialize in?"

"You do what you have to," I replied. "I guess I'm most noted for my stint as an environmental subminister, before it became a full ministry."

"Ah . . . that does explain a few matters."

"Perhaps my worst failing was attempting to thwart the building of the Dutch Masters wing of the National Gallery." I shook my head. "The Speaker informed me that deficient architectural design did not justify a disapproval on environmental grounds."

Both officers laughed politely.

"So I retired when I could, and began to teach, and that is where I met Llysette."

"I never saw any teachers as beautiful on any campus," Sudwerth offered gallantly.

"There probably aren't at the military schools—you were Annapolis?"

Sudwerth nodded. "But I knew I'd go Air Corps all the time."

"How did you get here, if I might ask?" I smiled. I really was interested in what he had to say, if not for the reasons most might be.

"Russian was my language; my grandmother was Russian, and she insisted I learn some when I was a child. I studied more at the academy, and a lot of my collateral duties helped." He shrugged. "Once you've had a squadron, you have to get staff experience or embassy experience, if you want to go on, and I couldn't see myself flying difference engines and filing cabinets in the federal district annex. So . . . they sent me here two years ago."

"We all go where we're sent." I fingered my chin, then inclined my head. "I presume you've met, at least socially, some of your peers in the Russian armed services. How would you characterize them?"

"People are people. They don't generalize well." Sudwerth laughed.

I laughed ruefully. "You're right about that. I guess I didn't say what I meant very well. We have a command structure that relies very heavily on what I would call experienced professionals, people like you. The Brits have a few from Sandhurst, but equally as many from their public schools, while the New French train all their officers practically from childhood. I don't know about the Russians, though . . . and? . . . ." I left the question hanging.

"I don't see too many of them, but I'd have to say that, in a way, the Brit model comes closest." Sudwerth pursed his lips. "The best of the Russian officers are very good. Some come from the old nobility, and some come from the sons of professional people in St. Petersburg, Moscow, a few other cities."

"They could use more of the best?"

"Couldn't we all?" countered Sudwerth.

"And how in general terms are they organized? I mean,

we have the marines, the Air Corps, the Navy, the Naval Air Corps . . ."

The colonel nodded. "Much the same—they have the Imperial Rocket Corps, the Aviation Corps, the Navy, and the Army."

That told me one thing. "I assume they have elite units . . ."

"Oh, yes." Sudwerth's next laugh was hearty, rueful, and genuine. "The Blue Cuirassiers, the Horse Guards Artillery . . . but every unit thinks it's elite in some way. Just stay out of any discussions along those lines." He fingered his watch, then looked up. "If you'll excuse me . . ." With a bluff smile and a nod to Llysette, he was gone.

Sudwerth had to have known about my involvement with the Nord scandal, but he'd never mentioned it, never even alluded to it, and that bothered me, along with a lot of other things.

"Interesting man," I mused, studying Commander Madley.

"He was commended for his command of the First Off-Shore Attack Wing, you know?"

"No . . . I didn't know. I imagine he's not exactly fond of the Austrians, then."

"He doesn't say much, sir. When I asked him about it earlier, his voice got a lot harder."

"Ah . . . Minister Eschbach!" Ambassador Hagel's voice cut in before I could reply.

I turned. With the ambassador was a tall and blond man, solidly built, but not heavy or overweight, probably in his late thirties or early forties.

"Piet, I would like you to meet Minister Eschbach. Minister Eschbach, this is Piet Darwaard, the first secretary. And this is the renowned soprano, Miss Llysette duBoise. Minister Eschbach had either the luck or the talent to ensure she married him."

"Luck, and her grace." I bowed slightly.

Llysette smiled, politely.

"I'm honored, Minister." Piet Darwaard bowed, offering an open and warm smile.

He was old-country Dutch from name to appearance, tall, blond, blue-eyed, and broad shouldered, with the kind of honest face that made every man want to slap his back and every woman bring him home to meet her daughter. I distrusted him instantly, perhaps unfairly, but anyone who had made first secretary in a major embassy with those physical attributes needed to be watched.

"I am also most honored to meet you, Miss duBoise. The St. Petersburg papers have made much of your coming concert appearance."

"Thank you," Llysette replied. "I hope I will not disappoint. It has been a long journey, and there is much yet to do."

"I am certain that if you delighted the Saints, you will delight people here even more. They love fine music here, more than in any place where I've been." He offered a warm smile.

"So I have heard."

"I wanted you both to meet Piet," the ambassador said, "because he's the one who really runs the embassy. He's already set up some things for you, Minister Eschbach, and he's making sure that Hamilton Tavoian is taking good care of you, Miss duBoise."

"I certainly wouldn't want to talk business so soon after you arrived," the first secretary said. "So I'll just mention that you both have meetings at nine-thirty tomorrow. I'll be meeting with you, Minister Eschbach, and Hamilton— he's in charge of cultural affairs—will be meeting with you, Miss duBoise." He smiled again and bowed.

A chime began to ring, and the voices in the lounge died away.

"I think we're being summoned," the ambassador said. "Best we go, or Annette will be telling me that everything ran late because I kept talking."

I had the feeling that we'd be seated with the ambassador and his wife, and probably with Drummond Kent, and that we'd talk pleasantries, and that I'd learn very little new, no matter how hard I tried, because Hagel was a well-trained politician and could talk forever while only seeming to impart information and because he knew very little of what was going on and because Drummond Kent knew even less.

I was right.

Thankfully, the dinner wasn't too long, and we did stumble back up to our opulent guest quarters, where it was scarcely difficult to fall asleep. I did remember to bolt the door and set the alarm. I should have done more, but I was far too tired to think as clearly as I probably should have.

24

THE ALARM WENT off far too early, and it took me several moments to discern where I was, because it was still fairly dark. Then, seven o'clock was before dawn in December in St. Petersburg.

"Johan . . ." Llysette mumbled.

"I know. It's dark."

"Cold . . ."

"It's St. Petersburg." I managed to beat the alarm into silence, if not submission, before struggling into a sitting position on the side of the bed. Finally, I stood and staggered out of the enormous bedchamber and through the salon and into the minuscule kitchen. There wasn't much there, except teabags and a kettle. There wasn't even sugar, and that meant I'd have to choke down bitter tea.

While the electric kettle began to heat, I decided to see how effective Christian had been in obtaining news. I peered through the spy hole first, but the corridor was empty. In the wooden box affixed to the wall beside the left-hand door was a newspaper and a sheaf of standard pages stapled in the upper left-hand corner. I brought all the papers inside, rebolted the door, and went back to the kitchen, where the kettle was groaning but not yet boiling.

I didn't try to read the *Times* of London but began to skim the summaries put together by the embassy staff.

... prices of kerosene and crude petroleum still rising in major markets ...

... two more Austrian submersibles said to be patrolling the Indian Ocean ... denied by Foreign Minister vonBraun ...

... Fifteenth Austrian Mountain Division posted west of L'Vov ...

... King Constantine protests Austro-Hungarian pressure to allow unlimited access to Greek ports by Austrian warships ... and lease of land for a military aerodrome ...

... Austria may plan detonation of a "massive" nuclear device at its North African proving grounds to counter recent Russian tests of the Perun missile ...

... Minister of Defense Holmbek refused to comment on the report that Columbia was increasing its capabilities to wage a cold weather war ...

A particularly loud groan, followed by a hiss and then a shriek, informed me that the kettle was boiling. I poured the boiling water into the teapot. The tea was old, and I'd had to use a strainer because I couldn't find a tea ball, and that meant loose fragments in the tea, which I didn't care for ... but old tea with dregs was better than no tea, especially as we were still adjusting to a rather radical time change.

I carried two cups to the bedroom, where I tendered one to Llysette, who had managed to prop herself up with pillows and turn on one light, the closest bedside lamp.

"Thank you, Johan." For a time, Llysette sipped the tea slowly.

"What's your schedule?" I finally asked her.

"At eleven o'clock, we will practice here. At half past

two, we leave in an embassy *voiture* for the theatre, and we have but an hour there."

"And then?"

She shrugged. *"Et toi, mon cher?"*

"I supposedly have two meetings. They may lead to something. They may not." I took a sip of the tea. It was bitter. "I'm going to take a shower."

"Always you hurry . . ." But she smiled warmly.

"Always," I admitted, setting the teacup down on the bedside table.

I finished showering and dressing before Llysette. So I took an armchair in the long salon and began to read through the *Times* of London. Most of the interesting articles were merely elaborations on the embassy news summaries, but there was one other interesting article, although I wasn't quite sure that everyone would find it as interesting as I did.

St. Petersburg (Special Report). How Many Students? Who knows? Even in well-ordered Russia, students can occasionally ruffle more than egos. Last month's student riots have had an interesting outcome. The disruptions went further than demonstrations in halls and courtyards. The registrar's office has admitted that there are more than a few missing records. Even the paperwork section of the Okhrana, an organization well known in Imperial Russia and elsewhere, and renowned for its expertise in finding and keeping every known form of documentation on individuals, has admitted that it cannot find the current student registration list at the University of St. Petersburg. Last century's class lists, of course. Even last year's list, but not this year's lists. Students will be students, and even a tzar can't order them not to be. . . .

There was something about it, but I couldn't finger it, not exactly.

"Johan?" called Llysette from the master chamber.

"I'm out here. Are you ready to go down for breakfast?"

"Mais oui." Llysette emerged wearing a black woolen suit with a deep blue silk blouse and a multicolored silk scarf that somehow tied everything together.

"You have your key?" I asked.

"You plan to leave me so soon?"

I almost fell for it, but just grinned. "You're feeling better."

"Sleep, it always helps."

Terese didn't join us as we walked down toward the elevator, but after her performance on the turbo, I wouldn't have been surprised had she had been up for hours and out running the streets of St. Petersburg.

As we left the elevator, I could hear voices from the corridor that led to the "business" side of the embassy. Although it was still dark outside, the wheels of commerce and diplomacy started early, even in St. Petersburg. Just slightly after eight, and it appeared as though we were about the only ones in the dining area. Apparently, the working day started very early for even the senior staff, although I doubted that the ambassador or his wife ate in the dining area. Maybe he was an early riser, too. He'd been a one-term senator from Nebraska, as I recalled.

"Tea, coffee, sir, madame?" asked a steward who had appeared from nowhere. The accent was pronounced, which meant he was probably Russian.

"Do you have chocolate?"

"Yes, sir."

I glanced at Llysette, and she nodded. "Two chocolates, with breakfast."

There were no menus, and we ended up with eggs halfway between scrambled and omelets, link sausages that were slightly better than Scottish blood sausages, but not much, toast just short of blackened, stewed tomatoes, and a huge pot of marmalade.

Nine-thirty found us on the second floor of the embassy, Llysette headed into one office, and me into another. Piet Darwaard's office was as I imagined most of those in the embassy. The cherry-paneled walls remained, as did the narrow floor-to-ceiling windows, the high ceilings, and the carved chair rail and crown moldings. The once-painted or gilded ceilings were off-white, and where there had probably once been velvet hangings framing the window casements, the only window treatments were wooden-slat blinds, which had been raised to show a gray morning.

"Good morning, Minister Eschbach."

"Good morning. You have a good view here," I observed, before taking the chair opposite the too modern oak desk that fitted neither in color nor in style the room itself.

"I don't have much chance to enjoy it." Darwaard's smile was a shade warmer than polite.

"Tell me about the meetings you've set up, if you would. I'd gotten a preliminary list which had a meeting with a Dimitri Vlasovich at the Ministry of the Interior."

Darwaard handed me two folders, each blank on the outside. "Today, you have two. The first is at eleven o'clock with the number-two man at PetroRus, a Kyril Kulikovsky. I don't recall his patronymic, but it's in the folder. The second is the one with Vlasovich at three o'clock."

I flicked through the folders, but both happened to be exactly the same as the dossiers I'd already gotten from Harlaan. "What else can you tell me about Kulikovsky?"

"He's cultured and personable. He'll probably be at the concert. He's the one Pyotr Romanov uses to meet and screen everyone. If Kulikovsky doesn't pass on you, you don't meet anyone of import. He's sort of a high-level gatekeeper. No one thinks he makes any decisions, but you can't get to see anyone who does without meeting him first."

"What's his passion? Or what does he hate?"

Darwaard frowned. "I couldn't say. I've never seen him other than composed and charming."

"What about Vlasovich?"

"He's got two or three engineering degrees, one in environmental engineering from the University of Assen.

He's one of the few to get into the top four ranks of the civil servants without money or blood behind him. As soon as he heard that you were coming, his office contacted me. The word is that he lives, breathes, and dreams engineering in some form or another. He'll also steal any engineering idea that's not walled away."

"Is he married? Or does engineering serve that function, too?"

"He is married, to a French woman he met at one of the engineering schools. She teaches at St. Petersburg University."

"What happened with those riots? There were stories in the papers, even in New Bruges."

Darwaard lifted his shoulders. "The students were demonstrating for a constitutional monarchy, and removal of the tzar's absolute veto over any laws passed by the Senate and Duma. Things got out of hand."

"How much out of hand? One set of reports suggested hundreds of students were killed; others said very few."

"We don't know. It couldn't have been very many, because there weren't any new ghosts there at the university, but there had to be some because the university has been shut down until next semester. I'd speculate that part of the reason for the closure is to analyze what happened and make sure it won't occur again, and partly to ensure that tempers cool down."

"And partly to track down the instigators?"

"The Okhrana is very effective in finding student trouble-makers. They always have been; that's why there's still a tzar."

I nodded. "How about the rest of the week?"

Another folder appeared, which Darwaard passed to me.

"That's where things stand right now. There are one or two other possibilities, and I should know about them by this afternoon. I was led to believe that you would add to your schedule."

"I do hope so." I smiled politely. "I appreciate all you've done already."

"That's what we're here for." There was the briefest pause. "An embassy vehicle is at your disposal, with a driver, for whatever you need and for as long as you need it. The driver is Olaf. He's Swedish, but he's been with the embassy for years and comes well recommended. The drivers have a lounge on the main floor."

"Good," I replied.

Darwaard steepled his hands, a gesture I'd never liked, then began to speak slowly. "A few points to consider, Minister Eschbach, if you don't mind. As a subminister appointed by the Speaker, in general terms you rate the comparable address of 'your excellency,' but as an unofficial envoy of the Columbian government, you'll probably be addressed as 'your high excellency.' I suggest you look offended, or insulted if one of the more snobbish civil servants offers 'your honour.' It may not seem like much, but here in St. Petersburg, titles do matter, at least to the tzarists and the old aristocracy." Darwaard smile's verged on the patronizing.

"I can see that."

"Also, I understand from Colonel Sudwerth that Commander Madley will be accompanying you."

"I think Commander Madley is a fine officer, but I have a problem of sorts with that," I said. "I'm an environmental expert, not a military person. With even a senior junior officer accompanying me, wouldn't that convey an impression that I'm here at the military's behest?"

Darwaard frowned. "I can see your concern, but, remember, everything here has military overtones. I don't see as that would create too much of a difficulty."

"There's also the status question." I waited.

"Status?" Darwaard replied blandly.

"You know," I said with a laugh. "The number of retainers determines status. That's particularly true in some places."

"We're rather short-staffed, Minister Eschbach."

"I know that. You know that. It needn't be anyone essential. What about that young fellow . . . what's his name?"

"Christian? He knows the Russian language, and the requirements for exit visas and trade paperwork, and that's about it."

"That's more than enough, and it shouldn't put too much of a drain on the embassy, I'd think. With Commander Madley, Christian, and a driver, it would show that I'm more than a gesture. Christian can handle errands, that sort of thing, so that I won't have to be bothering you or others."

"That . . . yes . . . that is a good point . . . I suppose young Christian could be spared."

I needed both. Madley was intelligent, but he knew little about the current politics. Christian knew less directly, but I'd have bet he knew the embassy, and where at least some bodies were buried, and he seemed bright enough to have learned more than he knew he had learned, and I did need at least a small entourage to make the point that Columbia was quietly behind me.

"One moment." He picked up the handset. "Could you have Christian come up here in about five minutes? Thank you." Darwaard looked at me. "Since Christian will be detailed to you, it would be best if he showed you where things are."

"Makes sense to me."

"While we're waiting, there's something else to remember. The Russians have a saying. Offer a man a finger, and he will take your hand—if not your arm. It's not just a saying; it's the way many of them operate. Those in the underworld here are so brutal that a low trupp of Asten or New Amsterdam looks like a philanthropist by comparison."

"Nice folks. What do they handle? If the Okhrana is as ruthless as they're reputed to be, I can't imagine that these fellows would be exactly plentiful."

"Most of what they do is assassinations. Imperial bureaucracies do have a market for removals, and with all the paperwork of bureaucracies . . . well . . . sometimes high officials would rather not have fingerprints."

I got that message as well, but I smiled. "I can't imagine

that environmental engineering will provoke much controversy."

"I wouldn't imagine your environmental work would, either."

There was a knock at the door.

"Come in," Darwaard said.

Christian DeWitte stepped into the office. "You called for me, Mister Darwaard?"

"I did. Because of the special nature of Minister Eschbach's mission here, you've been detailed to act as his junior staffer while he is in St. Petersburg."

"Now, sir? I barely got started on the exit—"

"Those will have to wait, Christian. Some of Minister Eschbach's work is most time-sensitive. You'll be working for him beginning right now."

"Yes, sir."

I didn't much care for Darwaard's hearty open smile. So I offered him one in return. "Thank you very much, Piet. I appreciate everything that you've done, and I hope you can firm up those other appointments." I gave a minimal bow, then nodded to Christian. "We have to get organized, and the first secretary has a busy schedule."

Darwaard offered his professional smile as we left.

Christian looked sideways at me after I closed Darwaard's door behind us. "What do you want me to do, sir?"

"It's pretty simple. We have a car and driver. The driver is Olaf. We need to meet him, then find Commander Madley and make sure he's ready to go with us for the eleven o'clock with Kulikovsky."

"You're lucky with Olaf."

"You mean because Piet doesn't like him?" I didn't have to let that go, but I needed a reaction.

Christian's face froze for a moment, only the briefest of instants, but I was watching. "Piet's not quite so clever as he thinks." I laughed. "But we've got work to do."

Christian actually smiled, and that was a good sign.

We headed for the stairs and to round up the rest of my motley crew, and to change some currency, if we had time.

25

LESS THAN A half hour later, the four of us were in another internal-combustion-engined sedan, something called a Volga, which bore a large chrome hood ornament consisting of a stag with its antlers back in a rather unnatural position above a spread chrome "V." Christian sat in the front seat beside the gray-haired Olaf, while Madley and I sat in back.

The PetroRus building wasn't that far from the embassy, but to the east of the Tauride Gardens, where the Duma still met.

"Olaf . . . what do you know about the PetroRus building?"

"Sir? The PetroRus palace? Once it was a girls' boarding school—the Smolny Institute—and then for a time it was a reeducation center, and then Tzar Mikhail—the third one—had it torn down, and they built the PetroRus Centre there. That was when they had more cash from the Caspian oil fields," the driver said. "That was what First Secretary Darwaard said."

"He knows a great deal," I said. "He was probably over there a number of times."

"Not that I know of. He mentioned that when he went down to the general staff building."

"He seems like a very well-educated man." I turned to Christian. "Do you happen to know what he studied, or where?"

"He's from Waalford, outside of Asten, he said, and he went to the University of Assen as an undergraduate and to the University of Virginia for his graduate work."

It seemed that I couldn't escape The University, even in Russia. "Petroleum geology?" I asked lightly.

"International studies. He speaks Russian and Swedish, and some French, I think," Christian said.

"Wasn't he posted to Stockholm for a time?" I asked.

"Five years." Surprisingly, that was Commander Madley's comment.

"He's definitely talented. We're fortunate to have him." I could see a more modern building ahead, still of granite, but with almost slab-sided walls interspersed with sheets of green glass that seemed to catch and hold the winter sun. The roof was also slanted more than the older buildings and shimmered despite the weak light. "Is that the PetroRus building ahead?"

"It is, sir." Olaf pulled into a wide stone-paved drive and inched forward until we were under the archway and just behind another black Volga.

Despite the faint sunlight, the air was chill and damp as we got out of the sedan.

"How long will you be, sir?" asked the driver.

I smiled and shrugged. "A half hour, an hour. I'd be surprised if it were longer."

Olaf nodded. "I'll be waiting here."

Before we headed toward the modern glass door set in the square granite arch, I turned to Madley. "If you don't mind, Commander, I'm going to have Christian do most of the announcing and translating. I'd like you to watch and listen. Unless it's urgent, save any observations until after we leave."

The commander nodded.

Christian tilted his head quizzically but didn't say anything.

There were four guards in the lobby, not in Imperial Russian uniforms, but in rich green hard-finished fabric, trimmed in silver. Even without insignia, they still looked military. The lobby itself had smooth polished walls of a reddish granite and dark gray stone floors that glistened. There was a desk in the middle of the lobby, with a single clerk behind it.

I nodded to Christian. "Just tell them who I am and try to explain that I have a meeting at eleven o'clock with Kyril Kulikovsky. Oh, and make sure that you get in that I'm his most high excellency Minister Johan Eschbach."

"Kyril Kulikovsky?"

"That's right."

Christian marched forward and delivered an impressive-sounding spiel, the only words of which I recognized were my name and "Columbia."

I stood there and looked bored and above it all.

"He's good," Madley murmured.

The clerk nodded, nodded some more, looked at a clipboard, and then picked up a handset. He spoke on it and looked vaguely surprised. Then he hung up and motioned to one of the guards.

Christian turned. "His high excellency Executive Director Kulikovsky is waiting for you, Minister Eschbach."

The armed guard in green escorted us past the clerk's station and to the far side of the foyer, where there was a bank of elevators, if three could be considered a bank. After we entered the elevator, so did he, inserting a key and pressing the button for the sixth floor.

We got out on the sixth floor and stepped back in time. Although one wall to the right of the elevator was entirely of greenish glass, the interior wall was polished cherry, with both a carved chair rail and a matching crown molding, and three portraits in gold frames graced the wall leading to an ornate cherry reception desk. The woman behind the desk was blonde, wearing a black suit, a red blouse, and a warm smile.

The guard stood beside the elevator and watched as we stepped up to the reception desk, or rather Christian did, explaining once more.

Her smile broadened before she replied, in lightly accented English. "Your Russian is excellent, and Executive Director Kulikovsky will be with you all in just a moment."

She hadn't even finished her words before a tall, slender, dark-haired man appeared, wearing a gray suit that would've easily have graced either Philadelphia or the federal district.

"Minister Eschbach ... gentlemen, it is so good to see you." He glanced at the commander and Christian, "Elenya will find you refreshments while the minister and I meet."

With that, and a hidden smile, I followed Kulikovsky through a solid cherry doorway and down a short corridor to a windowed office, neither large nor small, which was furnished in what I would have called Russian modern. I liked the older and more ornate style better.

The Russian executive sat down in one of the chairs in front of his desk. I took the other.

"Minister Eschbach, I am so glad to see that you could be here." Kulikovsky's English bore only the barest trace of an accent.

"I'm more than happy to be here." I smiled and waited.

"The first secretary of your embassy ... I must say that he was less than forthcoming about why you wished to come to visit PetroRus."

"First Secretary Darwaard is of old Dutch stock," I replied. "They find it hard to offer much information unless they are absolutely certain of matters." I shrugged. "I had asked to meet with colleagues and those who had, shall we say, a practical interest in environmental matters."

The slightest frown appeared and vanished before Kulikovsky laughed. "A practical environmentalist! That is ... what would you say ... a term that contradicts itself?"

"An oxymoron. Perhaps. But we live in an uncertain world, and those of us with a practical disposition are always looking for others who would like to look into practical solutions."

"Ah . . . always to the practical. Dutch indeed you are, Minister Eschbach."

"I'd understood that practicality was also a valued Russian trait."

"For some. For some." Kulikovsky tilted his head, as if pondering whether to add to what he had said. "For others, ideals matter more. Is that not so in your country?"

"If you're not practical, I've found, it can be difficult to hold on to your ideals," I pointed out. "That's something the ideologues have trouble understanding."

"So you are a practical, idealistic environmental specialist?"

"Among other things." I shrugged.

"You think that what is practical for one country or one organization is so for another?"

"Sometimes." I laughed. "I doubt that environmentally sound warm-water drilling technologies would be terribly practical for Arctic oil extraction efforts. But some technologies are practical in many lands and applications."

"Practical . . . but are they affordable?"

"Affordable," I mused. "That's an interesting concept. That depends on who pays, and what. It's always better if people can trade benefits. That way, no one has to explain the budget, and each party can take credit for the increased revenues or production or whatever."

"If that is possible." Kulikovsky's voice was skeptical.

"It's always possible if both sides have something to gain and nothing to lose."

"Nothing to lose?" Kulikovsky laughed, a harsh but hearty sound. "You sound like a salesman, Minister Eschbach. Does not someone always give up something of value?"

"Not always," I countered. "And sometimes something is not of value or of far lesser value for one party than to another. Then it makes sense to trade. If you are a champion skater, the best skates in the world are of value to you. To me?" I shook my head. "Likewise, I have a steamer at home that operates on kerosene. Here, your vehicles run on gasoline. A tank full of gasoline is useless to me, but it could be valuable to you."

"Were it that all matters were so simple." Kulikovsky smiled.

I returned the smile. "I've often found that people make matters more complicated than they should be. When one understands his own basic interests—or his country's—it becomes more simple."

Kulikovsky leaned forward. "What are your interests? Personally."

"To help my country and my wife."

"Those do not sound personal."

I offered a heartfelt and hearty laugh. "They're *very* personal. My wife has made my life a joy again, and I'd like to help her gain what she was denied by Ferdinand, and frankly by my own government. Second, if I can't help my country . . . then I won't be able to devote my full energies to what I enjoy doing, and that's consulting and teaching."

"And your country's interests?"

"There's no secret to those. Columbia needs a broader range of dependable fossil fuel supplies." I looked at Kulikovsky. "It's your turn."

"My personal interests do not matter so much." He paused. "That is because they are tied to Russia's interests." There was the slightest glimmer in his eyes as he asked, "What interest of Russia's do you propose to satisfy?"

"Several. You have some pressing environmental concerns that Ferdinand continues to exploit. There are efficiencies in energy extraction and production that might be possible, and there are possibilities for granting energy concessions to Columbian firms that will result in near-term hard currency inflows."

"You Columbians . . . even in circumspection, you are blunt."

"No. I'm not a diplomat," I admitted. "I'm a practical man. I have trouble talking in circles. I prefer to recognize and solve problems, instead of pretending they don't exist."

Kulikovsky nodded, then pursed his lips. "If you would excuse me for just a moment . . ."

"Certainly."

With a smile, he stepped out a side door.

I'd either made progress or totally destroyed it. I *thought* I was getting somewhere, but who knew?

Kulikovsky was gone about five minutes before returning and reseating himself in the chair he'd vacated. "My wife and I, and a friend and his wife—your wife is the diva, is she not?"

"Yes."

"I know the time is short, but could you join us for dinner at the Imperial Yacht Club at eight? It would be such a treat. You do have formal attire, no?"

"I can manage that."

"Elisabet would be so pleased. Our daughter studied the voice at the conservatory, and she insisted that we must go to the concert."

"Will your daughter be there, at the concert?"

"Oh, yes, and with her husband." The PetroRus executive smiled, and the smile seemed to be one of relief. "If you would meet us at the club just before eight . . ."

"Llysette and I will be there."

"Good. And I will think over what you have said."

And that was that.

Kulikovsky and I walked out smiling, and Commander Madley and Christian rose from their chairs, and everyone bowed and smiled, and in minutes we were on the elevator headed downward—without a guard.

Commander Madley waited until we were outside and in the Volga before speaking. "I'm under the impression that most Russian bureaucrats don't come out and greet guests personally." He looked at Christian.

"I haven't been at one of these meetings before," Christian answered, almost apologetically. "What I've heard is that most make you wait and come to them. Many are very rude."

"That could be because he's spent a great deal of time in either Britain or Columbia. Oh . . . his wife is a great admirer of Llysette's. They've asked us to dinner at the Imperial Yacht Club tonight. Formal attire."

Christian's mouth opened. "The only one in the embassy who's ever been asked there is the ambassador."

"It helps having a famous wife," I suggested. "Is there somewhere that we could get something to eat—you, too, Olaf, before we go to the Ministry of Interior?"

"There is a café not far off the Nevsky Prospekt."

"Let's try it." I was glad I had roubles in my wallet.

Olaf parked the Volga on the street, not fifty yards from the café, something impossible in any Columbian city, and we got out. I hadn't taken two steps when a wisp of white appeared before a door nailed shut with a black bar. The ghost held up her hands, as if begging, then murmured something, although murmur wasn't correct because everyone heard ghosts in their thoughts, not aloud. I didn't recognize the words, except that they were Russian. Then she dropped to her knees, as if pleading—and vanished.

I didn't shake my head, though I felt that way, as we walked into the café.

The small café was better than the image I had from the outside. The wooden tables were battered, but the black-and-white marble floor tiles were clean, if scarred from years of use, and the windows were wide enough to let in the icy winter light. My breath didn't quite steam, although I was perfectly comfortable in my heavy winter overcoat.

In the end I had something I couldn't pronounce that seemed to be a cross between a potato pancake, lace potatoes, and a crepe, rolled around a stewed meat filling. It was tasty, and filling, and after paying for four meals and teas, more than half my roubles were gone.

"I hope you two talked to Elenya," I said after swallowing a mouthful of strong and not quite bitter Russian tea.

"Christian did most of the talking," Madley said.

"What did you learn beyond the chitchat?" I asked, taking another sip of the tea.

"Not much," Christian said. "She's married, and she has two children. She likes working for PetroRus, and especially for Director Kulikovsky. It's been a cold winter already, with more snow than usual for November and December . . ."

I made a note to remember that.

"She also said something about Christian's accent being more sophisticated than other Columbians she had met," Madley added.

"Other than that, sir . . ."

"I imagine she's been told to be polite and say nothing important." I turned to the driver, who was finishing off the last crumbs of his lunch. "Olaf, you spend more time than most people in the embassy with the everyday Russian people, don't you?"

"Most of all, I see drivers and imperial guards, and city police . . . and my neighbors."

"You've lived here how long?"

"Twenty years, since I met Irenya."

"How are prices? For things like food, rent, that sort of thing," I asked.

"They are going up, every week. It was not always that way."

"Even petrol?"

Olaf nodded. "But the bread is the worst. A single loaf costs twice as many roubles as it did last spring."

"Has this happened before? Do people talk about it?"

"I do not remember it being quite so bad, but it has been a cold year." He didn't quite look at me.

"What about ghosts? Does St. Petersburg have a lot?"

Olaf glanced toward the door, then shrugged. I understood. More than anyone wanted to talk about, it appeared.

So I finished my tea, and since everyone else had finished before I had, I stood. "We'd better be going, I'd guess."

I didn't see the ghost beside the black-barred door on our way back to the black Volga sedan, even though that side of the building was in shadow from the afternoon winter sun that wasn't about to last, not with the clouds coming in from the north.

The main Interior Ministry building was little more than two blocks east of the Neva, off the area that Olaf called the English Embankment. Like every other government building we had passed, it was of gray stone, with pastel-painted panels to add some color, but the Interior Ministry had chosen a pastel green that somehow looked sickly.

Christian had a bit more trouble explaining who I was and why I was there, but in the end we all piled onto another not quite obsolete elevator that only took us three floors.

According to the backgrounders, Vlasovich was the director of engineering technology for the Ministry of Interior, and it was clear that a director wasn't on the top of the bureaucratic pyramid, because he met us himself, introduced himself, and suggested that Madley and Christian wait in two very uncomfortable wooden chairs that looked even older than the building.

Vlasovich had a far more modest office than had Kulikovsky, barely fifteen feet square, with a single window that looked out on a black-gray stone wall. When I stepped into his overlarge closet, he closed the door, then walked behind a desk that might have been new a generation before and surveyed me for a time. I just waited.

"The famous Minister Johan Eschbach." He shook his head. "You do not look two meters tall, like Peter the Great. You do not have the cold eyes of a Koba. You do not have the sensuous lips of a Don Juan. Yet you have made great men weep, broken more revolutionaries than the Okhrana, and swept into your arms the most beautiful diva of the century. I congratulate you." His accent was somewhere between Brit and old Dutch with a touch of French, probably reflecting his schooling and his wife.

"What exactly can a mere representative of his Speaker say to that?" I asked with a laugh that I hoped wasn't too forced.

"Very little." He dropped into his chair and gestured to the single chair across the ancient desk from him.

As I took the seat, I noticed that the difference engine on the stand beside him was as modern as anything in Bruce's shop. "How about the esteemed and respected Dimitri Vlasovich, engineer par excellence, known for his ability to beg, borrow, steal, and adapt every engineering idea that is not walled away—and even some of those?"

Vlasovich laughed, a deep belly laugh of the sort that everyone took to mean a truly jovial soul. To me, men who could laugh that way were twice as dangerous. "Even Pyotr Romanov would not say that to my face. To my back, but not to my face."

"Pardon my ignorance." I tried to keep my tone ambivalent.

"I want all the environmental technologies you will give us. What do you want?" Vlasovich's dark brown eyes bored into me.

"The concessions for Columbian Dutch Petroleum to explore, extract, and transport Alaskan north-shore oil for a reasonable royalty payment."

A broad smile crossed the face of the director of engineering technologies. "You see? It is very simple. I say what I want. You say what you want. With PetroRus, it will take you two meetings, perhaps three, and you may get nothing. They are what you call bureaucrats, and they call themselves businessmen. I am the businessman, and they call me a bureaucrat."

I nodded. "So how do you propose to get what you want, and for me to get what I want?"

"That is harder. If I say we need the technologies, the minister will approve, but he will not cross Pyotr Romanov, and Romanov will not approve unless those he trusts also approve."

"What you're suggesting is that if I can get PetroRus to approve of the proposition, the Interior Ministry will agree, provided the control of the environmental technologies goes to you?"

"Ha!" That got another belly laugh. "You could be Russian, Minister."

I doubted that, and doubted more that I'd want to be. "How many other obstacles are there that I don't know about?"

"In the great land of Imperial Russia, you talk of obstacles? Your high excellency, how could one imagine such? Certainly, it is possible that our great and glorious Air Corps might be persuaded to do without fuel it could never refine . . . Yet, how would the Imperial Rocket Corps—" He broke off abruptly. "But I wander. Best you consider the obstacles you face, about which this poor functionary knows nothing. I only know that they must exist, or you would have your concession, and I would have your technologies."

"In everything, there is someone who would rather build a small empire and die with it than see his country prosper." I was temporizing, but what else could I have said?

"In the west, certainly not in great and Imperial Russia, most of those are soldiers, for they long for the days when a sword and a strong right arm would build empires. Today, in your land, it might be an aircraft, but they feel the same, whether that man is serving in an embassy or in an office in your federal district."

I laughed. "I won't return the favor, because I don't know enough to offer an epigram that would be both accurate and witty."

Vlasovich shook his head. "It is a terrible thing to be a scientist in our world. If one pursues a science that improves all the world, then one is silently condemned for not serving one's fatherland. And if one pursues a science that grants a fatherland or a motherland a great military advantage, then one must live with a troubled conscience."

I understood that, even if I weren't a scientist.

"But always, I wander and ramble. You were kind to see me, Minister Eschbach, and I will do as I can." He paused. "Have you seen the Bronze Horseman?"

"Not yet," I admitted, "except from across the square."

"You should see it up close, especially after the sun sets. At five o'clock tonight, perhaps quarter past, if you are lucky, you can see one of the ghosts of the white nights. They are said to determine Russia's future." He smiled. "They have determined our past. That is certain."

"I'll see what I can do."

"Be careful, though." He gave a crooked smile as he stood. "If you do not see the ghosts, you will miss much. If you concentrate on one ghost . . . you may not see the others."

I stood. "Thank you."

He watched, his face blank, as I left the small office and rejoined Commander Madley and Christian in the small reception area, where there wasn't even a receptionist.

I didn't say anything until we were back in the Volga and Olaf was driving us through the early twilight caused by the clouds and the late afternoon, back to the embassy.

"Sir," ventured Christian, "how did it go?"

"Like everything else," I replied. "I think he'd like to see things work out, but he's not the only player." That was safe enough.

"There was almost no one in the building," Madley added.

"I'm not surprised. That's why he wants any assistance we can provide him."

Both actually looked surprised, but then, as I thought about it, I hadn't actually mentioned anything along those lines. I decided not to explain.

By the time we got out of the Volga in the embassy courtyard, it was already past four-thirty.

"Commander Madley, would you mind checking with

Colonel Sudwerth to see if there's anything I should know about?"

"Now, sir?"

"Why not? I'll tell Olaf about tonight. I don't think you or Christian will be needed to go with us to the yacht club."

My tone was dry enough that the commander did smile as he answered, "I don't imagine so, sir."

"I'll be in the guest quarters later."

With a nod, Commander Madley was gone.

I turned to Olaf. "You'll be the one driving us in the evenings as well?"

"Yes, sir."

"How long does it take to get to the Imperial Yacht Club?"

"A quarter hour . . . no more."

"My wife and I—or rather Mademoiselle duBoise and her husband—have been invited to dinner at eight. If we are down here at twenty before the hour, will that be early enough?"

"Yes, sir . . . at that time."

I checked my watch again—four forty-five. "Christian, we need to go look at the Bronze Horseman—up close."

"Now, sir?"

"Now's as good a time as any."

"But Commander Madley . . ."

"He doesn't need to come on a bit of sightseeing, does he?"

"Olaf . . . if you wouldn't mind?"

"Not at all, sir. You'll be impressed. It's good to see."

So we slipped back into the Volga, and Olaf drove southward and then along one of the canals—the Moika, I thought, but I could have been wrong—before following the Lvov Prospekt back toward the Neva and the Senate Square. He parked on the east side, and we got out. The darkness was almost eerie so early in the evening, and intermittent fat flakes of snow drifted out of a dark sky. Streetlights set on tall and curved iron brackets provided illumination of the square, except that they were set far enough apart that there were really patches of light and darkness, although the reflection off the snow created a more even but much dimmer secondary lighting. Even in the early evening, there were passersby scattered throughout the area.

We walked across the carefully swept stones toward the monument. While most of the area was swept, there were sections where the snow had been piled, almost like irregular gray-white walls. Then, everything in St. Petersburg seemed to take on a certain grayness.

The Bronze Horseman stood in the Senate Square, if I understood the translation correctly, facing the River Neva beyond the Admiralty and the English Embankment. On the back of the rearing horse was the figure of Peter the Great. Even after more than two hundred years and even in the dim light, with fat wet flakes of snow falling, I could still see—and feel—the intensity of the ancient monarch's eyes. The single block of red granite from which bronze rider and horse reared, sculpted centuries before into the shape of a cliff, seemed to take on the color of long-faded blood, not quite washed away by time or the waters that had periodically inundated St. Petersburg. I had to look to make out the snake that had been crushed by the mount's hoof, but it was there.

As we circled the monument more closely, I could see that Vlasovich had been right. A series of ghostly figures flickered in and out of sight.

"I haven't seen that before," Christian offered.

"Have you been here at twilight or early evening?"

"No, sir."

"They're probably mostly older ghosts. Some might date back to the Decembrist massacre."

"I thought you didn't know much about Russia."

"I don't." And I didn't, not any more than I'd been able to cram in reading about between teaching and everything else in the month between finding we were headed to St. Petersburg and boarding the turbo in Asten. I'd learned but a fraction of what a good agent needed to know, but I was surprised that Christian didn't know about the ghosts.

I could see a man walking slowly from the direction of the Neva, and turned to the young diplomatic officer. "Christian . . . just walk over to the other side of the horse, please."

This time, he didn't question me. He just casually walked away.

The man who had been approaching had a black wool overcoat and an equally black and well-trimmed beard. He wasted no time. "Minister Eschbach. You look like your picture. A friend said I might find you here." His English was heavily accented, so much that I had to concentrate to catch what he said.

"A recent acquaintance suggested I look at the Bronze Horseman at this time of day."

"What do you think?"

"Magnificent," I said. "The ghosts have been here for a time as well. Do they have a name?"

"Some call them the ghosts of the white nights." He laughed. "But many ghosts are called such in St. Petersburg."

"That seems paradoxical. I imagine they're hard to see during the white nights."

He laughed, gestured toward the intermittent wet flakes of snow. "This is another kind of white night, the kind that has brought ghosts and misery to too many for too long." He paused. "In our modern age, even ghosts are vanishing." He laughed again. "Some have said you have detailed plans to clean up the Dnepyr . . ."

"That is possible . . ."

"It is also said there is a price for those plans . . . a high price for those who love Russia."

Trying to avoid the price issue, I smiled indulgently. "I don't operate that way. I'm looking for something that benefits everyone involved. I'm someone who wants clean rivers anywhere. I have to confess that I'm also someone who doesn't want Ferdinand to obtain any more of those rivers." I shrugged.

"What good will clean rivers do people who cannot enjoy them?"

"Not much," I admitted. "But they'll do even less good to people turned into ghosts or put in Ferdinand's work camps." I could see his eyes narrow at the mention of ghosts, but he nodded at the work camps.

"There is that. It is not much, but it is something. These technologies? Do they work?"

"The majority have already been used. Some are just being adopted."

He nodded. "We will see." He stopped and gestured at the massive figure of Peter the Great that loomed above us. "He thought he did what was best. For forty years there were so many ghosts in St. Petersburg that no one lived here who was not compelled to by the tzar. Those were the first ghosts of the white nights. Some say that the ghosts saved Alexander II seven times. They failed the eighth time. One cannot always rely on ghosts, even in the city of ghosts. There is a legend that the ghosts of the white nights will save the tzars and St. Petersburg. A silly legend, but comforting. Men may create ghosts, especially those who would challenge even the skies and the white nights, but ghosts create little but sadness."

Alexander II had been fortunate for a long time before his assassination in 1886, and Russia had been even more fortunate that he had managed to push through his great reforms in 1881, and that his reactionary son had ruled for only eight years and his even more reactionary eldest grandson for but six. "I try not to rely on ghosts, but on people."

"Here, for all I have said, ghosts may be more reliable, Minister Eschbach. I wish you luck, for all of us." With that, he turned and disappeared into the shadows not lit by the tall and curved iron street lamps.

Wondering exactly the purpose of our exchange, I began to retrace my steps across the square, along the stone path swept clean of the snow, back toward the Volga sedan and Olaf. Christian joined me but did not say anything.

I could feel a chill from somewhere . . . almost like the feeling of a ghost appearing or being created, and I turned, whirled really, to see another man in a heavy greatcoat running behind one of the lines of piled snow toward us, something in his hand. "Run!"

"Sir?"

"Christian! Run like hell!" I didn't have any idea of the range of Bruce's pen zombie-projector, but it was the only weapon I had that was instantly ready for use.

I triggered it, probably from too far, but at least that might buy me time.

The man stood there, shaking his head for a moment, then looking at the object in his hand.

I could sense the ghost-tension rising around me, and threw myself over one of the piles of snow and dropped as low as I could while scuttling away from the half-stunned fellow. I got perhaps thirty yards when there was an explosion, followed by the sound of fragments, falling like a quick rain shower on the stones.

I moved more quickly but didn't stand erect until I neared the street and Christian.

"Are you all right—"

"I'm fine. We need to get out of here." That was a line from a third-rate spy novel, but true nonetheless.

"You're still a spy, aren't you, sir?"

"Let's just say that it might be better not to mention this, Christian. If you feel you have to tell *someone,* then tell Commander Madley and let him decide."

"But you didn't want him to come."

"I don't care if he *knows.* I just didn't want him to be seen here."

"Is he? . . ."

I laughed. "No. Commander Madley is exactly what he seems."

"Olaf!" I called as we neared the Volga. "We need to get back to the embassy."

The driver frowned but said nothing as we climbed into the back.

"I think I went sightseeing on the day a revolutionary decided to throw a bomb at the monument. I decided discretion was the better part of valor."

"There was one last month, and the month before. They closed the square each time. No one said anything. There was nothing in the papers. There would not be." The driver made a sound that was half grunt and half laugh.

As the black Volga carried us back to the embassy, I tried not to frown. I didn't understand the bomb. What purpose was there for Vlasovich to set me up? There was no way he'd get what he wanted—assuming he really wanted what he said he did. But if he didn't, why say he did so directly and enthusiastically? To get my words recorded? What I'd said wouldn't surprise anyone, even on the front page of whatever paper was circulated in St. Petersburg. It probably wouldn't even offend most people.

The first man had been sent by Vlasovich, but he hadn't said that much beyond platitudes—or had he? What had he said? Even Vlasovich had said little directly, except about the part of my mission that no one really cared if it became public. Everything else had been veiled in sarcasm or innuendo, and in a language foreign to the Okhrana.

And what if the second man had been the target? In the patches of light and darkness, that also was possible . . . but was what he had tried to convey that deadly that someone wanted one of us dead? Again . . . it had been set up in a way that wouldn't necessarily call attention to my presumed death as being linked to the real issue—whatever it might be. I'd just have been a stupid Columbian diplomat poking around after dark, and an easy target for extremist revolutionaries in a country known all too well for its xenophobia.

I couldn't say that I understood all the pieces of the puzzle, but those that I did understand bothered me more than a little.

The other thing was that a ghost had tried to warn me.

Or so it seemed. Was that what had happened with Alexander II? Or were the ghosts of the white nights just drawn to the tension of violence, and their appearance served as warning for those who were sensitive? Either way, I owed ghosts—those of the white nights and Carolynne, who in becoming part of my soul had left me more sensitive.

When we got back to the embassy, we made our way up to the second floor where I had Christian check with Darwaard's office to see if I had any messages or any additional appointments for Tuesday or later in the week. Although I stood back, Darwaard was out, and his clerk looked up at Christian, and then at me, and smiled very politely.

"When he left, Secretary Darwaard said there weren't any updates."

I couldn't say I was surprised, but I didn't say anything until we were well away. "I'm going up to our quarters to rest and get ready for this dinner. I'll see you in the morning, say about ten, in the waiting area outside Piet's office."

"Yes, sir." Christian's smile was somewhere between amused and troubled.

That was about the way I felt as well as I headed for the back corridor that led to the private elevators.

26

❧

Since Llysette was already taking a bath, the first thing I did after I reentered our spacious quarters was look around for suspicious signs. Finding none, the second thing was to change the battery in Bruce's pen projector. The third was to lay out a spare set to slip into the pocket of my formal wear. I might not be able to get back to the embassy for a change the next time, although I doubted I would need the miniature weapon at dinner.

Then I knocked on the door of her bathroom.

"Johan?"

"*C'est moi . . .*" I slipped inside into the steamy air.

"The theatre, it was cold. My teeth they chattered, and Terese's fingers, they were frozen. So a hot bath I am having."

"I noticed." I leered slightly.

"Johan . . . *j'ai froid*. Later, *mon cher*."

That was more than enough for me. "How was the piano?"

"It is very good, and it was tuned."

"How did the rehearsals go?"

"*Comme si, comme ça . . .* still we are both tired, and could use more sleep."

I nodded.

"Sleep I am not getting?" Llysette raised her eyebrows.

"We've been invited out to dinner tonight. Formal wear. We still have to eat somewhere, and I'm not sure that you want to spend every meal in the dining area here."

"To where must we go?" Her voice was wary.

"The Imperial Yacht Club. The number-two man at PetroRus has asked us. His daughter is a fan of your singing, and so is his wife, and a friend."

"This will not be late?"

"No. You're the diva. When you're tired, we beg to depart. But we'll probably get better food than anywhere I know to go."

"Plus que ça, je crois."

"Probably, but it can't hurt to have supporters among the extended Romanov family."

She raised her eyebrows.

"It can't," I repeated. "Have you seen any of the others on the concert?"

"Robert Thies. He arrived this morning. He came to practice as we were finishing."

"What's he like?"

"He is shy. Most quiet. He plays well."

"Good." At that moment, I heard a chiming in the bedroom. I slipped out of the bathroom and looked around. It repeated itself. I realized it must be a door chime, necessary because of the size of the suite, and I hurried through the salon to the door of the guest quarters. I peered through the peephole. Commander Madley was standing there.

When I opened the door, he stepped into the foyer.

"I'm sorry for the intrusion, sir, but you and Miss duBoise are going to the Imperial Yacht Club tonight, sir. It's always formal."

"I understood that. I have black-and-white wear."

"You need your medals," Madley pointed out. He held up a set of miniatures designed to go on a formal uniform. "You'll also need them for the concert on Thursday."

I recognized all but two of them. "Medals? I'm a civilian these days."

"Ah . . . sir, that distinction doesn't exist for the Russians, not in the upper civil service ranks. I had looked into it before we left Columbia and had this set put together. I'm sorry I forgot to give them to you earlier. If you show up with no decorations, people may talk to you, but it will be much harder, and among some of those you might face a certain disdain. The rank order is roughly equivalent to theirs. The red medal with the blue border means that you're a second level civil servant, the same as Deputy Minister Kent, and the green one with the four stars signifies twenty years of service—that seemed to be right from what we could figure."

"That's about right. Military and civil service totalled twenty-four."

"The others are your military medals, and you know what each of those mean."

It made sense. The Russian aristocracy had always moved in and out of the military and the civil service. "Thank you. That's something I really hadn't thought about."

"You seem to have a number of matters somewhat more pressing. Christian told me about this afternoon. Minister Holmbek suggested something might occur. Is there anything I can do?"

"For the moment, keep it between the three of us. If anything should happen to me, let Minister Holmbek know, but not anyone here until you've reported to him."

"I thought as much, sir." He looked very young, suddenly, and about ready to salute.

Recalling how long ago it had been since I'd been a lieutenant commander, I felt very old. "We've got another appointment in the morning, at eleven, with a Colonel General Kaselov, who happens to be the head of canals and waterway engineering for the Imperial Army."

"Yes, sir."

"I'll see you and Christian at ten, in the second floor embassy office foyer."

"We'll be there. Good luck tonight, sir. They say the food there is excellent. I envy you the dinner."

After I closed the door, and bolted it, I carried the miniatures back to the bedroom before slipping back into the bathroom, where Llysette still luxuriated in the steamy warmth.

"That was who?"

"Commander Madley. He brought me a set of miniature medals to wear. I'd forgotten that people still wear medals everywhere around here. At least to formal dinners."

Llysette smiled. "I have never seen your medals."

"You will."

We finished with bathing and showering and a few other matters and still were down in the doors to the inner courtyard at twenty-five before eight. Llysette was wearing the same formal gown she had worn to the president's arts dinner, the black and green one. I felt overdone with the medals on my chest, and grateful to put my heavy black wool overcoat over the formal wear.

Olaf bounded out of the Volga and opened the door for Llysette. "Mademoiselle . . ."

"Thank you." Llysette bestowed a dazzling smile.

Olaf returned the smile with a half-bow, then returned to the chauffeur's position and drove out through the open iron gates of the courtyard.

From what I'd dug up, the Imperial Yacht Club was a relatively new structure on the Neva north of the French Embankment, not all that far from the PetroRus building. The older building had caught fire and been gutted during the confusion of the Winter War of 1936 when the young Tzar Vladimir I had been stupid enough to respond to the Austro-Hungarian gambits over the Polish raids; and by spring, when the snow melted, Austrians held the western half of Poland, and Finland was independent, if only technically, and a protectorate in fact of the Swedish confederacy. So far as I could tell, it was the only winter conflict the Russians had ever lost, and probably because General Schiffen had been smart enough never to invade what might have been called "old Russia" and because the Finns were even better at cold-weather guerilla warfare than the Russians. In any case, that had been the last major war the Russians had fought. No one was counting all the minor insurrections fought in the Caucasus or the border skirmishes with Chung Kuo.

As we turned off whatever embankment we were traversing, I caught a glimpse of a figure in white, or I thought it was, amid the now lightly falling snow—a ghost in another kind of white night?

It was less than ten minutes later that Olaf guided the Volga off the avenue and under a gilded covered archway. The area under the archway was brightly lighted.

"I will wait here," Olaf said as the doorman in crimson and gray stepped forward and opened the door for me and for Llysette to get out.

"You could get something to eat . . ."

"No. I will be here."

"Thank you."

As we stepped toward the doors, heavy cherry with etched and gilded glass windows set in them, another doorman opened them for us, ushering us into a modest coat foyer, where a young lady in the feminine version of the gray and crimson uniform took our coats. Then we stepped though the second door, opened by yet another doorman in gray, into what was the main entry foyer. No sooner had we stepped into that foyer than Kyril Kulikovsky came forward to greet us.

"Minister Eschbach . . . Mademoiselle duBoise . . ."

There were bows all around. The man with Kulikovsky was also tall, both of them slightly taller than I was, if somewhat more slender. I could never be called slender, even with all the exercising and running. As Commander Madley had predicted, they were wearing medals, but only three, the first two almost identical matches to those Madley had added to my array.

"Serge Yusupov and Adyna Yusupov," Kulikovsky announced. "This is my wife, Elisabet."

Yusupov took a quick but almost furtive inventory of the stuff on my chest.

"Llysette duBoise, who is the singer, and incidentally, my wife," I returned.

"He is the distinguished visiting minister from Columbia."

"Most distinguished, I fear," I said lightly, "for my taste in finding and luck in marrying Llysette."

"You are gallant as well as handsome." The dark-haired Adyna Yusupov smiled.

So did Elisabet Kulikovsky, but she did not speak.

I finally managed to finish studying the entry foyer of the Imperial Yacht Club, from the polished warm cherry-paneled walls to the replica shimmering bronze sconces that held electric candles to the custom woven hexagonal carpet laid over the pale green marble tiles, each edged in bronze. The single portrait, set in a recessed section of wall, was that of a young-faced tzar on horseback. It wasn't Peter the Great, and while I couldn't see the rectangular plate at the bottom of the gilt frame, it was probably Mikhail I. It couldn't have been anyone else at the Imperial Yacht Club.

"Shall we?" asked Kulikovsky, gesturing toward the carved cherry archway, attended by a maitre d'hotel, or the Russian equivalent, dressed in black, but with white trousers.

The dining room was large, and the tables were set much farther apart than in even the best of Columbian top-level restaurants. In the far left corner was a raised dais, and upon it sat a string quartet, playing something that sounded like Mozart. We found ourselves at a circular table in the far right corner.

The menus were in Russian and French, and the cuisine seemed to be mainly French.

"Is there anything that the chef is most known for?" I asked.

"Here, it is all good," Kulikovsky said. "I often have the veal *impérial*."

That was something I'd never heard of, which probably underscored my unfamiliarity with the most elite of restaurants, but, then, retired government spies and university professors are not endowed with the kind of resources to frequent such often.

Llysette had the veal oscar, and I opted for the *impérial*.

Kulikovsky ordered the wine, and I wasn't surprised that it was a chardonnay, although the vintage was one I hadn't ever seen—Red Opal—from Australia.

"To our lovely guest," offered Serge Yusupov.

The wine was a good chardonnay, if not so good as the best from Sebastopol, and went well with the paté, a far lighter type than I'd ever tasted.

"Kyril . . . did he mention that our daughter studied voice . . . at the Conservatory? . . ." Elisabet's English was deliberate, but not that strongly accented.

I wondered how many Columbian petroleum executives could have seated themselves and their spouses at dinner with a Russian diplomat and carried the conversation in Russian. I knew the answer, and in a way, it was most depressing. I had to console myself that I could have done it in French or German.

"Does she sing now?" Llysette asked.

"Not now. She sang in the chorus with the opera, but the children are small, and . . . her husband is a major with the Blue Cuirassiers . . ."

So she really shouldn't have lowered herself to singing at all—but I kept that thought to myself and merely nodded. So did Llysette.

"Can you tell us what you will be singing?" asked Adyna. "At the concert?"

Llysette offered an embarrassed and rueful laugh. "The Russian songs and arias, mostly. From Rimsky-Korsakov, Tchaikovsky, and Rachmaninov. Others as well, perhaps."

"The tzar will like that."

Kulikovsky nodded somberly. The women smiled. I

watched, and that was the way it went all through dinner, and dessert.

I had a *flan Russe* to finish the meal, and shouldn't have, but flan has always been a weakness of mine. I was debating whether to take another mouthful when Adyna Yusupov turned to Llysette.

"You must see the Pavlova porcelains . . . you must. They only make one hundred of each, and each is promised years in advance. Even the tzar gets only one." The dark-haired Adyna smiled cheerfully. "You cannot come to St. Petersburg and not see them. The yacht club is one of the few places where there is a complete set on display. One is even modeled after the great Kshesinskaya. She was a ballerina, not a singer." She shrugged. "Perhaps someday . . ."

I wondered what that meant.

Llysette gave me a quick glance that told me she understood what was happening, and that she was leaving to see the porcelains only for my benefit.

"You might stop and look at them on the way out, Minister Eschbach," Kulikovsky said. "Not that roubles are everything, but one could sell the least valued of those porcelains for enough to purchase the most luxurious Volga, or three of your most expensive Stanleys."

"They must be superb," I said. More than fifty thousand dollars for a porcelain doll?

"They are," Yusupov agreed.

"You are an interesting man, Minister Eschbach," offered Kulikovsky once the women were out of earshot. "This is our second meeting, and you have asked nothing. You have hinted that you might be helpful in some fashion. Your embassy does not know why you are here, but has been asked to do your bidding. Would you care to speculate on how you might be helpful?"

"Good environmental information is always helpful," I said with a laugh. "Especially if it's used in the right place and time." I fingered my chin. "Let's just take a hypothetical example. Say there are two nations. They both produce petroleum. One prefers to produce more than it needs, in order to finance other requirements. The other tends to use more than it produces, and, as a result, has always been spending money on research. There is research on how to produce petroleum better in cold weather, research on how not to waste petroleum in transport, research even on cleaning up rivers that have been contaminated by petroleum and petrochemicals. All of this research is necessary, because the second nation never seems to have quite enough petroleum. Does the first nation need this research?" I shrugged. "Probably not. Or not until the first nation cannot produce as much petroleum as it would prefer. Even then, some in the first nation might not be interested. Even if they were, it could be hard to determine what such research might be worth."

Yusupov nodded. "I can see where, in your hypothetical case, of course, determining interest might be rather hard. For example, what if, and we are being very hypothetical, the research were suited to one climate and not another? Or, if for tactical reasons, the first nation could not afford to admit publicly any necessity for such research, and yet all payments for services are reviewed and made public?"

I smiled. "You describe the problem very well. I suppose there are ways around that. Intelligent people often can work out such."

"Hypothetically, you understand, how would one go about that?"

"Well . . ." I drew out the word. Here I was going to have to be careful, not to give away the details while outlining the principle. "It would seem to me that the answer, theoretically, you understand, would be for each party to understand the needs of the other. The second nation needs an additional and more reliable source of petroleum. The first nation needs to expand its production without seeming to do so and while still appearing to dictate the situation." I spread my hands. "Surely, there would have to be a way for such conditions to be met?"

"An interesting, if theoretical, proposition."

"At this point, it is theoretical," I conceded, "but all such propositions start in theory. Then, someone has to make them practical."

"You Columbians . . . you are so amusing. Some even find you naive, it is said."

"In many ways, we are indeed naive," I agreed. "We are a young nation. Still . . . sometimes, if one looks on a problem with a touch of naiveté, solutions that are difficult for the cynical can become possible. Someone in my country made a comment along the lines that solutions are always possible if you are willing to let someone else take the credit." I grinned. "I am a retired minister. You both know that. I am here because of my wife. I have little need of publicity, except for her, and less for credit."

"Such altruism . . ." The cynicism was most evident.

"Hardly." I laughed. "Hardly. Llysette obtains greater recognition. She gets more concerts, and she is happy. I'm happy because she is getting what was withheld. I'm also happy because . . . well . . . if my naive approach works, then I know that I was right, and everyone benefits." I let my voice harden. "Except Ferdinand." Then I smiled. "Altruistic? Naive? I think not."

The two exchanged glances.

"An interesting approach . . . it might even bear considering. Theoretically, of course. We will have to think about that." There was a shrug from Yusupov. "Turning theories into practice is often much harder than spinning the theory."

"True—but that's what makes life interesting and rewarding." I paused. "Just suppose, only suppose, that you obtained technical information on technologies for enhanced oil recovery methods suited to your needs. And suppose, just suppose, that you could also act as the provider of certain environmental technologies designed to clean up rivers, such as, say, the Dnepyr." I shrugged. "And suppose, again just theoretically, you could recommend granting a concession that would also return hard currency to the Imperial Treasury or to PetroRus for production in a locale that would be exceedingly costly for you to develop, but whose concessionary income would be significant." I smiled politely. "Just naive supposition."

"Most naive . . ." murmured Yusupov. "Yet intriguing."

"That's Columbia, naive and intriguing." I thought they were very interested, but interest didn't translate into results, and I wouldn't exactly hold my breath. So I took a sip of wine, a very small one.

"All of this is fascinating, but how does one turn theory into practice?" Kulikovsky grinned and added, "Theoretically, of course."

"One talks, to start with," I suggested. "If such a concession existed, theoretically, then those in Russia with the power to grant it would talk with those involved from . . . say, Columbia. If the talks appear to progress, then it would obviously be in the practical interests of those in Columbia to ensure that information on certain recovery technologies and perhaps even on some equipment became available. Each side offers more as matters progress."

"Could not one side just, as you Columbians put it, lay the cards upon the table?"

"That's certainly possible," I admitted. "Except, if, say, I held such cards and laid them on this table, you might be inclined to take them and not encourage further progress, or others might suggest the same to you. That also assumes that, if someone like me did so, people would value what was laid down."

"Naive, but not stupid . . ." murmured Yusupov.

"Willing to trust, in hopes of both benefiting, I'd say."

"And what if more than one Columbian party wished the concession?"

I'd wondered that from the beginning, and I was glad I'd asked Harlaan. "That would go down to practicality, I would say. Were that the case, I would suggest granting the concession to the party that had the greatest resources, and the greatest experience in cold-weather extraction, and the greatest ability to come up with immediate hard currency."

"You put matters so succinctly, Minister Eschbach. Yet there could be other considerations . . ."

I offered yet another laugh. "There always are. Someone offers a side concession, or a political interest, or a possible military considerations . . ." I shrugged, seeing a slight tension in Yusupov. "But your business is petroleum. You have to operate where you know what you do. If you don't, well, then, everyone else determines your business, and it won't be petroleum, and, at least in Columbia, you won't be running the business much longer." I thought I caught the quick flash of looks between the two and quickly added, "The other consideration is always national interest. When I was more active in government, there was always some ministry that had its own agenda, but usually that agenda was more in the interest of the minister than of Columbia." I offered a wry smile. "I'm sure that doesn't happen here."

"Of course not," replied Yusupov dryly.

Kulikovsky glanced up. "I believe the ladies will be returning in a moment. Still . . . you present an interesting, I believe you call it a scenario."

I just nodded. Saying any more wouldn't do anything. There is always a time to stop, and I hoped I hadn't already passed that point.

At that moment, the three ladies did in fact reappear, but the conversation was limited to a few minutes of small talk, centering mainly on what we should see, if we had time, and then we were all bowing and being most polite in our departures.

I glanced at the Pavlova porcelains as we left, and they were indeed exquisite, more like fine porcelain jewelry, or the equivalent of a Fabergé egg, but I wasn't sure I'd ever be an enthusiast of porcelain dolls.

Olaf was waiting outside the club and offered another broad smile as Llysette appeared, wrapped most securely in her heavy coat, against snow that had become harder and finer, and a wind that was gusting more strongly.

Once we were inside the Volga, I turned to her, and,

with a smile, asked, "How were the porcelains?"

"Johan . . ."

I grinned. "You're cute when you do that."

"Baby ducks, they are cute." But her pout was a put-on, and we both knew it.

Olaf did get us back to the embassy, and it was only eleven when we climbed into the massive bed, both exhausted, if for very different reasons. I was so tired that I fell asleep trying to put together the jumble of the day's events, even as my mind insisted that I needed to think things out. I put an arm around Llysette and told my subconscious to work on the problems. My conscious mind wasn't going to be conscious that much longer.

27

I WAS UP very early the next morning, letting Llysette sleep, while I went back over the briefing materials Harlaan had sent through Commander Madley. I'd hoped that there might be more background material on Serge Yusupov.

There was. Not a great deal, but the picture matched the man I'd met the night before. Yusupov was in effect the director of operations for PetroRus, although his position was somewhere between an independent director and special assistant to Pyotr Romanov. The analysis suggested that Pyotr Romanov listened to Yusupov. That was fine, *if* Yusupov had liked what I'd said.

Next I checked over the materials on Colonel General Vasily Kaselov. There wasn't much, not even a picture, just basically a position description. I set down the folders and tried to think, sipping the bitter tea I'd fixed.

What was beginning to bother me was that almost any diplomat should have been able to do what I'd done so far, and probably better. That meant that either I was deluding myself, that our diplomats weren't that good at their jobs, that the real problems were ahead, or that Harlaan had me in St. Petersburg for another reason entirely, and that I was expected to work out the petroleum negotiations as cover for something else that I had yet to discover.

I was doubtless missing things, but I couldn't figure out what in any specific terms. So I went and retrieved the news summaries and the paper. The summaries were as expected, except I didn't realize what was missing from them until I saw a tiny article in the *Times* of London.

Federal District (WNS). "Treason at worst, misfeasance at the very least!" That was how Congresslady Patrice Alexander (L-MI) charged Rocketrol—the chemical division of AmeriSun. According to Alexander, the second largest Columbian petroleum firm had leaked the components of a prototype solid rocket propulsion fuel being developed for the Columbian Ministry of Defense to its Russian subsidiary—the former Putilov cartel. Neither the Colombian Ministry of Defense nor AmeriSun had any comment.

I looked blankly into the darkness outside the window of the small kitchen. Definitely interesting—and getting murkier all the time.

I was in the second-floor office foyer of the embassy early, even before ten o'clock, because Llysette and Terese had wrangled more practice time at the Mariinsky Theatre—at nine-thirty—and they were off in the sedan assigned to her. I hardly had a chance to look around before Piet Darwaard appeared.

"If I might have a moment of your time, Minister Eschbach."

I followed him into his office and let him close the door behind me. I didn't wait to be invited to sit down.

"I understand that you've been approached several times, by various individuals," Darwaard said smoothly.

"It depends on what you mean. I've had sightseeing tips. I've had people draw me aside and ask why I might be offering detailed technical assistance and question its value if it is being given for virtually nothing—"

"If I might ask, since the ambassador will certainly want to know, what did you tell them?" Darwaard's smile was close to patronizing, but it was the professionally patronizing expression adopted by too many second-level bureaucrats.

The details of my work were none of his business, but there wasn't any point in picking a fight . . . yet. "I told them that it wasn't for nothing; that if it keeps more Russian territory in Russian hands, that helps Columbia."

"I don't think you understand how dangerous St. Petersburg is, Minister Eschbach. Everything appears so quiet and civilized, but nothing is as it seems. A sightseeing tip might be from a Septembrist who would like nothing more than to get you in an unprotected situation so that he could create an incident to destabilize the tzar. In fact, I'm led to believe that you barely escaped something like that."

"That's possible, Darwaard." I used his last name to remind him, not quite gently, who was who. "Everything is a risk. But the biggest risk at the moment is doing nothing."

His eyebrows lifted, and the pleasant look vanished from his face. "It's not in the news, but it's everywhere else. Anyone who is anyone in St. Petersburg knows that the embassy car assigned to you was parked on the edge of the Senate Square yesterday, and it drove away just after a bomb exploded in the square."

"We did hear an explosion," I admitted. "Do you happen to know what it was?"

"It was a bomb, and I was informed this morning that it appears the man who was carrying it was a Septembrist."

"Septembrist?"

"A member of the most radical revolutionary group. They feel that Russia belongs to Russians, and that the tzar is but a creature of the west."

"Interesting. I gather that the theory is that I'm here pushing some radical commercial or environmental idea that will further subjugate Russia to the degenerate west?"

"Something along those lines." Darwaard paused for a

moment. "If the ambassador should ask . . . or if the speaker should inquire . . ."

I wanted to tell dear Darwaard that I'd be happy to answer to either personally, but decided against that. I smiled. "Actually, we had a few minutes, and I'd read all about the Bronze Horseman. So we went and saw it. It wasn't planned, and it was a spur of the moment decision. Those, I've found, are usually safer."

"That was the first bomb in a public place in months. The Okhrana has doubled their street patrols this morning."

"Was anyone killed?" I didn't point out that Olaf had indicated there seemed to be bombs going off more often.

"Only the one person was killed, and he was one of the Septembrists," admitted the first secretary.

"The bomb must have malfunctioned, then. Most convenient for the Okhrana, then." I smiled. "While I'm here, do you have any additional appointments I should make?"

"I'm afraid not, Minister Eschbach. The embassy has opened what doors it can." His smile was bureaucratically correct and followed by a shrug.

"I understand. You've been most helpful." I stood. "As matters develop, I'll let you know."

Christian was standing outside the office door when I emerged. I checked my watch. "How long does it take to get to Colonel General Kaselov's?"

"He's in the general staff offices. No more than fifteen minutes, sir."

"Good." I beckoned for him to follow me.

Once we were out in the corridor away from the clerks, and Darwaard, I said what I had in mind. "Piet has indicated that he has reached the limit of what he can do in opening doors. I'm on my own from here on out. I don't want to cover ground that's already been gone over. Is there any place in the embassy records that lists meetings that have been set up or even requested?"

"Yes, sir . . . but . . ."

"I understand that the meetings are often confidential. I wouldn't want the records. I'd just like to know what Russian government and nongovernmental organizations have met with or requested help in matters involving the environment and energy—just in the last two months or so. The organizations and a key name. That way I'll have some idea."

"Ah . . ."

"We've got almost an hour. I'll meet you here in fifty minutes, and we'll go over what you've got. I need to go over some matters with Commander Madley."

"I think he's in with Colonel Sudwerth, sir."

"He won't be long. I'll wait for him here. You see what you can find."

As I had predicted, Lieutenant Commander Madley appeared within five minutes after Christian left.

"Minister Eschbach, were you looking for me? I thought you weren't due to meet General Kaselov until eleven."

"I'm not. I wanted your thoughts on the reason for the meeting before I stepped into it." I gestured. "We can go downstairs and sit in a corner of the dining room. There's no need to stand in the corridors."

Madley nodded.

I began to retrace my steps to the stairs. There was no sense in taking an elevator for one floor. "How is the good colonel this morning?"

"He seemed the same as always."

Madley was a bit too straightforward to lie well, but I let it pass for a time before making another comment. "I imagine he has a lot on his hands with the current situation."

"He's had a large stack of papers on his desk every time I've been in his office, and they're never the same ones." The commander shook his head.

The dining room door was shut but not locked. No one was in the room, and we sat at the nearest table.

"Is there anything I should know about?" I asked.

"Nothing that isn't in the news. You're getting the summaries, aren't you?"

I nodded. "What I don't quite understand is why there's

not more maneuvering over energy supplies. The Russians have relied on their Caspian fields for hard currency for years, and the combination of increased demand and decreasing production have to be squeezing something."

"What's to maneuver, sir? The military gets whatever they need; heavy industry gets the next priority; the well-off have to pay exorbitant prices; and that leaves some for export."

The answer was too pat, like a lot of those I was getting, but in an autocracy, it might just be correct, and that was also depressing.

"How did your dinner go?" Madley asked.

"It was a marvelous formal dinner. Everyone wanted to talk to Llysette. The food was excellent, and Kulikovsky and his wife were charming. Their daughter studied voice at the Conservatory. They'll probably be at the concert on Thursday. As for anything else . . ." I shrugged.

The commander and I went back upstairs at ten-thirty, and Christian was pacing back and forth. So I didn't let him wait.

"What did you find, Christian?"

"There have only been a few. There were meetings with Putilov—"

"I thought they were a munitions outfit," I said misleadingly.

"They're also the Russian branch of AmeriSun, sir."

"Ah," I nodded. "I'm sorry. Go ahead."

"The others were Colombian Dutch Petroleum—they met with both the first secretary and the ambassador—and AAVO."

I didn't have to try to look blank at the second name, although it sounded familiar.

"That's the Swedish firm that holds most of the North Sea oil. They met with the first secretary, and the Swedish ambassador met with Ambassador Hagel."

"What about SAAB?" I asked, just to see if I got a reaction.

"No, sir."

"Why do you think they'd be interested, sir?" asked Madley.

"I'm not sure. I was thinking that military turbofighters burn a lot of fuel, but I suppose they leave those considerations to the Swedish embassy." I paused. "But you'd said on the flight in that we had to avoid Swedish territory. Are things that tense between Russia and Sweden?"

"Oh, no. The Swedes used to do joint exercises with the Russians, but they didn't work too well," Madley said. "They both worry about the Austrians, but they couldn't trust each other. The joint exercises were the tzarina's idea."

"She's Swedish, isn't she?"

"The sister of the king," Christian replied.

"With a direct wireline like that . . ." I laughed. "So the airspace problem is because they're both so worried about the Austrians that they have a tendency to shoot first?"

"It's not that bad yet, but Minister Holmbek didn't want us to be the first bystander casualty."

"Makes sense."

So we headed back down the steps to find Olaf and the Volga, but he was waiting in the rear courtyard under the cloudy sky.

I gave Olaf the address. He nodded, and we were off.

"That's not in the main building of the General Staff complex," Madley observed.

"I'd be surprised if it were," I replied. "He's an engineer in charge of canals and keeping rivers clear of obstacles. The combat types wouldn't consider him that necessary. You should see where our engineers have their headquarters."

The Russian headquarters annex building was tucked away a good two blocks farther east of the river from the main buildings of the general staff complex. The structure was of stone, but unlike the Winter Palace, the Admiralty, and the other major structures, it was just solid gray stone, with no pastel sections to relieve the monotony.

The inquiry by the clerk was almost routine, and there

was but a single guard in the dingy and cold stone lobby. We walked up two floors without an escort. The elevator wasn't working.

The colonel general didn't keep us waiting, either, and this time, I took my entourage in with me, not that it was a problem because Kaselov had an aide-interpreter as well. His aide was a military officer in a formal gray and blue uniform, but I couldn't read the rank symbols. That meant five of us were sandwiched into an office space barely ten feet by fifteen, with a desk for Colonel General Kaselov, a straight-back wooden chair that might have dated to the Winter War beside his desk for his aide-interpreter, and three other uncomfortable wooden chairs for us.

Kaselov said a few words in Russian, no more than a handful.

The aide began in English. "The general has heard that you may be in possession or be able to be in possession of technical information that could be used to develop technologies to clean up contaminants from rivers."

"I am here on an environmental mission," I admitted, waiting for Christian to translate before continuing. "Such technologies do exist."

Kaselov replied briefly, and the aide spun out the reply. "The general is responsible for the maintenance of open traffic on the waterways. He is concerned to know if using any of these technologies would affect river traffic."

"There are technologies that have been used in the past that would do so. They were not terribly effective and often created worse environmental problems. We would not recommend any of those."

A broad but somehow wry smile crossed Kaselov's narrow face as his aide translated.

"What benefit would such technologies provide?"

"I can think of several. First, it would remove the Austrians' grounds for provoking an incident. Second, it would improve Russian fisheries, which would make food in the areas both better and less expensive. Third, it would save you the expense of developing the technologies . . ." I shrugged. "I'm sure I could come up with more benefits."

The officer only offered a sentence.

Christian looked at me. I nodded. Christian then added several sentences in Russian.

Kaselov inclined his head, not quite dismissively, nor peremptorily, before replying.

The Russian aide looked to Christian, who translated the response.

"It's your business to offer the benefits; it's mine to see if they really benefit us."

"That's fine with Columbia," I replied. "You'll find that they are worth a great deal."

"That may be. We will have to see. Both the Ministry of Interior and the Ministry of War work together on such matters."

"As they should. When the Interior Ministry pursues the matter, I presume you will be the one to whom copies of the materials should be sent?"

I understood the single emphatic syllable.

There were a few more polite sentences, and then the general stood, offered thanks through the interpreter, and we were soon headed down the stairs.

Again, no one said anything until we were back in the Volga.

"His translator was from army intelligence," Madley said.

"Why did he even want to meet me?" I asked. "Just so that he could say he'd looked into the situation? Or to give the intelligence officer a look at me?"

"Both, I'd guess, sir."

"What next, sir?" asked Christian.

I wished I knew. "We go back to the embassy, but the long way."

"The long way?"

"Olaf, I'd like to drive past the university."

"That's on the other side of the river."

"That's fine. We have some time."

Christian and the commander exchanged glances, and

Olaf pulled away from the dingy annex building and immediately turned westward, toward the Neva, and whatever bridge would take us over the river and onto Vasilevsky Island.

The trip didn't take that long, less than fifteen minutes.

The university campus did not look that different from the rest of St. Petersburg—gray buildings, snow, swept gray stone walks. In fact, it didn't look all that different from sections of the University of Assen in winter, except that St. Petersburg University seemed deserted.

"Stop the car, please," I said abruptly. "Just somewhere along here."

Olaf did so, but I could sense his puzzlement.

"I need to get out for a moment."

This time another set of quizzical looks passed between Christian and Commander Madley.

I stepped out of the Volga, under the gray skies. Commander Madley followed me, a step or two back, clearly nervous.

As I walked, slowly, deliberately, I glanced in the direction of the Neva, although I couldn't see it, then back toward the building that looked more like a palace. As I recalled, there was a palace adjoining the university area, but I couldn't remember whose it was or had been. The street was nearly deserted, and only a few sedans rumbled past on the stone paving blocks.

Looking back up at the long building that could have been classrooms or dormitories or both, I noticed that all the windows were shut, and all looked the same from the outside—on all floors except the ground floor, where the windows were longer.

Except for the passing cars, the area was silent, as I supposed it would be with the colleges of the university closed until after the beginning of the next year.

I strolled farther, listening and just trying to absorb the feel of the area, until the absolute quiet on all levels got to me, and I turned and walked briskly back to the Volga.

Because I couldn't have explained what I'd learned,

even to myself, I didn't try, just sat back and tried to think on the way back to the embassy.

The chance to retreat and ponder didn't offer itself. As soon as I stepped out of the Volga in the embassy courtyard, under a sky that was hard and bright blue, with a chill wind that cut right through my heavy black wool overcoat, a clerk I didn't know was running up to me. He had to have been freezing, because he was only wearing a topcoat, not even a vest.

"The ambassador was looking for you, Minister Eschbach."

"I'll be right up. His office is on the second floor at the end, isn't it?"

"Yes, sir."

As the young clerk scurried away, both Commander Madley and Christian looked at me.

"I haven't any idea."

"Ah . . . sir . . ." Christian ventured. "This afternoon?"

"Unless someone else wants to meet with us, I'm going to go with my wife and listen to her rehearsal. Then we'll have dinner somewhere."

"Yes, sir," Christian replied.

"If you want to go to the rehearsal, either of you, it's at three at the Mariinsky." I smiled and turned out of the teeth of the wind and toward the doors to the private side of the embassy.

The honorable Charles Hagel was waiting for me, or presenting a reasonable facade of doing so when I stepped into his spacious office. His wide windows afforded a front view, more down the street toward the Nevsky Prospekt. He looked at me, almost quizzically, then gestured toward a black leather upholstered and comfortable chair across the desk from him.

I sat down and waited, absently noting the chill from the closed windows behind him. Winter was definitely headed to St. Petersburg.

"It appears as though you're making progress, Minister Eschbach, but I'd appreciate a little information." Hagel offered one of those warm, charming, sincere, and utterly false political smiles, the kind that makes most people feel like the center of the universe. It just made me uneasy. "Walt said you had a unique style, and it's pretty clear you do." He laughed. "But it does put me in an awkward position if I can't report something to Minister Vandiver and the Speaker." The smile vanished. "It is rather difficult to explain the proximity of a senior Columbian minister to a terrorist bombing."

I shrugged. "First Secretary Darwaard warned me about sightseeing. Apparently, I didn't take him seriously enough. You can check with Christian DeWitte. We were sightseeing. One fellow was friendly, and he left, and then I saw a suspicious-looking fellow. I did exactly what I would have done in Philadelphia or Asten or the federal district. I got out of there as quickly as I could. I never even got a good look at the man." All of that was true.

Another charming smile followed the nod. "You were fortunate."

"I still run a great deal. It helped."

Hagel ignored that. "Do you have any more plans or meetings?"

"The ball's in their hoop now. I thought I might take in Llysette's rehearsal at the Mariinsky this afternoon."

"I just got a wirecall from Elston Hayworth. He's the negotiator for the Ministry of State's Alaskan Petroleum concession. He's been invited to preliminary talks with PetroRus and a representative of the Russian Minister of Interior. He said you did something."

"I've had a meeting or two with Kyril Kulikovsky," I admitted. "I just emphasized that in an uncertain world cooperation for mutual practical benefit has many advantages. He said he'd consider what I offered. I've also met with the general in charge of rivers and waterways, and with a representative of the Ministry of Interior."

"I see. For less than two days in St. Petersburg, you appear to have been very busy."

"Busy . . . but we will have to see." I didn't think my

official schedule was nearly so busy as it should have been, for reasons about which I was getting more and more concerned, even if I had little enough proof. From what I'd heard so far, I wasn't about to claim more or to hand over anything of substance to the Russians until much greater interest manifested itself. Much greater interest.

"That we will." Yet another smile followed. "I don't want to keep you, Minister Eschbach, but I trust you understand my position."

I stood before he could. "I certainly do. I'll let you know if anything develops."

I had walked less than a dozen paces from the ambassador's office when Colonel Sudwerth appeared.

"Minister Eschbach, the man I've been looking for. Might you have a moment, sir?" asked Sudwerth in his hearty and polite voice.

"A few minutes, but I'm going to try to listen to Llysette's rehearsal this afternoon, and I'll have to get something to eat before that."

"This won't take long."

I followed him to his office, smaller and far more spare than the first secretary's, and with the only view that of the rear courtyard.

Sudwerth closed the door but didn't sit down, as if to underscore that he intended to be brief. "I just wanted to know how your meetings were going and whether I might be able to offer any assistance."

"I've met with the people who were interested, and now we'll have to see."

"I understand you saw Colonel General Kaselov."

"That was this morning. He was concerned that any environmental technology might have an adverse impact on the usability of canals and rivers for transportation. I think I was able to reassure him on that score. What do you know about him?"

"He seems to be what he is."

"Unlike many of their military?"

"Russia is an autocracy, Minister Eschbach, and they

have a secret police that is very thorough and effective. The Ohkrana has no fear of dealing with military officers. Anything that supports the tzar and the motherland is considered acceptable in some circles."

"That's scarcely a new idea," I temporized. "Besides, I'm just offering environmental expertise that will result in improved energy recovery techniques and riverine cleanups. I doubt that they have much problem with saving roubles, not with Ferdinand knocking on the south door."

"The Russians' great strength is that they will take any losses necessary to destroy an invader. That hasn't changed since Napoleon."

"The Russians haven't changed, but the Austrians have," I said mildly. "Except in the case of the March to the Sea and the fall of the Low Countries, they're content to take little bites, to provoke the other land, and then to chop up attacking forces. That's why they effectively hold all of continental Europe, except Sweden and Russia." I watched Sudwerth closely as I added the next sentence. "Unless Russia has something newer and more powerful than anyone has been able to discover, the Austrians will do the same thing they've been doing—most successfully. They'll just nibble away at Russia the way the Poles did in the tenth century or whenever it was, or perhaps they'll nibble up enough of the Ottomans to control the Bosphorus directly, and then turn their energies to Russia."

"You may be right, Minister Eschbach, but I'd advise against saying so loudly outside the embassy."

"I may be wrong, Colonel. I often have been. So I'm most unlikely to venture a public opinion."

Sudwerth laughed. "I've probably kept you . . ."

"No problem. But I do need to find my wife." I offered a last smile and slipped out his office door, keeping the expression in place until I was well away.

I needed to know more, but that was getting more and more difficult, largely because I didn't speak Russian, and I wondered, not for the first time, why Harlaan had really wanted me in St. Petersburg, as opposed to someone who did know the language and the culture far better.

28

THE MARIINSKY THEATRE looked like a circular stone arena rising out of ornately rectangular buildings added on at irregular intervals, except it was tall, a good five or six stories. At a first impression, it didn't look as if any part of the theatre had more than a few yards of surface that were not broken by a projection, a pediment, a faux column, or stone casements, but all were tied together by the pastel blue-green painted over the flat sections of gray stone. I could honestly say its exterior was like no other theatre or opera house I'd ever seen.

Llysette's driver from the embassy pulled up on one side of the theatre, and we got out, into a steady wind that had dropped the temperature to well below freezing. I held the case with Llysette's music, although she'd never even carry it onstage, and followed her and Terese through a side door. A thin man in a gray jacket led the way. Eventually, we ended up in the wings of the theatre, stage right.

As we stood there, I could hear the piano. In the center of the stage, lit by a single spotlight, a young man was obviously concluding a section of a piano concerto, playing with what seemed to me to be both great energy and talent.

"Beautiful," murmured Terese as the other pianist finished. "I'm looking forward to hearing the entire concerto tomorrow."

The pianist—Robert Thies—stood, then bowed, as if he had an audience, and walked toward us.

"How is the piano?" Terese asked as Thies approached.

"It's still a little stiff on the bass." Thies had a warm and somewhat shy smile. "It's not as cold in there today." He looked at me. "You must be Minister Eschbach."

"I only heard the last of your playing, but it sounded magnificent."

"That it did," Llysette added.

"I'm glad you didn't hear the first part."

"We did the other day, and it was good," Terese said.

Thies smiled apologetically. "I've done it better, and I will tomorrow."

Llysette slipped out of her heavy coat and gloves and looked at me. I took both. Terese had laid her coat and gloves over a chair and was already headed out onto the stage, where the piano was still spotlighted. I added Llysette's coat to the pile and watched.

"Your wife is quite something," Thies murmured as he stood beside me.

"She is." More than he would ever know—or should.

As Llysette neared the piano, the spots vanished, and the full stage lighting came up. The theatre was dark, except for the stage, and I couldn't see any way to get out front, at least not without tripping over something in the dark. So I just eased back slightly along the wings and stood beside one of the dark velvet curtains and listened.

After a few minutes of warm-ups, Llysette and Terese began on the Rimsky-Korsakov piece, which was based, I understood, on a Pushkin poem—or maybe it was the Tchaikovsky "Nightingale" that was based on Pushkin. Either way, even though I didn't understand the Russian, I thought she was wonderful, but after she finished, she turned to Terese and murmured something. Then they did it again. What they'd fixed I didn't know, but it was somehow subtly different and better.

Next came the first Tchaikovsky piece, the one set to the Goethe poem, except that Llysette was doing it in French. She'd learned it in both French and German, but French was far more appropriate than German in St. Petersburg. That went smoothly, and they went on to the next Tchaikovsky piece—"Last Night."

In the end, they spent their entire allotted hour on the stage, and the Black Mesa Chamber Quartet was waiting to step onstage when Llysette and Terese walked out.

I gave my diva a warm smile as she approached. I held her coat but didn't offer it yet because she was hot from the exercise of rehearsing. Most non-singers don't realize how athletic singing really is.

Llysette didn't speak to me, but that was normal. She was still in her own world, going over the rehearsal, and I didn't try to break in as we made our way down a set of stairs into a lower backstage area.

There were several young women waiting down below, some younger than Llysette's students at Vanderbraak State, but they looked like singers, rather than having the almost emaciated look of dancers, although the Mariinsky was home to both the Ballet Russes and the Imperial Opera. The youngest-looking stepped forward, probably urged on by the older students. She didn't look at Llysette directly, but held forward what looked to be a glossy flyer with Llysette's picture—and a pen.

"What is your name?" Llysette asked as she took flyer and pen.

The girl looked blank.

"Que vous appelez-vous?" Llysette asked.

When the girl didn't respond, I almost repeated the question in German but decided against it. The Austrians and Germans weren't exactly beloved in Russia. "To a singer to be," I suggested, "or something like that."

She wrote something like *"Pour la chanteuse des années d'arriver."* The girl might not have understood spoken French, but she beamed as she read the words.

A tall white-haired woman appeared, standing back as Llysette signed several more flyers. The older woman smiled as each of the girls stepped away, then said something in Russian. The young singers all turned and bowed to Llysette.

"I am Irina . . . Arkhipova," said the woman.

"You sang at the Bastille Opera," Llysette replied.

"Many years ago." The older woman laughed. "Many years ago. Before you were a student."

"Just after I was a student, alas."

Both singers laughed.

"I am glad you are here. My students heard you sing, and now they will not think that only Makarina or Gorchakova can sing the Russian songs."

"And so they will try the French *melodie,* the English art songs?"

"One hopes," replied Arkhipova.

Llysette smiled. "One never knows."

"No. That is true." They both smiled, wistfully and ruefully. I knew why.

Llysette stepped away, back toward Terese and me.

"I thought the three of us could go out to dinner somewhere now," I suggested. "It can't be too late, but if we go back to our rooms too early . . ."

"I will worry."

"Food would be good," Terese agreed.

Robert Thies apparently was waiting for us, because he stepped forward. Farther back, halfway up a flight of stairs, on a landing, Irina Arkhipova had stopped to talk to one of the Russian singers.

"We'd thought about going out to get something to eat," I said to Thies.

"I could use it." He grinned quizzically. "Where?"

I looked back. Arkhipova was still talking to the student. "Let me ask her. She might have some suggestions. Who knows, maybe I can get her to come with us."

"That would be good," suggested Llysette.

So I walked up the steps and edged toward the white-haired singer, waiting for her to finish her conversation.

Abruptly, both stopped talking and looked at me.

"Yes?"

"I beg your pardon," I said. "I didn't mean to interrupt you, but I was wondering if you could recommend somewhere to eat nearby."

The older singer tilted her head. "There are several . . ."

"Would you like to join us?" I asked Arkhipova. "We'd like to have you, as our guest."

"I could not . . ."

"Please do. I hope I'm not imposing, but we would feel better if you came." I grinned. "We also wouldn't get lost."

The young student singer said something, in Russian, and Arkhipova laughed and said something in return, almost gently.

"You are . . ." The student pointed to Llysette.

"I'm her husband," I said. "I'm the only one who isn't a musician."

Arkhipova nodded. "I will go."

I still wondered about the conversation between the two as we walked toward the others. "Miss Arkhipova has agreed to join us and guide us."

Llysette smiled broadly at Irina. "I am glad you will come."

"My student said that I would have more stories to tell if I come."

"*Je crois que non . . .*" Llysette murmured.

"Where are we going?" asked Robert Thies.

"If we . . . are welcome . . . the Winter Swan is good."

I liked the name, and so did the others, because they nodded.

Arkhipova guided us back out through another convoluted set of steps, and we found ourselves out on the cold street. As she and Terese led the way toward the embassy car, Llysette bent her head toward me.

"So charming you were, Johan." Llysette gave me a wicked smile. "How could any woman refuse?"

"As I recall, you did for quite some time."

"That, I did not." She elbowed me gently. "Never did you ask."

"Yes, my dear diva."

"Johan . . ."

I didn't say more as Arkhipova gave more directions to the embassy driver, most of which I couldn't catch or make sense of.

". . . across   Voznesensky   Prospekt . . . Ekaterina . . . left . . ."

Whatever I thought, the driver understood, and, as soon as we crowded into the Volga, we were off, through streets moderately crowded, under a dark purpled sky, with bright stars and a cold wind that seeped into the embassy vehicle. Less than ten minutes later, we were climbing out of the Volga beside yet another gray stone building, back into the chill and biting wind.

From outside, the Winter Swan's windows were bright, welcoming against the cold and windy evening and the gray buildings looming seemingly in every direction.

I wouldn't have called the Winter Swan either a restaurant or a café . . . more like the Russian version of a bistro . . . with tables almost too small for the number of people— but with linen tablecloths, and cutlery—especially with the five of us crowded around a table designed for four. The driver had decided not to join us but to come back in two hours. I had the feeling he didn't want to deal with another two hours of conversation about music.

Llysette and I let Irina order for us. Robert Thies apologetically asked her questions about half of what was chalked on the menu board, and Terese asked Arkhipova to order her whatever was the best fish dish, and I vaguely remembered that she preferred vegetarian or fish dishes, something I should have asked before I fixed that first dinner for her.

Then the conversation got around to music, while Llysette and I sipped Russian tea, and the others more alcoholic beverages—Arkhipova a red wine, Thies and Terese white wines.

"*Lady MacBeth of the Mtsensk District* . . . you sang Katerina, *non?*"

"Not often . . . the tzar's father . . . not fond of Shosta-kovich . . ."

". . . liked his *Symphony for St. Petersburg* . . . "

". . . wrote that when he thought how close the Finns came to taking the city in the Winter War . . ."

". . . wasn't that his eighth?"

"I would like to have heard Chaliapin as Holofernes," Arkhipova said, her voice slightly louder. "Everyone . . . they all think of him as Boris Godunov. My great-aunt said he was magnificent as the Assyrian. That was how Golovin painted him."

I had to nod to that, because, although she had spoken in English, the only words that were really familiar to me were the name Boris Godunov, the upstart tzar, and the name of the opera by Mussorgsky. I'd never heard or seen the opera itself.

I ended up eating what I thought might be the Russian equivalent of a meat pie, but for all I knew it could have been Ukrainian, Tatar, or something else. Whatever it was, it was good.

". . . claim operas do not represent the people . . ."

"Music must lead people, don't you think?" asked Thies. "If it follows whatever the popular taste happens to be, then what's its value?"

"That's the argument about elites," I pointed out. "In-tellectual *noblesse oblige*." I grinned. "The problem in any society is that, if the elites don't lead, who does? And what happens?"

Arkhipova lifted her eyebrows. "But . . . who is elite? Does birth . . . tell . . . who is this elite? If the elite are . . ." she paused, as if trying to remember a word, "able, who says what is able?"

And that had always been the problem, and probably was even more so in Russian, although some of the New

Bruges old Dutch patroons weren't much better than the extended Romanov clan, I suspected.

There was a momentary silence, into which I plunged. "Has anyone written an opera about the ghosts of the white nights?"

"No," replied Arkhipova bluntly.

"I'm surprised that no one has written an opera about them."

"Operas are about heroes and leaders. The ghosts are not tzars. They are not living heroes. Some say that the ghosts saved Tzar Alexander II, but there is already one opera about a peasant hero who saves the tzar."

I looked blank.

"It is *A Life for the Tzar*. Glinka. It is not performed often in these times." Arkhipova smiled knowingly.

"I just wondered," I offered. "I was sightseeing the other day, and I saw the Bronze Horseman just after sunset, and there were ghosts there."

"St. Petersburg has many ghosts. It is a city built on ghosts. But few wish to dwell on them. Many would have them vanish, because they remind us of that which was less than good. Is that not so in your land?"

For some reason, her words—"many would have them vanish"—struck a chord, but again, I just nodded and sipped the last of the tea, and tried to listen and follow the conversations that swirled around me.

" . . . Rimsky-Korsakov . . . he should not have tried to rewrite *Boris Godunov* . . . Mussorgsky understood Russia . . . oh, he understood Russia . . ."

In one sense, as I listened, I was beginning to understand, not Russia, but Columbia, as far more Byzantine than Imperial Russia, even though Russia retained the Byzantine aspects fostered by the Eastern Orthodox Church, even though all in Columbia doubtless thought Russia the more cruel and Byzantine than Columbia.

I knew better.

29

I DIDN'T EXPECT anything to happen on Wednesday morning, and it didn't. There were no messages, direct or indirect. No requests for meetings. No inquiries. Even the news summaries showed nothing new, just rehashes of the existing international questions and tensions.

The embassy appeared happy to ignore me, and Llysette was busy in the salon room of our quarters, practicing with Terese.

The wind had died away, but the sky remained a clear and cold blue, unusual, I understood, for December. So I went for a walk, accompanied by Christian. First, we walked up to the French Embankment, even though there was no longer a France to name it after.

"That used to be the French Embassy." Christian pointed to the building across from the one on the corner that bore the Austrian flag. "I suppose it still is. It's empty now."

We waited for a break in the traffic and then crossed the embankment road. Maybe the enbankment and the road were both the French Embankment, but, in any case, we turned westward along the Neva. As the poets and the novelists had written, the waters of the river were a steely gray.

"If this weather continues, it will freeze before Christmas. Christmas is later here. Eleven days, I think," Christian said.

"The Eastern Orthodox Church never changed the holy calendar?" I asked.

Christian shrugged.

We continued walking toward the Troitsky Bridge, named for an obscure reformer, and I kept surveying the traffic and the few others walking. So far as I could tell, no one was tailing us, at least not closely.

The large and ancient structure on the north side of the Neva became clearer and clearer, especially after we passed the bridge. The tower of the cathedral stood out against the blue sky.

"Is there anyone in the Peter and Paul prison?" I asked.

"People talk about it. It's where they dump the student dissidents."

"The ones that caused the uprising at the university last month?"

"If they imprisoned any, that's where they'd be."

"They must have imprisoned some of them," I pointed out. "They claim that they didn't kill more than a handful. There aren't hundreds of ghosts around the university. In fact, we didn't see or sense any, and there aren't any students."

"They closed the university until January."

"I wasn't aware they allowed disagreements, but I suppose that's one way."

"It's getting harder to control them. Difference engines are getting smaller and cheaper, even here. The Ohkrana raided a stationery supply warehouse last month. They claimed the business was a front for an Austrian plot to distribute difference engines and printers to the Septembrists."

"Was it?"

"How would we know?"

That was a very good question. I could certainly see the Austrians supporting any group that had a good chance of creating a civil war in Russia, but I could also see the Ohkrana and the tzar creating a plot where none existed to focus discontent away from St. Petersburg, and the Romanov autocracy.

We were walking into the embassy past the guards and through the private courtyard, and I was thinking about catching Llysette so that we could have something to eat together, when Commander Madley caught us just inside the doors.

"Sir, this came for you just after you left." He extended an envelope, a heavy parchment envelope with the PetroRus seal embossed in gold and my name written in elaborate script.

I turned it over, then opened it. There was a single sheet of PetroRus stationery with a short message.

If you are available at two this afternoon, perhaps we could meet again at my office.

The note was signed, and underneath the Russian signature was the script-printed name: Kyril Kulikovsky.

"PetroRus wants to talk some more. I have another meeting with them at two." I looked to Christian. "The embassy has some duplicators, I assume."

"Yes, sir."

"We need to duplicate a chapter or two from a technical manual. I'll meet you both in the office section in ten minutes."

The two of them were still looking at each other when I walked away and toward the elevator. No one else was on it, nor in the corridor to our rooms. I did hear Terese playing something through her door as I passed, but I couldn't say what the piece was.

Llysette was stretched out on the chaise longue in the bedchamber. She had a sheaf of sheet music in her hand, but her eyes were closed. She bolted upright as I walked in. "Johan . . . you surprise me."

"I didn't mean to."

"The Russian . . . I know it, but I do not."

"You don't feel as comfortable with it as with French or English?"

"Or even German."

There wasn't much I could do about that, since my knowledge of Russian was nonexistent. "Could I interest you in something to eat in about a half an hour?"

"Half an hour?" She looked down at the music. "That would be good. We rehearse at three."

"No dress rehearsal tonight?" I'd just assumed there would be a dress rehearsal for something like the cultural exchange concert, and dress rehearsal were usually the night before at the expected performance time.

"The Ballet Russes, it is performing tonight." She shrugged. "That, they will not cancel for us to rehearse. We rehearse at three."

"I'm sorry."

"It is nothing. For what they pay, we rehearse when we rehearse."

Even with the power of a government behind her, Llysette was running into the same kinds of space conflicts she faced at Vanderbraak State. The problems were the same, but the conflicting parties were just more prestigious.

"I'm still sorry." I slipped my briefcase from under the small desk and opened it. It didn't seem to have been tampered with again, and I pulled out the two manuals that I'd been sent by the Columbian Ministry of Interior.

"You? You have another meeting?"

"PetroRus wants to talk some more."

"Talk, it is cheap."

"I know, but we'll provide a little bait today. We don't meet until two. I'm going downstairs to make copies of what I need, and then I'll be back."

"I will be hungry then. But these I want to look over once more." She held up the music.

I was already hungry when I headed back down to the office section, the pair of manuals in the case I carried.

"What are we copying, sir?" asked the waiting Christian.

"Sections two and five," I said.

Christian frowned, but it was a questioning frown.

While I didn't have to explain, someone needs to educate the young public servants, preferably before they become older public servants. "Section two lays out all the technologies. I don't want to tell them how many there are. Section five clearly implies that there have to be five, but the ending leaves the impression of more—it says something like 'the next technology is a variation on this, while those that follow offer totally different approaches.' " I handed him the Russian version. "You copy these, and then we'll cross-check." Then I looked at the commander. "There's no need for you to hang around following me until around one-thirty. After we get this copied, I'm going to have something to eat, probably in the dining room, with Llysette. So I won't be leaving the embassy again until we leave for PetroRus. You probably ought to get something to eat."

"Yes, sir." Commander Madley looked as though he wanted to say something.

"Christian . . . where are the duplicators?"

"That room there."

I handed him the Russian version. "Start copying section two. I'll be there in a minute."

Once Christian had hurried away, I asked Madley, "What did you have in mind, Commander?"

"I have to say, sir, that I worry about your safety. You took that walk this morning, without any armed escort, and . . . then you went off to dinner last night, and . . . well, no one knew even where you were."

"I appreciate your concern. I'll try to do better. That's why I wanted you to know about this afternoon." I didn't say that I'd probably been safer at dinner at the Winter

Swan than at any other time since I'd been in St. Petersburg. "I promise I won't leave the embassy until we go to PetroRus." I paused. "Is this something that Colonel Sudwerth mentioned?"

"Yes, sir."

"I see he's looking after us." I smiled. "That's good. I'm going to check the copying first, then have lunch. You can watch or join us later." After the briefest of pauses, I said, "Then, again, maybe it might be best if you asked Colonel Sudwerth if he has any specifics on what we should be aware of or any places we should avoid. Could you do that?"

"Oh, yes, sir."

Christian already had the first section copied by the time I got into the hot copy room. After the second was done, I had Christian read the first part of the Russian version of each section aloud while I scanned the English version just to make sure the sections were the same. They were. They also came to more than sixty pages, which I replaced in my briefcase along with the originals.

"Who do I charge them to?" asked Christian.

"If there's an account for me, use that. If not, wherever you think best, and blame it on me after I leave." I grinned. "Now . . . if you'll excuse me, I have a date for lunch with a beautiful diva."

"Ah . . . yes, sir."

Christian was figuratively scratching his head as I left the copy room to go back up to the fourth floor, lugging both my originals and the copies.

Llysette was almost ready, and, after I took the originals from my briefcase and returned them to the traveling case, we walked down to the embassy dining room. There were just two choices for lunch—a baked unspecified white fish and a club sandwich. Both seemed rather unsuited to the elegant imperial decor of the embassy dining room, but unspecified anything, especially fish, left me uneasy. We had the club sandwiches with the tomato soup, and I managed to prevail upon the waiter to bring me chocolate.

Llysette had tea. My chocolate was bitter, and even four spoonfuls of sugar didn't remove the edge.

"This meeting, will it help?" she asked after nibbling at a wilted salad.

"It should help, but whether it will help enough, who knows? I don't think the Russians really understand the huge long-term diseconomies of environmental degradation, or the costs involved. They're just interested in picking up technology they don't have to spend capital to develop and test."

"They should develop it if they can get it from you?"

She had a point there.

"The problem is that they may not know what it's worth. They probably don't care." What I was certain Kulikovsky and Yusupov cared about was the promise of large and immediate cash payments by Columbian Dutch Petro. Vlasovich might care greatly, but how much pressure he and his minister might bring was far less than what other ministries might have to weigh against them.

"You must make them care."

I'd have to think about how I could pin their survival on supporting the agreement.

Unhappily, lunch and even the dry club sandwiches were over too quickly, and I was back in the embassy car, being driven back to the PetroRus building with both Christian and the commander.

This time, there was even less of a delay. We were waved upstairs, with a guard, but the guard was smiling, and all he did was turn the key and punch the buttons on the elevator. When we stepped out on the sixth floor, the charming Elenya was standing by the elevator—and so was Executive Director Kulikovsky.

"You are always prompt, Minister Eschbach. You do not make time a game of position."

"Oh, but I do. My time is important. So is yours. When I waste neither, you find yourself indebted to me." I offered a slightly crooked smile, hoping he'd smile or laugh.

He laughed.

Behind us, as Kulikovsky escorted me down a corridor, I heard Elenya saying, "I have some Russian cakes for you two."

We walked past Kulikovsky's office and into one furnished more in what I would have called Russian traditional, with more ornately carved and darker furniture, the upholstery in dark green velvet, set off by silver piping. Behind the desk sat Serge Yusupov. He stood and gestured toward the chairs. "Greetings, Minister Eschbach."

I sat down and set my briefcase by my knee.

Kulikovsky bowed and left, closing the door behind us.

Yusupov tilted his head slightly to the left. "You have suggested a few possibilities, but we have not gotten into specifics."

"No, we haven't." I opened my case and handed across the first section—some twenty-eight pages, at least in English. I hadn't counted the Russian pages, but I thought the translation was shorter. I closed the case, leaving the second section inside.

Yusupov took the section and began to read. After perhaps three pages, he stopped, then flipped to the back and read more before looking up. "Very interesting. In Russian, and on white paper. How thoughtful."

"It might make matters somewhat easier."

"You are not concerned that . . . There is the matter of, shall we say, credit?"

"If you intend to steal it, removing identification markings would be easy enough. Besides, Columbia, as we discussed earlier, is interested in other matters. This way, PetroRus could take a greater share of . . . credit . . . for your ingenuity, at least."

"In some ways, Minister Eschbach, you are a pleasure to deal with."

"Obviously, someone isn't pleased," I said with a laugh.

For a moment, Yusupov frowned. "That is true. I do not think Marshal Putin is pleased with your appearance, but we are."

"Putin? I don't recall his name. Is he with the Air Corps?"

"*Nyet* . . . the Imperial Rocket Corps."

"Ah . . . I presume, because of the Putilov connection?"

A look of something—not quite surprise—flickered across his face before he spoke. "I would not speculate. Prince Romanov might, but I would not."

"When one is less directly related to the tzar, one must be more circumspect?" I suggested.

"One must always be circumspect in St. Petersburg. Sometimes one must be even more circumspect." He cleared his throat, then lifted the section. "This is most useful . . . yet how would one know that there might be more, that this is not . . . ."

"A bluff . . . a teaser?" I shrugged. "That would be in bad faith. If we acted so poorly, I don't doubt you could come up with reasons to void any agreement. That wouldn't be in our interests."

"I know that. But . . . I do not make the decision. I recommend." This time, he shrugged.

I gave a dramatic sigh.

He knew it was dramatic but managed to keep a straight face.

I bent down and extracted the second section—thirty-three pages—and extended it. "This might help."

He read some of it, checked the pages, and read the last section, then grinned. "You knew I would ask."

"I thought you might."

"And if I wanted more proof?"

I held up the empty case, open so that he could see it was empty. "It's your turn."

"It is." He stood. "We have enough to consider. I appreciate all you have done."

"I trust we can work something out," I said as I rose from the green velvet-upholstered chair. "It's to your benefit, and to that of PetroRus and Russia, as well as to us."

"There are things we must consider, but we will."

The door opened, and Kyril Kulikovsky was waiting to escort me out.

Yusupov smiled, and so did I.

As we walked back along the corridor, I turned to Kulikovsky. "What is his title or position?"

Kulikovsky laughed humorously. "He has no title. He doesn't need one. He says it would hinder him."

So much for that.

"Besides Prince Romanov, you could talk to no one better, but I would not mention such in your embassy. Not until the matter is decided."

"I appreciate the advice."

"Advice, I can always give." He laughed again as we entered the foyer, where Christian and Commander Madley were talking with Elenya, in Russian.

Everyone bowed or the equivalent, and we took the elevator down to the main floor, where the clerk at the desk smiled and inclined his head, and the eyes of the guards followed us, more with speculation, I thought, than outand-out distrust.

"Did you learn anything this time?" I asked once we were in the car and headed back to the Columbian embassy.

"Not too much," Christian conceded.

"She did hint that everyone knows who you are," Madley said. "She wanted us to know that."

Christian looked surprised.

"Did she say that?" I directed the question to Christian.

"Not that way . . . it was more like . . . you must be very honored to be working with such a distinguished minister . . . is it true he was a hero and a high government minister? And then she said something like . . ." Christian glanced to the commander and swallowed before going on. "It isn't often that a hero and the world's greatest singer are married and come to St. Petersburg . . ."

"I did take the liberty of telling her just how few Republic Air Crosses have ever been awarded," the commander added.

"Besides that, we talked more about food," Christian said.

"Did she suggest any good places to eat?" I asked.

"The Parizhmuzyka . . . the first secretary ate there once, I think . . . and La Metropole . . ."

"Was there anything else?"

"I can't think of anything." Christian glanced at Madley. "Can you, Commander?"

The aviator shook his head.

The rest of the short return drive was silent, as I tried to sort out what had been said, what had been meant, and what had been implied—and what had not.

The saying was that you never saw one ghost, but a plethora, or it never rained, but it poured. Either way, it works out the same, and this time, as I had left the Volga on my way into the embassy, there was another diplomat, a shorter and wiry man, with a darker complexion. It took me a moment to pick out his name from my memory—Hamilton Tavoian, the second secretary.

"Minister Eschbach . . . there's someone to see you."

"I'd be happy to see them." I glanced around. "I don't have an office . . ."

"Ah . . . First Secretary Darwaard is meeting with the ambassador, but he said earlier in the week that you could use the conference room next to his office if you needed it."

"I guess I need it." I paused. "Who wants to see me?"

"The AmeriSun representative in St. Petersburg. His name is Clinton Mills."

That surprised me—and it didn't.

"I . . . took the liberty of having him wait in the conference room."

"That's fine." I didn't sigh. I just turned to Christian and Commander Madley. "I won't be needing you two for a while."

"I can catch up on exit visas," Christian said cheerfully.

"I'll see if Commander Sudwerth has anything new," added Madley.

We all followed Tavoian up the stairs, and then my de facto aides went different ways, and I went to the conference room. The only thing cheerful in the entire room was the large cherry conference table. The chairs were upholstered in green leather so dark it was almost black, and the only wall decorations were faded etchings of scenes of the federal district.

The man who was waiting for me was a good half foot taller than I was, with the broad and cheerful smile of a professional lobbyist, which was certainly what he was. He stepped forward and extended his hand, even before Tavoian had closed the door behind him, leaving the two of us alone in the conference room.

"Clinton Mills, Minister Eschbach. I do appreciate your taking the time to see me."

"I'm happy to see you, but I can't imagine what I can do for you, Mister Mills." I dropped into one of the chairs and gestured for him to sit down.

He did, but easily, with the grace of an athlete who knew that he was too big to sit quickly or heavily.

"What did you have in mind?" I asked.

"I just wanted to give you some background. I don't know if anyone at the embassy explained my concerns. I'm from the corporate headquarters of AmeriSun in Philadelphia." He smiled winningly. "Actually, my assignment is here in St. Petersburg, but I report directly to McCoy Johnson. He's the president of AmeriSun."

"What is your assignment?" I managed to keep smiling.

"Liaison, mostly. I'm sure you know that Putilov is a wholly owned subsidiary of AmeriSun. Under Columbian and Russian law, for very different reasons, the president of Putilov must have the freedom to determine the company's goals and objectives."

"So AmeriSun can fire the president, but not direct his actions?"

"Exactly." Mills spread his hands. "That's where I come in. Fyodor Ilyinsky certainly doesn't want to undertake initiatives that will be viewed . . ."

"Unfavorably in Philadelphia?" I suggested.

"You might say that I'm here to make sure that there are no surprises on either side."

Like too many professional politicians, Clinton Mills had the kind of personality that focused on the person he addressed, so much that almost everyone felt special. As with the politicians, I just felt uneasy. "That explains what you do, and why it's necessary. I'm still a bit puzzled as to why you wanted to see me."

He offered that warm smile. "The word is that you're trying to broker some sort of deal between PetroRus and Columbian Dutch Petro." He held up his hand. "I'm not saying it's true. Rumors have a way of taking on a life of their own. I hope it's not true, especially because, well . . . that could put our government in a delicate situation, and you've had a most distinguished and admirable career."

I laughed. "Far less noted and distinguished than you're implying."

"All the world knows of you, sir." That statement arrived with an honest and open look of deep sincerity.

"I do doubt that, but . . . go on. You were about to discuss the delicacy of a situation about which I'm clearly totally unaware. What is this situation?"

"As you may not know, sir, through its Putilov venture and its connections, AmeriSun has been working to build a closer relationship commercially between Columbian business and Russian interests. This has taken a considerable investment of time and capital over a number of years, and it has been a gradual process, of necessity . . ." Another smile followed his words, this one half apologetic. "If political considerations were to supersede agreements being developed through mutual understanding and commercial benefit . . ."

I wanted to laugh. Since when hadn't both politicians and business types incessantly meddled in each others' affairs? But I didn't betray any humor or disgust. I just nodded soberly. "I think you may have misunderstood why I am here. My background is environmental. I am indeed trying to work out something, but . . ." I paused. "You may have heard that Ferdinand has objected to the level of pollutants and the effluent characteristics of the Dnepyr River? That he has complained of the impact on the Romanian fisheries?"

The faintest touch of a frown crossed Mills's face before the smile reappeared. "I had heard words to that effect, but . . . I was under the impression that was more pretext than anything else."

I nodded again. "Indeed the complaint may be a pretext, but with the unstable state of the world today, isn't it worth denying Ferdinand any pretexts? One sends a retired minister, a few environmental references and methodologies . . . it costs little enough." I shrugged.

Mills presented yet another of his array of smiles—this the one of honest relief. "That makes a great deal of sense." He paused, and a look of reflection followed the smile. "You do have contacts, Minister Eschbach, and I would offer my own personal observations that perhaps it might be to the Speaker's advantage if you were to convey our concerns. In your case, we obviously misunderstood, but the existence of such persistent rumors might lead many to believe that if an effort to assure an Alaska oil concession to Columbian Dutch is not in progress, it might well be soon. Our years of experience here would lead us to believe that would not be wise. Russia can be a very dangerous place when rumors take on a life of their own."

"I think that's true anywhere, Mister Mills. Still, I do appreciate your sharing that experience. I can't promise that anyone listens to a retired minister of the opposing party, but I will convey your words and concerns." And that, I fully intended to do.

After he'd taken in the words, I stood. "I do appreciate your taking the time to stop by, and your courtesy in sharing your insight and experience."

"I hope I've been of some small assistance, Minister Eschbach."

"You've been of very great assistance, Mister Mills. I

can't tell you how helpful your words have been."

I waited for a time after he left the conference room before heading back to our rooms on the fourth floor of the residence wing. I knew Llysette wouldn't be back for a time, and I had more than a little thinking to do.

30

W ITH NO MEETINGS scheduled for me on Thursday, and Llysette's performance coming that night, we slept in later than usual. The sky was actually getting light by the time I struggled into my shower. When I dressed, I did take the precaution of slipping the bullet-resistant vest liner into place. The situation was already interesting and unfortunately promised to get more so.

The news summaries I retrieved from the box outside our door and read while Llysette was dressing didn't help much, either.

Austria detonates "massive" nuclear fusion device at Birel Aswad in North Africa . . . device estimated to be 250 times more powerful than previous weapons tested by Austro-Hungary . . .

. . . DeGaulle claims sightings of more Austrian submersibles in Caribbean . . . denied by VonBraun . . . Holmbek only confirms that a submersible that was not Columbian or New French was sighted "somewhere north of Antigua" . . .

Third and Fifth Ottoman Janissaries posted to Sli-

ven on the northwest border of the Bulgar province
of the empire . . .

That wasn't good. In thirty years in the military and
public service, I couldn't recall the Turks moving additional troops north and west of Istanbul—away from Russia and more directly against Austro-Hungary.

Unidentified sources indicated that a fire in the Salz-
burg Neurological Institute that had been explained as
an electrical fire was in fact deliberate arson. Dr. Jo-
achim Heisler, recently appointed director of the institute, denied the speculation . . .

Heisler—the head ghost technology researcher for Ferdinand—had a new position? That made me uneasy, but
since Heisler had created many of Llysette's troubles, anything about the man tended to make me uneasy.

Austrian foreign minister asks for neutral inspection
of Perun rocket installations to verify "scientific" purposes of the rocket . . . denied as totally unreasonable
by Russian Communications Minister Lamanov . . .

I shifted to the *Times* of London, but the lead story was
the Austrian fusion device. The only new aspect of the
story was the claim by British "experts" that it would take
several years for the Austrians to streamline and reduce
the device into a deliverable weapons system.
There was no mention anywhere of the cultural
exchange concert.
I didn't mention that to Llysette as she entered the salon.
"Are you ready to find some sustenance?"
"I could use more than bitter tea, Johan."
"So could I."
The staff was about to close the dining area when we
arrived, but Llysette smiled, and they didn't say anything.
We did get served very quickly, and the toast was under-

done, rather than burned. I didn't say much until she had more than a few bites and the color had returned to her face.

"How do you feel?" I finally asked.

"It will be a good concert." She offered a little frown. "The Russian worries me. To learn it from recordings and the IPA, it is not the same."

"You'll be better than good, much better." I grinned.

"You say that because you love me."

"I love you, but I say that because you are a great singer."

"*Non* . . . one judges not before the performance. Not in a foreign land with a foreign tongue."

I decided to get off that track, and quickly. "What do you feel about Russia?"

Llysette took another sip of tea, then tilted her head, thinking for some time before responding. "I do not know."

Waiting, I took another sip of tea. I hadn't been able to get chocolate, despite having it on other mornings.

"The Russians, they have deep feelings. These feelings are strong. But feelings, they are poor self-control. One must think, and balance what one feels. Never to ignore the feelings . . ." She shook her head and then shrugged. "I do not know, Johan. There is only what I feel."

"Maybe that's why there are so many ghosts, and why everyone talks about them. People who die with strong feelings are more likely to be ghosts."

"*Peut-être* . . ."

I laughed. Her "perhaps" was more than dubious, but she kept me from going too far into theorization, which is always a danger for a professorial type.

When Llysette finished the last of her tea, we stood and departed, probably to the relief of the embassy staff, and walked back to the elevator, and then to our spacious quarters. My eyes strayed to the blank stretch of wall, behind which was reputedly the ghost of the lover of one of the daughters of Tzar Mikhail II.

While Christian or Commander Madley might appear at my door, there was no guarantee that messages would get to me. So, after escorting Llysette back to our quarters, where she planned to rest and warm up slowly, and after promising to reclaim her for a late lunch, I girded myself and headed off to the second-floor office section of the embassy.

The first familiar face was that of the good Colonel Sudwerth.

"How are things going, Minister Eschbach?" asked Sudwerth.

"It's far too soon to say. Some of this may not play out until well after we've returned to Columbia." I smiled. "Environmental negotiations and technologies are both complex, and the Russians don't have that much experience in more advanced technologies of this nature. As we both know, their emphasis has always been military and industrial."

"With their neighbors, how could it be otherwise?" Sudwerth said jovially.

"That's an interesting question. They're also neighbors."

"In Alaska? That border's never been a problem to us."

I shook my head. "I meant that the Russians are neighbors to the Austrians, the Ottomans, the Chinese, and the Swedes, and they weren't exactly peaceful in years past in lopping off Turkish territory, or in taking chunks of Poland before the Austrians grabbed it in turn." I gave a rueful smile. "You could also ask the question the other way. With the Russians as neighbors, how could anyone on their borders be otherwise?"

"You aren't justifying the Austrians, I trust?" Sudwerth's laugh was slightly strained.

"Me? Hardly. I have far more reasons than you'll ever know, Colonel, to detest the Austrians. I have to say, that were I in their position, I'd certainly be wary of the Russians, and the current situation isn't based on what we think it ought to be, but on what they think about each other." I grinned. "That's easy enough to say, and harder to do anything about, don't you think?"

"True enough, Minister Eschbach." He paused. "Do you have any more meetings?"

"Not today. Not unless something has happened in the last few minutes. But . . . one never knows."

"One never does." He inclined his head. "I trust you will have a good day."

"Thank you." I smiled and continued toward the small cubicle that was Christian's.

He looked up from a pile of papers as I peered inside. "Yes, sir?"

"Any messages? Anyone else who wants to hear my environmental spiel?"

"Ah . . . no, sir. Not that I've heard. The first secretary hasn't said anything either."

I nodded sagely, although I felt anything but sage. Russia wasn't where I'd been trained to be, even by the Spazi, and I knew all too well that had I known a fraction as much about Russia as about Austria I could have done a great deal more. That also meant someone didn't want me to do a great deal more—but only what I'd been sent to do. The problem was, as usual, that to accomplish the mission always meant doing more than anyone had anticipated. But try telling that to skittish politicians.

"Sir?" Christian's polite question interrupted my brief reverie.

"We should take a drive around St. Petersburg while we have the time." That would give me something—a better feel of things—and keep me from pacing around and disturbing Llysette, who didn't care much for nervous husbands hovering around before she performed.

"Sir?"

"Olaf and you are going to give me a tour between now and lunch. That will help me, and you'll still have the afternoon to go over those papers."

"Yes, sir." His tone was cheerful. Forced, but cheerful.

I hoped the drive would show or tell me something.

31

T HE DRIVE AROUND St. Petersburg, despite Olaf's careful descriptions, didn't tell me much, except that there were a number of very wealthy Russians, and a huge number of not very well-off workers crammed into seemingly endless buildings, long and institutional structures of gray stone or red brick. The worker housing surrounded the wealthier areas of the central part of St. Petersburg like an enormous ragged cloak cast over a glittering uniform. The wide streets and the gray stone, and the snow—they all somehow emphasized the enormous difference between the well-off and the clearly not so well-off. As usual, for all that, it was what I wasn't seeing that probably held the keys to my understanding what was happening around me.

After I returned, I just ran errands for Llysette and kept my mouth shut, at least as much as I could.

Llysette and Terese and the other performers left the embassy at around six-fifteen. I would have preferred to go with her, but the ambassador and Deputy Minister Kent had requested that I accompany them. At six forty-five I was trying not to pace around the small foyer leading to the rear courtyard of the embassy, waiting for those two worthies, when Colonel Sudwerth appeared, in his formal blacks, under a military dress coat. Because I was still inside the embassy, I hadn't fastened my wool overcoat.

Sudwerth smiled as he glanced at the miniature medals that I'd reluctantly affixed to the breast of my black formal jacket. "Good. I see you're wearing your medals. One of the trials of functions in St. Petersburg. The ambassador asked me to remind you that there will be a reception at the theatre afterward, not that I imagine you would be one to forget. Deputy Minister Kent has reserved a receiving room. We don't know if the tzar and tzarina will be there, and, if they are, they may choose to receive people in their box. It's just down the corridor from the room. Commander Madley and I, and Hamilton, will be following you four to the Mariinsky Theatre in the military car."

"Will you be in the box with us?"

"In the back row, where we can't be seen." Sudwerth shook his head. "You dignitaries are who the people want to see."

"Minister Eschbach?"

I turned to see the ambassador and his wife, followed by Drummond Kent and Hamilton Tavoian. Annette Hagel wore a deep and brilliant blue gown that swirled out from underneath the near full-length ermine coat, a coat which emphasized that Ambassador Hagel or his spouse had means far beyond those of an ambassador's income.

"Greetings," I offered with smile.

"And to you, Minister Eschbach," returned Annette. "I'm very much looking forward to hearing your wife."

"She's looking forward to performing. She always does." That was an inane comment, but any response would have been, if considered fully.

When we stepped into the courtyard, there were two vehicles waiting—the embassy limousine, with the Columbian flag on the short staff on the front left fender, and another black Volga. I gestured for the ambassador and his wife to enter first, letting them have the forward-facing seats, while Deputy Minister Kent and I took the rear-facing ones.

As we cleared the open iron gates of the courtyard, Annette Hagel smiled at me. "This must be routine for you."

"Watching Llysette perform is never routine. Anything can happen in live performing. One time a bat swept into the hall where she was singing, and it started to swoop lower and lower." I laughed. "She finished the song—something by Debussy, as I recall—and the bat flew out."

"Wasn't your wife kidnapped right after the Salt Palace performance?" asked the dark-haired woman.

Drummond Kent stiffened, but said nothing.

"Yes . . . but that was a mistake. They weren't after her."

"You?"

"I'm afraid so. They thought I knew more than I did. Very unfortunate circumstances. With the help of the Columbian embassy and the Saint head of security, we managed to right the whole mess, and they returned Llysette unharmed." I hoped she'd stop there.

"Wasn't there something about you offering yourself . . ."

I repressed a sigh. "I did work out a trade. It was the only way to persuade them that I couldn't do for them what they wanted."

"Which was?"

"They wanted to overthrow the government of Deseret." I offered a rueful laugh. "That was well beyond my capabilities. I managed to stall matters until the Saints could bring in reinforcements, so to speak, and then escaped in the confusion."

"There's more of a story there, but it's one I'm not likely to get." She grinned at me, almost like Llysette did, and the expression made me like her a great deal more than I did her husband.

"There are always stories . . . and some are better not told in depth. Then, all the mystery and glamour vanishes."

I'd barely stopped talking when the limousine eased to a stop under a series of lights before the Mariinsky Theatre. Outside the theatre, there was a line of people queued up, a relatively long line, probably two hundred people.

"We'll have some crowd," I observed, as I slipped out to hold the door for the ambassador and his wife.

Drummond Kent stepped out beside me. "Hamilton told me that there were very few seats left, and that was at noon."

"How much are the tickets?" I asked.

"That was a tricky business." The ambassador laughed as he helped his wife from the limousine. "We didn't want to make a profit on the concert, and the Mariinsky people didn't want us undercutting their normal schedule. So the price is what they normally charge, but all the profits after the theatre's costs are going to the tzarina's favorite charity—that's a hospital and home for disabled children."

I looked at the line again. Paying customers were always a good sign. I could remember when I'd first met Llysette, and she'd been lucky to get two hundred people for a free recital in Vanderbraak Centre. But that had been before Carolynne . . . and before she'd been rediscovered.

By now, those in the second car had joined us, and Second Secretary Tavoian was leading us to one of the doors beside the main door, where he flourished something and waved us all through.

The staircases were covered with heavy carpet, and we must have climbed at least three levels before Tavoian held open a door to a box. From what I'd read, when the theatre had last been remodeled, the tzar's box had been moved more toward the center, and expanded so that it was twice the size of those on each side. The box offered to Ambassador Hagel apparently belonged to one of the Romanovs, but whoever it was, and I suppose it could even have been Pyotr, was either in the tzar's box or elsewhere.

"You and Deputy Minister Kent have the two center seats on the lower level," murmured Hamilton Tavoian as we entered the box, with its gilt and green walls and the two stepped rows of green velvet armchairs. "You both outrank the ambassador."

After hanging my coat on the rack in the back corner, I sat down. The area below was already half full, and the boxes I could see all had people in them. The Mariinsky Theatre wasn't as big as the Salt Palace in Deseret, supposedly holding a little more than half the audience, but that was still more than 1,500 seats, and with the gilded tiers that seemed to rise forever above the mezzanine, it seemed larger and far more substantial.

"You don't see theatres like this in Columbia," Drummond Kent said quietly.

"No one wants to pay for them," I pointed out. "They have to make a profit, or at least an attempt at it so that whoever makes up the difference doesn't feel like they're subsidizing opulence and waste. The problem is that one person's elegance is another's waste."

Kent frowned but didn't say anything.

I glanced down the program—or rather at the translated version that the embassy had supplied and which I'd put inside the official Russian version that had been left on the holder before my seat—just at the section for Llysette.

The Nightingale
Nikolay Rimsky-Korsakov (1844–1908)

Opus 6, No. 6
"None But the Lonely Heart"
Pyotr Il'yich Tchaikovsky (1840–1893)

Opus 60, No. 1
"Last Night"
Pyotr Il'yich Tchaikovsky (1840–1893)

Opus 16, No. 1
"The Cradle Song"
Pyotr Il'yich Tchaikovsky (1840–1893)

Opus 21, No. 5
"The Lilacs"
Sergei Rachmaninov (1873–1939)

"Air de Lia"
from *L'Enfant Prodique*
Claude Debussy (1862–1918)

Vocalise
Sergei Rachmaninov (1873–1939)

Mme. Llysette duBoise, Soprano
Mme. Terese Stewart, Piano

The Black Mesa Quartet was first, and they led off with *Quartetto I*, a later composition from Janáček, the Czech-oslovakian composer who fled to Britain around the turn of the century when it had become all too clear that Czech nationalists, particularly artistic ones, were going to be the first to be wiped out under the increasingly more stringent Austrian control over its provinces, a control that had later turned into a total political assimilation of Czechoslovakia.

Their second, and final number, was a Beethoven string quartet, the one in F Minor.

The crowd obviously preferred the Janáček to the more traditional Beethoven piece, as did I, although I suspected Columbian audiences would have preferred Beethoven.

During the brief intermission, while they changed the stage and rolled out the piano, the hum and buzz of con-versation drifted through the theatre. Unlike in theatres in either Deseret or Columbia, or even in Quebec, New France, or Austria, I hadn't the faintest idea of what that humming buzz might represent.

"The ambassador tells me that you've been quite busy," offered Drummond Kent.

"Somewhat busy. In this business, it's hard to tell if you've made any progress at all. Environmental techniques and technologies aren't exactly on the top of anyone's pri-ority list, unless there's an environmental disaster at hand."

"There is that." Kent stretched slightly, his eyes flicking to the back of the box, but both Commander Madley and Colonel Sudwerth had slipped away at the beginning of the intermission. "Then, there is the matter of your past affiliations. That lends a certain air of mystery to your presence. I'm not entirely unperceptive, and it appears as though Colonel Sudwerth has shown a great interest in you, as opposed to your beautiful and most talented wife."

I nodded. "I'm sure that's because he can't figure out how a former military pilot ended up a spokesman for the environment. The colonel would be happy to pulverize the environment on behalf of Columbia, but I'm not sure he has quite grasped the idea that cleaning up polluted rivers can sometimes avoid conflicts in places where we'd rather not fight—or have others fighting."

"The Dnepyr situation?"

"Something like that."

"Will it work?"

I laughed. "It's worth trying. If it doesn't, I'm sure someone will think about returning to military pulverization techniques."

The lights flickered, twice, and the door at the back of the box opened. Hamilton Tavoian, Colonel Sudwerth, and Commander Madley returned. I had to wonder why Piet Darwaard wasn't there, unless there was a policy that one senior staff member had to remain in the embassy.

When Robert Thies appeared on the stage below, several minutes later, he smiled his shy boyish smile, and then went to work.

Like Llysette, he'd clearly tailored his program to the audience, beginning with Prokofiev's *Sonata No. 3 in A Minor*. The Russians recognized it and clapped heartily when he finished. He concluded with Rachmaninov's *Three Preludes* . . . and got an even heartier round of applause that took a long time dying away.

Then there was another intermission, and about that time, my palms began to get sweaty. I tried not to fidget in the chair, while keeping a polite smile on my face.

Llysette swept into the middle of stage, wearing a long shimmering gown, the bodice and skirt a silvered green, topped by a short black and silver sequinned jacket. She'd decided on that when she had learned just how cold that tall stage was, even despite the heat of the lights. Terese wore black and quietly seated herself at the piano.

The Rimsky-Korsakov *Nightingale* was the first song, and Llysette did it in Russian. I thought she was wonderful. There was the sort of silence that was between surprise and awe for a moment after she finished, before the applause came, then died away, almost as if they all wanted to hear more.

Tchaikovsky's "None But the Lonely Heart" was one she'd learned in France, and she did it in French, but the next one, "Last Night," another Tchaikovsky song, was in Russian, and the applause showed that the Russians did like that touch. "The Cradle Song" was in French, followed by Rachmaninov's "Lilacs" in Russian, and then the Debussy aria in French.

With each song, the applause built, until, after the Rachmaninov *Vocalise,* the crowd started to stand. The whole effect, with all the tiers of the theatre, was deafening, and it didn't fade away until Llysette gestured to Terese for an encore.

The encore was a Columbian piece, Gershwin's "Summertime." But they even clapped and stamped their feet for that.

As the stage darkened, and the clapping finally died away, Drummond Kent looked at me. "I'd heard. I had no idea."

"There's no one like her," I said. But then, even as my eyes burned in gladness for her, I could never say why. "No one."

Finally, I stood and followed Kent out of the box and down a corridor that had apparently already emptied.

Colonel Sudwerth and Commander Madley flanked the doors to the reception room, along with Tavoian, effectively acting as door keepers.

Once inside, I looked around the reception room, but I didn't see Llysette. In fact, as functionaries in black and white and in formal uniforms of various colors and cuts and women in elaborate dresses began to drift into the room, the only performer I saw was Robert Thies.

"I really enjoyed your pieces," I told Thies, "especially the last prelude."

"I'm glad I played before her." He shook his head. "No one could have followed her. I'd heard she was wonderful, but . . ."

"Words don't describe it," I finished.

"There she is," he said.

As I turned, I could feel an enormous smile cross my face and fill me as I looked at her, and for a moment, we were the only two people in the increasingly crowded room. Her smile answered mine, and I stepped forward and hugged her. "There aren't words. You were wonderful, and more."

"It was good."

The very understatement of her words emphasized just how good she had been.

Thies bowed. "I've never heard better. Not anywhere."

"You are most kind."

"I'm not kind. I'm truthful. I can't tell you how glad I am that I played before you sang."

At that point, Ambassador Hagel and his wife moved through the crowd toward us. "Magnificent. Just magnificent." He was beaming from ear to ear, as well he might, since the concert would certainly reflect well on him.

Drummond Kent was also beaming, and while they congratulated Llysette, I slipped away to get her a glass of wine, and edged through the crowd to bring it back to her.

"*Merci, mon cher,*" she murmured between thanking and responding to well-wishers.

Something caught my eye, and I turned. Despite the formal black and white, and the red decoration with the silver starburst, I recognized the man who stood at the end of the table that held various gourmet items neither Llysette nor I had had time to sample.

He nodded.

I returned the nod, but had to wait for almost ten

minutes while Llysette dealt with well-wishers. In the meantime, Terese had drifted into sight from somewhere, and she and Robert Thies were talking animatedly. I hadn't seen the Black Mesa Quartet.

When there was a break, I touched her arm. "Llysette, I'd like you to meet someone."

"Mais oui, mon cher." She turned.

I bowed to the man, smiling broadly. "I'm Johan Eschbach, and this is my wife, Llysette."

"Dietre Fontaine, at your service." He bowed to me, and then more deeply to Llysette. "Your singing continues to enchant the world, mademoiselle."

The last name Dietre was using was different, but that wasn't a problem. "Dietre and I have run across each other a number of times over the past years. He always shows up in surprising places." I turned to Dietre. "What are you doing these days?"

"I've been detailed to the New French embassy to offer my expertise in energy matters . . . and others."

"I have to offer my thanks for your last venture in that area."

"I am glad all turned out well." He nodded to Llysette. "Your singing was without peer, and I am most glad to have been able to hear you once more in person. You are far better than the disk from the Salt Palace would indicate, and now the Russians will know that."

"We sang what we hoped they would like."

"They did—most clearly. It is a pity that you were required to leave France and go to Columbia. Some of us had so hoped you could have gone to New France." Dietre smiled. "As Johan knows, I am an elitist at heart."

Another man in formal dress—with a blue ribbon and sunburst of some sort—appeared beside Dietre.

"This is Marshal Gorofsky," Dietre offered. "Of the Russian Imperial Air Corps."

"For now, at long last, you are popular in Columbia, mademoiselle. You would always have been acclaimed and rewarded in Russia," Gorofsky said after bowing.

I raised my eyebrows. Gorofsky had something in mind.

"You are most kind," Llysette replied.

"The great problem that the arts have always faced in countries where the populace has too great a say in their funding is that what is funded must reflect popular taste, and, as we in Russia know all too well, popular taste is seldom excellent. Here, we show them what is excellent, and they are grateful."

That was well said, and mostly true, even if aristocratically pompous. "Do you think that is true only in the arts, Marshal?"

"It is more obvious in arts, I submit, Minister Eschbach. Popularity is an element in any system, even the most autocratic and regimented, because it is so much easier to count heads or hands than to evaluate excellence."

"Perhaps we should have some tea or a drink someday and discuss that and solve the problems of the world."

"It has many. Where does one begin?" Gorofsky laughed. "Perhaps we should, when we have a long afternoon." He bowed to Llysette. "You were magnificent. I hope you will return, perhaps in the time of the white nights, so that you may see Russia at its brightest as well, and so that we may hear you once more."

Llysette inclined her head.

"And you, Minister Eschbach, I understand you now teach."

"The economics, technical basis, and politics of the environmental and natural resources," I admitted.

"Ah . . . you have considerable expertise there. But it is a pity you could not also teach the same with regard to military science. You were a most distinguished pilot, and someone should teach those who will lead that excellence in the military cannot be based on technology alone, no matter how advanced and how fantastic. Nor can it be based merely on economics or body counts." He laughed. "I wander. Perhaps we should have that drink or tea someday and compare stories."

"I'd look forward to that."

The marshal slipped away, past two men in formal dress I'd never seen before.

"Until later, Johan." Dietre offered a French hug. I almost didn't feel the envelope slipped inside my jacket until after he had stepped away. "Take care of your wife. None of us would wish to lose her."

"Thank you. I will."

With a brisk nod, he stepped away, and I turned toward Llysette. "He is very taken with your singing. He was also at the Salt Palace concert."

Colonel Sudwerth, carrying a clear drink of some sort, untouched, appeared, with his jovial smile in place. "You move in interesting circles, Minister Eschbach. Did you know that man—he calls himself Fontaine now—is the head of New French espionage in St. Petersburg?"

Behind him, Commander Madley watched, holding a drink of his own, also untouched.

"I can't say that I did." That was true enough. I laughed. "We only talked about the concert, but I appreciate the warning, and I'll certainly be on my guard if I run across him again."

"Try to be on your guard before you run into him. He's an especially nasty type, I've been told."

I knew that already, but I just smiled. "I'll be very careful."

Sudwerth gave me a perfunctory nod and headed toward someone in a Russian uniform. I don't think I'd ever seen a place where so many men wore uniforms.

Abruptly, Drummond Kent appeared at my elbow, accompanied by Hamilton Tavoian.

"You are both invited to meet the tzar and tzarina . . . they will see you in their box."

So we followed Deputy Minister Kent and a pair of tall guards in uniforms to the doorway to the imperial box, guarded by yet another set of guards.

Tzar Alexander IV was tall, a good two or three inches taller than I was, but balding. He stood on one side of the box, flanked by the icy-blonde tzarina. "Please . . ." He gestured, and we stepped forward, but I lagged a bit so that Llysette was the one in front. It was her night and her concert.

"You are not Russian, but you sang those songs like a Russian and an angel, and that is why all in the theatre wept." The tzar offered Llysette a warm smile. "Always, you will be welcome in St. Petersburg and Russia."

Llysette bowed. *"Merci, votre majesté."*

"No . . . we owe you thanks, and we always will." He looked at me and smiled, an expression somewhere between bemusement and courtesy. "Your wife sings like an angel, but I understand you're like the seraph who protects her."

"I do what I can, your majesty." I suspected he deserved some more exalted title, but since no one had briefed me on that, I couldn't offer it. I doubt anyone really expected we would meet the tzar personally, or, if they did, they wanted me to botch it. "Wouldn't any loving and devoted husband?"

He laughed. "Minister Eschbach, you amuse me. Would that you were Russian, but we can do little enough of that in these days."

"I'm glad to have brought you that amusement, your majesty." I inclined my head slightly, a head upon which he wished to bestow some honor or which he wished to remove, or both.

"In these days, the profession of autocracy is fraught with danger. We can, of course, be more forthcoming in culture than in commerce and government." He turned and murmured a few words to the icy figure of the tzarina.

She smiled, and the momentary warmth was almost like frost shattering off a statue in brilliant sunlight.

The effect vanished almost immediately when the tzar returned his gaze to Llysette and asked, "You will be here several more days, will you not, Mademoiselle duBoise?"

"Oui, votre majesté."

"Would you consider giving a short private concert for our family, some close friends, and relatives, in the concert hall in the Winter Palace . . . perhaps, this Saturday night?"

"Delighted, we would be." Llysette bowed her head just slightly.

"Excellent! The children and many others will hear what they should have heard tonight." The tzar smiled patronizingly. "I understand that you cannot do an entirely new program, but if you could add one or two songs we did not hear . . ."

"We will do what we can." Llysette offered a true diva's curtsy, mixed with a warm smile.

"Then we will see you on Saturday night. I will send a note."

There must be something about royalty and tzars and the like, because we could sense, without a word, that the audience was over.

We followed Minister Kent back to the reception area, but it was already almost empty except for embassy people. After reclaiming our heavy coats, we walked back down the stairs and out to the limousine. I gathered that the other performers had already left.

Perhaps fifteen students had waited outside, huddled inside coats, under a clear sky, with a biting wind out of the north. As they saw Llysette, they inched forward, and one called something.

"They'd like your autograph," Commander Madley translated.

"I will sign."

So we all stood in a circle behind her.

"If you would tell me their names . . ." Llysette smiled.

Although she was shivering under the heavy coat in the night chill, Llysette patiently wrote down the transliterated names and signed programs for close to twenty young people.

When she was done, as we turned toward the limousine, I saw a patch of faint white by one of the stage doors. Several of the departing students stopped and pointed as well.

"Can you hear what they said?" I asked the commander.

"I couldn't hear it all, sir. Something about the ghost of a singer."

"Pauvre femme," Llysette said in a low voice before we climbed into the limousine for a quiet trip back to our quarters in the embassy.

I didn't even put a hand near the pocket where Dietre's envelope rested, not until we were back in our quarters, and I took off my jacket and laid everything in it on the highboy. After hanging the jacket up I unsealed the envelope.

There were only three sheets of paper there.

The first was a slightly yellowed newspaper clipping—from the *Times* of London, dated January 17, 1994—nearly two years ago.

St. Petersburg (BNI). "Heavy bombers will be dinosaurs," claimed the Russian Minister of War Putyatin last week. Putyatin also stated that Russia could not afford to build useless heavy bombers that would soon be "obsolete," but would concentrate on "the weapons of the future." Many interpreted that to mean that the Perun rocket was being developed as a prototype of a multiple warhead delivery system. . . .

This morning it was revealed that Putyatin had died suddenly of an undisclosed illness in St. Petersburg. Details were not available. . . .

This is not the first time that a high minister has died unexpectedly after revealing information that might be considered harmful to Russian interests. . . .

The Russians contend that, as a prototype, the Perun is not yet a weapons system and does not fall under the provisions of the High Frontier Treaty.

The second clipping was also from the *Times* and dated May 23, 1995, more than a year later.

St. Petersburg (BNI). Refuting Austrian claims that Russia was systematically flouting the High Frontier

Treaty, Minister of Communications Lamanov stated, "The Perun is being developed strictly for research purposes."

"Research is a convenient fiction," retorted Austrian Foreign Minister VonBraun. "Last year it was a weapons system of the future. Now it is a research tool. . . ."

The third item in the envelope was a single sheet of paper, on the top of which had been typed a single line: "This might be of interest." It might have been except it was all in Russian. Then I looked again. A single table had been circled in red, and I didn't need to read Russian to understand it. It was a plot of frequencies, and I knew them all too well.

At that moment, I did swallow. Hard. I'd been wondering why Dietre had sought me out, but I wasn't wondering any longer. Now, I was just scared.

I almost missed the two names at the bottom of the page—also typed in manually. The one I didn't know was Yelensov.

We only had another week in St. Petersburg, and I hadn't the faintest idea of how to deal with what stared me in the face, only that I needed to do something—and still get an oil agreement signed.

"Johan . . . are you all right?"

"No. I'm not." I handed her the items in the newspaper and watched while she read through them.

Finally, she looked up. "All this, I understand but the chart."

I bent forward and whispered in her ear, "Ghost formation energy frequencies."

She turned almost as pale as I felt.

"What will you do?"

"I don't know . . . yet."

Neither of us said more for several minutes, and I felt absolutely rotten for dropping the Arctic Ocean on her after such a glorious concert, and she didn't know the worst of it.

"Do not . . ." she murmured, kissing my cheek. "It was not you."

Maybe not, but I felt like I had been the one who'd spoiled the euphoria of her concert.

32

AFTER ALL THE excitement, despite my tiredness, I didn't sleep well, and I had to do my best not to toss and turn. The size of the bed helped keep me from disturbing Llysette too much, but I was up well before it even started to get light on Friday morning.

The news summaries did contain a brief mention of the concert; at the end of the summaries were two typed sheets with what were translations of what had appeared in the St. Petersburg papers. I skipped over the comments about the quartet and Thies, except for noting the quartet got polite mentions and Thies was well-received.

> Many foreign sopranos have been disappointing when they have performed at the Mariinsky. Last night was no disappointment. It was a triumph for the French-born Columbian soprano Llysette duBoise. Unlike some, she understood she was in Russia, and all but one of the works on her program were by Russian composers, although she sang several in French. Even so, her Russian was close to flawless . . .

I shook my head. Llysette would agonize over the phrase "close to flawless."

. . . and her delivery, soul, and musicianship beyond compare. Those at her performance left the concert wishing she were Russian. So did this listener. The great Russian soprano Arkhipova claimed that the Mariinsky would not see the equal of duBoise for decades, if not generations. From what was heard last night, she may be right.

That brought a smile. Of course, Arkhipova was right. How often was there a singer who was a diva from two generations with the soul of two great singers?

The second review was similar, except it noted that her encore performance of the Gershwin piece was also a treat.

After that, I almost didn't frown at the headline in the *Times* of London: AUSTRIA CLOSES PERSIAN GULF. The story was straightforward enough. Ferdinand was claiming that New France and Columbia had closed the Caribbean to international shipping to protect their energy supplies, and Austria was forced to do the same.

I sighed and looked into the darkness outside the window that was fading into gray.

As Llysette peered into the tiny kitchen, I couldn't help smiling. I stood and thrust the translated reviews at her. "They thought that it would be generations before another singer like you came to the Mariinsky."

"Johan . . . it is early. That good, they could not be."

I poured a cup of tea for her as she read through the reviews.

"My Russian . . . I told you . . . it was not good enough."

'Close to flawless' is outstanding for less than six weeks of preparation in a foreign language."

"You are kind." She sat down at the small table and sipped the tea. "Irina said she would come this afternoon to work on the Russian phrasing with us. I will be better tomorrow night. Terese has a small recorder, and we will record. That way, I can recall the phrasing when we return to Columbia."

"You'll sing them again?"

"Mais oui."

"Just remember," I said gently, "my beautiful and talented diva, that you have conquered two national capitals."

"Not yet," she replied with a smile. "After Saturday . . . we shall see."

"You are a skeptic."

"I am hungry."

So we cleaned up, dressed quickly, and went down and caught the last of breakfast.

After that, we went back to our quarters, but I was there only long enough to gather my overcoat and gloves. I had some more sightseeing in mind, if of a particular nature, but I needed to check a few more items. The last thing I did was make sure I had fresh batteries in the calculator that was more than a calculator, before I slipped it into my side coat pocket. The projector pens went into my shirt pocket, beside the more bulbous special pen, and a couple of spare batteries.

Then, overcoat folded on my arm, I went to find Commander Madley. He was in the conference room, reading a sheaf of papers. After alerting him, we went to Christian's office. The younger man was looking over exit visas at his desk.

"Yes, sir?" asked Christian.

"I have a request of you two. I need to see if either of you can find out anything about a man named Viktor Yelensov."

Madley stiffened.

"I see you know of him."

"If . . . if he's the same man, there is a Viktor Yelensov who is considered one of the . . . he's very involved in the rocketry projects."

"The Perun work?"

"I can't say, sir."

Madley had already said enough.

"He's a payload or warhead specialist then. Otherwise, you could have said more, because they used all the Goddard work for propulsion systems."

"Sir . . . I really can't say." Madley screwed up his mouth. "His degrees are in physics, and he's written papers that have been published on electrical wave theories and ELF propagation propensities."

I managed to keep my reaction to a nod. "Outside my field, clearly. You can comment on that, can't you?"

"As far as I know, sir, Viktor Yelensov has nothing to do with either energy or environmental efforts."

"That's all I need to know." I pursed my lips. "I still have to wonder . . ." Then I shook my head. "Christian . . . could you check and see if there's anything in the past news clips or summaries about him, particularly about energy-related matters. There may not be, but I need to know that."

Madley frowned but didn't offer anything else.

"While you're checking that out, I need a moment with Colonel Sudwerth."

Madley didn't relax a moment with that, and I'd thought he would. All he said, almost stiffly, was, "I'll see if I can help Christian, sir."

"I won't be very long, I'm sure. That's if the colonel's even around."

Colonel Sudwerth was standing in the doorway of his small office.

The last thing I wanted was to be behind closed doors with the colonel at the moment. So I stopped and asked, as innocently as I could, "Colonel, you have some understanding of the situation in which I find myself, I trust? After a week, I still find very little happening."

"Minister Eschbach, attempting to work out anything quickly in Russia is time-consuming and frustrating."

"It also leads one into strange places," I mused.

"The ambassador has noticed that," said Sudwerth. "He mentioned that there was an explosion right after you left the Senate Square, where I understood you were sightseeing."

"I'd always wanted to see the Bronze Horseman, and we had a few minutes between appointments. I understand there was a Septembrist there. I gather we were both lucky and unlucky."

"A few minutes later, and you might have been another of the ghosts of St. Petersburg, Minister Eschbach."

"Lucky, as I said." I looked at Sudwerth. "Have you ever heard the name Viktor Yelensov?"

"It's not the most common of names."

I could tell. He'd heard the name. "I'd asked Christian and Commander Madley to see if they could find out anything about him, but they couldn't find anyone like that in the environmental area. Or in dealing with energy. His name was passed to me, but I don't know why. It's certainly not a name I've run across, and it wasn't in my briefing materials. Someone suggested I even should meet the man, but I don't have any idea why."

"That name didn't come up as any of those Darwaard asked me to check out," mused Sudwerth. "I can look and let you know. If I find him, would you like a meeting?"

"I suppose so. I would hate to tell the Speaker that I had overlooked anything."

"I'll see what I can do."

"Thank you very much, Colonel."

I hadn't retraced my route back toward Christian's office more than a half dozen steps when I saw him turn the corner and walk toward me, followed by an embassy guard with a folded sheet of paper.

"Sir, there's a gentleman here, waiting outside. He asked me to give this to you."

I looked at the paper and read it quickly.

"Was nearby. Do you have time for tea at the café in the next block?"

There was a signature, and a "G" after it.

"Christian . . . if you'd keep looking for Yelensov. I'll be back in an hour or so."

"Sir?"

"An old friend. I didn't expect to see him, and this is the only time we can talk. I'll be back. Don't worry."

I left him standing there. The story wouldn't hold up

longer than a few minutes, but that didn't matter, so long as I got out of the embassy quickly.

After trotting down the steps from the second floor, I walked out the business door of the embassy, into the wind, and fastened my coat, then pulled on my gloves. Under a gray sky that seemed to be lowering, it was colder out than it had looked. I patted my side pocket in a passing way, ensuring the calculator was still there.

I was headed toward the Nevsky Prospekt when Gorofsky walked up beside me. He wore a plain black overcoat, although he had a uniform on beneath.

"So good to see you, Minister Eschbach. You will not be here that much longer in St. Petersburg, and I did want to have that talk about evaluating excellence. It is a problem here, but one that cannot be discussed among peers."

"I can see that. It appears that all too many of those in the upper ranks of the imperial government have, shall we say, ties to the tzar."

"It has been that way for four centuries, starting with the Tolstois and the Miloslavskys. One must work with it, as one can." He pointed to a glass-fronted door and a narrow glass window. "I said it was not far."

I entered first, with a certain trepidation. The café was small—only six or seven tables—and barely ten feet wide and twenty deep. The tables were of polished wood, without any coverings, and the chairs were the solid straight-backed armless wooden kind—battered and nicked. There were two white-bearded men in heavy gray overcoats—military greatcoats stripped of braid and insignia. They sat at one corner table, hunched over steaming cups.

Gorofsky led me to the other corner table, gestured to the man standing in front of a curtained arch, and said something in Russian. The man vanished. "I ordered tea. You do not mind?"

"Tea is fine."

"Before he died, my father used to come here."

"Was he a military man?"

"Many of us have been. The first General Brusilov was

my great-great-uncle, and he understood men and how to use them. He told my father that the most important thing was to show strength of will, not when matters were going well, but when they were going badly." Gorofsky took a sip of the tea. "Matters are going badly, and few will admit it. Matters are not going well in Columbia, and few there will admit it either, I hear."

"That could be." I laughed gently. "In a democracy, one must not alarm the people unduly, because they immediately blame those who sound the alarms. I suspect that in a tzardom, the same is true, except one must worry not about the people, but the tzar."

"There is always someone." Gorofsky shook his long-faced head morosely, then smiled as the waiter set two huge mugs of tea on the table. "But you are here."

I took a sip of the tea, welcome after even one long block of walking through a chill wind. I glanced out through the window, noticing that the day had darkened and that fine white flakes of snow had begun to drift down.

"Your wife, she is magnificent."

"She is."

"It is a pity that she would not have come here, were not matters so . . . unsettled." He laughed. "We understand the politics of Columbia. A man like you, who knows what must be done, he is never sent unless they see no other way."

"Does all of St. Petersburg know that?"

He shook his head. "A few. Pyotr Romanov suspects. Colonel General Kaselov knows, but can do nothing and will say less. Director Yelensov thinks you are a politician and beneath notice."

I wanted to ask about Yelensov, but decided to let Gorofsky tell it his way—with a little prompting. "You seemed to indicate that too much technology, especially fantastic technology, might be more of a curse than a blessing."

"That is when it is used wrongly." He cocked his head. "I am getting to be an old military man, and once I was a young pilot. You are a senior minister, and once you were a young pilot and a hero." He waved off my disclaimer before I could make it. "I think we might see matters in the same way. It is an ill-kept secret that the Austrians have a device that turns soldiers into zombies. It is a slightly better kept secret that we have the basics of that technology. You know both, or we would not be having tea together. Someone got the idea of trying to develop that device in an untried way along with two other unperfected technological innovations. There is a great deal of the War Ministry's funding that will go into building something." The marshal snorted. "If it works, it will not reach most of the Austrian troops, and it will give the Austrians the provocation to launch heavy bombers that we do not have enough interceptors to stop. If it does not work, then roubles that could have been spent on working technology will be wasted, and Russia will be weaker."

"I assume that the director was that someone. That could be a problem. Can you do anything about it?"

Gorofsky shrugged. "If the project director were removed, discredited, almost anything, something might be possible. If anyone in the Air Corps acted first, then it would be perceived as professional jealousy and spite. The tzar discourages infighting, often with exile, sometimes with executions."

"And the arguments you've just presented would be regarded as excuses? That is, if you acted first?"

"That is true."

"Hmmm . . ." I took another small swallow of the tea, actually finding it not too bad, despite its strength and the lack of sugar. "I can see your problem. It would also seem that, theoretically, you understand, that should anything happen to this director, not much would change. He has a team. . . ."

Gorofsky snorted again. "He has a team. They are lackeys, and he has not shared the information with anyone. They say he has not written any of it down so that no one will dare remove him."

Perhaps occupational paranoia might actually be helpful. I took another sip of tea. "The man who introduced us . . . he told you?"

"Only what the device was. I had to find out the rest."

I nodded. "All I can say is that I will look into the matter." I wasn't about to promise anything in public with a man I'd never met before the previous evening.

"I will do what I can . . . but it would be better . . . if the first action were taken by others . . . second steps are also necessary."

I understood that, as well. I just didn't know if Gorofsky happened to be mostly trustworthy, partly trustworthy, or totally untrustworthy. "I can tell it's important, and I will look into it."

"That is all I can ask of you." He took a long swallow and finished his tea, setting a bill on the table. "The tea is mine." Then he stood.

"Thank you. Will I see you at the Winter Palace?" I stood.

"No." He laughed. "I am not family. Do tell your wife that I hope she can return and sing for all of us again."

"I will."

Outside, he walked south and then west, and I headed back to the embassy, thinking . . . and worrying a great deal, especially about just how many players there were. So far, without digging that deeply, I'd discovered at least five.

33

WALKING BACK TO the embassy through the wind that remained gusty and chill, with the fine-falling snow that feathered away from my boots with every step, I was definitely grateful for my heavy overcoat and the lined black leather gloves. It was only a bit after eleven, which surprised me, when I walked into the rear courtyard of the embassy.

I needed to do a little reconnaissance of my own—across the Neva to take another look at the University of St. Petersburg. I really wanted to confirm something, because I was operating far too much on feel and intuition. So I began to look for Olaf.

I didn't get very far when a marine appeared in a heavy winter greatcoat. "Sir . . . your driver didn't show up this morning, and Colonel Sudwerth asked me to fill in, sir. We're a bit short on drivers. Also, sir, he left this with me for you." The marine handed me a sealed envelope.

I opened it and read.

V. Yelensov has agreed to a meeting with you at eleven. I'm meeting with the ambassador, but will try to join you.

There was no signature, just a scrawled initial that looked like an "S" and an address below, on the Tolstoi Prospekt.

"Do you know this address?" I offered the note to the marine.

"Yes, sir."

I glanced up at the courtyard, then took a deep breath, knowing the next few hours were going to be very dicey. But if I didn't play it out, I had this feeling that much of Europe would be zombies and black glass. I turned and smiled ruefully at the driver. "We'd better be going. Which car?"

"The Volga at the end, sir."

I climbed in, and the driver guided the car through the iron gates, nodding at the sentry as we passed.

From what I could tell from the maps I'd studied, and from what Olaf had said in carting me around the city, we were nowhere near the headquarters of the Imperial Rocket Corps, or anything else, but then I'd figured that was likely. I'd already slipped the calculator out of my pocket and had the projector pens in hand.

Abruptly the Volga turned down a narrow lane, then started to slow.

I slid to the curb side of the car, opened the door, and stumbled out onto snow-slippery stones before the embassy Volga totally stopped.

Three figures in black coats appeared, all with rather long knives, but I was a good twenty feet from where they had obviously expected me.

Before they took three steps, I'd already inserted the pens in the calculator and pressed the delete key.

Two went down like undercut trees, but the third shook his head. He was either ghost-zombie resistant or I was out of power. The calculator went on the top of a small heap of snow as I kept moving.

I still had muscle power, and before the third thug recovered fully I stepped inside the knife hand and put an elbow through his larynx, and a knee somewhat lower. He was trying to retch and turning purple.

Then I turned and yanked the bulbous pen from my breast pocket.

The hard-faced Republic marine was lifting the forty-five when the zombie beam hit him. I was too far away, which was probably a blessing, because, like the third thug, he just staggered.

I wasn't as tough on him, but I wasn't gentle, either. I snapped his knee with a side kick and then broke his gun wrist. The semi-blankness in his eyes meant he probably wouldn't be too coherent about what had happened, and that was just fine.

I borrowed his forty-five and used it on all three of the toughs. Since two of them hadn't any minds left, I wasn't doing any more than I'd already done—just changing the appearance of their virtual deaths into physical deaths.

Then I emptied the weapon and left it several feet from the dazed marine. Moving quickly, I scooped up the calculator and the pen antennas—one had jarred loose and I had to dig through the loose snow to get it.

I walked briskly out of the narrow lane, hoping I could reorient myself and get to where I needed to be.

Behind me, I could hear windows opening, and voices, in delayed reaction to the shots, I was sure. In an autocratic police state, especially in winter weather, people are inclined to wait a bit before investigating gunshots.

There are also certain advantages to being graying and older. People don't think of graying men with lined faces as able to act quickly. Someday I wouldn't be able to, and that day was probably closer than I wanted to admit. The way I was panting was more than enough indication of that.

It was a *long* walk through the cold wind and snow, past what seemed too many canals and innumerable gray stone buildings, only a few of which were lightened with the pastels one saw in the tourist guides. It was close to two o'clock when I trudged into the lobby of the glass and slab-sided PetroRus building. The granite that had been reddish in the sunlight when I'd come before just appeared dull now.

The clerk at the desk in the lobby looked at me blankly.

"Minister Eschbach for Director Yusupov."

The clerk didn't understand, or pretended he didn't. I pretended not to understand him, which wasn't that hard, since I didn't, except in general terms. He said something, and I repeated who I was and who I wanted to see, and he shook his head. I stood there and repeated what I had to say.

Finally, he picked up the wireset, then smiled wanly at me and pointed to it.

I nodded and pointed upstairs.

He shrugged.

Shortly, some young and junior type emerged from the elevator and walked toward me.

"There seems to be a misunderstanding here," he began.

"I'm sure we can work it out," I said firmly. "I'm Minister Johan Eschbach of Columbia. I've had several meetings, the last one with Director Yusupov. I have some urgent information for him. Personally. I think he'd like to hear it. At the very least, he should hear that I am here."

"You are . . . the husband of the diva?" He smiled. "She was magnificent!" His face fell. "But Director Yusupov is not here."

"Then I suggest you inform either Director Kulikovsky or Prince Romanov."

He frowned.

"Just ask," I suggested.

Finally, he nodded and vanished back into the elevator.

I stood there stoically, in a semblance of a military parade rest. I really wanted to pace back and forth, but that would have given away too much.

Less than ten minutes later, the young executive or clerk reappeared, looking more than a little puzzled. "Prince Romanov has requested to see you."

This time, the elevator went all the way to the top. By

then, the tips of my ears had finally thawed out. A young woman, blonde and poised, met the elevator.

"Minister Eschbach?"

"Johan Eschbach," I confirmed.

"Prince Romanov is most interested in seeing you. Might I take your coat?"

"Oh . . . yes. A moment." I slipped the discharged calculator into my suit coat pocket, and put the pens in my breast pocket. "I hope I don't need these."

She smiled tolerantly and took the coat and the gloves I'd put in the pocket.

Pyotr Romanov's office was on the northwest corner of the PetroRus building. The prince was standing beside a most traditional and ornate Russian desk that was a good two centuries old. One wall had an ancient wooden bookcase that towered floor to ceiling, filled with leatherbound volumes, books of different ages, sizes, and shapes, not designer ones.

Through the broad green glass windows behind him, I could see the spire of the cathedral in the middle of the Peter and Paul Prison and, also, that the edges of the Neva were beginning to freeze.

"Prince Romanov, Johan Eschbach," I offered quietly.

A broad smile appeared on Romanov's angular face as I stepped forward. "Please be seated." Impossible as it seemed, his smile broadened. "You are an interesting man, Minister Eschbach. You arrive without a car and without an escort. That is the sign of a most confident man—or a most desperate one."

I laughed. "Some of each, I think. I'm very confident that we can put together something that will benefit both our countries, and strengthen Russia in dealing with Ferdinand."

"We do not need help—"

I brushed off the disclaimer. "The Russian winter and the endless number of Russian peasants are useful only against massive attacks deep into Russia. Ferdinand will never attack Russia in that way. He will nibble your borders away, and let you attack him, and that will allow him to use all of his weapons in self-defense. And when your armies are gone, destroyed to the last man, he will advance, perhaps a hundred versts, perhaps two hundred, and he will consolidate his gains, and then, in a generation, his successor will use similar tactics, just as Ferdinand's father did."

"The Imperial Rocket Corps?"

"Even if you had a warhead as deadly as Ferdinand's nuclear devices, right now you don't have the roubles and the production capacity to produce enough of the Perun or whatever its successor may be. The arrangement I suggested will buy you time and provide hard currency from Columbia. Very hard currency that does not depend on politics. That currency can be used to strengthen whatever branch of the military the tzar wishes."

"And *you* can deliver this?"

"I wouldn't be here if I couldn't." And I'd make sure that Columbian Dutch Petro didn't welsh on their end of the deal, even if it meant using every political card and dirty trick I knew.

"A most confident man."

"A man sent to put together a deal, not to make political points, or make large organizations happy."

"You are not giving this away."

"Absolutely not. I want three things."

Pyotr Romanov raised his bushy eyebrows, so at variance with his angular and almost reptilian face.

"You want? What is to prevent us from taking what you offer?"

"You might get the raw technical data, but you won't get the support that will make it easier, and you can't get the hard currency rolling in year after year without giving." I smiled. "I can deliver the raw technical data within days. That's the token of good faith. That's what you show the tzar or whoever to prove you're getting."

"Not all that data will come to PetroRus."

"No. The environmental technology data goes to the

Ministry of Interior and Director Vlasovich. You get the enhanced technology recovery equipment data—and whatever technical advice you need to make sense of it."

He nodded slowly. It wasn't a nod of agreement. "What are your three things?"

"A signed agreement granting the Alaskan north-slope oil concession to Columbian Dutch Petroleum, along with an easement and the right to build a pipeline to our Northlands. That's the first. The second is even simpler. I want Viktor Yelensov—the director in the Imperial Rocket Corps—to be at the private concert where my wife is singing at the Winter Palace tomorrow, and I want a few minutes to talk to him alone there after the concert."

That definitely got a frown, as much of puzzlement as anything else.

"And the third thing?" he asked.

"Your word of honor that you will support the concession agreement so long as royalties are paid to PetroRus or whatever Russian entity is to receive them."

Romanov laughed. "Your third condition . . . is what Kulikovsky would call naive."

I laughed for a moment, then fixed my eyes on Romanov. "I don't think so. You're part of the longest existing royal lineage in the world, at least the longest with real power. If you choose to offer your word of honor, you and I both know that if you break it, you'll be the one to live with it. I'm not asking PetroRus. I'm asking you."

Romanov's next laugh was rueful. "You know the Russian code?"

"I do."

"You are ten years older, perhaps more."

I smiled, and waited. He'd agree. He couldn't afford not to.

"You realize I will have to escort Yelensov myself."

"I thought that was possible."

"Marshal Putin will not be pleased, nor will my cousin."

"The marshal would not risk angering the tzar for such a simple request. A concert and a reception in the Winter

Palace for one of his more promising scientists and project leaders. And surely the tzar would not begrudge a few minutes."

"The marshal will complain later. So will my cousin."

"A meeting will cost neither you nor the tzar roubles. That part of the price is cheap. The marshal may complain, if he does not think it through. He also could use the increased revenues to the military."

"Why do you wish to talk to this Yelensov?"

"Let us just say I need to see him in person, and let us say that he probably doesn't want to see me."

Romanov nodded. "Pardon me . . . but you know you cannot carry weapons into the Winter Palace?"

"I brought no side arms, no weapons, even to Russia, and I won't have any on me tomorrow night. That would be stupid and more than foolish."

"That it would, and I do not think you are a foolish man, Minister Eschbach." He smiled. "I will bring this . . . Yelensov to the concert for your meeting. That is my gesture of good faith, and you will bring the entire package of technical data to me on Monday."

"Agreed."

He stood, then smiled again. "It is still snowing. Would you be offended if I offered to have my limousine return you to your embassy?"

I laughed as I also stood. "Scarcely. My driver seemed to have forgotten me. You are most gracious."

"It is my pleasure."

He must have pressed a button, because the door opened, and the blonde young woman was there, with my coat, to escort me out and down to the garage.

Romanov's limousine might have been a Volga, but it was twice the size of the embassy limousine—it seemed that way to me. It flew a flag on a jack staff set on each front fender—one flag being the Russian flag and the other the PetroRus flag, I thought.

Riding back felt better than walking through cold streets

in a city I barely knew, although I at least knew I could find my way back to the embassy.

The driver stopped in front of the main embassy door and then came around and opened it for me, bowing.

"Thank you very much."

His "You are welcome" was heavily accented, but far better than I could have done in Russian.

Sudwerth practically came running after me as I walked through the business section of the embassy toward the guards that blocked the way to the rest of the embassy. I was ready to present my passport when he charged up.

"Minister Eschbach! I didn't see the embassy car."

I turned and smiled ruefully. "Your driver didn't have a very good sense of direction. He let me off in some forsaken section of St. Petersburg, and then drove off. I haven't seen him since. Next time, I think I'll wait for Olaf—or for you."

"We'd better go upstairs," he said politely.

I shrugged.

Neither of us said anything until we were on the second floor.

"My office is here." He gestured.

I entered, then turned. "You seem upset. What's the problem?"

"The driver hasn't returned, and that was more than four hours ago."

"That's his problem," I said tiredly. "I wasn't exactly pleased with him. I never could find either the address or Yelensov, and I ended up walking to my second appointment."

"Your second appointment?"

"I finally got a meeting with Pyotr Romanov, the head of PetroRus."

Sudwerth's mouth almost opened, but he managed to keep a professional demeanor. "Congratulations."

"Not yet. It's looking favorable, but you can't count on things until they're actually completed." I shrugged. "I should know in a few days." I paused. "At least, I hope I will."

"About the driver?" Sudwerth said. "Where did he take you?"

"I have no idea. It didn't look like what I thought Tolstoi Prospekt should look, but I don't read Cyrillic. He pointed to a building and said it was the place. I got out, and he was gone. So I went up and inside. It was an office of some sort. There was a clerk who wanted to know if I was there about bills of lading. I asked for a Mister Yelensov, and everyone just shook their head. One of them said I was in the wrong part of town and gave another address. I wasn't about to try to find it, not with another meeting. So I walked until I found a canal and followed it and finally got to the PetroRus building."

"And you had your meeting and walked back, I suppose?"

"No. I had my meeting, and Prince Romanov loaned me the use of his limousine to bring me back, since my driver had obviously gotten lost. So I had to apologize for the embassy's incompetence." I looked hard at Sudwerth. "I don't like apologizing for incompetence, Colonel."

"Perhaps if Commander Madley . . ."

I just looked at him. "It's been a long day, and it would have been a waste if I'd had to rely on your man. I'm going to have dinner with my wife. Good evening, Colonel."

I smiled and walked out.

Behind his half-smile he was fuming.

Then I walked over to the ambassador's office. "Is he in?"

"Ah . . . sir."

"I'll be just a minute." I walked to the door and opened it.

Both Darwaard and Hagel looked up—almost guiltily—from where they sat on opposite sides of the ambassador's desk.

I closed the door behind me. "Gentlemen. I have a slight problem. Or rather, you do. This morning, I asked Colonel

Sudwerth to see what he could find out about someone whose name was passed to me. When I returned from a visit with an old friend, who I thought might help, the colonel had left a note and a driver." I extended the crumpled note, first to Hagel and then to his first secretary, but didn't let them have it. "The driver abandoned me in the middle of St. Petersburg, and I had to walk to my appointment with Pyotr Romanov. Scarcely a good sign, and although Prince Romanov was gracious enough to send me back in his limousine, that was not good, either. I no sooner walk into the embassy than Colonel Sudwerth is complaining that his driver is missing, as if I had anything to do with it."

I looked from one to the other.

"Sir, Minister Eschbach . . . that note . . ." Darwaard said. "That's not the colonel's writing. I get all his reports."

"Then," I said slowly, "I think you all have a much, much bigger problem. And I do not think the Speaker will be pleased."

Hagel looked like he'd been gut-punched. Darwaard appeared mildly concerned.

I smiled. "It's not my problem, except that whatever it is made it a bit harder to deal with Pyotr Romanov. What I was asked to do is hard enough without this sort of blunder. But I am most certain that you two and the colonel will find a way to resolve it." I paused, before adding, "I am most certain you will."

"Ah . . . yes, Minister Eschbach," Hagel said slowly.

Neither said another word as I left, but after I heard the door close, before I stepped away, I could hear the ambassador's voice, and it wasn't gentle, although I couldn't make out the specific words.

Colonel Sudwerth stood by the desk of the ambassador's secretary.

"I'd wait a few minutes if I were you, Colonel," I suggested.

"I appreciate the advice, Minister Eschbach." Beneath

the polite tone, there was a chill colder than all the snow still falling outside.

I kept smiling as I walked toward the elevator that would take me upstairs.

34

L LYSETTE AND I had dinner in the embassy dining area—early and alone at one of the smaller tables—and I told her exactly what I'd told the colonel and the ambassador. From my expressions and gestures, she understood that there was much more, and that there wasn't anything to be said where we were. She was also worried.

So was I, but I had a very good idea that nothing would happen—not until after Saturday night, when all bets were off.

Even with all the tension, I did fall asleep fairly soon. That was what walking around St. Petersburg in the cold had done for me. I just didn't sleep that late.

Llysette did. So I was in the small kitchen a little after sunrise the next morning, suffering through tea that was too strong and too bitter . . . and going through the news summaries, and the *Times* of London. The Speaker had issued a statement saying that the Caribbean was open to all merchant shipping of any registry and invited Emperor Ferdinand to follow his lead. There had been no response from Vienna, and probably wouldn't be. Complaining about the Caribbean had just been an excuse for Ferdinand to extend Austrian control over another area of the globe, and little short of war would see an Austrian back-down there.

The quarters bell chimed. Even as I rose to get it before it rang again, I wondered who it could be so early on a Saturday morning.

Both Colonel Sudwerth and Commander Madley were standing outside in working undress blues. They looked most unhappy.

I opened the door.

"Colonel, Commander . . ." I just looked from one to the other.

"Might we come in, Minister?" asked Madley.

"Certainly, but I'd ask you to speak quietly. Llysette is still sleeping, and she has to perform tonight."

"Of course." That was the commander.

Sudwerth just nodded.

We sat on three adjoining chairs in the salon, and I waited for one of them to speak.

Finally, Sudwerth cleared his throat. "Your driver? . . ."

"Olaf?" I didn't have to act puzzled on that.

"No . . . Corporal Bromwood."

"Colonel . . . if you're talking about the man who drove me to the wrong place yesterday, he wasn't my driver. He was your driver. Now . . . what's the problem?"

"The Russians are charging the driver with murder."

"Murder? What did he do? Go off and try a burglary or break into some woman's house?"

"No."

I sighed. "Why don't you tell me what happened? I told you about my problems with the corporal."

"The embassy car was found on a side street in a bad district in St. Petersburg yesterday around noon."

"And you didn't find out about it until now?" I let my voice rise and sound half incredulous, half annoyed.

"We didn't find that out until after eight o'clock last night. The embassy got a call saying that one of our soldiers had been injured and was in the St. Petersburg hospital in serious condition. Captain Austin went to the hospital. He found a guard posted at the door to Bromwood's room, but no one would tell him why."

I waited.

"This morning," Sudwerth continued, "just about a half hour ago, we received a visitor from the Ohkrana. He informed me that Bromwood had murdered three Russians. They said the ballistics tests say that his forty-five killed the three men." Sudwerth snorted. "There's a problem with that. He's got a shattered knee and a broken wrist. He's still in shock and can't remember anything. If he killed the three, how could he have done it in that condition?"

"They attacked him, and he probably fired at them after he realized they were serious." I frowned. "It could be that there were several more attackers, and they got to him before he could shoot any more of them. It could be any number of things," I pointed out.

"One of his attackers had a crushed throat. He probably would have died of suffocation if he hadn't been shot."

"And?" I asked.

"You were the last person we know that saw Bromwood." Sudwerth was sounding far less deferential. Far less.

I nodded. "I've told you what I know. Bromwood left me somewhere I couldn't possibly recognize and then drove off. All the signs were in Cyrillic, and, from what I could tell, it wasn't anywhere near where I was supposed to be. I'm standing in the snow, in the middle of St. Petersburg, wondering where I am and where you are, and where your driver's gone. Whatever it is, I'm sorry the driver got mixed up in it, but . . ." I spread my hands helplessly. "I haven't any idea of what I can add to this mess. Your driver made a mess of my day, and put me in not the best of lights with PetroRus, and now he's getting the embassy into trouble at a time when what I'm trying to work out is at a most delicate stage."

"I'm trying to find out what happened, Minister Eschbach."

I sighed loudly. "Colonel. I have told you three times

what happened. *Your* driver left me in the lurch. I couldn't find the address, and I had to walk to my second appointment. Prince Romanov was well aware that I *walked* to his office. I wouldn't have wished this on anyone, but I have to tell you that I wasn't exactly pleased, and if the way he handled me was any indication, I really can't say I'm surprised."

"You don't sound terribly sympathetic."

I took a long deep breath. "Your driver left me in a desolate part of St. Petersburg, where I was supposed to meet you. You didn't show up, and the driver left me to fend for myself. Now you're acting as though it's my fault that the man didn't do his job and got into trouble. I'm sorry he's in trouble with the Russians. I wouldn't wish that on any innocent person, but if he'd escorted me to the right place, it's clear none of this would have happened." I fixed very cold eyes on Sudwerth. "If you'd been there, this wouldn't have happened. I didn't create this mess. If anyone's responsible for it, you are."

He stepped back.

"Maybe you have a problem with your military personnel, Colonel. Maybe you should look into that before arriving at my door ready to blame me."

"Is that all you have to say?" He was still clearly angry.

"No." I stood up and glared at the colonel. "I have one other thing to say. When matters go wrong at the bottom, there's usually a problem at the top. I suggest you look into that most thoroughly before you imply blame to someone who's been in Russia for exactly four days." I looked at Madley. "Commander, I need to talk to you." Then I turned my eyes back on Sudwerth. "Good day, Colonel. I suggest you look elsewhere for the cause of your problems."

Sudwerth was furious, which was exactly the way I wanted him. He looked at Madley as if to say something.

"Commander Madley was detailed by the Minister of Defense to work for me, Colonel. I suggest you remember that, as well." I gestured toward the foyer. "Good day, Colonel."

Madley stood there, half dazed, if not in outright shock, long after the door had closed behind a departing Sudwerth. Acting the situation hadn't been that hard, because Sudwerth had been the reason for the mess.

Madley wiped his forehead. "Sir . . ."

"You're wondering why I was so hard on the colonel and worried that I've put you in an impossible position." I laughed. "If I hadn't done that, you'd be in an even worse position."

"I can't say I understand, sir."

"You will. Just think about this. Sudwerth arranged the meeting I was supposed to go to; his driver relieved Olaf. If you look into it, I suspect you'll find Olaf was detained or sent on an errand."

I extended a piece of paper. "I was given this. Either Sudwerth wrote it or his driver forged it or someone else forged it who knew I was tracking Yelensov. At that moment, there were exactly three people in the embassy besides me who knew—you, Christian, and the colonel. Did you tell anyone?"

"No, sir."

"Did Christian?"

"He couldn't have, not for a while, because I helped him go through the records. We were together for at least an hour."

"That leaves the colonel, Commander, because I had that note less than an hour after I told you two." I paused. "Analysis will show it's not my writing. If Sudwerth sent me on a wild hare chase . . . that's not exactly good. If he didn't, then it shows that his detachment isn't what it should be. Either way . . ."

"That's a pretty serious accusation, sir."

I sighed. "Commander . . . just ask yourself two questions. Why am I here, and why are you here?"

After a minute, his eyes dropped. "This isn't a good situation."

"If it were, would you have been detailed to answer to my orders?"

"Probably not, sir."

"There's nothing you can do right now, Commander, except keep an eye on the colonel and keep an accurate record of what happens."

"Yes, sir."

After he left, and the door closed a second time, Llysette slipped out from the bedchamber into the salon. She looked at me. "You have troubles, *mon cher*."

"Colonel Sudwerth's driver—the one who left me on my own—has been charged with murder by the Russians. The good colonel thinks I had something to do with it. He doesn't seem to understand that he and the driver caused the problems, not me."

"*Toujours,* that is the way of those like him. They would blame everyone but themselves."

"He's more than a little angry, and I worry about what he might do."

"You will do what is necessary, *n'est-ce-pas?*"

"We each have our jobs to do." I smiled. "What will you wear tonight?"

"The other recital gown."

"You thought something like this might happen. Performing for the tzar, I mean."

"*Non.* It could happen. That I knew, but to count on it, *non.*"

"After you get dressed, we need to eat."

"After you offer me tea, *mon cher,* I will dress." She arched her eyebrows.

I laughed for a moment before I hugged her, trying not to think about what would happen after her performance.

35

I WAS MORE than a little nervous going to the Winter Palace on Saturday night. It had been made clear that Llysette's performance was for the imperial family and friends, not for dignitaries. The ambassador was not invited, nor was Deputy Minister Drummond Kent. There were only four of us in the embassy limousine—Terese, Llysette, Commander Madley, and me. I'd insisted on the commander as both an aide for us and as a translator, and the Russians had apparently agreed.

"This is really a command performance," Terese said. "I wish I had a chance to practice with the instrument. I don't know how it will even feel. It's nerve-wracking enough to play for an imperial tzar, without even knowing the piano."

"That's why the huge fees," I said dryly. I shifted my weight. The pen projector with its new battery, and the spares inside my jacket, felt huge, and yet simultaneously, I felt as though I were about to walk into a battle unarmed.

The driver turned off the Palace Embankment and eased the limousine through the left hand archway in the lower level of the Winter Palace, the only one whose iron gates were brightly lighted. Once inside the huge courtyard, the limousine pulled up under a covered portico, where footmen uniformed in gray with green piping opened the doors.

Once inside, we walked through a large mesh arch, a detector of some sort, and Llysette had to open her metallic purse, apparently because the metal sequins blocked the scanners. Llysette looked disconcerted when the attendant motioned for her to open the purse, but there wasn't much in the velvet-lined purse—just a compact, a lipstick, a folding brush, and similar items.

Partway down the corridor were three women in identical dark blue velvet dresses. One stepped forward and said something.

"She wants to take your coats," explained the commander.

We surrendered our coats, and then another functionary, this one in gray and gold, appeared to escort us, taking us up a huge staircase and then back through what seemed endless halls, most of them with parquet floors of intricate and original designs that changed from hall to hall.

The concert hall was on the second level of the Winter Palace, although they called it the first floor in the European tradition. I also wouldn't have called the room a concert hall. There was a small raised built-in dais against one wall; it looked to be an elongated hexagon lifted only a foot above the mixed and polished woods that comprised the elaborate parquet floor of the rest of the space. The walls were white, with intricate moldings, including what I would have called a ledge molding all the way around the hall about fifteen feet off the floor. The ceiling rose at least another ten feet above that. Etched glass doors were set at intervals on two sides of the hall.

There were close to two hundred seats set out in an arc, and each seat was an armless upholstered wooden chair—except for the larger throne-like upholstered armchairs set apart from the others just in front of the wall opposite the performing dais.

Somewhere around fifty people, all in formal attire,

stood in the open spaces around the chairs, and the low buzz of conversation ebbed and flowed.

I looked for the four chairs to the left and in front of the tzar's chair. That was where the four of us were to sit.

As we sat down, more people appeared in the room, until it was almost full. Then, another set of doors opened, and everyone stood. So did we. The tzar and the tzarina entered, preceded by three children, a girl and two boys, all roughly between nine and twelve, I would have guessed.

When the tzar was seated, everyone else sat, and so did we.

Then a functionary in a gold and green uniform stepped out and looked toward us. Terese and Llysette rose and stepped onto the low dais. Terese did take a few moments to run through a scale or two and to get a feel for the piano.

As at the cultural exchange concert, Llysette began with Rimsky-Korsakov's *Nightingale,* her voice soaring and filling the hall, yet with a warmth and a delicacy that was more obvious in the smaller space.

That got sighs, before the applause. Next came the three Tchaikovsky pieces, with more nods, sighs, and greater applause, especially for the Russian version of "Last Night." Then she did "The Lilacs" before going to her French heritage with Debussy's "Air de Lia."

That's where she added another French piece, "Air des bijoux," Marguerite's "jewel song" from Gounod's *Faust,* before doing the Rachmaninov *Vocalise.* Even though it was a vocalise, with no actual words, with Llysette's interpretation and feeling it sounded angelic, powerful, beautiful—and very Russian.

There was a respectful moment of silence after the *Vocalise,* before enthusiastic applause.

Llysette gestured to Terese, conveying that there would be another song, and murmurs passed around the room for a moment.

They finished with Mozart's "Alleluia," which, of

course, was in Latin, and the applause was even greater.
There were enough cries of something, which Commander
Madley translated as "encore" for me, that she sang the
Gershwin "Summertime" as the encore. They wanted
more, and after a moment, she and Terese turned to each
other and spoke. Then Llysette did the "Adieu, forêt" aria
from Tchaikovsky's *Orleanskaya Deva,* which I'd been
told meant "Maid of Orleans." The tzarina liked that, and
there was more applause, but Llysette and Terese just
smiled and bowed.

Before they could leave the dais, the tzar beckoned, and
a functionary in a gold and green uniform stepped forward,
carrying a moderately large black lacquered box and a
smaller box.

The smaller box was tendered to Terese.

"You are most skilled, madame, and allowed a true talent to flower for us all." The tzar smiled. "That too is
talent, and to be rewarded."

Terese inclined her head, but the tzar had already turned
to Llysette, as the functionary extended the larger lacquer
box to her.

"This was painted by the younger Golovin, years ago.
He did not paint many. Our other gifts are inside. For both
of you." The tzar smiled, and so did the tzarina. "You were
even more magnificent tonight than the other night. Your
power is evident at the Mariinsky, but here your warmth
is more obvious. The children will remember this for many
years."

Even from where I sat, the nod made it clear that Llysette was dismissed. She curtsied, as did Terese, and then
they bowed and moved sideways, off the dais and back
before their seats next to me. There was the faintest sigh
of relief from somewhere, as though someone had worried
the two women might turn their backs on the tzar.

The tzar stood, as did the tzarina, and, after a moment,
everyone else, as the immediate ruling family stepped toward the doors through which they had entered.

Llysette eased to my shoulder.

"Minister Eschbach?" The angular face of Pyotr Romanov was above my shoulder.

"I'll only be a few minutes." That was what I hoped, and what I told Llysette. "You stay with the ladies, Commander."

Commander Madley frowned momentarily, then nodded. "Yes, sir."

I followed the prince—but not all that far—only a few yards through a foyer and into another room. On the way, I palmed the pen projector.

"This is the Malachite Room," explained the angular Romanov. "It used to be a favorite of the tzarinas, years ago, but has fallen into less favor as being too ornate."

I glanced around, noting the elaborate opulence, with the carvings that festooned every molding, and vases and paintings, and the malachite green that seemed everywhere. A thin-shouldered but tall man rose from one of the settees as we neared. His pale face showed every sign of his not wishing to be there, and his eyes burned.

I just smiled.

"Viktor . . . this is Minister Eschbach. He very much wanted a few words with you." Pyotr Romanov bowed. "I will rejoin you both in a few minutes."

I knew Yelensov had to speak English, however badly, and it might make matters easier, but I didn't say anything until the prince vanished. "Good evening, Director Yelensov. I did want to meet you face-to-face."

"You have. Now I will go." His English was heavily accented but understandable.

"I don't think so."

"This is outrageous. I have work to do."

"I'm sure you do, but not on a Saturday night. How close are you to using a fusion reaction to powering a one-time zombification projection?"

Yelensov stared at me. "Prince Romanov said you were an environmental minister."

"What you're trying to do has environmental impacts, don't you think? People are part of the environment."

"You Columbians. Why are you here?"

"Isn't it obvious? Colonel Sudwerth is worried you won't be able to complete the job. They're putting pressure on him for results, and if anyone in Congress finds out . . ." I shrugged.

"You won't leave St. Petersburg." His voice almost hissed.

"Why don't we worry about that later?"

Yelensov laughed, very softly, menacingly.

I was glad I'd already palmed the pen projector. I just hoped I'd read the man right. "So you've actually tried combining de-ghosting boosted by an atomic device, and it didn't work. What makes you think it ever will?" I asked conversationally.

Yelensov's face narrowed.

"It's an interesting proposition," I said carefully. "But conceiving of it and putting it into practice are two different matters."

"Anything that can be conceived can be developed. Is that not the goal of science?"

Even through the heavy accent, I could hear the archness of his tone of voice.

"And you and your team need to put science in the service of the motherland to keep Ferdinand at bay?" I asked.

"I need no team."

"You need no team, for what, boosting the effect across twenty versts? When all you can do is twenty yards?"

"Twenty versts?"

He still hadn't said anything. So I prodded again. "What good will that do with an impact of only twenty versts across? You couldn't build enough rockets, and Ferdinand has all his headquarters shielded. Anything that will block nuclear radiation will be more than enough to block your little gadget—if you can even build it."

"Twenty versts? One can do that from a tower. Why not two hundred versts?" His hand slipped toward the slit pocket in his jacket and the bulge beneath.

Two hundred versts? I tried not to wince, even as I unpalmed the pen and triggered it.

Yelensov just looked at me blankly as I rummaged through his coat pockets. I was right, except his gadget looked more like a miniature pistol with twin antennas. I pointed it at the floor and discharged it—for a long time—then bent one of the projection antennas.

"Hold this . . . it discharged accidentally when you tried to point it at me."

I put a fresh battery in my own pen, thought about replacing it in my pocket, but instead slipped it up inside my shirt cuff, where I could let it slide into my hand quickly.

I backed away.

Of course, there were guards at the door to the Malachite Room, in the foyer between the room and the concert hall, which although yards away might as well have been versts. Military guards, and they had pistols pointed at me. Beside them was a broad-shouldered and smiling officer, wearing the insignia of the Imperial Rocket Corps.

"You were waiting for me, Major?"

"Colonel . . . Colonel Kerachev . . ."

"I beg your pardon." I turned over my open hands to suggest I wasn't carrying anything in them.

"It's almost a pity you carry no weapons," the colonel said. "That would have made it far easier."

They'd obviously seen Yelensov still standing when I'd opened the door, and hadn't drawn the right conclusion—yet. But it might not be long.

"If I ran, it might be hard to explain shooting me in the back, especially since I was invited to the Winter Palace, and especially with the concert hall not that far away."

"Those few left would not dare move if they heard shots from here. Not with the tzar already safe in his private quarters. Why, his private musicians are probably already playing military marches, or he is listening to a disk of them. The tzar likes his music very loud."

I was far from an expert on Russian physiognomy, but I didn't believe him. Not totally.

"Where are we going?"

"Does it matter?"

"I suppose your friends don't speak English."

"How perceptive of you."

I triggered the pen, keeping it half palmed. His face blanked, and then he crumpled. I still didn't understand why some people went down, and others just stood there blankly. Strength or weakness of soul and spirit?

The soldiers looked at him, and I swept them with the last fragments of the charge.

They shook their heads, blinking, as if they couldn't see. I probably fumbled, but I managed to open the pen and put in another battery before giving them another jolt. One stood, and one went down.

There I was, just outside the Malachite Room, once a favorite of one of the earlier tzarinas, with three bodies who would wake up zombies, and two standing around. I hoped I didn't have to explain too much or too long, but even if I didn't make it out of the palace, I'd done Harlaan's dirty work and at least delayed a military and ecological nightmare.

I pointed to the door to the Malachite Room. The soldier began to walk.

In the end, I left four zombies in the Malachite Room and walked back through the foyer to the concert hall, nodding at the guards by the door as I stepped back inside. I had one of the military side arms in the inside pocket of my formal vest. That was a risk, but not great compared to the ones I'd already taken.

The room was almost empty, although Llysette was talking to a girl who appeared to be about ten.

Pyotr Romanov eased toward me. "Are you satisfied?"

I motioned for him to follow me a bit away into a corner of the almost-deserted concert hall. "Yelensov is a zombie, a soulless man. He was carrying some sort of device. Some soldiers followed us into the room. He told me to get away.

I did. He did something, and four of them are without spirits."

Romanov started to flush. "You . . ."

I glared at him. "Yelensov was going to double-cross you. He wanted the oil concession to go to AmeriSun. He was getting solid rocket propellant formulas from them through the Putilov connection. They wanted the oil concession." I held up a hand. "The Imperial Rocket Corps has those formulae already. What's done is done. You'll get the oil concession, and a lot more in royalties from Columbian Dutch. No one from Columbia will say a thing."

The anger in his face was slowly replaced by a combination of relief and amusement. "What was the device that turned men into zombies?"

"I don't know how he got it." That was technically true. I had my ideas, but I didn't *know*. "I do know that Ferdinand is supposed to have something like that. It might have some military use, and I'd guess that Yelensov's staff knows all about it, but you'd know how to handle that far better than I. Yelensov was still holding it when I left. I didn't want anything to do with it."

"I should explain this?"

"Don't explain anything. Say that Yelensov wanted to double-cross you, and that Russia would have suffered because AmeriSun can't pay the same amount of royalties." I smiled. "Unless I've read things very wrong, you need both that technology and that hard currency far more than you need a superweapon that will only result in more disaster to Russia than anyone else."

He started to protest, studied my face, and gave me a resigned look. "You will ensure all goes as you said."

"I will."

"You and your diva had best leave with your ambassador, now. I would also recommend that you not leave the embassy until your aircraft takes you back to Columbia."

As Prince Romanov and Commander Madley escorted

us back to the courtyard and the waiting embassy limousine, I knew I'd be more than happy to get aboard the big Curtiss, but that wasn't until Monday, at the earliest, or so I'd been told—if I could survive until Monday.

I watched closely as the driver guided the limousine back though the iron gates, but they didn't close, and no one came running after us or started shooting. I took a slow and silent deep breath.

After that, I didn't say all that much in the limousine, except to keep congratulating Terese and Llysette.

"You see . . . the tzar was pleased. You could tell it from his face, and even the tzarina smiled." I paused. "Who was the girl you were talking to?"

"She was the daughter of one of the grand dukes," explained Commander Madley.

"She wanted to know if she was too old to begin to sing." Llysette laughed. "I asked her if she could play the piano." She adjusted the metallic black purse that seemed heavier than it looked.

"She sat down and played part of a concerto some of my college students have trouble with," added Terese.

"At her age, if she has the voice . . ." I began.

Llysette nodded. "*Mais,* the voice . . . who can tell?"

At that point, the limousine swung past the sentries and into the courtyard of the embassy. I struggled out and held the door for the ladies.

"Will you be needing me more tonight, sir?" asked the commander.

"Not that I know of."

"Tomorrow?"

"I'd doubt it," I answered. "I expect I won't hear from PetroRus or the Ministry of Interior until Monday. If you're not tied up sightseeing, you might check tomorrow afternoon. I think Llysette and I will try to unwind."

At that point, I really wished we had a bottle of wine, and I know Llysette did, but I hadn't thought about that. Again, I'd been too wrapped up in my project to think about her need to unwind. She'd had some time to do that

at the reception after the concert, but the private recital at
the Winter Palace had been strange, to say the least. In a
way, I'd expected a reception—or something—but maybe
there had been, and we were the hired help and not invited
into such exalted circles.

The commander did escort us all up to our rooms, then
bowed and departed. I checked the quarters quickly before
he left, but no one was there. Then Llysette and I stood
by the piano where she'd set the black lacquer box.

I wondered about opening the box, but somehow, with
the exquisite scene upon it, and the tzar's reference to Golovin, I doubted that it would be explosive. Still, since it
had no lock, I found a coat hanger and made a hook and
padded it.

"Johan . . . this, it is necessary?"

"Probably not . . ." I grunted as I eased up the cover,
which was no chore, so easily did it open. The grunts were
partly for effect, and partly because I was doing it in a
way so as not to scratch the finish.

There were two items in the box—an envelope and a
narrow velvet box. Llysette opened the velvet box first. It
contained a heart-shaped emerald pendant on what seemed
to be a platinum rope-style chain. The emerald was easily
ten carats in size.

We both swallowed, looking at a jewel that was probably worth more than all we owned and might ever own.

There was a *click* from the foyer, and we both turned
as Colonel Sudwerth appeared, wearing not his undress
uniform but a black flight suit.

"Greetings, most honored Minister Eschbach." Sudwerth's voice was jovial as he walked through the small
entry foyer and into the salon. "Pardon my walking in, but
I knocked, and the door was ajar."

It hadn't been.

At the sound of Sudwerth's voice, Llysette set down the
velvet jewel box on the Haaren and clutched the black
metallic handbag that was both larger than the usual evening bag she carried for performances and also didn't quite

match the black and silvered green performing gown.

"Good evening, Colonel. How can we help you?"

"You're a bungling idiot, Eschbach."

No fancy titles, now.

"Oh?"

"I could report you straight to the Okhrana . . . for murdering Yelensov."

"Murder? I'm not aware that I murdered anyone."

"You turned him into a zombie—like you did Corporal Bromwood."

"I don't recall seeing you at the Winter Palace, Colonel."

He just smirked before going on. "All you think about is how pure you can make things and how you can make money for the merchant bankers of Asten and New Amsterdam. The rest of us have more important things to worry about. Things like the survival of Columbia. . . ."

"I worry about it, too, Colonel," I pointed out. "And like you, I've fought for her."

"I don't understand you," he said. "What did you do to Yelensov?"

"I didn't do anything. Or rather, I stopped him from doing something to me. He pulled out a gadget, except I thought it was a gun. It went off, but it had antennas, and it stunned him. I decided to leave him with the gadget and slip away. But it was really a setup, because there were some elite Rocket Corps soldiers and a colonel waiting for me . . . but, then, you knew all about it. You helped set it up."

"Why would I do anything like that?"

The question was a dead giveaway.

"Because you're the conduit between the Columbian Air Corps zombie project, or whatever they call it, and the Imperial Rocket Corps." I really didn't want to use the pen projector on Sudwerth. That would have been extremely hard to explain, even if I could have gotten it out of my pocket without his noticing it. Even if I could have, it was discharged, and I had no more batteries nearby.

"You're both traitors." The gun that appeared in his hand was on me, but his eyes darted back and forth between Llysette and me.

"You're part of the conspiracy that turned zombification and de-ghosting technology over to the Russians—not to mention the AmeriSun solid rocket fuel—and we're traitors? Could you explain that, Colonel?"

"We can't stop Ferdinand by ourselves, Eschbach. Look at the failures, year after year. Time after time. You're here, practically begging the tzar for the right to purchase his oil. That's strength? That's a foreign policy?"

"And you wanted to give the Russians rocket technology and spur them into developing a nuclear-powered zombie-bomb? So that they could turn sections of Europe into lands populated only by zombies? And what would Ferdinand do then? He'd send his heavy bombers eastward and turn all of Russia east of the Urals into black glass. Is that the world you want to live in? Or leave to your children?"

"Better that than the world you'd leave, with everything under Ferdinand's thumb, with work camps everywhere."

My zombie pen was discharged and out of batteries, even if I could have reached it, and the Russian side arm was inside my vest. In short . . . I was out of luck. I'd anticipated that Sudwerth would do something stupid, but I hadn't thought he'd actually break into our quarters in the embassy right after Llysette's performance in the Winter Palace. So he was smarter about that than I was, and I had just come up against the fact that I was getting too old for the game in which I'd once excelled.

"Work camps . . ." Llysette swayed, and then crumpled.

I started toward her.

"Don't move, Eschbach. It's better this way. I'll get her next. You don't think Yelensov was the only one with a 'gadget,' did you. Poor woman, couldn't stand the shock of an Austrian assassin killing her husband." He raised the side arm, and I realized that it wasn't any official Columbian issue, but smaller.

That made sense, too.

I waited until he started to squeeze, then lurched sideways, to his right.

I didn't hear the first report, but I felt like a sledgehammer had smashed into my chest. The second shot ripped into my left arm, half spinning me.

There was a third report, a sharper *crack*, followed by a fourth and a fifth, but they came nowhere near me.

I blinked, finding myself half on my knees, half against one of the salon chairs, trying to ignore the blazing in my left arm, and the dull aching from the impact of the first shot against the vest liner. I fumbled to pull the Russian sidearm out from inside my vest. Sudwerth looked at the splotches of darkness on his chest and, with shaking hands, slowly turned his weapon toward Llysette, who had fired from the floor.

I finally fumbled out the Russian side arm, more quickly than it seemed, aimed it, and squeezed. It did go off, and Sudwerth went down, and he wasn't going to get up. He might not have, anyway, from what Llysette had done, but I'd wanted to be sure he didn't fire at her. That was the least I could do to atone for my stupidity.

I wasn't sure I was going to get up, either, as stars flashed in front of my eyes.

I was only out for a few minutes, I thought. But I was stretched out on one of the love seats, Llysette bending over me. Again, as once years before, she had bound my arm, and I could see Commander Madley standing behind her.

"Greetings, Commander," I croaked, half wondering how he'd gotten there so quickly.

"Hush," Llysette said. "The embassy doctor, he is coming."

Madley looked at my arm. "He shot you. Sudwerth shot you."

"He tried. It can't be that bad, or I wouldn't be here."

"You've lost some blood and then some," Madley replied. "Doctor Emsworth will be right here. He said not to move you." After a moment, he asked, "Colonel Sudwerth?"

"The good colonel saved our lives, I think, by stepping in front of an Austrian assassin. The assassin escaped—regrettably. I don't know that it should be made public, but we should report the facts . . . and let his superiors determine what kind of commendation he should receive."

"The colonel, he tried to kill Johan. He was a traitor," Llysette said. "But . . . it would not be good to tell the world. He said an assassin was here to kill us. The colonel—he stepped in front of the bullets to save me."

Weak and dizzy as I was, I could see the cold strength in her eyes.

So did Madley. He took a step backward. "The guns . . . they have prints . . ."

"They do not," Llysette replied. "The assassins wore gloves. They will find no prints." She looked at me. "Nor anything else."

I hadn't seen her wipe the guns, but I didn't doubt it. I also got the message about Sudwerth's "gadget."

Llysette and Madley were both right about one thing. I did need help. There were stars flashing in front of my eyes. Then I couldn't see anything.

36

THE DOCTOR, LLYSETTE, and Commander Madley wouldn't let me meet with Pyotr Romanov until Tuesday, more than two full days later, although they said he could have come to see me.

What I had to say didn't belong inside the embassy, but I did ask for an armed guard from the embassy to escort me to and from PetroRus, and Commander Madley carried the case with all of the data and techniques I'd promised. The armed guard wouldn't have stopped the Imperial Rocket Corps, but it would have been far too embarrassing for anyone to try to overpower a detachment of Columbian marines—and it would have raised questions I knew no one wanted reopened.

So, with my arm still in a sling, mainly because it was going to take a while for tissue and muscles to heal, I walked into the PetroRus building, flanked by a Republic Naval Air Corps lieutenant commander and four Republic marines.

This time no one asked any embarrassing questions, and Commander Madley and I were escorted to the elevator and whisked to the top floor.

Pyotr Romanov and Serge Yusupov both were waiting in the foyer on the top floor.

Pyotr Romanov looked at the arm that was in a sling.

"I'll explain . . . in a moment. It's why I'm a day late." I turned to Madley. "Commander, if you'd open the case and give the documents inside to Prince Romanov."

Madley did.

Interestingly, Romanov didn't hand them to Yusupov, but held on to them and looked at me. "We need a few minutes, do we not, Minister Eschbach?"

"We do."

"Serge will provide some background to the commander while we talk."

So I followed the prince back to the ornate office that overlooked a gray St. Petersburg, although the temperature had risen to around freezing.

After he closed the door and we sat down, he nodded toward my arm. "You were well when you left the Winter Palace."

"I was." I gave a rueful smile. "The palace was safer than the embassy. It appears as though an Austrian agent, possibly an intermediary, penetrated our embassy. The agent was determined to stop the oil agreement, because the Austrians see that as a Columbian move to strengthen Russia. He thought he could do so by shooting me."

"It is an interesting story, Minister Eschbach."

"It's not only interesting, but the way it was reported." I smiled. "I'm ready to have that agreement signed today."

"These things take time," the prince temporized.

"I was shot. A senior colonel was shot protecting me. The colonel was killed with either a luger or a Russian Maxim belonging to a zombie who was once a senior project manager for a most dubious adventure by the Imperial Rocket Corps."

"It is said that such an 'adventure' would restore greatness to Russia."

"There's great doubt that it will ever work." I laughed, bitterly, ignoring what that did to my chest, upper arm, and shoulder. "Even if it did work, it would guarantee that all inhabited areas of Russia east of the Urals would be turned into black glass by Ferdinand's heavy bombers. The Swedes would immediately move into all areas that weren't radioactive, and Russia would be back in the tenth century so far as sovereignty happened to be concerned."

"Oh . . ."

"Prince Romanov . . . I don't play games. The Putilov people sold the Rocket Corps and the tzar a bill of phony goods. I don't deny that the basic de-ghosting technology exists. Ferdinand already has it, and, if Russia uses it to build mobile defensive projectors, you can certainly ensure that you can't be invaded—not without even greater costs than those created by the Russian winter."

His face remained impassive.

"Now . . ." I emphasized. "You—or Russia—have gotten some good defensive technology, and you got it for next to nothing. You've just gotten the basis for oil recovery technology that cost others hundreds of millions, if not billions. I've just saved you from a worldwide disaster, and it's time for a gesture in return."

"You think I can provide such?" The eyebrows waggled.

"Of course. You had your doubts about Yelensov and his projects from the beginning. You just didn't have the clout or the position to stop him. Neither did the Imperial Air Corps. Otherwise, you wouldn't have made sure that Yelensov came to the Winter Palace. If the tzar looked into that closely . . . at the very least, you might not be quite so favored. He may even have had some doubts, but wanted someone else to act." I smiled. "So you recommend the Columbian Dutch Petro concession and get it signed because it offers more cash—hard dollars—and that will strengthen your position. And Russia."

"Putilov gets nothing?"

"They got the solid fuel for your next-stage Perun, and Fyodor Ilyinsky gets to keep his job and his head. That's fair, I think."

"Why should I give away Russian oil?"

I had the feeling we were backtracking, but you never know. "Look. You could do it as a joint venture, but joint venture means joint investment of capital and equipment, which you don't have. Nor do you have the shipping and other means to transport anything you did produce. You really can't safely bring in anyone besides Columbia, and, besides, only the Austrians have the capital to do it right, and Columbia would have some strong concerns there. I don't think the tzar would exactly want to cut a deal with the Austrians. So your options are fairly simple. Sit on it, and get no hard currency and no enhanced oil recovery technology and no environmental assistance and technology. Give the concession to AmeriSun, and get less money, and no enhanced oil recovery technology and no environmental technology. Believe me, after already finding out that the information was leaked to Putilov, the Columbian government will block anything involving AmeriSun. So you give the concession to Columbian Dutch Petro and get everything, plus a happier tzar and a much happier Columbia."

"You do not mention Russian interests."

"I just have. But if you're talking about the Imperial Rocket Corps, Marshal Putin is going to be much happier if nothing gets mentioned, and it won't be by Columbia if this works out. And Yelensov's staff can figure out how to build ground-based de-ghosting projectors and come out looking fine." I frowned. "I don't see that you have a problem . . . unless you make one."

"The tzar said he wished you were Russian. It is better you are not. No Russian would do as you have." Romanov shook his head. "You will have your agreement."

I wasn't sure. I felt like I'd renegotiated the agreement twice, if not more, and until the money was in the bank, or until the concession agreement was signed and publicized worldwide, I wouldn't count on it. "This afternoon?"

"This afternoon. From what I have seen and heard of you, Minister Eschbach, you will not stop until you complete your mission, or until you are dead. It would be most embarrassing to have you die, especially now, and . . . as you have pointed out, it is a most beneficial agreement for both sides." The prince offered a smile less reptilian as he stood. "And your wife is the most outstanding diva of the generation."

I rose as well, almost gracefully, and we walked back out to the foyer where the commander and Serge Yusupov waited.

Once I had a signed agreement, six volumes of environmental technology—the ones in Russian—were going directly to Director Vlasovich. If Vlasovich got a second set from PetroRus, he certainly wouldn't mention that he'd already received a set. That way, I could be sure Vlasovich had a chance of cleaning up the Dnepyr . . . as well as making sure I kept my word.

37

I N THE GRAY mid-morning on Wednesday, Llysette and
I watched as two marines loaded our luggage into the
embassy limousine. Commander Madley stood beside us
in the rear courtyard of the embassy that had once been a
world-class hotel, and was yet haunted with ghosts. I was
thankful Colonel Sudwerth wasn't one of them. Perhaps
that was because he'd been so arrogant he hadn't believed
he was dying, even as he was.

"How do you feel about being detailed to replace Colonel Sudwerth for a while?" I asked the sober-faced officer.

"It wasn't something I planned, sir." A crooked smile
crossed Madley's face. "It's probably better this way. Also,
everyone knows I worked with you, and that association
doesn't hurt. Everyone knows that you have a way of getting things done."

I wondered about that.

"You were skeptical of the colonel for a while," I said.
"You didn't do anything."

Madley offered an embarrassed smile. "Minister Holmbek told me to stand back unless your life was in danger,
sir. He said you had . . . a unique . . . way of operating."

"I appreciate his confidence. Any more uniqueness, and I'd have been dead." I glanced toward the embassy, then lowered my voice. "As for the first secretary . . . you know what I think . . . I'm sure."

"Yes, sir, and I wouldn't go against your judgments."

I hoped Madley could do something about Darwaard, who might well have been more guilty than Sudwerth, but there was no proof I knew of, and Darwaard had certainly been skillful enough to avoid me for days without seeming to do so. Sometimes, the villains do get away with it—at least for a time.

The doors to the private side of the embassy opened, and the ambassador stepped out and walked toward us. Smiling broadly, Ambassador Hagel bowed to Llysette. "Your concert was magnificent. Annette and I will remember it forever."

His smile was strained as he turned to me. "Minister Eschbach . . . I trust you will have a safe flight home and that you'll be fully recovered before long."

"Thank you, Ambassador," I replied. "I'm sure that you'll have no trouble with the implementation of the petroleum concession, now that the tzar, PetroRus, and the Interior Ministries have approved it, and I'm certain that you'll see that the first secretary agrees that it's a good idea." I emphasized the last phrase slightly.

"The first secretary has already agreed. There's a name circulating about you, I've heard." The ambassador tilted his head, then looked at Commander Madley.

"Oh?" I looked at the commander.

Madley looked back at the ambassador.

"A Marshal Gorofsky, I believe, wired Commander Madley to pass on a message." The ambassador grinned. "He said that you were the latest incarnation of the ghosts of the white nights. Or was it that you were fortunate to escape being the latest ghost of the white nights?"

I laughed, ruefully and gently. "The latter, I'm sure."

"There is a legend that Peter the Great declared that the ghosts of the white nights would always save the city,"

Madley said. "It goes with the one about the Bronze Horseman."

"St. Petersburg can have the ghosts," I said. The city needed them, and perhaps the tzar most of all, if he would but look at them.

"They have more than enough," announced Drummond Kent as he and Terese joined us. "I would like to leave them behind, and I do believe we're all here."

The Black Mesa Quartct and Robert Thies had left on Monday, for Stockholm, where they were appearing in separate concerts. I didn't envy them. The touring life wasn't what most people thought. The few appearances that Llysette was making were wearing enough. I couldn't imagine doing it day after day, week after week.

"Have a safe trip home," the ambassador called cheerfully as Commander Madley and the four of us climbed into the embassy limousine.

Once outside the iron gates of the embassy courtyard, the driver headed southward, eventually along the Lvov Prospekt, toward the aerodrome.

Leaving Russia was far easier than entering it, and Republic Air Corps 2 was even less crowded on the return trip. Llysette and I had one of the table areas to ourselves. Terese was kind enough to take another to leave us some privacy. We didn't say much until we were airborne.

"You're getting to be a wealthy woman," I teased her. "Cheques from everywhere. Fiftccn thousand from the government, twenty thousand from the tzar, and an emerald. Such an emerald." I grinned, knowing she was wearing it under her high-necked dress, because she said there was no other safe way to carry it back.

"That I did not expect." She shook her head. "Nor the cheque from the tzar. Terese . . . she was also surprised at hers."

Actually they had been bank drafts of some sort, but imperial drafts, the kind we'd probably take a photograph of, just to remind us that it had happened.

As I looked past Llysette and out the window of the turbo and down at the lines of white and gray that were St. Petersburg, and the areas of darker gray that were the Neva and Lake Ladoga, both fringed with white that showed they soon would be frozen, I had to wonder. Peter the Great had built St. Petersburg as a window to the west, and to the world, but what really was behind that window? Although Llysette and I had seen very little, there was far, far more to the vast land than St. Petersburg.

In retrospect, what had happened was so obvious. The tzars had built a bureaucracy of highly educated men, a thin layer of expertise that had enabled the Romanovs to maintain order and control. The very thinness of that veneer had allowed me to do as I had, but even though I had seen very little except for that expertise, I had great doubts how much longer the Romanovs could maintain such absolute control.

The student revolutionaries—they had wanted real change or real ghosts to show the brutality of the Ohkrana, but the de-ghosting technology had destroyed that. That destruction was also why the university area had felt so dead when I had looked around it. No one would ever know, but my guess was that hundreds, if not thousands, of students had died there, their ghosts removed, and the student records obliterated, so that no one would ever know for certain. So, for the Ohkrana and the tzar, the answer was simple. No ghosts meant no unrest, and de-ghosting was yet another tool for maintaining the autocracy.

Yet the intermittent Septembrist bombings continued, despite difference engines and the Ohkrana, and I wondered if they were not as inspired by the ghosts of the white nights as discouraged by those restless and endless spirits that infused the city of gray stone and skies.

Would the ghosts of the white nights again save the Romanovs, or would the coming new millennium see the end of the dynasty—either through the advancing tanks of

Ferdinand or through the slow erosion of the image of the tzar?

Ferdinand controlled a system and a bureaucracy; I had the feeling that both controlled the tzar, much as he denied and protested it. And I had no doubts that the de-ghosting technology would reappear in Russia, and doubtless before long. I hoped that the Duma and those more perceptive than the tzar had a chance, perhaps a few more years, to make changes before the tides of revolt again surged in— and a chance is all any of us get.

I couldn't see Marshal Putin making the de-ghosting technology widespread. It was too easy for rankers and even peasants to abuse. But word would leak out that Russia had the technology, and that would cool Ferdinand's rhetoric and efforts, because, if it did come to a war, the Russians would use *anything*.

I shivered at that thought, because Pyotr Romanov had said that I had not acted as a Russian would. I feared I had, because I had used just about anything as well. Was it wrong to do what I had? Or was it a case, as the near-forgotten Speaker Breckinridge had once said, where everyone was wrong.

"Pauvre homme," murmured Llysette, laying her head against my good shoulder. "You worry much."

I did have one question, one I hadn't been about to ask while in Russia, and I laid my lips against her ear, whispering, "How did the luger . . ."

"Inside the lining of the metal purse." She smiled. "There is lead in the sequins."

How far we had come. She'd shot me, in the beginning, and now had used the same luger to save my life.

38

B OTH LLYSETTE AND I were just happy to get back to
Vanderbraak Centre, even if a northeastern winter
storm blanketed the town and most of New Bruges within
hours of our return. We were happy to be snowed in for
the next day or so, and Llysette didn't complain about the
cold. But, she didn't have to. I kept the woodstove in the
parlor stoked, and there were plenty of staples laid aside
in the cellar, even if little was fresh.

And that was that. The world teetered on. The doktor
and the diva had done their bit, and no one said a word,
because saying something would have revealed just how
close matters could have come to disaster, and because
none of us involved could really have proved how dangerous the situation had been. There were some indications
in the weeks after we returned to New Bruges, if one knew
where to look.

The head of the united Columbian defense staff died
unexpectedly when his limousine was hit by an AmeriSun
petro hauler that burst into flames, and four other senior
generals took early retirement for unspecified reasons. The
clean-cut Verner Oss had vanished from my classes, probably headed off to another assignment, and I still had no

idea whether he'd been detailed from Holmbek to protect me or from the Air Corps for less friendly reasons, but his disappearance was a good sign in most ways, except I missed having him as a bright student.

The chief executive of AmeriSun's Rocketrol chemicals division died from a gunshot wound to the head, but no suicide note was ever found, although the gun did bear his prints. Columbian Dutch Petro was beginning to drill exploratory wells in Russian Alaska, and building highways. The Northlands tar sands petroleum conversion plants came on line and began to send kerosene south. I supposed all that showed that representative governments, so long as they represent everyone, and neither just the elite nor just the mob, can in fact muddle through.

Back in Russia, ionization and filtration equipment was being installed on the Dnepyr, and his high excellency Dimitri Vlasovich had become a deputy minister in charge of environmental improvement—that was what the short note I'd gotten from him indicated, along with thanks for the materials and contact lists. Ferdinand changed his tack and now was complaining that the change in the water purity would disrupt the Romanian fisheries.

The Russians announced the Firebird, the successor to the Perun, and said that they were building it for research purposes, but that it could be easily reconfigured to carry multiple warheads if necessary. They didn't say what kind, but I had an idea that they were "less fantastic," as Marshal Gorofsky would have termed it, after Marshal Putin died when his transport crashed on takeoff from St. Petersburg. And I never did find out if anything happened to Piet Darwaard, although I doubted it. His type was far too careful.

Llysette's students began to do recitals, and she spent too many nights up at the music and theatre building. But . . . as a result of the St. Petersburg concert, Llysette received another half dozen invitations throughout Columbia—and two from abroad. One from Quebec and one to perform in Citie de Tenochtitlan, sponsored by Franco-PetEx. I suspect Dietre had something to do with that, since he'd been in Deseret as their "representative," but I doubted that we'd ever know for certain, unless he showed up at the concert—which wasn't beyond probability. He did get around, and he did love Llysette's singing.

Then, on the first Saturday in March, three packages arrived at the post centre. A smiling Maurice had a padded registered letter to me, registered from the Office of the Speaker. There was also another thin letter from International Import Services, PLC, Columbia City, Federal District, and a much larger package from the Presidential Palace, addressed to Llysette.

I'd been going to go to McArdles' and do the grocery shopping. Instead, I eased the Stanley through the slush from Thursday's snow, back up Deacon's Lane.

Llysette was at the door.

"What . . . Is something the matter?"

I couldn't help smiling as I carried the packages and envelopes into the study. "I don't think so. We received some packages, of sorts."

I opened the thin letter from International Import Services, Harlaan's "consulting" front, wondering if the envelope held the "fee" he'd promised months ago, and if it did, whether it would actually amount to something. I swallowed. There was no letter, just a cheque, for fifty thousand dollars. I had to read the numbers twice. Then I showed it to Llysette.

"*Mon cher,* you are the wealthy one now."

"Only until your next two concerts," I pointed out.

The padded letter from the Speaker was next. There were two pieces of paper in the letter from the Speaker. I read the formal letter first.

Dear Minister Eschbach:
    On behalf of the government of Columbia, I would like to be the first to congratulate you on your most successful efforts to facilitate the cleansing of the Dnepyr River and to provide environmental expertise beyond anyone's expectations . . .

I would like to invite you and Mme. duBoise to attend the Speaker's Honors Dinner in June, where I would like to present you personally with the Columbian Civilian Achievement Medal.

While I wish the government could offer greater recognition of your services, I do wish to offer my deepest thanks and appreciation.

The handwritten and unsigned note was briefer.

Our deepest thanks for what will never be known.

I wondered about both sentiments. Thanks of those in power are brief, and everything becomes known in time. Still, I'd at least delayed the development and deployment of the zombie bomb—assuming that Yelensov had been right and it could be built at all.

Llysette tapped me on the shoulder. I smiled and handed her both sheets of paper.

"At last . . . they recognize you."

"At last," I agreed. "David and the dean will enjoy telling the world about another distinguished faculty achievement."

"You are not pleased?"

"I am, and I'm not."

Llysette nodded. She understood.

I looked to the second package. It was from the Presidential Palace, addressed to Llysette, and was fairly light, but not small. "You open this one."

Llysette opened the first box carefully to find a second inside, bearing inscriptions in Russian, German, French, and English, and from the three that I could read, they all meant the same thing—"Fragile." The inside box also bore the name "Pavlova" and an envelope fastened to it. She then opened the unsealed envelope to extract a card. The card was unsigned, but bore the words: "This was sent to the president for transmission to you."

"If it's what I think it is," I said, "be very careful."

Llysette raised her eyebrows, but she was careful.

I was right. Inside the box was a small display case, and in the case was an exquisite Pavlova miniature porcelain— that of a dark-haired singer in a shimmering silver-green gown, with a short black and silver jacket. The figure was less than a foot tall, but small as it was, I could recognize Llysette's every feature replicated there.

From what I could tell, she had been given the second of one hundred limited edition figures.

"It is *magnifique* . . . "

"You were *magnifique* . . . " I insisted.

"Not I," she said gently, looking up from the porcelain, "you were the one who saved the world . . . all would be zombies and ghosts . . ."

I wasn't sure I'd done that. I think Llysette had done that, for without her songs, no one would have listened to me, and the memories of her songs in St. Petersburg would last far longer than the rumors of what I'd done, and that was certainly for the best.

But . . . the world goes on, lurching from danger to danger, as would any world, and the spies are forgotten far sooner than the great singers, and that, too, is as it should be.

Look for

LEGACIES

By

L. E. MODESITT, JR.

Now available in Hardcover

I

⚜

IN THE QUIET of the early twilight of a late summer day, a woman sat in a rocking chair under the eaves of the porch, facing east, rocking gently. Except for the infant she nursed, she was alone, enjoying the clean evening air, air swept of sand grit and dust by the unseasonal afternoon rain. So clear was the silver-green sky that the still-sunlit Aerial Plateau stood out above the nearer treeless rise that was Westridge, stood out so forcefully that it appeared yards away rather than tens of vingts to the north and east.

She rocked slowly, looking down at her nursing son, a child already with dark hair, more like deep gray than black. Through the open windows set in the heavy stone walls, she could hear the occasional clatter of platters being replaced in the cupboards, and the squeak of the hand pump.

The glittering and scattered light reflected from the quartz outcroppings on the top edge of the distant and towering Plateau died away as the sun dropped farther. Before long, pinlights that were stars appeared, as did the small greenish crescent that was the moon Asterta. The larger moon, Selena, had already set in the west.

She brought the infant to her shoulder and burped him.

"There . . . there, that's a good boy, Alucius." Then she resettled herself and offered the other breast.

As she began to rock once more, a point of light appeared off the north end of the porch, expanding into a winged feminine figure with iridescent green-tinged silver wings. The nursing mother blinked, then turned her head slowly. For several moments, she looked at the soarer, a graceful feminine figure somewhere in size between an eight year old girl and a small young woman—except for the spread wings of coruscating and shimmering light, which fanned yards out from the soarer's body until it bathed both mother and infant.

The woman chanted softly,

> *"Soarer fair, soarer bright,*
> *only soarer in the night*
> *wish I may, wish I might*
> *have this wish I wish tonight . . ."*

For a long moment after she had completed her wish, the woman watched. The soarer's wings sparkled, their movement seemingly effortless, as she hung in mid-air, in turn watching mother and child, less than twenty yards from the pair on the porch. As suddenly as she had appeared, the soarer was gone, as was the green radiance that had emanated from her.

Slowly, the woman murmured the old child's rhyme to herself.

> *"Londi's child is fair of face.*
> *Duadi's child knows his place.*
> *Tridi's child is wise in years,*
> *but Quattri's must conquer fears.*
> *Quinti's daughter will prove strong,*
> *while Sexdi's knows right from wrong.*
>
> *Septi's child is free and giving,*
> *but Octdi's will work hard in living.*

Novdi's child must watch for woe,
while Decdi's child has far to go.

But the soarer's child praise the most,
for he will rout the sanders' host,
and raise the lost banners high
under the green and silver sky."

She looked beyond the north end of the porch once more, but there was no sign that the soarer had ever been there.

Within moments, the door to the house opened, and a lean man stepped outside, moving near-silently toward the woman in the rocking chair. "I thought I saw a light-torch out here. Did someone ride up?"

"No . . ." She shifted the infant and added, "There was a soarer here, Ellus."

"A soarer?"

"She was out there, just beyond where you put the snow fence last winter. She hovered there and looked at us, and then she left."

"Are you sure, Lucenda?" Ellus's voice was gentle, but not quite believing.

"I'm quite sure. I don't imagine what's not there."

Ellus laughed, warmly. "I've learned that." After a moment, he added, "They're supposed to be good luck for an infant."

"I know. I made a wish."

"What did you wish for."

"I can't say. It won't come true, and I want it to come true for Alucius."

"That's just a superstition."

Lucenda smiled. "Probably it is, but let me have it."

He bent over and kissed her forehead. "For him, as well as for you."

Then he pulled over the bench and sat down beside her as the evening darkened into night.

2

I N THE WARM sun of a clear harvest morning, five people
stood beside the stable door, two men, two women, and
a small boy. The child had short-cropped hair that was a
dark gray, rather than true black, and he clutched the hand
of the younger woman and looked up at the man who wore
the black and green uniform of the Iron Valley Militia.
Tied to the post outside the stable were a roan, saddled,
and a gray mare. The gray tied beside the roan had no
saddle, but a harness and two leather bags of provisions
across its back.

"Father?" offered the boy.

The uniformed man bent down and scooped up the
child, holding him against his shoulder so that their faces
were but handspans apart. "You'll be a good boy for
Mother, won't you, Alucius?"

"Yes, Father." His words were carefully articulated.

"He's always good," offered the older woman who stood
back from the couple.

"You'd say that anyway, Veryl," countered the older
man.

"I might," Veryl responded with a smile, "but Alucius
is good. Lucenda knows that."

"You'll be careful, Ellus," said Lucenda. "You will, won't you?"

"He'll be fine," boomed the older man. "Best officer in all Iron Valley. Just going after brigands, that's all. Not like the border wars with the Lanachronans when I was his age. They had Talent-wielders. Not very good, but they did call out sanders—"

"That was then, Royalt," pointed out Veryl. "You and Ellus can compare stories when he comes back. Reillies, sanders, Talent-wielders . . . whatever you want."

The three other adults smiled at the dryness of her tone.

Ellus handed Alucius back to Lucenda, then bent forward and hugged her, kissing her on the cheek. "You two be good. I shouldn't be gone that long."

Alucius squirmed, and Lucenda set him down beside her, and threw her arms around her husband, holding him tightly.

Alucius looked up at the pair, embracing, then to the corral not two yards from where he stood. His eyes met the black-rimmed red orbs of the lead nightram, and he gently let go of his mother's trousers, taking one step, then another toward the black-wooled ram with the red eyes and sharp horns.

"Alucius!" Lucenda cried, lunging toward her son.

"Let him go," came Royalt's voice. "Best we see now. He's protected by the fence. Rams don't hurt children, unless the children hit them, and Alucius won't do that."

Lucenda glanced from Alucius to the fence, and to the nightram on the far side of the four rails. Then she looked to Ellus. His lips were tight, his eyes fixed on their son.

In the silence that had settled across the stead, Alucius took three more steps, until his chest was against the second railing. The nightram stepped forward and lowered his head, until his eyes focused on the child. The curled and knife-pointed black horns glittered, reflecting the sun from their lethal smoothness, standing out from the light-absorbing all-black face, and from the black fleece that was so deep in color that the ram was darker than any night.

Even the sharp-edged hoofs were night-black.

The boy smiled at the nightram, then reached out with his left hand and touched the beast's jaw, fingertips from the sharp teeth. "Good! Good ram."

For a long moment, the nightram's eyes took in Alucius. Then the ram slowly lowered himself to the ground, so that his eyes were level with those of the boy.

Alucius smiled. "He's a good ram."

"Yes, he is." Lucenda's voice was strained.

"He likes me."

"I'm sure he does."

Deliberately, slowly, Alucius lifted his hand away from the nightram. "You be good, ram." He stepped a-way from the railing. The ram slowly rose, lifting his head and sharp horns, but only watched as the boy stepped toward his mother.

"He was a good ram."

Lucenda swept Alucius up into her arms, hanging on tightly. "Yes, he was. But you must be careful with the nightsheep."

"I was careful."

The ram tilted his head, before turning and walking to-ward the far side of the corral.

"He'll be a herder, for sure, Ellus." The older and broad-shouldered Royalt laughed. "He's already got a way with them. He'll be ready to take the flock with us when you get back."

"That's good to know—and so young, yet." Ellus smiled and straightened the green and black tunic. The smile faded as he looked Lucenda and Alucius. He stepped over to them and hugged both of them for a moment. Then he looked at Alucius, his face serious. "You'll take care of your mother while I'm gone, won't you?"

Alucius nodded.

"Good." Ellus smiled once more. "I'll be back before long. Sure as there are five seasons, I'll be back."

"I'll be here," Lucenda replied.

Still holding the smile, Ellus untied the roan and

mounted, leading the gray as he rode down the lane toward Iron Stem. He turned in the saddle and waved as he passed the end of the outermost section of the southernmost corral.

The older man and woman took several steps back toward the main house, before stopping and watching the rider. The younger woman stood by a fence post, ignoring the nightram on the other side, tears streaming down her face. The fingers holding her son's hand did not loosen as she sobbed.

Alucius looked at the departing rider. "Father . . ."

"He'll be back," Lucenda managed. "He will be."

Alucius watched until his father was out of sight. To the south, above the high road that lay beyond vision, an eagle circled upward into the open expanse of silver-green sky, a black dot that also vanished.

3

OUTSIDE, THE EVENING was darkening, with neither moon to offer illumination. Inside the second lambing crib, with only a small, single-crystal, light-torch to dispel the blackness, Alucius watched. His mother held a bottle filled with goat's milk, feeding the small nightlamb. The lamb sucked greedily for a short time, then stopped, lowering his head slowly.

"You have to drink more," Lucenda told the lamb gently. "It doesn't taste right, but you have to drink it." She stroked the lamb.

"He doesn't like the sand. I wouldn't like sand in what I drank," Alucius said solemnly.

"It isn't sand. It's quartz. It's powdered as fine as we can make it with the crusher."

"But why?" Alucius gave a small frown.

"The ewes have it in their milk. They get it from the quarasote shoots. So we have to put it in the goat's milk so the lamb will grow strong."

Alucius could sense the doubt in his mother. "He's very sick, isn't he?"

"He isn't as strong as he should be. It's hard for lambs who lose their mothers. The other ewes don't have enough

milk for two. Sometimes, they don't have enough for one."
Lucenda tendered the bottle, and the lamb sucked for a
time, but the amount of milk left in the bottle remained
almost the same.

"He doesn't feel good," Alucius said. "He's tired."

"He has to eat, or he won't get well," Lucenda said
evenly.

"Will he die?"

"He might."

Alucius sensed the concern in his mother's words, and
the darkness behind them. He looked at the lamb, then sat
down on the old horse blanket beside the animal. Slowly,
he reached out and drew the small creature to him, his
arms around the lamb's neck.

The lamb bleated, then seemed to relax, looking up at
Lucenda. Alucius waited.

She offered the bottle once more.

Alucius held the lamb until the bottle was empty.

Lucenda looked to her son. "How is he?"

"He's tired. He'll be better."

"He made a mess of you," Lucenda said.

"I'll ask Grandma'am how to wash it off." Alucius
yawned and lay down on the blanket next to the lamb.
"I'm staying here. He needs me. He'll be better."

"For a while, dear."

"All night. He'll get well. You'll see. He will."

"If you say so, Alucius."

"I just know he'll get stronger." The child's treble voice
held absolute conviction. He yawned again, and then
again. Before long, his eyes closed. So did those of the
lamb.

Lucenda looked at the sleeping child and the sleeping
lamb. A faint smile crossed her lips.

4

THE WIND OF late fall whistled around the dwelling, but the warmth from the big iron stove in the main room had infused the front parlor as well, as had the heat from the kitchen, with the associated smells of baking apples, biscuits, and mutton. Because it was Decdi, when Royalt did not graze the nightsheep, the older man sat behind the table desk, studying the black leatherbound ledger. He dipped the iron pen into the inkwell and added several figures to the column of figures. Then, with a satisfied half-smile, he swished the pen in the cleaning bowl, wiped it gently with a scrap of cloth and set it in its stand. After closing the ledger, he stood and put it on the top shelf of the bookcase. As he lowered his hand, his sleeve slipped back over his herder's wristguard, a seamless band of silver, with a strip of black crystal in the center.

Alucius watched from the leather hassock by the bookcase, his eyes on the herders' wristguard for a long moment. While chores still had to be done on Decdi, the day ending the week seemed special, perhaps because there was time for the adults to talk, and Alucius could listen, and no one urged him on to the next chore.

"Could I play a game of leschec with you, Grandfather?" asked Alucius. "A short one before supper, if you wouldn't mind?"

"You finished your lessons?"

"Yes, sir." Alucius pointed to the lesson book on the one shelf that was his, and that held his learning books as well. "Do you want to look at them?"

"You say they're done, they're done." Royalt leaned forward and offered a wide smile. "You've been watching us, haven't you?"

"Yes, sir." Alucius did not move from the hassock.

"Supper'll be ready before long." There was a twinkle in Royalt's eyes as he watched his grandson. "We're having an apple pie. You can smell it."

"I know. I helped mother pick the best baskets at market. This afternoon I cored the apples and sliced them."

The herder frowned slightly. "How did you did pick the apples?"

"I was careful. I just said some baskets looked good." Alucius put both slippered feet on the polished wooden floor. "You said I had to be careful."

"I did. A good herder has some of the Talent, and most people are not comfortable with it. They especially don't like children with it."

"I was careful," Alucius said again.

"I'm sure you were, boy." Royalt grinned. "You think you can beat me?"

"Probably not yet," Alucius replied. "I can't see far enough ahead."

"None of us can, boy. We'd always like to see farther than we can. That's being human." Royalt took the board from the shelf and set it on the table, followed by the plain lorken box that held the pieces.

Alucius stood and pulled the hassock to the side of the table opposite his grandsire. Then he knelt on the hassock.

"You want black or green?" asked Royalt.

"Don't we choose?"

Royalt laughed. "You pick. I'll choose."

The boy took two of the footwarriors, one green and

one black, and then lowered his hands below the table, switching the pieces between hands several times before lifting both hands, backs up, and presenting them to his grandfather. Royalt touched Alucius's right hand. The boy turned his hand over, opening it and showing the black piece. Then he turned his left hand and displayed the green footwarrior.

"Black it is."

Alucius quickly set up the pieces, beginning with the foot warriors in the first row, and ending with the soarer queen and sander king.

"Do you have any questions before we start?" asked Royalt.

"No, sir . . . except why is the soarer a woman and the most powerful? Sanders are powerful, too, and they kill nightsheep. The soarers don't." He paused. "Do they?"

"No, the soarers don't." The older man laughed. "I can't tell you why the soarer is the most powerful piece. It's always been that way."

Alucius waited for his grandfather's move. Not surprisingly, it was the fourth footwarrior, two squares forward. Alucius matched the move, so that the two blocked each other. His grandfather moved the pteridon out, and Alucius countered by moving his fifth footwarrior a single square forward.

By several more moves, Royalt was smiling. "You *have* been watching. You're playing like your mother, but that last move was like Worlin's."

Royalt attacked, taking Alucius's lesser alector, but losing a pteridon, and a footwarrior; before capturing the boy's greater alector, at the cost of the other pteridon.

"Supper's ready!" called Lucenda from the main room.

"We can finish after supper," Royalt suggested.

Alucius studied the board before looking at his grandfather. "No, sir. You'll win."

"I might not."

"You should win," Alucius said. "But could we play another tomorrow?"

"I think I could manage that, if I'm not late bringing in the flock." Royalt stood. "Before long, you'll be besting me." Royalt laughed. "Time to wash up, boy."

Alucius followed Royalt to the washroom off the kitchen where Royalt took the lever of the hand pump and put it through several cycles, until the chill water was flowing into the basin. Alucius waited and then took his turn, before returning to the kitchen.

Royalt sat at the head of the table, at the only chair with arms, facing into the kitchen, while Veryl sat at his right, closest to the serving table. Lucenda set a wide platter of mutton—from a town sheep bought the week before—on the table, and then seated herself at the end of the table, with Alucius on her left.

Veryl cleared her throat gently, and the other three bowed their heads.

"In the name of the One Who Is, may our food be blessed and our lives as well. And blessed be the lives of both the deserving and the undeserving that both may strive to do good in the world and beyond." Veryl smiled and looked up, glancing at Royalt.

The herder returned the smile, and then speared a slab of the mutton and set it on his wife's platter before serving himself and passing the platter to Veryl, who in turn passed it to Lucenda. Lucenda served Alucius and herself. The gladbeans, doused and lightly fried in sweet oil, followed. Alucius took one biscuit after his grandfather passed the basket to him.

"You can have two," offered Veryl. "You're a growing boy, and there's more than enough. We got some of the best honey from Dactar last week."

Alucius grinned. "Thank you, Grandma'am." He knew about the honey, having already snitched the smallest of samples several times during the week.

"Of course," his grandmother continued, "there isn't quite so much honey as there might have been."

Alucius flushed.

Lucenda shook her head, in what Alucius knew was

mock-disapproval—or almost mock-disapproval.

"It was awfully good," Alucius admitted, "and I only had a little."

At the end of the table, Royalt coughed to smother a smile.

"You might have asked," suggested Lucenda.

"You would have said no."

"Sometimes that happens," his mother replied. "We can't always have what we want. You know that. Get too greedy, and you might get a Legacy of the Duarches."

"Yes, ma'am." Alucius wasn't too sure what that meant, but it didn't sound good.

After the momentary silence, Royalt spoke. "Been wondering if we'll be having a long and cold winter this year." He took another slab of mutton, and ladled gravy over it.

"You think so, dear?" asked Veryl.

"Haven't seen a sander in near-on a month. Not many sandwolves, either. Or even scrats. Saterl says the sandwolves have moved closer to the town, that folks there are losing dogs, and the wolves are going after food sheep. They all forget that the wolves don't leave a scent, and that food sheep don't sense them. Most times, sandwolves don't like town sheep, unless they're starving. Last time that happened this early in the fall was in the big winter, fifteen-sixteen years back." He took a swallow of the weak amber ale. "Wind's colder early, too."

"Do you think we should lay in another town sheep or two in the holding barn?"

"Three, maybe. And some of the big sacks of dried beans. We've got the coins."

Alucius hoped that his grandfather happened to be mistaken, because Alucius hated the beans. But he knew that Royalt had a feel for weather, and his own feelings had already told him it was going to be cold.

"And some of the dried maize," suggested Lucenda.

"You never did care much for the beans, did you, dear?" asked Veryl.

"You know that, Mother." Lucenda grinned. "Neither

does Alucius. One of my faults that has been passed on to him."

"One of your few faults," suggested Royalt. "If you'd pass the biscuits, Alucius?"

Alucius looked around the table, at the three adults, and took another biscuit, smiling, before handing the basket back to his grandsire.

5

❧

THE DUARCHY OF Corus blessed all the lands with peace and prosperity, for generation upon generation, from the times of the Forerunners onward. Never was there so fair a realm, so just a world, and so blessed the peoples of a world.

The Myrmidons of Duality and their pteridons controlled the heavens, and they conveyed dispatches, orders, and messages from one end of Corus to the other, from the northern heights of Blackstear to the warm waters of Southgate, from Alustre in the east to mighty Elcien in the west, all so that the peoples of the Duarchy might prosper, and that their children and their children's children might do so as well.

Likewise, the Alectors of Justice and the Recorders of Deeds made sure that evil gained no foothold in any city, not even in the courts and chambers of the Duarches, nor in the meanest of city quarters, for without justice, nothing endures for long.

The Engineers of Faitel created the mighty eternastone highroads that crossed Corus from west to east, and south to north, excepting only the Aerlal Plateau and the Anvils of Hel. Upon these highways moved all manner of goods and travelers, each secure in the knowledge that all were safe from any manner of harm.

Even the oceans fell under the sway of the Duarchy, with the fleets of the Duadmiralty built of dolphin ships so swift and fierce that no pirate and no brigand could contest or escape them, and the ways of the seas became as highways upon the waters, bringing goods and travelers to all manner of places.

The sun shined its favors out of a silver-green sky and blessed the Duarchy and all its peoples through all five seasons of each year, every year.

Then came the Cataclysm, and the old ways and webs weakened, and the world changed for all time . . .

History of Corus [fragment recovered from the Blue Tower at Hafin]

6

〜

Mist sifted from the clouds overhead, and fog covered most of Westridge, bringing with it a faintly acrid scent of damp quarasote mixed with that of night-sheep dung. The supply wagon stood outside the stead stable. Wearing his oiled leathers and a battered brown felt hat, Royalt held the leads to the dray horses. He sat on the left side of the wagon. Beside him, slightly more to the middle of the wagon seat, was Alucius, who wore an oiled leather cloak over his nightsheep jacket.

"It's miserable weather to go to town." Lucenda stood bareheaded under the slight overhang of the stable eaves.

"Best weather to go," replied Royalt. "We don't miss grazing time. We need the salt, and the flour. Your mother's not up to taking the team . . ."

Alucius sensed that his grandma'am might never be up to taking the team. Something about her leg hadn't healed right. He felt that he should have been able to do something. Not that he hadn't tried . . . when no one was paying attention. Sometimes, she felt better, but it never lasted.

Lucenda looked at her son under the oiled leather cloak that was too big for him. Alucius returned the gaze with a calm smile.

"Alucius will be fine. He needs to get off the stead more, daughter."

"I suppose he should," Lucenda replied. "You be good for your grandfather, Alucius."

"Yes, Mother." Alucius smiled. "I'll be good."

Lucenda flushed. "I don't know why I say that. You're always good."

Royalt flicked the reins, and the pair of dun horses moved forward. "Should be back around supper time."

Neither the man nor the boy spoke until the wagon was on the narrow track that led southwest, through the treeless expanse of low and barely rolling rises, covered with scattered quarasote, toward the main road.

"You take it to heart, don't you, boy?"

"Take what?" Alucius wasn't sure he understood.

Royalt laughed. "I could be wrong. Let me ask you something. Do you remember what your father said before he left?"

"He said to be good and to take care of Mother."

"That is what I meant," Royalt said.

Alucius turned in the wagon seat and looked at his grandfather. "Did I do something wrong? You sound angry." Except that wasn't right. Alucius could feel it wasn't anger behind the words.

"I'm not angry." Royalt shook his head, and a strand of light gray hair flopped across his forehead. He brushed it back absently. "No, Alucius. You haven't done anything wrong. You never have. That was what I was talking about."

"I threw stones at the grayjays."

The grandfather laughed. "That wasn't wrong in the same way I was talking. You didn't mean to hurt them. You listen. Suppose that's what comes from growing up without any brothers or sisters and so far from other steads."

Alucius nodded. "I have you and Grandma'am and Mother. You play leschec with me."

"You're already better than I am, young fellow."

"That's because I can think about it more," the youngster said solemnly.

Royalt laughed.

The wagon bumped and jolted along the track from the stead for two vingts, and it seemed like it had taken glasses to cover the distance when Royalt finally spoke. "Here we are—the old road. Don't have to worry about sinkholes, washouts . . . and it's a smoother ride." Once he had the wagon headed south on the gray stone road, Royalt shifted his weight in the seat and smiled. "Good roads. Have to admit the ancients built good roads."

The ever-present red dust had drifted into piles beside the road, now dampened by the mist, and in places, encroached slightly on the gray stones that, even when scratched or cut—and that was hard to do—showed no trace of damage by the next day. The road ran straight as a rifle barrel from north to south between Soulend and Iron Stem. That much Alucius knew. He also knew that not many people lived in Soulend, and that it was much colder than in Iron Stem or in any of the more southern Iron Valleys.

The boy glanced back over his shoulder. The clouds had lifted some, and the mist-blurred Aerial Plateau scarcely looked any smaller or any farther away, even after two vingts of travel. If the clouds did not descend again, the Plateau would look almost the same from Iron Stem, he knew. His eyes went to the empty gray stone road ahead.

"This is a good road, isn't it, Grandfather?"

"That it is, lad."

"Not many people travel it."

"When it was built, back before the dark days, there were more people in the world, and it was a road many people traveled."

"The dark days were a long time ago," Alucius pointed out, hoping that his grandsire would offer more than his usually clipped explanation.

"That they were." Royalt paused, glancing sideways at the boy. "So long ago and so terrible that we can't count exactly the years." He paused again. "They were dark years, because everything changed. Some of the legends say they were dark because the sun did not shine for a year. Others said that was because the Duarchy ran dark with the blood of men and women who fought demons from beyond the skies. Still others claimed that those days were so terrible that no one will ever know what happened except those who died or lived through them." He cleared his throat once more before continuing. "Life changed. We know that. Iron Stem—do you know where the name came from?"

"From the iron mines and the mill, you said. That's all you said."

"Iron Stem had the mines and the big mill, and the mill used to make iron ingots as big as a man, and they put them on huge wagons and drove them down to Dekhron and put them on barges. The barges carried the iron to Faitel, and the artisans and engineers there formed the iron into tools and weapons and beams that held up buildings all over the Duarchy."

"An iron ingot as big as a man?"

Royalt nodded. "Some were bigger than that. I saw one, when I wasn't much older than you. They found a stack of them, buried under clay, coated in wax or something. Looked as if they'd been formed maybe a year before." He laughed. "Took a double team to move each one. Sold them to the Lanachronans. Town had golds for years."

"What happened? Why did the mill stop?"

"The weather changed. That's what they say. Some say the soarers did it. Whatever caused it . . . it takes lots of water to make iron, and it stopped raining. We used to have forests here, like the big trees on the river. You have to have rain for that. People needed the trees and cut them, but new trees didn't grow. It was too dry. The air got bad in the coal mines, and then there were creatures there, like black sanders . . ." Royal shrugged. "No coal, no water . . . and for a long time, no one needed much iron. So many people died everywhere that there were tools and weapons enough for anyone left."

"That's sad," Alucius said.

"Well . . . we wouldn't be herders if it hadn't changed," Royalt pointed out. "Nightsheep need the dry and the quarasote bushes. They say there weren't any quarasote bushes before the Cataclysm—and no nightsilk anywhere. There's little enough now. That's why the Lanachronans pay well for our nightsilk. They can't raise nightsheep there." He snorted. "That's also why we need a Militia. Didn't have one, and they'd be here, taking everything we have."

"Did the dark days change anything else?" asked Alucius.

"They changed plenty." The older herder pointed. "There's the tower. Won't be that long now."

The first building that was considered part of Iron Stem was the ancient spire that loomed over the Pleasure Palace. Its brilliant green stone facing could be seen from several vingts to the north. Alucius flushed as he recalled the first time he had asked about the name.

After they had crossed several low rises, the long wooden sheds of the dustcat works appeared to the left of the road, a warren of enclosures, all sealed to the outside.

"Have you ever seen a wild dustcat?" Alucius knew the short answer, but hoped Royalt would say more.

"Not since I wasn't much older than you. You know that."

"They aren't many, you said."

"There are more than most folk think. The dustcats aren't stupid. They know people are trouble, and want to capture them, and they've moved into the rock jumbles just below the Plateau or into the deeper swamps of the Sloughs. They still hunt people, but they only do it in packs, and they won't attack unless they can kill, and make sure that the hunters won't survive."

"Are they that smart?"

Royalt frowned, then replied. "Old man Jyrl used to say that the soarers warned the cats when hunters were around.

Claimed he'd seen it happen. Said that was why he never hunted them again, that any man who had both dustcats and soarers against him was as good as dead."

"But people still hunt them, and they keep them in the sheds there."

"And the cats kill one or two scutters a year."

"I don't understand. Why do people work there if they are going to be killed."

Royalt sighed. "It's hard to see it when you're young. But the dust—it's dander really—that comes off the cats makes some people feel . . . well, the best they've ever felt, better than a good meal, better than . . . lots of things. That's why the scutters work for so little. They're around that dust all the time, and they never think about anything else except gathering the dust. Gorend and his son Gortal sell the dust to the Lanachronans—and anyone else who will pay good golds for it, and they'll pay ten or twenty golds to hunters for a cat that's healthy. Ten golds is more than most crafters make in a year, Alucius. It's a huge amount of coin."

"Do you make that much?"

Royalt laughed. "We don't bring in the kind of coins Gorend does, but we make enough."

"I don't think I'd like caging the dustcats like that."

"Good, because I don't think much of those that do. But keep that between us, boy."

"Yes, sir."

Before long, the wagon rolled over the low rise and past the empty green stone tower and the lower building next to the road. Despite its brilliant color-faced stones laid in an alternating pattern, the structure looked more like a nightsheep barn, garishly colored, and was only fifteen yards in length, with almost no windows. The five lower courses were of alternating blue and green stones, and the six above had blue alternating with a faded yellow.

The tower stood alone, fifty yards north of the smaller building, its gutted interior empty.

"Grandfather?" Alucius asked tentatively. "The people

who built the building in front—" He didn't feel he should use the term "Pleasure Palace," especially since it was anything but a palace—"why didn't they just alternate the yellow, blue, and green stones from the bottom?"

Royalt laughed. "Asked myself that very question for years. I can't tell you, boy, because the place was old when I was your age."

"Are the same . . . people there?"

"Sanders, no. The women there change, they say, sometimes as often as the wind shifts the sands around the Plateau. Some stay. Most don't. I wouldn't know, for sure." Royalt cleared his throat and went on quickly, "Hope Hastaar has some of those sweet yams they bring up from Dekhron. Your grandma'am would really like them."

Alucius understood. "I hope he has some of the early cherries. They're good."

Royalt kept the wagon moving toward the center of Iron Stem, past the empty vingt or more separating the Pleasure Palace from the nearest cottage. Despite the chill and the mist and rain, the reddish-brown shutters were half open, as were the shutters of the cottages closer to the square.

Alucius leaned to one side, watching intently as they neared the metal shop. He listened for the hammermill, but the mill was silent, although the odor of hot metal and a line of smoke rose from the forge chimney. The road flattened into an absolutely level stretch more than a hundred yards from the square. The buildings around the square were all of two and three stories, and although boarding houses, all were well-kept and swept, if not always painted so well as they should have been.

On one side of the square were the trade buildings—the cooper's, the chandlery, the silversmith's. On the corner adjoining was the inn, with its blue-painted sign, showing the outline of the old mining mill. Alucius had only seen the mill once, a cavernous and empty set of walls on the far west side of Iron Stem.

In the center of the paved eternastone square was a short line of carts and wagons, several with canvas awnings to protect either produce or goods from the threatening weather. Alucius wondered why. Even the worst storms produced little rain, just winds that were more likely to damage the awnings than the goods.

Royalt eased the wagon over to one of the stone posts on the west side of the square. After setting the wagon brakes, he climbed down and threaded the restraint ropes through the iron rings on the back of the harness of each dun dray horse, then tied both the ropes and the leathers to the big iron ring on the posts. Then he took out the two watering buckets and motioned to Alucius, who had just finished folding the cloak and slipping it under the wagon seat.

"You can water them, can't you? The public pump's right there."

"Yes, sir."

"I'll be over checking to see if Hastaar's got any of those yams. Likely be from last harvest, but he sometimes brings 'em."

After taking the buckets from his grandfather, Alucius pumped what he felt was enough water into one bucket and then the other, and carried them back to the horses. He set the buckets before them, and then stood back.

"Don't see how you herders do that," came a voice from beside him. "I'd risk having them kick it over."

"They won't do that." Alucius turned and looked up at the older man in a shapeless gray jacket, wearing a battered gray felt hat.

"You're Royalt's grandson, aren't you."

"Yes, sir."

"I'm no sir, young fellow. I just run regular sheep south of town, where it's wet enough we don't worry about sanders."

Alucius nodded politely.

The man returned the nod, before turning and walking toward the nearest produce wagon.

When the horses had had enough, Alucius reclaimed the buckets and took them back to the pump, where he rinsed them out before replacing them in the back of the wagon. Then he walked toward the end-most cart, where two boys stood, admiring the display of knives on the dark cotton.

One of the boys looked up. His eyes scanned Alucius, and he used his elbow to touch the other, before whispering something. Both nodded to the itinerant knife-smith and stepped away.

"Are you interested in something, young sir?" asked the gray-haired man.

"I don't have any coins, sir," Alucius said. "You don't mind if I look, do you?"

The man, younger than Royalt, smiled. "Look all you want. I come here every Septi during the spring, summer, and harvest seasons. I'll even make special knives when you're ready for one."

Alucius could sense the friendliness—and a hint of something else, sadness perhaps. "Thank you." He looked over the array of knives. Most were for use in a kitchen or stead, but a handful, on one side, were clearly weapons. Alucius thought that the two on the end were a matched pair of throwing knives, but there was no reason to ask.

After a time, he nodded to the knife-smith. "Thank you, sir."

"Thank you, young sir."

Alucius rejoined Royalt by a cart containing a few small baskets of breads and some half-bushels of early cherries from the south.

Royalt glanced down at the boy. "I was thinking . . ."

"She'd like the soft bread, with all the raisins and the browned sugar . . . and the cherries."

Royalt raised his eyebrows.

"I heard her talking to Mother. They won't ever ask for anything, Grandfather. And Grandma'am won't let Mother ask for her, either."

Royalt burst into a loud laugh. "You know more at ten than I did at twice your age." He turned to the redheaded woman at the end of the wagon. "How much for the cherries?"

"Had to bring them up from south of Borlan. I'd say three silvers, but I'd not want to carry them back."

Royalt nodded. "What about two silvers, and throw in two loaves of the soft current bread there?"

The woman pursed her lips, calculating, as her eyes ran over the nightsilk covered herder's jacket that Royalt wore.

Alucius waited for a moment, then added. "It's for my grandma'am. I have one copper."

The woman shook her head. "Done. Two silvers and a copper." She looked at Alucius and added, "Let your grandsire pay them."

Alucius noted that his grandfather actually handed over two silvers and a pair of coppers, not just one.

"You carry the bread, Alucius."

"Yes, sir."

The two walked back toward the wagon through a mist that was getting cooler and heavier, under clouds that had once more thickened and lowered.

"I'd stay longer," Royalt said, "but there's not as much here as I'd hoped. Happens when you come mid-week. We need to go out to the mill for the flour and hope Amiss has some salt."

"Yes, sir." Alucius didn't know what else to say.

"The produce woman, she wasn't going to let those go for less than two silvers and five." Royalt stopped beside the wagon. "You knew that, didn't you, you imp?"

"Yes, sir."

Royalt covered the bushel with a cloth before easing it into the covered bin behind the wagon seat. He wrapped the two loaves of bread in another clean cloth before easing them onto a position on top of the coarse sacks of potatoes and yams he had apparently gotten while Alucius had been looking at the knives.

While Royalt untied the horses, Alucius climbed up into the wagon seat.

Then the herder swung up into the driver's seat. He released the wagon brakes, and gave a gentle flip to the reins. "Won't take long for us to get out to Amiss's place.

Should make it easy for us to be back to the stead by late afternoon. That way, your mother and grandma'am won't be worrying. And if it starts to mist more, you need to put the cloak back on."

"Yes, sir."

As Royalt guided the wagon onto the westbound road out of the square, Alucius could see the two boys returning to the knife-smith's cart.

"Why do people think we're different?" Alucius asked.

"You saw that, didn't you?"

"Yes, sir."

Royalt sighed. "Herders are different. You know when the horses have had enough to drink, don't you? Or when a nightsheep is hurt? Sometimes, even when people are hurt inside?"

"Sometimes," Alucius admitted cautiously.

"Most people can't do that. To be a herder you have to have some Talent. Not much, but some—I've told you that—and most people don't have even that much Talent. People are afraid of the Talent. Some of them even think that Talent was what caused the dark days."

"It didn't, did it?" asked Alucius.

"It doesn't matter whether it did or didn't, boy. What matters is how people feel. If they think the Talent caused the Cataclysm, then they're going to be afraid of people with Talent, and nothing we say is going to change things. That's why some people don't care much for herders. Something you have to get used to, if you want to be a herder."

"Is that why herders wear the wristguard?"

Royalt laughed. "No, boy. We know we're different. You can tell a herder, young as you are. It's a symbol, in a way, something to remind us who we are."

Royalt eased the wagon to the right edge of the road as a rider neared, coming from the west. The man tipped his battered felt hat to Royalt. The herder returned the gesture.

Alucius nodded to the rider, as well, even as he still wondered why people would want to believe things that weren't true.